Cactus Heart

WHYNOT
BOOK 1

CLIO EVANS

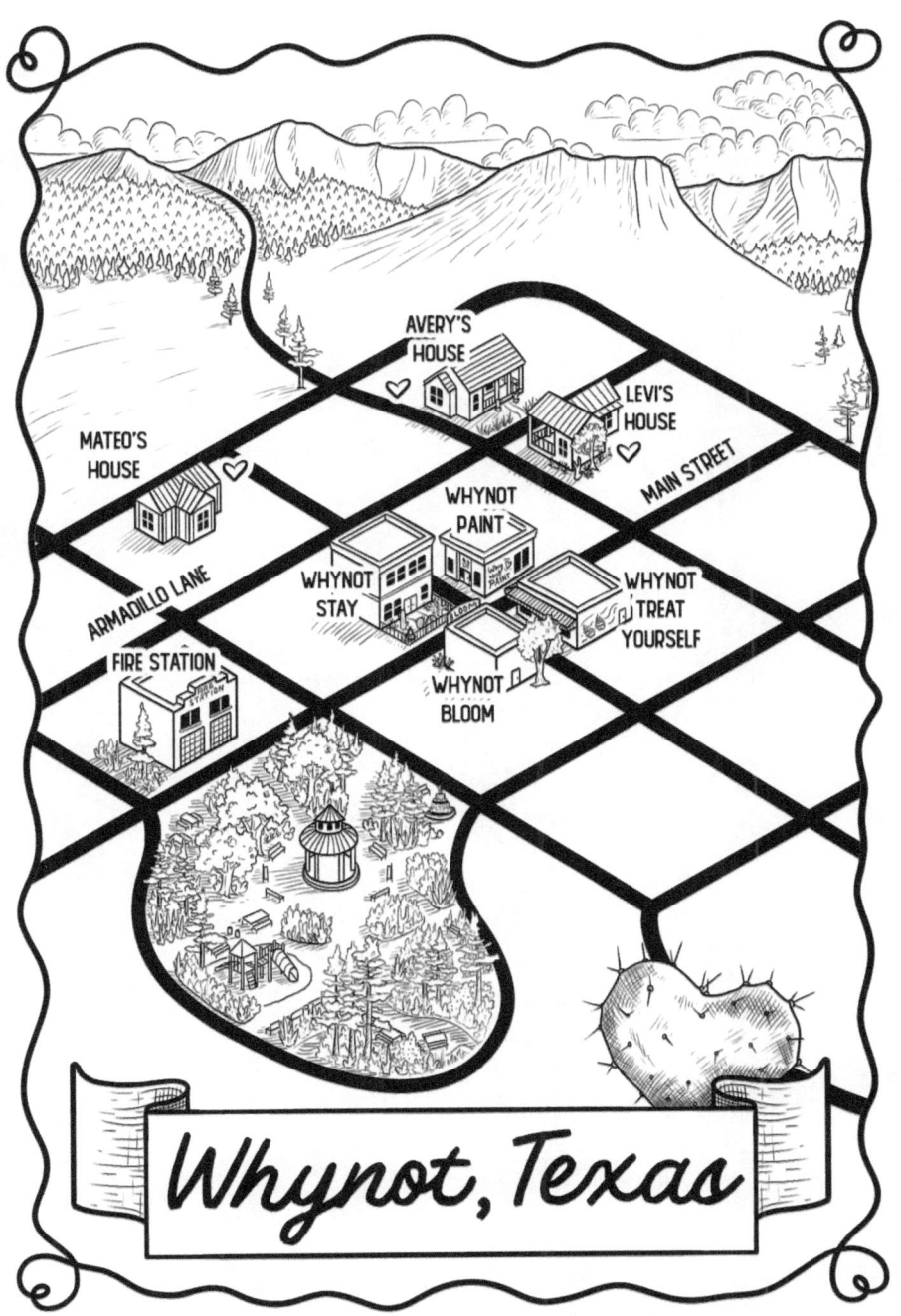

For anyone who loves a soft man with a mustache and slutty little glasses

Content Warning

Hello! Thank you for picking up Cactus Heart to read. Please check the contents below.

• *Detailed* sex scenes with: BDSM Dom/sub dynamics, praise, spanking, biting, ball gags, blindfolds, cock cage, collaring, leashes, voyeurism, forced orgasms, orgasm denial, Shibari, bratting, impact play with bruising, oral sex, squirting, throat fucking, anal sex, spreader bars, a man with slutty glasses who pushes them up the bridge of his nose, mustache riding, and more.

• Discussions of domestic violence

• Discussions of parental death (from heart attack, not on page)

• Discussions of mental health

If you have any questions regarding content warnings, please reach out to me clioevansauthor@gmail.com

 *Levi*

One Week Ago

> You've done it this time, Rayburn. Your face is plastered all over the fucking NHL. Is this some sort of sick joke? A prank?? Did you get drunk and send out this email?

> Why wouldn't you have told me you were going to make that announcement? Where did this even come from? YOU ATTACHED THE PRESS TO IT TOO. This is a NIGHTMARE

> LEVI FUCKING RAYBURN, ANSWER YOUR PHONE

> > Sorry, Robin. Need a break. Getting on a flight, I'll text when I'm ready.

> CALL ME NOW YOU JACKASS

I read the last text message from my agent, then pressed the button on the side of my phone until the screen turned black.

There.

Peace.

Finally.

I exhaled deeply as a weight lifted off my back, my shoulders dropping with relief.

In the last two hours alone, I'd had an avalanche of messages. Notifications for over three hundred unread texts and countless voicemails and emails cluttered my phone. I hadn't even dared to check my social media accounts. My entire fucking career was up in flames, and I'd struck the match.

I was done.

Plain and simple.

Done.

At least for now.

When I started this career, I'd dreamed about being one of the outliers. Playing until I was fifty-two, making a shit ton of money off sponsorships and ads, and riding into my golden years like a damn king.

But I couldn't do it anymore.

At thirty-six, my body felt like I was eighty. The countless injuries I'd had left me in pain all the time. There were some mornings I'd wake up and try a yoga class, only to find I could barely touch my toes. And I could deal with that part of it, but really, it was everything else that had pushed me too far.

The social media. The constant pressure of being perfect. My life being under a microscope. I didn't even know myself anymore.

I was done with it all.

"Now boarding group one for Midland, Texas."

I slung my backpack over my shoulder and winced as pain flared through my joints. I ignored the few glances from strangers around me, adjusting my face mask and keeping my eyes forward as I headed for the gate. I wouldn't be able to breathe easy until I was driving toward the dusty little town I remembered fondly from my summers growing up.

Escaping to the middle of nowhere was the only thing that sounded good right now. I doubted anyone would remember me, aside from the Whynot family. Austin was my best friend in the summers I spent there, and we'd kept in touch after I officially moved up to Saint Paul, Minnesota to go for the league. Maybe it was sad, but I still considered him my best friend, even though we only caught up once a month or so.

My entire life had always been split between Texas and Minnesota until that point, so it felt right that I'd be going back to find some peace.

God. My agent was going to kill me. Robin had worked her ass off for me over the last decade, and I was flushing it all down the toilet by announcing I was out for the season—and probably every season after that. It was June and the drafts were coming up in a couple of weeks, so I'd let management know through email that they'd need to find another goaltender.

Yeah, it was shitty. Yeah, it was unprofessional. Yeah, I'd been on this team for years and we were at the height of a winning streak that was putting us up there with the best teams in the NHL.

But I was breaking apart like a puzzle smashed to the ground. I had missing pieces too. I wasn't even a *good* puzzle.

The messages I'd glanced at were from my coach, my captain, my agent, and a few of the other players. All the rest pouring in had to be from every fucker who thought they had some sort of stake in my career or thought they knew me.

That was another reason I needed to go to Texas. Even not having seen Austin in over a decade, he knew me better than anyone else in my life.

The need to escape the constant prying eyes clashed with my need to finally be seen, sending mixed signals to my brain. It was par for the course. Something inside me was broken.

I shuffled forward to let the flight agent scan my paper

ticket. Her eyes widened slightly as if she recognized me, and I was gripped by panic. Was she going to say something? Was she going to ask me why I was a failure? Why I'd ruined everything?

But she didn't say anything.

Autopilot kicked in, propelling me down the flimsy jetbridge. I ducked my head as I crammed my massive body through the door of the plane.

I had flying down to a science. Window seat. First class. Headphones so no one would talk to me. Dramamine so I didn't vomit on whatever unlucky son of a bitch sat next to me.

Fuck, I was really doing this.

Soon, the pale pink of the Minnesota dawn would give way to the bright baby blue of the Texas sky.

It'd been years since I set foot in the little town of Whynot.

But just like the name, *why not* run away from all my problems? *Why not* go back to the one place that had been both my hell and heaven?

Why not go home?

CHAPTER ONE

My face was stained blue.

"Oh. My. God."

I'd really done it this time.

I snatched a wad of makeup wipes out of the package and furiously scrubbed my cheeks and forehead until my skin looked like a cooked lobster.

Oh god. It's not coming off.

"Fuck me."

My jaw dropped at the horror of my appearance.

It was my fault for attempting to color my own hair. My chestnut waves were a frizzy pain in the ass half of the time, so after a bad week, I thought it would be *fun* to attempt to turn them—*what did the package say?*—anime blue.

I was a painter after all, right? Couldn't be that hard to apply some hair dye.

Wrong. Now my hair was still the same shade of Whynot family brown, and I looked like I'd fucked a Smurf.

A string of curses flowed from my mouth in an unladylike manner that would have had my mother choking on her iced sweet tea. Although after twenty-six years of fighting me tooth and nail, she'd partially given up on turning me into the perfect daughter. I took too much after Dad, and since he passed, she'd stopped hating me so much.

Small comforts. It was too bad it took him dying for her to love me.

Oof. That thought stung a little too much and so I tossed it away like a dirty pair of jeans. I planted my hands on my hips and stared at myself in the mirror.

What the hell was I going to do?

Panic was setting in. I wouldn't be blue forever, right? The dye had to come off *somehow*.

The good news was that I owned an art studio, so I was always covered in acrylic splatters of color. No one would notice . . . probably.

I picked my phone up and frantically searched how to get hair dye off my skin. I fanned myself with the flattened box of *anime blue* as sweat pooled in my pits.

"*Shit.*"

My gaze flicked back to the mirror and I turned my head, checking the Bob Ross clock hanging in the kitchen down the hall. Bob was always twenty minutes early, and I'd never bothered to fix him.

But that meant I was *late*.

There was no time to do everything Reddit was telling me to do. Every Wednesday morning, I had to be at Whynot Paint before 9 a.m. or face the wrath of the small town's elderly students for being late. Ms. Carlson, in particular, was a pain in my ass. Listening to a retired math teacher lecture me on tardiness was the last thing I needed this morning.

I grabbed a scrunchie off my vanity and swept my hair back into a messy bun. Five more makeup wipes in the trash, and I was only slightly less cartoonish.

As long as I avoided my brothers *and* mother *and* friends

while in town, I'd avoid hearing about this little incident for the rest of my life.

My *final final final warning* phone alarm screeched. I winced, turned it off, and rushed to my bedroom.

This is what I got for wanting to make a change in my life. Everything had always been the same since I'd moved back to Whynot. The little Far West Texas town was slower than molasses, and the people here were nuttier than Evie's famous pecan pie.

The last census showed that there were 2800 people in Whynot, and since I was raised here, I could name almost every single one of them. My four-year escape to the University of Texas in Austin for my fine arts degree would forever be referred to as my glory days from here on out.

Well, aside from the time spent dating a piece of shit who made me doubt *everything* about myself. But that was besides the point.

The only thing we had going for us here in Whynot was that it'd become a tourist destination over the last few years. Artists, photographers, and travel gurus alike flocked here throughout the summer. They came for the aesthetic, then left to escape the heat.

Since my dad passed away, my brothers and I did our best to carry on his legacy in the town. With the Whynot name, we were at the center of everything we could do to help this place.

I owned his old art studio and worked with the community to bring art to our schools and anyone else that was interested. I was also on the Whynot planning committee for the annual fall festival and an ear for everyone's complaints.

Basically, I had three jobs, was bluer than a Texas summer sky, and had no romantic life because my two older brothers were menaces to anyone who batted an eye at me.

I had a love-hate relationship with those two. Of course, I

7

loved them. But I was sick of my love life being treated like something they could swoop in a ruin any time they wanted. It was funny when I was a teenager, but now I was creeping toward thirty and could count on one hand how many people I'd dated.

The problem was, the last person I dated not only had been Dallas and Austin's friend, he'd turned out to be manipulative. Mean. Abusive. I was still angry at myself about dating him for so long. I ended my relationship with Kevin the moment he left bruises on my arm in an argument, and then two days later, my dad unexpectedly passed away.

Needless to say, my brothers had their reasons for being overprotective. Even if they drove me nuts.

Dallas was a mechanic. Four years older than me, liked to keep to himself—which was unfortunate for him, because being a *Whynot* in *Whynot*, Texas meant you never had a moment of peace.

Between him and our oldest brother, Austin (another city name, because my parents embraced their Texas pride a little too much), Dallas was the least annoying of the two assholes.

Austin was the worst. Everything had to be *a certain way* in his world. The pressure he put on himself to be perfect spiraled out to everyone around him which made him completely insufferable at times.

My "messy" aesthetic? It drove him *insane*.

But, I had to hand it to him, Austin did his best. He also had too much on his plate, by his own fault, between running Whynot Stay, the library, and being head of the city council. He was thirty-five, and I was certain that with his stress levels, he'd be dead before forty.

But what the fuck did I know? I was the youngest of us three, and those dicks never listened to me.

I was probably going to grow old and die alone in my cute little house with a thousand vibrators and an addiction to one of those ridiculous dating shows Evie and June loved so much.

I threw on my favorite gray T-shirt, slipped into a faded paint-stained set of overalls, and rushed through the house snatching up everything I needed to get out the door. My bag was tossed over my little green velvet sofa, my sunglasses on the sunflower-tiled kitchen counter, my boots kicked apart in the entryway.

June and Evie were going to lose it if they saw me today. I should have asked June to do my hair to begin with, but my ego had gotten in the way.

Speaking of my two favorite devils, my phone buzzed.

> June: Have you seen your new neighbor yet?
>
> Evie: Oh yeah, I've been waiting for an update. What's he like?
>
> June: Hey, we don't know for sure if the neighbor is a guy. We just heard that from the grapevine. Could be a sexy woman
>
> Evie: or a hot enby
>
> June: All nonbinary people are hot
>
> Evie: So so true. Avery, we need updates

I shook my head. It was too early in the day for this level of ridiculousness, but I was used to it.

Supposedly, the house across the street from me had been rented by a mystery man a couple days ago. No one had seen him yet, so I had no idea what he looked like or if he was even real.

I stepped out the front door and regretted it. It was summer and the heat was a sweltering, looming pressure on my body.

The sun wasn't even blazing yet, but sweat sprouted on my skin like a damn sprinkler.

My little house sat on a quiet street that was a four-block walk to the studio. Normally, I'd take that walk, but today I was opting for my '67 Ford truck that'd belonged to my grandfather instead.

I side eyed the house across the street as nonchalantly as I possibly could. There was no movement. No mysterious neighbor. Just a pretty sports car in the driveway that was nothing more than a pink ribbon on a pig.

Whoever my neighbor was, I knew one thing alone by seeing that car. They were *annoying*.

Haven't seen him yet . . .

> June: Are we sure he's not dead?

> Evie: You should barge in and find out

> Y'all have lost your damn minds, absolutely not

> June: Oh come on. Stir up a little trouble for once, Avery

> Evie: You deserve some fun with a hot stranger blowing through town.

> June: Get your freak on. We know you are one. And it's been too long

This is what I got for telling those two everything. They knew I was kinky, and liked to remind me of that anytime someone interesting (meaning not from here) visited Whynot.

As if I'd ever sleep with my temporary neighbor, let alone let them spank me or pull my hair. Those sort of acts with someone required trust. They required *connection*.

I shook my head as I climbed into the truck. As messy as I was at times, I still was a rule follower through and through. It was annoying, honestly, because I wished I could be the girl that would go knock on a strange man's door.

But nope, not me. I was a good girl who minded her business.

Most of the time.

CHAPTER TWO

Wednesdays were adult art class days.

The class was usually full of seniors, and occasionally a wine mom or two. Sometimes, June would stop in if business was slow at her flower shop and drape herself over one of my stools while she drank coffee and complained about the heat. Other times, Evie would bring me a piece of her famous pie for breakfast. On the rare occasion, I got both of them yapping up a storm.

This morning, however, I hoped I didn't find either of them there. I loved them *so, so* much, but I was still quite literally blue, and their snickers would send me over the edge.

Plus, the mystery neighbor was still . . . a mystery.

The tires screeched as I slammed on the brakes, and the truck tilted as I pulled halfway onto the curb behind the studio. I hopped out, keys jangling, and jogged to the back door of the studio, using my full bodyweight to barge it open.

Another alarm went off in my pocket. I threw all my things on a chair against the wall and swiped to turn it off as I headed through the hallway to the front of the studio.

Whynot Paint was split into three spaces. The front was the gallery and shop with my art for sale, along with some pieces from other local artists, and a showcase shelf for up-and-coming students in my youth classes.

Then, there was the classroom space: a large room with countless shelves of art supplies, huge windows letting in loads of natural light, and tables and stools for anyone coming in.

The last space was mine and mine alone. I'd painted the door bright blue and it remained locked. Everyone in my life knew that space was completely off-limits and to even think about stepping foot inside was against the rules.

Behind that blue door was a place that was full of magic. Skylights filled it with natural light. Stacks of canvases leaned against the walls. Half of them were landscapes or still-life studies, and the other half?

All my kinky paintings I needed to keep hidden from prying eyes. The last thing I needed was for Whynot to discover their small town darling was a thirsty, depraved harlot.

My studio was *my* safe-haven. Hopefully, I'd get to lock myself in there later tonight.

A knock echoed through the studio.

"Fuck. Of course they're here already." I plastered on a smile as I rushed to the front door.

Ugh. My *favorite* student.

Ms. Carlson's wrinkly face glowered on the other side of the glass. She radiated that scary math teacher energy like it was nuclear waste. "Oh there she is. She made it, everyone," she announced.

Great. I unlocked the door and smiled bigger. "Good morning. Ready for class?"

The little old bat pinched her lips. "You're late, little lady."

I glanced at my phone. "Only by two minutes, Ms. Carlson."

"And you're blue."

"I am, thank you. How about you go inside and grab your

favorite seat before anyone else? Would hate for you to end up at a different table this week."

I held the door open for her as she grumbled past me, beelining for the classroom. A few other familiar faces followed. Chuck and Grace, an older couple who argued like it was their love language. Whynot's version of the Golden Girls—Caroline, Betty, Lola, and Esmeralda. Tex, an eighty-four-year-old retired cowboy who liked to paint bluebonnets, even if that wasn't the subject we were working on.

One more figure loomed at the back of the little crowd that was unlike the others.

Holy shit.

"Well, I'll be damned." I planted my hands on my hips. "If it isn't Levi Rayburn."

It'd been at least a decade since I'd seen him, but I'd know that handsome face anywhere. Levi stood on the sidewalk looking completely out of place in my world. He was a solid foot taller than me with shoulders wider than a linebacker, biceps for days, and a slightly softer belly. His flaxen hair was pushed back, his beard glinting in the sunlight against his sharp jaw. He wore dark jeans, sunglasses, cowboy boots, and a shirt that was doing the lord's work.

Levi was my first crush. It was embarrassing, especially now. But, living between here and Minnesota worked in his favor in more ways than one. He'd gone off to be a big shot in the hockey world, and had come back looking like a rugged sports model.

Levi raised a thick brow and regarded me with a coolness that made my heart skip a beat.

I had the right guy, right? I knew that face anywhere. *Hell,* I'd dreamed about kissing that face.

"Do I know you?"

Jesus, there went every shred of my ego. Someone needed to run me over.

"Oh. Uh . . . I'm Avery. Avery Whynot."

"*Oh.*" His posture relaxed slightly, but his muscles were still rigid. "Right. Austin's little sister."

Of course. That's the only thing anyone ever knew me by. Every guy in this damn town treated me like a rattlesnake out of fear of looking at *Austin's little sister* the wrong way.

"I'm more than that," I said tightly.

"Right. You're . . . blue."

I crossed my arms. My temper flared. "And you look like you got your tan from a salon. Did running off to the big league knock your fucking manners from you?"

The corner of his mouth tugged. "Did this town dry up yours?"

I glowered until he held up his hands in surrender. His very strong, very sexy, very big hockey man hands.

"Sorry. I don't mean to offend you. I'm still getting my footing here."

He sounded genuine. I studied him for a beat longer, but then relaxed my shoulders. "It's fine. Are you coming to art class or not?" *Please say yes.* It'd be refreshing to have someone under the age of fifty in my class during the week.

"Well, I was actually looking for your dad. I haven't seen him in a while and wanted to pay a visit."

His words were a gut punch. My heart dropped out of my chest, my mind going blank.

God, I'd never get used to this. *Ever.*

I opened my mouth to tell Levi the truth, but another voice interrupted.

"Little Miss Whynot, why in the hell are you the color of a blueberry?"

Dammit. Had someone cursed me today? What had I done to deserve this?

With a sigh, I turned right as Mateo hopped out of his truck looking like a damn model. Seriously, he should have been in one of those firefighter calendars. Mateo had golden brown skin, dark brown curls on top of his head, a thick mustache begging for a ride, and a smile that made my entire body light up like the Fourth of July.

He wasn't dressed up like a firefighter right now. He wore faded jeans, a navy T-shirt with the Whynot Fire Department logo that showed off those heroic muscles, and as always, those damn *slutty little glasses*. They always magnified the crinkles at the corner of his eyes when he smiled at me.

I swallowed hard as he came up beside me with a broad grin and slid his arm around my shoulders in the *totally platonic* side hug that was actually going to be the death of me.

Ever since I'd moved back to Whynot two years ago, the two of us had become best friends.

And nothing more.

"Jimenez," I grumbled.

"Pff." He ruffled my hair playfully. It took every ounce of control not to lean into his firm hand like a cat. "What the hell did you do?"

I smirked. There'd been a missed opportunity to text him a picture of the messy sink earlier, which was too bad.

That was the thing about Mateo. I wanted him so much more than just a friend, but I just settled for having what I could.

Which was a really sexy, really good *friend*.

"I was going to dye my hair blue. Don't tell anyone I look like this."

Mateo twirled me toward him, his hands settling on my hips in an all-too-familiar, playful way.

Platonic.

Completely fucking platonic, even though I'd thought about his hands more than once at night.

"I'm texting the group chat immediately," he teased.

Dammit. Why did he have to be so cute when he smiled like that? Why the fuck did my brothers have to have hot friends?

"Why are you here, Mateo?" I asked. "Aren't you on the clock? You're wearing your shirt. You know I have class to run. Ms. Carlson is probably firing up the pitchforks now since I'm running behind."

Mateo's hands fell away and he crossed his arms. "Well, I may have taken a look at your art class schedule after someone mentioned in passing you were going to be teaching fumage."

Damn. That meant Angie had tattled on me.

Angie ran local dispatch and just loved to be up in everyone's business. She'd had it out for me ever since I stuck bubblegum in her hair in fourth grade. To be fair, it was warranted. She'd poured chocolate milk all over my art the day before.

Mateo's mustache moved as the corner of his mouth twisted with amusement. "And Avery, really? You're going to let *them* handle fire in a closed space?"

I stiffened. Fumage was an art technique I loved and wanted to share with more people. I'd learned about it in college and had been experimenting with it recently. To make a piece of art, you lit a candle and used the smoke to create impressions on paper or canvas. It was challenging and exciting, and you're damn right I was going to be teaching it.

"It's a beautiful art form and this class is for adults, hotshot. Some of the people in there wiped our asses when we were babies," I argued.

"Not mine. And now we all get to wipe theirs."

My expression pinched.

Levi cleared his throat and we looked up. He was staring at us awkwardly, his sunglasses reflecting the two of us. I saw how close we stood and immediately stepped away, my heart lurching.

Mateo offered a smile as he balanced his elbow on my shoulder. "Hi. Don't think we've met. I'm Mateo."

"This is Levi," I said as they shook hands. "He's also one of Austin's friends."

"Oh," Mateo said. "Wait, you're *Levi*? Sport Levi?"

Levi didn't smile. "I'm assuming so. Haven't seen him in person in years, though. Um, Avery—"

The door to the Whynot Paint swung open and I moved back before I got bumped.

"Miss Whynot! Some of us have bingo to get to in an hour." Sure enough, Ms. Carlson poked her head out. She looked like a snake about to bite me, but then her expression changed when she laid eyes on Levi and Mateo. "*Oh*, I see. We have new students. Of course, of course. Well, don't leave them in the heat, child, or else they'll get hot and sweaty."

Before I could run interference, she grabbed hold of Levi's bulky forearm and tugged him through the front door. His head turned and he looked like he was about to flee, but there was no escaping the Carlson claws once she had them on you, even if you were a buff hockey player. God help him now, Levi was going to be in this class, whether he wanted to or not.

Mateo hummed under his breath. His gaze landed on me and my skin prickled beneath the warmth of it.

"So that's the sports star friend?"

"Yeah." I put my hands behind my back, grabbing hold of my wrist out of sight and squeezing it. The motion had always grounded me. "He and Austin go way back. Looks like you got competition in town."

Mateo winked at me. "No competition, Blue. You know I'm good at sharing."

My cheeks turned hotter than asphalt at noon from the implication. "You *cannot* call me Blue."

His gaze lingered for a moment, and then he smirked as he slid past me. "I gotta after seeing you like this. Also, I definitely just texted the group chat."

I groaned and followed him inside.

At least I'd have two new students today. That was something good, right?

CHAPTER THREE

The last time I'd seen Avery Whynot, she was a pimpled teenager with stars in her eyes, pigtails, and a nasty sunburn.

When she called out my name, I'd thought *dammit*, someone recognized me, or someone had followed me all the way out here to this dusty shithole—but no.

Even worse.

Avery-*fucking*-Whynot had turned into a gorgeous woman with a tangle of silky brown waves, freckles dusting her smooth skin, and big brown eyes. The overalls she wore were a soft baby blue denim with paint splatters on them, her hips filling them out in a way that got my blood pumping.

Certainly not the thoughts I should have had about my best friend's little sister.

The good news was that I'd clearly annoyed her. That was good. It had to be good, because the other option was that she liked me, and I liked her—and again, after the hot flash of sexual thoughts that launched to the front of my mind upon seeing her, I couldn't take that risk.

The little old lady guiding me through the gallery had the grip of a goddamn defenseman. All my words failed me as I was dragged to the classroom inside.

Last time I was here at Whynot Paint, it looked a lot different—not nearly as lively or organized as it was now. In fact, I wasn't sure anyone ever ran art classes out of this place before. If I remembered right, Mr. Whynot used it as his studio and sold his work, and that was about it.

"Excuse me," I muttered, yanking my forearm away from the little old lady. "Don't touch me."

She scoffed. "Well then. Not very nice, are you?"

I bit my tongue. No, I wasn't very *nice* when strangers randomly grabbed me, little old lady or not. I'd been in too many situations where someone would touch me inappropriately or without my consent simply because of my job, which was why I valued my reputation as a total dick. It was an easy mask to pull on.

I ignored her glower and shuffled to the empty table at the very back of the classroom. Taking an art class was the last thing I imagined myself doing this morning, but I'd needed a break from the PT exercises that'd been sent over to me.

Right before my great escape from the best career I'd probably ever have, I'd gone to the doctor *a lot*. Countless appointments, countless recommendations, and ultimately a prescription—*give your body a break*.

I hated that. For years, I'd been the guy who was up every morning working out for hours. My diet was regimented. My life was a bunch of bottles of supplements, numbers on charts, and pushing myself to be perfect.

Now, I was broken in more ways than one.

At least I'd forced myself to venture out of the house I'd rented a couple blocks over. As much as I didn't want to interact with people right now, I had to admit it felt good to be out.

The man that'd interrupted us earlier followed Avery into the classroom. *Mateo.* I tried to keep my eyes off him, but it was impossible to. The charm that dripped from his body made my head spin as he sat down next to me. He leaned back in his chair, crossing his arms as he watched Avery with a certain attentiveness that made me wonder . . .

Were those two together? He'd certainly been pretty fucking friendly with her. Once again, my thoughts went where they shouldn't. The idea of those two together rolling around in bed was so unbelievably inappropriate, and yet I could not get it out of my perverted mind.

I needed to think of quite literally anything else.

I'd been in Texas for a week now. In Whynot for three days. Reluctantly, I'd turned my phone back on and the amount of notifications had only increased. My abrupt announcement had tipped everything upside down, and I had over a *thousand* unread text messages.

I didn't know that many people. At least, I didn't think I did. My phone said otherwise, though.

My social media accounts were flooded. My voicemails were maxed out. Every time I saw the little red number reminding me of how many unread messages there were, panic bloomed in my chest, and something in me felt dangerously close to breaking. Like my body, my life was made of glass right now.

It was just a break. Right? Whatever was wrong with me would pass. I'd had similar things occur over the years, although nothing at this level. But it made no fucking sense.

Pressure never got to me. Ever. So why now?

All I knew was I was only reading messages from my agent. Robin was in full-on crisis mode, but had given me six weeks to get my mind straightened out.

Six weeks.

Then she said we'd talk.

No one knew where I was aside from her, and it'd stay that way until I was ready to come out of hiding in five weeks.

Avery cleared her throat as she took her place at the front of the room. "Good morning, everyone. We're doing something new today. And lucky for us, we have the best firefighter in town to keep watch."

All heads swiveled to Mateo, who pushed his glasses up the bridge of his nose, completely at ease. My brain short-circuited as I studied him, trying to keep my attention off his mustache.

Damn, that was a fine mustache.

I liked kissing men with mustaches.

Get the fuck out of your horny head, Rayburn.

I tore my attention from him and refocused on Avery, as if that were any better. Whatever I'd said to piss her off earlier was clearly far from her mind as she gathered supplies, her dimples flashing as she spoke. I still wondered why her face was blue, but honestly? It kind of suited her. And the fact that no one seemed to really be fazed by it said something about her.

Something that piqued my interest.

"Today, we're trying out fumage."

"I don't smoke pot," one of the older women called from the front.

Avery swallowed a laugh. "Well, good thing we're not smoking pot, Grace."

"Well, damn, I don't want it then," one of the other women mumbled.

"Okay, okay. Please remember you're at a community art class. We don't smoke pot here. *Fumage* is an art form that involves using smoke to create art. We'll light our candles, and using the tip of the flame, you'll hold the paper and create abstract marks with it. You'd be surprised what you can make."

She dropped all the supplies in front of each of us before soaring back to the front. There was a canvas on an easel with fabric draped over it, and she tugged it away dramatically, revealing the piece underneath.

Everyone gasped and made approving sounds. I leaned forward, far more interested than I expected.

The art was really good. It was a black and white landscape with two longhorns in tall grass. Wisps of gray and black danced around them, abstract but calculated. The longhorns were done in such detail that I couldn't see how she did that with *smoke.*

Then again, I was no artist. Not like that, anyway. Photography was my hobby, but painting? It was impossible. The last time I'd attempted an art project of sorts was when I'd done wax play with an ex-lover.

"Did you do that, Avery?" an elderly man asked.

Her expression lit up. Suddenly, I didn't care about anyone else in the room.

"I did," she said. "This piece is for the festival auction in a couple months. However much it goes for will be donated to our library and keeping school lunches free."

Mateo leaned forward, his gaze locked on Avery with the same interest I felt. *Stop looking at him, dumbass.*

This was exactly why I'd gotten in trouble in the first place. I couldn't keep my expression in check most of the time, so I often ended up putting on a grumpy face to keep people from bothering me. My agent called it RLF, or *resting Levi face.* She'd even proposed we put that on stickers, but I turned that down fast.

God, I just knew Robin was burning a hole in my phone.

"So, let's give it a try. Y'all each got a candle and a piece of paper. Now, mind you, we are putting paper to flame, so it may catch fire. But if it does, I'll have buckets of water placed around the room."

Mateo cleared his throat. "Avery, are you sure about this?"

Avery flashed him a sassy smile. "I'm a professional, Mateo, so don't you worry your pretty head about it. Trust the process."

Mateo smirked. "I'm on the clock anyway, *Blue*."

She rolled her eyes at him, but I caught the hint of excitement that went beyond *friendly*. I raised a brow, invested in whatever *this* was.

See, maybe I had missed this small town. It was easy to sink back into speculating about two people I didn't know. Even more fun to think about what it'd be like to be with the two of them.

Now I knew I'd really lost my fucking mind. Maybe I needed to go back home and take a cold shower. Ice this damn lust out of my veins.

"Are you two dating?" I whispered to Mateo.

His expression flashed with surprise, and then he immediately shook his head. Shit, I should have kept my mouth shut.

"No. She's Austin's sister. She's off-limits." His tone was calm and serious, as if he'd rehearsed those words more than a few times.

"Right."

I distinctly recalled the bastard putting the fear of god into anyone who looked at her when we were kids. But that was before she was a full adult who could make her own decisions.

It had made sense then, but now . . .

The idea of him trying to control her love life didn't sit right with me. But, what the hell was I even thinking? I didn't know her. She certainly didn't like me. None of this was my business.

I looked away from Mateo, ignoring the heat that crawled up my spine. It'd been a long time since I'd felt a stirring in my chest like this. Maybe it was the fresh air or the fact that no one was stalking my every move here, but it felt nice to be interested in someone and not wonder if they had an ulterior motive.

Avery held up a lighter. "I'm going to come around and light all the candles. Don't do anything until I instruct you. Got it?"

Everyone murmured in agreement as Avery flicked on the lighter. She darted around the room to every wick until all of us had a candle with a flame.

Avery returned to the front of the class and lit one more candle for herself. She picked up the piece of paper and held both up, showing us how to angle the fire to the paper. I anticipated it would catch, but it didn't.

"What is this magic?" Mateo called.

That earned a few snorts. Avery ignored him as she moved the candle, soot darkening the page until she lowered it. She turned the page over, showing us the marks.

"Now how in the hell did you take that to *that?*" I asked, gesturing from the paper to the canvas.

There was something really special about the way her eyes lit up. Avery loved teaching, that much was clear. "There are techniques you do after this. You can use a paintbrush, a feather—really anything that can make marks to draw into the soot. You can also introduce other mediums too, like watercolors. For this one, I went over it with a paintbrush and pencil."

Damn. That piece would sell for thousands in some of the circles I used to run in. *Used to.*

Avery looked around the classroom. "Now, all of you give it a try. I'll get the water ready."

Mateo blew out his candle and stood up. "I'll help, Avery, if you just want to focus on teaching."

Her teeth sank into her bottom lip as she considered his offer. "You sure?"

Mateo nodded. "I'm no artist, Blue. Let me give you a hand."

"Ugh. I can't believe you're calling me that," she sighed. "But okay. Thanks."

I narrowed my eyes on the two of them again. Jesus Christ, they needed to get a room.

"Why *are* you blue?" someone asked.

"That's none of your business, Betty. All right, everyone. Make some art!"

I rolled my shoulders, ignoring the ache on my right side. I'd spent an hour this morning going through the PT exercises, and I hated them. Every moment of it was excruciating. Humbling. There was a fear lodged in my chest that I'd probably hurt forever.

Wrinkling my nose, I held the paper above the flame, careful not to let it touch the paper. It took some adjusting of the angle, but eventually a plume of soot licked at the paper, creating marks like brush strokes.

"Wow," I whispered.

"Good job." Avery's voice startled me, and I realized she was behind me. "May I touch you?"

I swore I could hear my brain synapses hissing. "Uh. Sure."

"Thanks." She leaned over me and grabbed my hand, steadying it slightly.

Her skin was soft against mine. Her fingers were long and slender and stained blue, her nails short. Heat jerked through me from her touch, but then I realized she could see my right hand was trembling and it all fizzled out into embarrassment.

"Sorry," I muttered. "My hand shakes on that side sometimes."

"You're doing great, Levi." The scent of her perfume washed over me and my mouth watered. Patchouli, rose, and berry hit me subtly like a sweet summer breeze. "There we go. Look, you're a natural."

"I'm not good at this."

"You're doing fine."

"I'm not." The fire was making me nervous now.

"You really are. You're doing great."

The praise kicked my heart rate up. I started to pull back, but the paper moved a little too close without me meaning to. The flame caught and I cursed as it lit up.

"Here," Avery said quickly. "I'll take it."

"No—"

"Give it to me, Rayburn," she growled, reaching for it.

I was being obtuse, but I snarled at her regardless. "I said no."

"You're being a dick."

I yanked back a little too hard and she stumbled forward, her long waves falling forward. In the blink of an eye, the flame caught her hair.

"Fuck!" I yelled, jumping up quickly. "Firefighter!"

Mateo rushed across the room in a blur and lifted the bucket. He threw the water straight on her, drenching her completely.

Avery squealed, her eyes clamping shut as the flame was snuffed out.

Everyone fell silent and stared as she sputtered, her cheeks blooming bright red. Her eyes flew open and burned with fury.

If looks could kill, I'd be a dead man.

"*Levi fucking Rayburn*," she hissed. "What the *fuck* is wrong with you?"

All my defenses rose up. "It's not my fault you didn't listen to me," I snapped.

Which was maybe not the best response I could have given to her.

"You didn't listen to *me*," she said. "I've been working with this art style for years. That's why *I'm* the teacher."

"I told you, I'm no artist."

"And as my dad used to say, everyone is."

Everything iced over. My eyes widened at the implication as her cheeks turned even redder.

Surely, she didn't mean her dad was gone. Surely not. Austin would have told me. We talked every month. We'd been talking *every month* for years. I would have known. Right?

"Used to . . . ?" I croaked.

Mateo winced, telling me what I needed to know without a word.

Avery's throat worked as she swallowed hard. She crossed her arms, her wet hair sticking to her face and neck. "Yeah. Sorry. Dad passed away two years ago. Heart attack. He's gone."

Two years.

All my bones were cold. I opened my mouth to apologize for putting my foot in it, but Avery was already moving to one of the other tables, completely ignoring me. Everyone's attention slid back to her, and even though she was drenched, blue, and on the verge of tears—she kept going.

Fuck me.

I needed to get the hell out of here.

Mateo pressed his lips together as he studied me. "You didn't know?"

I shook my head. "Austin didn't tell me. And I'm not very good at keeping up with people on social media anymore because of my job. Sorry for the trouble."

"Avery doesn't really talk about it," Mateo said, keeping his voice low. "Out of the three of them, she's more of a vault than Austin."

"Apparently not." Now the truth was staring me dead in the eye, and I didn't like it.

I was alone. Maybe more than I'd ever realized.

"Do you want to get brunch after this?" Mateo asked. "Since you're back in town, but also sort of new? We can grab tacos and go harass Austin. I like the idea of showing up with his best friend at my hip."

"No." I winced, having said that a little harsher than I meant to. "Sorry. I just need some air. I don't know what the fuck I'm doing here."

Before Mateo could say anything else, I pushed my chair in and headed for the door. Avery's voice haunted me as I hurtled to the front, my heart pounding as I ran from both of them.

One week in Whynot, and I'd already ruined everything.

CHAPTER FOUR

By the time dinner time rolled around, I'd taught four more classes without disaster and had managed to replay the situation with Levi a million times in my head.

I wished I lived in a city because then I'd never see him again. Instead, I was stuck in this tiny-ass town, and there was gonna be no avoiding him while he was back in Texas.

At some point I'd have to apologize for snapping, but that wasn't happening today.

It didn't help that Mateo had handled it the way he always did. After Levi left, he'd stayed to help for the rest of the class, and then he gave me a hug and left when it was finished.

That was it.

I could still feel him against me. His scent fucking haunted me. There'd been nothing sexual in his touch, just pure support, and that'd been enough to truly ruin my day.

A knock on the studio door had my gaze lifting from the front desk. I waved my hand at Evie, one of my best friends since high school. She was gorgeous as ever, not looking like she'd been up since 5 a.m. like I knew she had. Her blonde hair was pulled back into a ponytail, crimson red lipstick perfectly unsmudged. She wore a cute dress with strawberries on it that hugged her plus-sized body in a way that made me drool, the sweetheart neckline doing god's work.

Evie stepped inside and held up a piece of her famous pecan pie.

"I come bearing pie. I heard you might need it," she said.

I sighed dramatically. "Have I ever told you that you're beautiful?"

"You say that every time I bring you pie on a bad day, *Blue*."

I groaned and put my forehead down on the countertop as she approached. I'd forgotten that the bastard had sent the group chat a message about my little situation. I hadn't checked my messages all day.

Now, I was sure the entire town was going to be calling me *Blue* for the rest of my life.

"Oh boy. That bad, huh?" Evie sat the pie plate down next to me and stabbed the fork in it. "I was swamped all day, otherwise I would have rescued you sooner. June is on her way too. She's dropping off her niece at her brother's."

I raised my eyes to meet Evie's gaze with a frown. Both of us had noticed just how much more June had been caring for her niece, Laura. She hadn't talked to either one of us about it, which probably meant it was much worse than we knew.

"Do we need to run an intervention with her?" I asked hesitantly.

"Maybe. Too soon to tell. Her brother has never been my favorite person, but that's just because he's always caused her trouble. I know he's having a hard time right now." Evie pressed her lips into a thin line. "Tell me about today. Spill the beans."

"Well, today was a disaster," I said into the counter. I turned my head, keeping my cheek pressed to its surface as I broke off a bite of pie with the fork and shoved it in my mouth. The sugar rush eased the frustration around today just a bit.

"You're being a little dramatic," Evie snorted.

"I'm not," I protested. "Not only did my hair dye go everywhere this morning, I ran into Levi Rayburn, of all people. Then Mateo. Levi is even hotter in person than he is on TV. And Mateo makes me want to melt into the damn dirt, but he treats me like a kid because of Austin."

"Well, maybe remind them you're not a kid? I mean, you've been back for two years, Avery. Maybe it's time to stop pretending like you're just his friend."

I sat up, giving her a dirty look. "And how in the hell should I do that, Evie? Get a push up bra? Not everyone has tits like yours. I look like a boy under my overalls. Besides, Mateo and I can't be together. Austin would kill us."

Her laugh rang through the gallery as she dragged a barstool over from the wall, sitting down and resting her pretty face in her hands. "Okay, one, I've seen you in a bikini, you do not look like a boy. Two, Austin isn't the boss of your love life, regardless of the Kevin situation. Three, so far, all I've heard is you saw two hot men. What else happened?"

"Then they ended up in my fumage class and my hair caught on fire. Then Mateo threw water at me to put it out. I was wet and humiliated."

"I thought that was your kink."

"*Evie*," I hissed. "Be serious."

The door swung open and June burst in carrying two bags of hot fries from Whynot Burgers, a joint two miles outside of town and worth the calories.

June's hair was cosmos pink and cut into a wavy bob. She wore a green tank top and palazzo pants, her arms covered in flower tattoos that bloomed up to her shoulders. Most people in Whynot thought they were so *cute* given that she ran the local

33

flower shop—but Evie and I knew every single one of those flower tattoos were actually poisonous plants, which was just perfect for her.

Sweeter than sugar on the surface, but she'd rip someone's heart out through their throat if she needed to.

"Oh hell yes," I said. "Have I told you that you're beautiful?"

June flashed her dimples. "That bad of a day, huh? Why the fuck is your face blue? And why didn't you tell us this morning when we were asking about your new neighbor?"

"Because I was running late."

"And what's new?" June countered. "I could have helped you get the dye off. How do you think my hair stays so damn vibrant? I certainly don't let Betty at the hair salon touch it. If you're turning your hair blue, you need to bleach it first. I'll come over tomorrow to do it."

"You're an angel," I sighed. "I just want the ends done, honestly. I need some sort of change."

"So you woke up at seven this morning and decided to make one?" Evie asked.

I scooped up another bite of pie. "Have you met me?"

June plopped the bags on the counter and grabbed a stool, taking her spot next to Evie. The two of them exchanged glances and I frowned, wondering what they were thinking about me. Probably that I was a mess.

"Are you going to tell me the rest of what happened?" June asked.

I was being just a little dramatic, but I let out a long groan and made myself sit up straight. I dragged my pie plate closer and relayed everything I'd told Evie between the gooey bites.

"And in the end, I was an asshole to both of them. I'm certain Levi will never talk to me again and Mateo probably thinks I'm awful. But, I was just so embarrassed, and everyone kept asking about the dye. And I was running late, and I don't know. Well, and Levi asked about Dad."

Evie and June's expressions dropped.

"He didn't know?" June asked softly.

"No." I swallowed hard, suddenly losing my appetite. "Not his fault. He hasn't been back in Whynot in a long time. I think I was fifteen the last time I saw him."

At fifteen, a twenty-three-year-old seemed like an alien. He was completely in a different stage of life. And I distinctly remembered the last time I saw him, because he'd gotten into a fight with his dad on Main Street that ended with my dad and Austin pulling them apart.

"I've seen pictures of him in magazines and online," Evie said. "He's done some modeling. I mean, he's a hockey player. Well, he was one."

"What do you mean *was*?" I asked. "Isn't he some big league hotshot?"

Evie drummed her nails on the counter, clearly mulling over the info she had on Levi. "He quit last week. The only reason I know is because someone was talking about it at the pie shop earlier. They spotted him in town and were shocked to see him."

"He's probably looking for some privacy then," I muttered.

The silver sports car across the street from my house came to mind and I frowned.

Surely not.

Surely *Levi* wasn't the new mystery neighbor.

Evie shrugged. "Who knows. I just know the internet is losing their damn minds about his announcement. They're saying a lot of shit about him, both good and bad. His publicist is earning her paycheck, that's for sure."

June shook her head. "You know way too much about this, Evie."

She shrugged. "It's all over social media. Hard to miss when the algorithm knows you like hot beefy dudes rubbing all over each other."

I laughed as June pointed a french fry at her. "Good point. Send me the videos when you get a chance. Sharing is caring." She redirected the fry to me. "Are you still going to therapy?"

Dammit. "What a fucking segue. Can I finish my pie first?"

"Nope," June popped the *p.*

"Okay, well since we're talking, what's going on with Laura?"

June scowled. "Answer my question first, bitch."

"The answer is yes. I'm still seeing my therapist."

"And how are you feeling about everything?"

I scowled. The *everything* was so broad, but I knew what she was really asking. *Are you still fighting with your mom? Are you still having nightmares about Kevin? Are you still crying yourself to sleep missing your Dad sometimes?* "I'm totally fine."

Neither one of them bought it—and frankly, I didn't either. Most days, I *was* fine. But then there were days like today, when it hit me all over again: my dad was gone, the three of us Whynots were doing our best to fill his big-ass boots, and my mother was becoming a reclusive mess.

"Your turn," I said.

June ate a couple fries and then sighed, her shoulders tightening. "Laura will be spending more time with me. Ethan hasn't been doing well at all, and I don't know what to do about it. My mother still insists on babying him despite the fact that he's failing his daughter constantly."

"You can't keep stepping in," Evie said softly.

"I can and will. I love that kid. You know she called me 'Mom' the other day?"

Well, fuck. "She did?"

"Yeah. I got home and sobbed after that."

Evie leaned over and rested her head on June's shoulder. "Why didn't you call?"

June shrugged. "I don't want to burden you two."

"Don't you dare pull that card," I said. "Not after everything I've put on you guys in the last two years, okay? You could show up on my doorstep at 3 a.m., and I'd be there for you."

"Agreed," Evie said. "Lord knows I've shown up on both of yours. We've been friends since kindergarten, June. That's what we're here for."

"I know." She let out a slow, deliberate breath, her shoulders deflating like a balloon. "I'm starting to wonder if I should try and take custody of her. Financially, it might be a little hard. I was looking up how much raising a kid costs, and Jesus Christ. In this economy? I don't know. But I'd make it work."

"You know we'd help," I said.

"You already do plenty."

"Well, if you're doing more, so are we," Evie said. "If she ends up with you as her mother, she gets us as her aunts. That's how it works."

"Thank you." June let out a soft hum and shook her head. "My hope is that Ethan will get into a good rehab program and we can help him recover. I still believe in him. Plus, Mom would fight me on Laura."

We all knew that to be true. June's mother had always hated her in a way that made my own mother look like a damn angel. The way she treated June was bad enough that I'd long since dropped the niceties with that evil bitch. She was downright banned from taking classes at my studio.

Evie cracked her fingers and rolled her shoulders. "You know, I have two decades of pent up aggression I could take out on her if need be."

June's laugh lit up the room. "Okay, Rocky. We're not beating up my mom."

"I'm just saying, I could. Bakers muscles and all that."

The three of us burst out laughing. The knot in the back of my head eased a little. Even after a bad day, these two never failed to make me feel better.

Now, if I could just focus on that, instead of wondering just who my new neighbor actually was . . .

CHAPTER FIVE

"Maria, you can't be calling me every time this cat goes up the tree."

I cradled the ancient calico to my chest, wincing as she dug her claws through my shirt. Sweat dripped down my back as I climbed down the old oak, my boots smacking the dirt as I turned around and presented Frida to my cousin.

Frida hissed, baring her fangs at us like a little demon. At this point, I was pretty sure the cat had been alive longer than either of us.

"You know Abuela would kill me if this cat went missing," Maria answered, prying the beast off me. "Frida is her pride and joy. And I swear, she tries to get out any time I open the door. It's like she wants to die."

I snorted. "So you put in a call to the fire department?"

Not that I could really complain. There was usually nothing going on in our small town. Avery's hair catching fire on Wednesday was probably the most excitement I'd get all month, except that hadn't been exciting at all. If anything, it'd been painful to watch. Everything happened so fast.

Then her comment about her dad . . .

I pushed those thoughts away. I couldn't bring myself to

think about him or that night. It still gave me nightmares. Being the first one to the Whynot house that day would haunt me for the rest of my life.

"Oh sorry, Mateo. Were you *busy?*" Maria's voice snapped me back to the moment. "You think I'm climbing up that tree? I've got enough on my plate as it is."

"All right, all right. *Tranquilízate.*" I wiped my forehead with my shirt and adjusted my sunglasses. "I gotta head back to the station. You know, to keep being a hero and all that."

"Sure. Tell Austin I said hey when he inevitably brings you a snack because you two are bored."

I snorted, but didn't argue. Austin *would* be stopping by the station later to bring me dinner, but that was only because it was our routine during the week. Coming from a large Mexican family, I was used to having loved ones around to share good meals with. When I first moved to Whynot, I didn't have anyone but Maria and our abuela. Austin had become someone I enjoyed having around too, and it wasn't long before we developed a habit. Austin would finish up one of his miscellaneous tasks and come by to keep me company with carnitas, sweet tea, and small town gossip. Or we'd eventually bitch about how we were going to grow old and die without being loved because there was no one to date in Whynot.

Our running joke was *why not die alone?*

Maria smirked as she held Frida close to her chest and headed back into the house.

"*Te quiero!*" I called.

"Yeah, yeah. Love you too."

I shook my head at her as she stepped through the back door and shut it behind her. I loved my family. Truly. Even though Maria drove me a little nuts sometimes, I was closer to her and our abuela than almost anyone else in our family. While I missed everyone who lived in Lubbock and Odessa, it worked out that I loved those two the most—though that was a secret.

I planted my hands on my hips and craned my head back, glancing up at the sky. It was gonna be a hot one. It wasn't even noon yet, but the air wavered like the inside of an oven.

My radio buzzed from inside the truck and I jogged back to it, leaning through the open front door to listen.

"Helllooooo, Mateo? You there?"

I sighed. Our dispatch wasn't exactly the most professional dispatch out there. "Yep. What's going on, Angie?"

"Someone has a flat tire outside of town over by the 'Welcome to Whynot' sign. Some sort of pretty sports car. Dumbass ran over a cactus."

Oh boy. So an out of towner, then. I had a hunch who that might be, but then again, we were deep in summer and tourists were all over the place on weekends. "I'll head over."

"Also, I heard through the grapevine that Avery Whynot is going to teach another fire class . . ."

Of course she was. The Whynots were the most stubborn people I'd ever met in my life, and Avery was no different. "I'm sure she won't, but I'll check in."

"Thanks, Mateo."

I got in and started up my pickup truck. As a firefighter in a town this size, I put out every kind of fire but the kind with flames. Technically, I was the only fully trained and certified firefighter in town. Everyone else was on a volunteer and as-needed basis. I worked at the station Wednesday through Sunday, but otherwise stayed on call 24/7.

It wasn't exactly what I'd envisioned for myself after leaving Lubbock. I'd imagined going on to being one of those hotshot firefighters that was constantly saving people in danger.

Instead, I ended up being the only firefighter in a town the size of a speck of dust.

But, I *could* say I was the hottest firefighter in Whynot.

That had to count for something, right?

Five minutes later, I made it to the sign just outside the town limits.

"What the hell?" I snorted as I pulled off the side of the road.

A silver corvette was parked in the tall yellow grass. Next to it was a massive cactus that was no longer upright.

Neither of those were what made my brows shoot up, though.

It was the sexy hockey player down on his knees.

CHAPTER SIX

A line of sweat trailed down Levi's broad back. His gray T-shirt clung to his muscles as he inspected the car's tire. Wranglers made his ass look damn good, even if they were just a little too new and his boots definitely hadn't been broken in yet.

I'd seen him here and there in town—it was hard not to notice him. Usually he had a camera with him, and I had half a mind to ask what that was about.

I pushed my glasses up my nose and hopped out of the truck. "Hey, Levi. You okay?"

His head turned as he got up, letting out a low grunt. I didn't miss his wince as he stood.

"Are you hurt?" I rushed out.

"I'm fine. Shouldn't have rented a fucking sports car. A rabbit ran across the road, I swerved, and ended up running into that cactus."

Rogue cactus blossoms were strewn across the dead grass, the car slightly tilted on top of the saguaro. "You really need something cheap and hardy out in these parts. Especially if you go to the state park."

Levi was silent for a moment, but then broke it. "I take it someone called me in, huh?"

"Yep. Anyone new in town will grab attention, whether they like it or not. Even if you used to live here. Maybe especially so."

He tipped his head back with a groan. The Davis Mountains cut into the powder blue sky in the distance, a band of dark clouds hovering even further away. If we were lucky, maybe we'd get a sprinkle of rain. We certainly needed it.

"I guess it's a good thing, since my phone died." Levi pressed his lips together and then regarded me thoughtfully. "I was an ass on Wednesday."

"Well, I don't think you planned to set Avery's hair on fire."

"I didn't. I didn't plan to take an art class. I didn't plan to be here in Whynot. *Nothing* is going to plan."

I raised a brow. Up close, Levi was more handsome than should have been allowed. He had a ruggedness about him that felt out of place with the new denim and the flashy car. But then there were his eyes.

Green. Bright, grassy green. A shade of green that'd been haunting my dreams.

His beard looked soft and well kept. I thought about running my fingers through it, then shoved that dirty thought away. God, what the hell had gotten into me? *Something.*

Ever since the class with Avery and Levi, I'd been too horny for my own good. They were two threads I kept trying to yank free, but only pulled tighter with every tug.

The truth was, I'd always wanted Avery. That was one of my longest kept secrets.

But Levi?

One look at the hockey player had my body craving things I'd kept in check for two years. Since Avery moved back to Whynot, I hadn't dated or been with anyone. Why? Maybe because she was who I really wanted, but I'd just never crossed the line with her. Maybe because we lived in a small town where there wasn't really a chance to be kinky like there was in the city.

Either way, Levi's presence was disrupting all of my hard-earned self-restraint.

"I have a proposal," I said.

Levi crossed his arms. "And what would that be? Send me back to Minnesota?"

"No," I snorted. "How about I give you a ride? I know the mechanic and I'm sure he can get you taken care of. Well, actually, I'm sure you know him too. His name is Dallas Whynot."

Levi cracked a smile that was brighter than the sun. "Damn. I forgot he's the mechanic. Never thought he would end up in that career."

"What did you think he'd be?"

"A fucking librarian."

I barked out a laugh. Dallas was an interesting one, that was for sure. All he wanted to do was work on his cars and read books.

"You know, he has one of those little free libraries outside his house," I said. "Keeps it fully stocked and everything."

"Of course he does." Some of the tension melted from his shoulders. "I guess I'll take that ride, if you don't mind, Mateo."

My stomach did a cartwheel as he said my name. I swallowed hard. "Sure. Where are you staying?"

"I rented that little house over on Armadillo Lane. The one with the yellow door."

Oh boy. Did he have any idea that he was neighbors with Avery? Seemed like something one or the other would have mentioned by now. The tension between them was a movie on repeat in my mind.

Maybe I was just looking too much into things, but the way Avery had looked at him made me jealous—

I clipped that line of thought like an unruly weed. I had no business thinking about Avery. Especially like that. She was Austin's sister, for god's sake. She was my *friend*. Over the last couple years, we'd become a staple in each other's lives. It wasn't uncommon for her to show up on my doorstep with breakfast and coffee on mornings when I was off.

She was also a gorgeous, funny, smart mess—and I absolutely could never think about more than what she was.

A friend.

Just a friend I thought of every single waking moment of every single day.

Just a friend I wanted to fuck straight through my mattress.

"I'll give you a ride," I said tightly.

"Thanks. Actually, I've been meaning to go see Austin, I just haven't yet. I've been kind of keeping to myself. Probably not the best idea. Do you know where he might be?"

"Sure do," I chuckled. "He's probably working on the finances for the various businesses he's got his fingers in. Should be at the office at the little blue hotel downtown. I'm surprised you haven't texted him yet or he hasn't texted you."

"He probably has, honestly. I've been avoiding my phone. It's been off or dead since I got here."

I wondered why that was. It wasn't like me to pry, but I was undeniably curious about Levi. There was just something about him that made me want to get to know him, especially when he let that prickly guard down.

"Well, come take a ride with me. I'll get you over to him. Got anything in your car?"

"Just a backpack and my camera bag. I was going to go for a hike."

"In this heat?" I snorted. "You'd be roasted, Minnesota."

Levi stiffened for a moment, but then released a laugh from his gut. "You know, everyone has been calling me Tex for so long, it's kind of nice to be called that instead."

There was that flutter in my stomach again and a nervous smile tugged at my lips. What was it about him?

Levi leaned into the car and grabbed his backpack and water bottle, which was a relief to see. The last thing I needed was to be dragging him into the back of an ambulance with heat stroke. More often than not, that's how I spent my shifts during the summer.

I rubbed the back of my head as Levi popped the tiny trunk. He pulled a black duffle bag out and slammed it shut.

"Let me give you a hand," I offered.

"I got it."

"Come on." My heart skipped a beat as I reached for the camera bag, our hands brushing as I took it. Levi swallowed hard, his eyes tracking me as I headed back to my truck.

I had no idea what the hell was wrong with me. I'd lived in Texas my entire life and knew better than to be openly . . . *what*? Bisexual? Flirty with a burly man like Levi? I hated that I even had to think about it, but the last thing I needed was to deal with someone homophobic or asinine. He was friends with Austin and Dallas though, and since those two were also bi, I doubted Levi was homophobic. But I'd learned I could never be too careful here.

Levi opened the door on the opposite side, but this time his smile was a little more genuine, and his cheeks a little more pink.

And maybe not from the sun this time.

His brow lifted. "Do firefighters normally rescue guys like me?"

"You'd be the first to run over a saguaro." We both slammed the doors and got into the front. I stole another glance at him as I pulled onto the nearly empty road. "A nice bonus to my day, though. Before you, I was literally rescuing a cat from a tree. And I gotta say, you were a lot easier to pick up."

A husky chuckle left him. "Didn't think firefighters still did that."

"We do in Whynot."

He let out a soft hum and relaxed a fraction. "How long have you lived here?"

"A few years. Moved over from Lubbock after my fire-fighter and EMS courses. There was an opening here, and well, I have a cousin and grandmother in town. Just made sense." I stole another glance, noting the way his left thigh bounced up and down. Was I making him anxious? "Do you need a Gatorade or anything? I got some in a cooler in back if you do."

"I'm all right. I've been drinking plenty." His gaze focused on the buildings as we crawled along Main Street at fifteen miles per hour. "Do you think Avery hates me?"

Their interaction must have been on his mind as much as it had been on mine. Avery had a temper sometimes, but she never aimed it at people. The way she'd snapped at him wasn't like her, but between being asked about her dad and feeling embarrassed, I understood why she did.

"No. She went home and scrubbed the blue dye off her skin. And she's been painting and working her normal weird hours."

"What hours are those?"

I wasn't sure I should answer that, because then he'd discover I knew a lot more about her schedule than I should have as a friend.

"They're just all over the place. I'll park over by her gallery and we can walk over to the hotel. Maybe you can chat with her. I really doubt she's holding a grudge."

Frankly, I knew Avery could hold a grudge. Dallas and Austin knew that better than anyone else. The truth was, if she were still mad at Levi, she would have said something to me.

Not that we told each other everything.

Just *almost* everything.

Levi didn't say anything else as we passed by the coffee shop first. The front was painted bright pink, with "Whynot Community Coffee Roasters" gleaming on a custom hand-painted sign Avery had made a few months ago. I was halfway convinced there wasn't anything Avery couldn't do. Small tables sat outside, a few people lounging beneath the umbrellas and sipping on iced lattes.

Then there was the flower shop, Whynot Bloom, which was owned by June. It had the same bright colors as the coffee shop, like a cactus in bloom amid the neutral tones of the rest of the street. My favorite shops here were all the ones that went the extra mile with their storefront, such as Avery's gallery.

Levi leaned forward slightly, ducking his head.

"We got a theme in this town, as I'm sure you remember. Pretty much everything is named after the town."

"And *why not?*" Levi sat back in his seat with a smirk. "I know it gets old."

"It does. But I like it. Adds a bit of charm."

"So does the landscape."

He was right about that. A few miles north of our little town were the Davis Mountains, and then to the south was Big Bend National Park. Whynot had a lot of visitors passing through—including hikers and artists—especially during the summer. It was part of the reason I kept my truck fully stocked with water and emergency supplies.

"You planning to do some stargazing while you're here?"

"Maybe," Levi sighed. "I don't really know what the fuck I'm doing, honestly. I just needed to get away."

Hmm. What was Levi running from?

"It's a good place for that. If you need any recommendations, just let me know. I know things may have changed since you lived here." I slowed the truck as we passed Evie's famous pie shop. "That place has the best pecan pie in Texas."

Levi shook his head. "Not sure I'm buying that."

"It's true."

"In Whynot, of all fucking places?"

I grinned. "Yep. Evie has been in magazines and stuff. There are articles about it."

We were proud of her, that was for sure. I spent way too much of my paycheck on Evie's goods. The pecan pie was pretty damn good, but the tres leches cake with a dulce de leche glaze was the best.

"So, what you're saying is that I should get some pie later."

"Yeah, and know that it's all you're going to want while you're here."

Avery's gallery was on the right. I pulled up to the curb as the front door swung open.

Avery stepped out into a ray of sunlight, and my pulse shot straight up.

There she is.

I'd never get tired of seeing her. I swallowed hard as she gave us a devilish glare, her hands planting on her hips as I turned off the truck.

"I don't think she wants to see me," Levi said quickly. "Let's just go see Austin."

"She doesn't bite." Kind of wanted her to bite me, though.

Levi grunted, but we both opened the doors and got out. Avery crossed her arms as people left her studio, heading down the sidewalk toward their cars or another shop.

Her hair was drawn back into a loose bun today, wisps framing her face. Her bangs were messy and she'd caught a little bit of a tan over the last few weeks, and it made every freckle stand out. She was wearing olive green overalls with a tank top, paint streaks staining the fabric.

"What do you want?" Avery asked flatly.

"We're going to see your brother," I said as I met her on the sidewalk. Levi had yet to say a word. "Don't suppose you know where he is?"

"Mateo, you know more than I do. The two of you are joined at the hip." She turned her bright gaze onto Levi, and I almost felt sorry for him.

"What?" Levi grunted.

"What do you mean *what*?"

Jesus Christ. The tension radiating off these two was enough to make me sweat.

"You're looking at me like you expect me to say something," he quipped.

"I was looking at you expecting you to say something rude, and you did."

"Avery," I hissed, surprised by her attitude.

Her spine stiffened, her cheeks reddening. She blew out a breath and then looked away.

"*Avery*," I said a little more seriously.

Levi cleared his throat and started to slide past us to escape, but she caught his forearm. He turned in surprise, his expression softening as he looked at her.

There went that green-eyed monster again. Ugly and all consuming and scratching at my soul.

Avery released his arm. "I'm sorry, Levi. I overreacted. I didn't expect to ask about Dad and I didn't expect to ever see you again, and well . . ." She trailed off, her throat working. "I'm sorry."

"I'm sorry too, Avery. I've been thinking about you and couldn't get our interaction off my mind," he said simply. He held out his hand. "Truce?"

Avery gave him a soft smile and slid hers into his. Seeing how massive his hand was compared to her slender, paint-stained one made me think about what it'd be like to have them both roaming over my body.

God, they were still shaking hands.

"What in the actual fuck?"

An all too familiar voice broke our trance. I turned, spotting Austin Whynot walking straight for us down the sidewalk with a look in his eye that had me taking two steps back from Avery.

But, his gaze wasn't on me.

It was on Levi.

Specifically, Avery and Levi holding hands.

CHAPTER SEVEN

Levi was still holding my hand before god, the whole town, and even worse—my brother.

Or maybe I was still holding his.

Regardless, I didn't shake free until my asshole of an older brother was upon us. I forced a smile as Austin pulled Levi into a bear hug.

"Holy hell," Austin said. He cast me a side glance before he drew back. "Where in the hell have you been, Rayburn?"

"Oh, you know," Levi chuckled. "Everywhere but here."

Austin took his denim *Whynot, Texas* ballcap off, raking his fingers through his short, dark brown hair before putting it back on. He'd shaved recently, which was a good sign that he wasn't completely overworking himself. He was dressed in jeans and a blue T-shirt, his boots the same ones he'd been wearing for nearly a decade. They used to be Dad's, and at this point, I felt like he was going to be buried with them.

Between the four of us, Levi was still the tallest, but Austin wasn't too much shorter than him. Both of my brothers were taller than they should have been, in my opinion. At least two inches from each of them should have been mine, but instead, I was stuck at a solid five foot four.

Austin cracked a wide grin. "It's great to see you. It's been way too long. Never thought you'd come back here."

"Me neither, if I'm being honest." Levi took a step back and shoved his hands in his pockets. "How's everything going? Haven't heard much from you this last month."

Austin snorted, studying him closely. "I've been around. But what about *you*?"

The insinuation was there. The little tidbits I'd heard about why Levi was here . . .

"You could say I've also been around," Levi said.

I glanced down the sidewalk, but aside from a couple of regulars, it was just our little group. Even with it being Friday, the town wasn't too busy yet. This evening would be a different story, though. All the restaurants would be hopping and all hotels booked up as tourists came in for the weekend.

Mateo watched me closely as Austin and Levi talked. I raised a brow, met his gaze briefly, and then redirected my attention to Evie's pie shop across the street so I could pretend I was drooling over the baked goods instead of him.

It wasn't fair. Mateo was the problem. Because of him, I dreamed about sexy firefighters more often than I cared to admit. Mateo was on my mind all the time, and I had to just pretend like he wasn't.

"So, you're really back?" Austin asked, glancing from Levi to Mateo and then back to me. "And you've met my best friend and Avery again."

"He didn't recognize me at first," I chimed.

Levi shrugged his burly shoulders. "Last time I saw you, you had pigtails, pimples, and a sunburn."

Great. So that's how he remembered me. "Wow, Levi, you are so good for my ego," I sighed.

Mateo snorted, but didn't say anything.

"I'm back for now. I've actually been here for a week, I've

just been getting settled," Levi said. "I forgot how fucking hot this place is. And dry."

Austin nodded. "I heard. I texted, but when I never heard back, I thought people were making things up. You're staying over on Armadillo?"

Wait, what?

Levi nodded. "Yup. It's a cute little house. Way too small for me, but fine for now."

Surely fucking not.

"Yeah, the couple who redid that did a good job. They really spruced it up. I helped out with a couple of things when they first started the project. It's pretty popular with tourists."

Levi was my new neighbor? How in the hell had I not seen him over the last week? An entire fucking week? Had he even left the house?

"Are there even many tourists here?" Levi laughed.

"More than you'd think. A lot of outdoorsy folks roll through here."

I narrowed my gaze on Levi as the two of them chatted, thinking about the sports car I'd seen. Levi was driving *that* thing?

Austin chuckled as he slid his arm around my shoulders to give me that overprotective brotherly hug I knew all too well. *Oh boy.* I pressed my lips into a thin line, wondering what was about to come out of his mouth.

"Well, you can keep an eye on my baby sister then. She's across the street from you."

Levi's expression didn't change, but as his gaze met mine, everything inside me melted into a pool of panic. It was just my luck that he was my new neighbor. I didn't need to be thinking about the fact that he'd be right across the street from me.

"And you're just a couple blocks from Mateo," Austin said

casually. "His house is over there too. You'd have to drive to mine, though. And you should, assuming you got a car."

Mateo's mustache twitched. "Oh, he's got a car,"

Levi let out a deep hum, but smiled. "Maybe not anymore. It's currently on top of a cactus outside of town."

"I'll call Dallas and have him tow it," Austin offered.

"I think it just needs a tire changed," Mateo said. "Should be easy."

"That's good. What kind of car?"

"A little sports car." Levi sighed and ran his fingers through his beard. My gaze lingered on the motion a little too long. "Should have rented a truck. Mateo rescued me."

"Sounds like Mateo. He keeps us all from falling apart."

Well, that was the truth. I glanced up at my brother and narrowed my eyes on him. The circles under his eyes were a little darker than usual, and that haunted look he'd worn since Dad died lingered beneath the happy mask he always put on.

I poked him in the ribs. "You look fucking tired."

"Hey." His smile slipped slightly "Nice to see you too. Why have you been a stranger lately?"

"Because you annoy the shit out of me. You keep scaring all the good men off."

"Hey," Austin quipped.

Mateo smiled, but it didn't make his eyes crinkle like normal. Levi raised a brow, watching me closely. I leaned into Austin a little more despite the fact I was telling the truth. He *did* annoy me, but I also loved him.

I just wished he'd stay out of my love life.

And stop making his friends feel like they had to babysit a full adult.

When I'd gone to UT, he'd been less of a menace for four years. I'd dated whoever I wanted without any sort of oversight and it'd been great. It'd been normal. Then, Kevin moved from

Whynot to Austin, and we started hooking up. Then we started dating. Then he suddenly wanted me to quit being an artist, settle down, have his children, and become his trophy trad-wife stay-at-home mom. We started fighting, and those fights spun out of control.

When Dallas and Austin found out what Kevin had been saying and doing to me, they drove across Texas and showed up at my apartment. When they saw the bruises on my arms that he gave me during our breakup, Austin damn near put Kevin in the hospital.

My entire apartment was packed in a few hours. Austin paid for movers to drive my stuff all the way to Whynot and never said anything else—just that I was coming home.

The phone call about Dad happened on our drive back.

I'd blocked out those few hours. Everything was a blur.

My therapist said that trauma did that sometimes, and then would try to prod me about it. It was like pressing a thumb into a partially healed scab and asking if it hurt. It always hurt.

To top it all off, ever since the situation with Kevin, Austin and Dallas had been cockblocking me like two cowboy nuns.

"If I wasn't annoying you or scaring guys off, I wouldn't be doing my job." Austin looked directly at Levi. "I gotta protect you from jerks and guys just passing through town."

The message was loud and fucking clear, but Levi didn't seem affected. If anything, he just smiled a little broader. "Don't tell me you're still trying to keep your sister from dating. She's an adult, isn't she?"

Austin narrowed his eyes, his body stiffening. "Yeah, *and?*"

"I'm just saying."

"Well, *I'm* just saying my sister isn't up for dating anyone. She's got enough on her plate. She's busy being a strong, independent woman."

Jesus fucking Christ. Surely that wasn't where he was going to go with this.

"A strong independent woman can make her own dating decisions," Levi countered.

"Or, a strong independent woman has brothers to beat the shit out of anyone who bothers her."

Oh my god. "Hi, hello. You both sound stupid and I'm standing right here?" I argued. Was this really happening? Austin wasn't usually so blunt out of the gate. I thought after not seeing each other for so long, this would be the last conversation to come up.

Mateo cleared his throat. "This is getting a little out of hand. You're overstepping, Austin."

Austin ignored him. I met Mateo's gaze again as Levi and Austin had a dick measuring contest right out here in the open on Main Street.

Levi crossed his arms. His muscles popped, the sunlight lapping at them the way I briefly imagined—before scolding myself. He was a wall of beard and muscles and had no right to be hotter in real life than he was on TV.

Had I spent the last forty-eight hours scrolling video compilations of *Levi Rayburn's Hottest Moments*? Possibly.

"I'm just saying it seems like Avery can hold her own," Levi said casually.

My heart did that stupid little somersault again. I liked that he was standing up for me, even if it meant nothing but trouble.

Mateo cleared his throat. "Maybe we should go get some lunch? Or go get a coffee? A beer even?"

Austin released me and crossed his arms, going boot to boot with the hot hockey player. "You show up in my town after how many years, and our first conversation is about my sister's dating life?"

"Once again," I said loudly. "I am standing right fucking here. My dating life is no one's business. I can date who I want."

"When you come walking up like a fucking bodyguard, I sure do," Levi growled.

"From my point of view, it looked like you were holding her hand."

"Well, I was, dipshit. Because we were *shaking* hands," Levi said. "Apologizing for our interaction yesterday. Got off on the wrong foot, you see."

"Seems like you haven't changed in that regard."

Levi and Austin stared at each other for three seconds . . . five . . . ten.

Fuck, this was unbearable. I was teetering between anger and bursting out laughing. Mateo met my gaze this time and shook his head.

Levi's jaw flexed. "We're a little too old to settle things how we used to."

"You just don't want to get your ass beat."

Levi's biceps flexed and my mind made a static noise. "Austin Whynot, are you going to break your hand trying to punch me or are you going to buy me a beer?"

"The verdict is still out."

"All right," Mateo interjected. "This has been great, but some of us want to get on with the rest of our day. Austin, you're being a dick. Levi is right about Avery, she can make her own choices. Also, aren't the two of you friends? What kind of greeting is this?"

"The kind you get when Austin is acting like an ass," I said. I held up my hands. "I'm done. I'm going back inside to paint. Have a good lunch, or whatever the fuck you're going to do while you discuss my sex life."

"We're not discussing that," Austin hissed. The horror on

his face was enough to shake his resolve. "What the fuck, Avery?"

"You fucking started it," I growled.

I couldn't stand this anymore. I opened the door to the gallery, embracing the wave of cool AC. There was a presence right behind me as I started down the hallway. I turned, expecting it to be Austin.

But, it wasn't my brother.

It was Mateo.

CHAPTER EIGHT

My gaze met familiar warm brown eyes, darker than a Texas storm.

Something crackled between us. Something that dug its way between the cracks of the facade I'd built over the last two years. Something that would get me in a whole lot of fucking trouble.

I raked my fingers through my hair, ruffling my bangs. "I'm so tired of this. I'm so tired of everything here. There are some days I just want to run away. Ever since Dad died, both Austin and Dallas have been ten times worse. I'm suffocating."

"I know." Mateo winced, trying to find some sort of half-assed defense like he always did for Austin. "That was stupid, but I think it's good Levi said something. Austin is just being an older brother."

"You mean an asshole?"

We both glanced back at Levi and Austin standing on the sidewalk. But they weren't fist fighting—they were laughing. That was a good sign.

Mateo pressed his lips together. "Do you ever . . ."

He trailed off, not finishing his question. My pulse raced as I became all too aware of the fact that we were standing so close and that he looked really damn good in his jeans. I looked up at him, drinking in the way the sunlight kissed his brown skin. He pushed his glasses up the bridge of his nose, his mustache making me wonder about what it would feel like against my inner thighs. *Down, girl.*

"Do I ever what?" I whispered.

"Nothing. It's nothing."

"Liar." I leaned against the wall, still embarrassed by what had just happened. But then I thought about what Evie and June had said about reminding Mateo that I was my own person. That I didn't need to be treated with kid gloves. "I love my brothers, Mateo, but they drive me insane. I'm always treated like a baby. Forever the little sister, but I'm an adult."

"You are."

"What were you going to ask me?"

"I shouldn't ask."

"*Mateo.*"

"I shouldn't."

"Mateo. I swear . . ."

"Fine." He turned his attention fully on me. Every cell in my body lit up with need. "Do you ever think about dating someone in secret?"

He was standing so close—there was barely any space between us. I could feel the heat between our bodies, heady, burning lust singing in my veins.

Do you ever think about dating someone in secret?

The question had run through my mind constantly, but I never considered actually trying it with anyone.

I'd always had eyes for him.

But Mateo always reminded me we were just friends.

"Why would you ask me that?" I asked.

Mateo took a step back, leaning against the opposite wall. His hands fell to his side, flexing. "I'm just wondering, Blue."

The way he said *Blue* this time put me on edge in a different way.

"We're just friends," I bit out. "You've told me that a thousand times. Just *friends*."

He held my gaze as he straightened slightly. "Did you really believe me?"

What? My mouth dropped. He was joking, right? Just playing with me. But his expression was serious. His tone was tender but firm.

Before I could say anything else, the door swung open to the gallery. Austin poked his head in.

"We've made up, kids," he called. "Want to go to lunch? You too, Avery. We can have Dallas meet us."

"No," I said. "I brought a sandwich. I have art to make and emails to answer."

"You're always working," Austin said sourly.

"Oh, don't even start with me," I snapped. "Go get some lunch. Take some time off. I'll catch you Sunday at dinner."

Austin flashed a grin and winked before letting the door shut. I breathed out, my thoughts racing. I turned my attention back on Mateo, but now he wouldn't look at me.

What did he mean by what he said? For two years, he'd insisted we were just pals.

Friends. *Buddies.*

He'd been there for me countless times and was always there to rescue me when I needed it.

He was always there.

When I let loose with Evie and June, he was the one I called to be our designated driver. Not Austin. Not Dallas. Mateo.

He had never let me down, never failed to be there when I needed him. As bittersweet as it had been, I'd tried so hard to accept the fact he'd always been so clear on—we were just *friends*.

But after what he'd just said . . .

Mateo headed toward the front door. I rushed after him and caught his hand in mine.

"Mateo," I breathed out.

He paused with one hand on the door and the other in mine. He still wouldn't look at me.

"*Should* I have believed you?" I asked. "When you said we were just friends? After all this time?"

"No. You shouldn't have."

Before I could get another word in, Mateo was out the door. I watched as my brother slung his arms around the hot fire-fighter and hot hockey player, and the three of them laughed as they sauntered down the sidewalk.

Levi was my neighbor.

Mateo was my friend.

And the two of them were my brother's best friends.

Which meant, above all else—they were off-limits.

CHAPTER NINE

Austin led us down the sidewalk to a small blue two-story hotel with a handcrafted sign out front that said *Whynot Stay*. A wraparound porch with an abundance of flowers and wicker chairs made it feel more like a home than anything else.

Before we got to the gate, Mateo's phone buzzed in his pocket. He answered it quickly and then winced. "I'll head over. Thanks, Angie." He clapped Austin's shoulder. "Gotta go."

"Everything okay?" Austin asked.

"Just a tiny fire to put out, but not the literal kind. Some kids being dipshits. I'll catch up with you later. Levi, don't be a stranger. You don't need to run over a cactus to get my attention." He winked at me, and that wink bolted straight to my cock. "Get my number and address from this dumbass."

Austin gave him a quick hug. "See you. Be careful."

"Will do."

"See you," I croaked as Mateo took off down the sidewalk.

We watched him go, and then Austin cleared his throat. When I looked at him, all the bright energy that'd been radiating off him disappeared. He suddenly looked beyond exhausted—nothing like the always happy guy I'd known growing up.

Every summer I'd spent here had been full of everything good and everything bad. But, Austin had always been one of those good things.

The thing was, even though we'd catch up every month over the last few years, he'd kept a lot from me. I was still mad at him. Hurt, even.

"Avery told me about your dad," I said bluntly. "Something you didn't mention in the many phone calls we've had."

He opened his mouth to speak, but then shut it.

"I was shocked," I continued. "I still am. And I don't understand why you wouldn't have said anything to me. That man raised me during the summers, Austin."

"I have things to explain. There's a little restaurant inside the hotel. Are you okay with me multitasking while we eat and catch up?"

"Multitasking while you tell me what the fuck is wrong with you? Sure."

Austin winced. "Great. I'm doing bookkeeping today and it's been a nightmare."

I sighed. I didn't like walking on eggshells, but decided to indulge him. "Didn't your mom used to do that?" I asked.

"Used to."

Austin offered a grim smile as he led me through the tiny picket fence gate. Water trickled from a three-tiered fountain, sun-warmed stones creating a path through yellow tufts of grass and bright pink flowers of the Texas sage. With the rocky soil and dry climate, the grass here was rarely green, but there was an appeal in that. It felt like home. I could almost feel the heat of the rocks through my soles, reminding me of when we'd run around barefoot chasing horned lizards.

I remembered this hotel, and they'd put in some work to

make it look like this. It used to be rundown and dull, but the paint job, landscaping, and careful renovations had really turned it around.

"Did you do all this?" I asked.

"Yep. Broke my middle finger installing that damn fountain. It's still slightly crooked." He turned and secretly flipped me off. Sure enough, it was slightly bent. Barely noticeable unless pointed out.

I laughed and shook my head as we bounded up the steps. A couple sat at a small table enjoying brunch despite the midday heat.

"Howdy," Austin called, putting on that mask again. "How's the food?"

"Great!" the woman responded. "You've got something special here."

"We sure do," he said warmly. "Make sure you get some pie from Evie's today before she runs out. It's the best in town."

They grinned. "We're headed there right after."

"Wonderful. You folks enjoy."

As we walked through the front door, we were met with the warm scent of woodsy vanilla. I breathed in deeply as I took in the space. Wooden floors creaked beneath our boots as we walked through the front lobby to an adjoining space that belonged to the restaurant. Large windows let in natural light, filling the brightly painted space with warmth. It was small, but not too much so, with booths that were perfect to sit and work at.

Austin had left his laptop and things out on the corner booth in the back.

"Wow," I said, looking around.

The walls were painted a deep forest green with acrylic paintings of Charros on horseback and women dancing in beautiful dresses framed in gold.

"From an artist a couple towns over," Austin said, catching my gaze on the art. "Lucia Pérez. She's really talented."

"She is."

A bar stretched around the space with velvet barstools, the scent of chorizo, bacon, and scrambled eggs wafting through the air. My stomach growled as we sat down in the booth. Austin pushed his laptop and papers aside.

I raised a brow. "You just leave your shit everywhere?"

"Everyone knows I work here often. And that I always sit at this booth. No one's going to mess with my stuff, city boy."

"Fair enough. I forget how trusting people are here."

"Not the same up north?"

"It's the same in a lot of places," I said. "Minnesota is great. Lot of trusting people there. Just maybe not leave your expensive laptop in a booth, leave the building, and walk down the street to see your friends and sister kind of trusting."

"*Fair enough.*" Austin relaxed in the booth as he studied me, tilting his head slightly. "I saw the news."

My stomach dropped. "Yeah?"

"Yeah."

By this point though, everyone probably had. At least anyone who cared about hockey. Thankfully most people in Texas didn't, so maybe I wouldn't have to be asked a million questions by strangers.

"You didn't mention anything to me about it last time we talked."

I narrowed my eyes on him. "Is that how we're gonna do this?"

Austin's cheeks reddened. "No." He looked up as a woman with black hair braided into a bun came up to us and slid a menu in front of me. "Hey, Maria. How's it going today?"

"Fine. Where's my cousin? I thought after saving Frida he'd be sitting here with you."

"That damn cat climbed up the tree again?"

She smiled. "Yeah. What can I say? She yearns for the wild."

Austin chuckled. "She does. Maria, this is Levi. He used to visit in the summers when we were younger, and now he's back in town. Levi, this is Maria. She works here sometimes, but otherwise, she's Whynot's best librarian."

"A librarian? That's really cool. I don't even know how one becomes a librarian."

"It's harder than most people think," she said casually. "But I love it. I love our library in particular because we've been able to expand some of the summer reading programs for kids. And we were able to add a library of things for folks to borrow, like power tools or ghost hunting kits."

I grinned. "Ghost hunting kits?"

"Yep." Maria beamed.

"Does the library have different hours on Wednesdays?" I asked curiously. "Or—"

"It opens later during the week," she said. "I usually work a couple hours here and then head over. The tips fund my love for special edition books. What brings you to Whynot?"

"Just visiting for a few weeks," I said. "Needed an escape."

"Got it. And out of all places, you chose *here*—when it's hotter than hell?"

"Yep," I said. "How'd you end up in Whynot?"

Maria smiled. "Got family here, so it was an easy choice. I'll bring y'all waters. Want anything else? Austin, your usual?"

"Yes, please."

"What's your usual?" I asked.

"We have peach cobbler pancakes that will probably be the death of me one day," Austin groaned. "They're fucking diabolical."

69

"Sold." I wasn't even going to worry about my diet for the next few weeks. "I'll take those too."

"Great. I'll be back in a bit."

"Thanks." Austin said. He waited until Maria was out of earshot, then his expression grew serious. "All right, Rayburn. Spill."

"I feel like I should tell you to go first." I hesitated for a moment, and then continued. "I'm sorry about your dad."

His shoulders deflated. "I'm sorry I didn't tell you. Honestly, our phone calls became a weird form of escape for me. And you had so many good things going on, I wanted to hear about those instead of telling you what a fucking disaster everything was here."

"But I would have come to his funeral. I would have flown down to support you. We've been friends for decades and you not telling me feels like a fucking gut punch."

"I'm sorry. I am. I should have told you. I just couldn't bring myself to. There was so much happening when he passed that it was easier to just . . ."

"Suffer alone?" I shook my head. "I know how you are. You always put everything on yourself. You should have leaned on our friendship."

"There's a lot I should have done," Austin said. "And truly, I am sorry. There's not really an excuse. I didn't tell you. And that was fucked up of me."

"It was fucked up." I leaned back in the booth and studied him. "I haven't been a good friend."

Austin's brows drew together. "That's not true."

"It is true. A good friend would have noticed something was off in our phone calls, right? I don't know."

He smiled despite the heaviness of our conversation. "It was bad, but easy to hide when talking with you. I think about him every day. I took on what I could. Avery ended up changing her entire life plan to come back here when she was supposed to be traveling the world painting and stuff. And Dallas . . . I don't know. He won't talk about it either."

"Dallas never was much of a talker, if I remember correctly. Although, it seems he's changed given that he's a mechanic now."

"Oh, don't worry. He's still a book nerd." Austin leaned his head back against the booth. "Mom has gotten less social. We all go over for dinner on Sundays just to try to keep some sort of normal routine. But she's pulled back from the community so much. I've tried pushing her out, but it's hard."

"You can't do everything," I said softly. "You've always tried to, but you can't. You're not Superman."

"I have to be," he said. "I don't have a choice. There's a lot of people who depend on me. A lot of families and small businesses. I've always been the one to help out, and always will be."

"And what about you?"

Austin shrugged. "I'll be fine."

I doubted that. I knew he did too. Neither one of us was convinced by his half-assed *I'm fine.*

"I'm sorry I haven't been there for you," I said.

"It's a two-way street, Levi. I'm sorry I haven't been there for you either. I'm sorry I didn't tell you about Dad."

"It's all right," I said. "I forgive you."

He nodded, and as we'd always done, we put it all to the side. He'd apologized, I'd apologized, and that was that. We didn't need to hash it out anymore.

"I'm just glad to see you, even if you're not staying." He narrowed his eyes on me. "Okay, I've bared my soul. What's up with you? You were at the height of your career, last I checked."

I blew out a long breath as Maria came back to the table. My mouth immediately watered as she set down the massive stacks of fluffy pancakes with syrupy peaches and a crumble on top .

"Enjoy," she said. "Holler if you need anything else."

"Thank you," I murmured.

"Thanks, Maria."

I waited until she was out of earshot and kept my voice low. "I'm in constant pain, Austin. My entire body has been destroyed by this sport. I fucking love it. I love the game, I love my team, I love the fans. But I just hit a point where I couldn't take it anymore."

"What was the breaking point?"

Well, that was the question of the century, wasn't it? I mulled it over as I forked a bite of the pancakes, letting out a soft moan as the sweetness hit my tongue. They were perfect.

"Don't worry, I'll wait forever," Austin teased.

"Fuck off," I chuckled.

It felt good to have our friendship falling back into place so easily, even with the weird Avery stunt. But, he'd always been over-protective of her. Dallas too, even if he didn't realize it.

"The Friday before I made that announcement, I woke up and could barely move. All my joints hurt. I've been pushing my body to be as perfect as possible. I've been on a fucking diet with no room for joy in it. I got up and tried to do some stretches, and just couldn't. Then got a text from someone I've hooked up with before who just wanted me for my connections . . . And I thought—what's the point of any of this? I don't have anyone in my life that loves me outside of what I can offer them. With my dad passing a few years ago, I don't even have family."

"What about your mom? How's she doing?"

"She's living her own life." Without me. Occasionally, she'd remember I existed outside of my half-siblings and would call, but it was usually only around the holidays or my birthday.

"Maybe we can make our moms be friends or something."

I raised a brow. "Doubt it. How's *your* mom?"

"I don't even know, Levi. She's not the same, though. Don't think she ever will be. She has treated Avery differently since Dad died." He made a face. "Sorry. Don't need to get into my family bullshit. All of that is to say, I'm sure you've been lonely."

"Yep. I have been."

My throat tightened. It'd been a hard pill to swallow, realizing that pushing myself to work so hard all the time meant I hadn't made many friends. If anything, I'd gone out of my way to avoid them. It'd taken my body breaking on me to look up and realize that I was missing out on life. Missing out on having people around me that wanted to know the *real* me.

"I've got it all and nothing at the same time," I said. "I needed to escape. I need to figure out what I want. But I don't think being a hockey player is it anymore. I'd rather become a college coach and take a pay cut than keep doing this."

"You've worked really hard to get to where you're at," Austin said. "Harder than most, since nothing was handed to you. Walking away from all of it . . ."

"I know it's not a good idea," I said. "I've worked my ass off for this for years. And like I said, I love it. I love hockey. But I'm not happy. We'll see how I feel in six weeks."

"I'll support whatever you decide," Austin said with a shrug. "But maybe you just need to take a season off?"

"Maybe," I said. "I've got six weeks, then my agent will be hunting me down. If I don't have an answer for her, she'll fly out here and drag me back to Minnesota. And I don't want that. She scares me."

Austin snorted. "She can't be that bad."

"She is. Robin terrifies me. That's why she makes so much money."

Not to mention, at the end of the day, she did hold my best interests at heart. If I decided to take a break from hockey, she'd figure out how to get me into other doors.

"We have a free yoga class on Sunday mornings at the park," Austin said. "Avery, Evie, and June usually go. Mateo and I sometimes join if they bully us into it."

"I don't know about doing yoga in this heat."

He laughed. "Hey, it's under the pavilion. It's not too hot in the morning. I mean, I always end up drenched. Even holding that tree balancing pose or whatever is fucking hard."

"It's definitely too hot for that. But, I'll think about joining. I have to do something active while I'm here or else I'll turn into stone."

"In theory, I should also try to do more. What is it about turning thirty and your entire body starts hating you?"

"It's bullshit."

"Agreed." Austin shook his head as he dug into his pancakes. I smiled to myself, feeling an easiness wash over me that I hadn't felt in a long time.

So long as I stopped thinking dirty thoughts about Avery and Mateo, maybe being back in Whynot would be good for me.

CHAPTER TEN

I brushed the pastel pink acrylic paint over my cotton canvas, working in broad strokes as I covered the entire piece. Rock music blasted through my studio and I hummed along, completely zoned out as I focused on my art.

This was my favorite place to be in the world. In my studio, listening to music, and painting a piece I'd been planning for a couple weeks.

This one was going to be a massive bright landscape with cacti in bloom and a couple at the center, I just wasn't sure who the couple would be yet. It'd be awhile until I got to them though.

For now, I had the shapes blocked out in pencil beneath the glaze layers and worked the pink around them. Usually, I was totally caught up in painting while I worked, but today my mind wandered to a place it shouldn't.

Mateo and Levi.

Especially Mateo, at least at the moment.

Since we spoke yesterday, his words had yet to leave me. We hadn't texted each other since then, which made things feel worse. I chatted with him almost as much as I did June and Evie. Not texting him to tell him about my burned dinner last night or how I'd found a scorpion in my shoe had been excruciating, but I wanted to hear from *him*.

It'd been a long time since I'd had sex. Even longer since I dated someone. Since moving back to Whynot, my love life had been nonexistent. Getting over Kevin and healing from that heartbreak had been important. But then, pining over Mateo while telling myself he was just a friend had become my default state of existence.

So, what the hell was I supposed to do now?

Kiss him? Take him on a date? Roll around in bed with him? Tell him I want him to tie me up and put me on my knees with a ball gag?

This wasn't a *get him out of my system* sort of attraction, though. I knew if we started something, it would either be the greatest thing in the world, or we'd fuck up and I'd have to live with that mistake for the rest of my life.

Taking the chance felt too risky. Not to mention, my brothers would lose their minds. Hell, everyone would. We'd be picked apart by the whole town of Whynot. I didn't like the idea of being scrutinized in that way.

The fact that Kevin had been Austin and Dallas' friend certainly didn't help anything. If Mateo and I started dating, they would have issues with us. It wasn't fair to Mateo to put him in that position.

You're getting ahead of yourself.

I wrinkled my nose as I dipped the brush in paint and spread more on the canvas, drawing in soothing breaths and releasing them as if I were meditating.

The plan had been to forget about the world and make art for the next few hours.

But it was looking like I'd paint for a few hours and forget everything in the world *except* the hot firefighter and hot hockey player.

Or ex-hockey player, if what Evie said was true.

Was that why he was back in Whynot? I remembered the last time Levi visited a few years ago, for his father's funeral. The two were never close, but he'd still flown down, and I remembered it because it was right before I left for the University of Texas. He hadn't even seen me, but I'd seen him.

I'd never really known his dad. I knew he was a hard-ass. I knew they didn't get along, and also knew my dad and brothers didn't like him much. More than once, Austin had argued with Mr. Rayburn. And truly, Austin was one of the worst people in the world to argue with. That son of a gun was worse than me when he was pissed.

The only other thing I really knew about Levi's family was that his mom lived in Minnesota, which was why he'd gone back and forth as a kid. Trapped in this hellish heat during the summer with his dad, he stayed at our house more often than not.

It all felt like so long ago. A different time. I'd felt so invincible back then. It'd been a lot easier when my dad was alive. He always made me feel like I could conquer anything in my life because he'd conquered everything in his.

Except for the heart attack.

I paused my painting and straightened my spine, uncurling myself so I didn't turn into a shrimp. Tears pricked my eyes. I was alone, so I didn't hold them back.

The rest of the town and my family needed to know I was reliable. Still invincible.

But here in this studio, surrounded by art that was just for me—full of all my sadness and happiness and desires—I could cry. My vision blurred as I loaded the paintbrush again and continued working.

There were no words to describe the loss a community felt

when someone so bright left it. The thing about brightness like that was that so often, it made you unable to see other things.

As an adult, I knew now that my dad had faked a lot of his perfection. My brothers and I had discovered the hard way that a lot of the finances were tangled between the businesses he owned. That he was behind on taxes. That the house we grew up in was on a loan that should have been paid off a long time ago. The truck he'd bought for Austin's sixteenth birthday had been a splurge he couldn't really afford. My tuition he'd so graciously paid for was something he never should have committed to.

It'd been a nasty wake up call.

Our mother hadn't known, of course. She'd never been involved in any of that. I wished that she would have been, but she'd always deferred to him.

As much as I loved my parents, their relationship had never been the blueprint I wanted for my own. At the end of the day, they loved each other though, and for that I could be thankful that they raised me.

Even if my mother would never really understand me.

To be fair, I'd never really understood her. I would never be the perfect daughter to her. If I would have gone on to be a doctor or lawyer, she might have loved me a lot more. But art was part of my soul. I couldn't not create it.

My phone buzzed in my apron pocket and I placed my paintbrush down on the palette. I answered without looking.

"Hello?"

"Hey." Dallas' voice surprised me. I immediately raised a brow. He rarely called. "What are you doing?"

"Working." I narrowed my eyes. I was suspicious. "I'm painting."

"Got it."

"Why?"

"Just curious. I'm about to go pick up Levi's car and take it back to the shop, and wondered if you were with him."

Why in the hell would he wonder that? My nostrils flared. Had Austin said something? Knowing him, probably. "Nope. I'd make a bet Austin's got him tied to his hip now. How about you call him up?"

Dallas chuckled and then let out a long sigh. Sometimes when he sighed like that, it reminded me of our dad. "I was just checking on you. You've been distant lately."

"I literally saw you last Sunday."

"Yeah, and? That was family dinner. We're always there unless someone is sick. I meant aside from that."

My throat thickened and I stood up, stretching from side to side. "I've been busy."

"Busy with what?"

"None of your business," I snapped. "God, y'all are always up my ass. You and Austin are pests."

"I'm just checking on you."

"No, you're *fishing*," I said. "You act like you're just a bookworm car guy, but you like gossip more than Mom does."

He feigned a scoff, but I could hear the hint of amusement. "All right, all right. Acting like it's a crime for your older brother to call you."

"*Dallas*," I growled.

"Fine," he sighed. "Jesus. I'll leave you be . . . Want to get lunch tomorrow?"

I pinched the bridge of my nose. "I guess. Nothing in town sounds good, though."

"We could make the drive somewhere."

I narrowed my eyes, torn between being suspicious and genuinely feeling worried about Dallas. It was rare he asked for one-on-one time, and when he did, that usually meant something was on his mind.

"How about I make lunch?" I offered.

"Absolutely not. Your cooking is horrible."

Now, it was my turn to scoff. "Okay, well, you cook then."

"All right, I will. Lunch tomorrow at my place."

"And try not to poison me. The last thing I need is to be shitting for the next week because you didn't cook something right."

"That only happened once."

"Once was more than enough." I wrinkled my nose, thinking about the time Dallas had offered to cook family dinner and gave us all food poisoning. I'd sent him a Venmo request for ginger ale and meds afterwards, along with "fuck your cooking forever" in the memo. "I'll see you tomorrow. Oh, can you do me a favor?"

"Sure."

"Can you tell Austin to lay the fuck off when it comes to my romantic life?"

"Nope. See you tomorrow."

He hung up before I could protest.

What a bastard.

I was starting to dream of the day Austin or Dallas fell in love with someone, because then I'd be able to give them equal amounts of shit. I was saving up years worth of frustration for them. I'd never take it out on their partners, of course—but I was *yearning* for the day I could wreak havoc on them.

Out of love.

I groaned and sat back down on my stool, glowering at my canvas.

The pink was drying into a nice shade, one I could build on well. My gaze swept around my studio and I stood up, giving myself a moment to take a walk around. A lot of the art in this room was locked away for very specific reasons.

One, they were personal.

Two, they were kinky as fuck.

Paintings of women with rope wrapping around their bodies on full, glorious display. Couples and throuples grinding together, kissing, fucking. One of my personal favorites was of a woman wearing a ball gag with spit dripping down her chin, her eyes full of pure submission.

A lot of people had misunderstandings about submission. They thought it was disgusting, taking women back decades. *Why would you ever submit to a man?*

It was never about that. It was about trust. It was about knowing I could trust someone so wholeheartedly that they could put me on my knees and make me beg for them. It was knowing they respected me enough to fulfill my desires in a consensual, healthy way.

But if anyone aside from myself ever saw these, I'd be banned from the town. *Small town darling turned deviant slut.*

A text buzzed on my phone and I pulled it from my pocket.

Mateo: I'm sorry I was weird yesterday

He was joking, right? My jaw stiffened, my fingers moving rapidly as I shot a message back.

Weird??? That's what you're going with? Don't act like what you said was less than what it was

Mateo: I shouldn't have said anything.

Now, I was seeing red.

> Well, too late for that.

> You did say something and now I've been sitting here wondering what it would be like

Mateo: You know we can't get involved

Mateo: I'm sorry, Avery.

> Tell me you don't want me then

Silence. I stared at my phone, waiting for him to text back. I could see that he'd read the message, for god's sake.

> I know where you live. So either answer me here, or I'll show up on your doorstep after you get off work

> You can't hide from me, hotshot.

Mateo: Dammit, Avery.

> Well?

Mateo: Got to go

> You're a coward

He left me on read. I threw my hands up and damn near chucked my phone across the studio.

I was cursed. That was the only answer. Cursed to live and die alone and to become an eccentric artist. I dropped my phone back into my pocket and picked up my paintbrush again, now truly good and pissed.

This was exactly why we couldn't date, though. Things were bound to get messy. Even now, it'd be awkward for a few days while I worked through being angry at him.

My phone beeped again. I kept painting, trying to ignore it. Shoving away the constant temptation to check it.

I lost that battle.

I pulled it out and stared at the screen.

> Mateo: I could never tell you I don't want you, Avery

CHAPTER ELEVEN

My body hated me for getting up this early.

After a couple weeks off my routine, my brain was starting to revolt. I squinted, wondering if I should have made myself a cup of coffee as I walked down the sidewalk toward the park. Not that caffeine could fix whatever was wrong with me.

Hopefully, my body would love me after giving this a try. I doubted it, but one could dream.

The last time I tried yoga, I'd ended up leaving about halfway through the class. My joints had been so angry at me, my muscles protesting the entire time. I'd been fucking embarrassed. And as a professional athlete, there was truly something horrifying about that. It picked at all the soft parts I did my best to hide. The parts that screamed I was never good enough to be a professional athlete to begin with. The part that screamed I should have listened to my coach about stretching more. It was clear I should have taken better care of myself over the years.

I had a spreadsheet for all the exercises I was doing now. I even made a weekly schedule table and checked each color-coded day off when I completed them. Even though I was off the team for now, I had to maintain some sense of normalcy, and having my life organized helped. It was what got me through college and through the pressure of maintaining my grades while being an athlete.

Keeping my life down on paper was something I preferred to do even with BDSM relationships. I had an entire spreadsheet full of kinks and how I rated them, along with blank forms for if and when I was with someone. I always deleted old files if the relationship ended, too. But I *loved* having everything outlined in little details.

I was a freak in *all* the sheets.

I liked having references to what my partner or partners liked. Although, I was a little rusty to all of that now.

The idea of filling out kink spreadsheets with Mateo and Avery was a huge turn on. And the moment it crossed my mind, I used all my strength to push it back out.

I carried my mat across the grass, adjusting my sunglasses to keep the sun from blinding me. The sun was barely up, but the heat already had sweat trickling down my back.

Yoga in the park. Who even was I? The sidewalk eventually turned into a path that cut through grass, leading to a gazebo large enough to host ten people. I counted a few familiar faces as I walked up, my lungs squeezing a breath out.

I hadn't thought about the fact that I'd be doing yoga with people who knew me. Also hadn't thought about the fact that Avery and Mateo might be here.

Avery was wearing yoga shorts. *Fuck me.*

"Hey, look who it is," Austin called.

He grinned as I approached, clasping my shoulder gently and dragging me into a hug.

"Morning," I grumbled, forcing myself to not immediately focus on Avery and Mateo and the way they were standing as far away from each other as possible.

Had I missed something? I was no mind reader, but the

energy between them was off. Avery wouldn't look at him. Mateo was only looking at her.

Two women stood next to Avery and one of them smirked at me while the other one with pink hair stared me down like I'd committed some sort of crime against humanity.

Avery smiled at me. "Surprised to see you here, Minnesota."

"I told him about it," Austin said proudly. "And for once, all of us got off our asses on a Sunday morning."

"Hey," Dallas quipped.

It'd been a while since I'd seen him, but I'd know Dallas anywhere. I held out my hand as he approached and he pulled me into a hug before drawing back.

"How are you?" he asked.

"Hanging in there. Regretting getting up this early."

"You and all of us," Mateo mumbled.

"I have zero regrets, actually," the pink-haired woman said. Tattoos crawled up her arms and my eyes widened when I realized they weren't flowers—they were poisonous plants. She arched a brow at me. "I'm June."

"Nice to meet you," I said.

"This is Evie," Avery said, gesturing to her other friend.

Evie beamed and waved. "Hi, Levi. Welcome back to Whynot."

"Thanks," I answered.

Her attention turned back to June and Avery, and the three of them formed a tight knit circle. Occasionally, June would shoot Mateo the side-eye.

I very much felt like there were two teams here, and I was batting on the wrong one.

"So, who's teaching?" I asked.

Dallas snorted and looked at Austin. "Great question. Who's teaching this Sunday?"

"One of the golden girls, probably."

"The what?" I asked.

Mateo closed in on our group, his back to Avery. "I heard Lola is teaching today."

"So we'll be starting twenty minutes late," Dallas said.

"Without a doubt," Mateo chuckled.

The three of them kept chatting and I took a moment to study Mateo. He wore a navy Whynot Fire Department shirt along with some athletic shorts, occasionally pushing his glasses up his nose. My gaze lingered on his mustache and the stubble along his jaw line.

"Earth to Levi. Levi?"

Austin's voice broke through my trance and I snapped my head up. "Sorry. Need caffeine. Or something."

"All good. Do you want to join the volunteer fire department?"

"What?" I shook my head. "You're gonna have to back up five steps."

Dallas chuckled. "He's just fucking with you. We were talking about—"

"Someone come help me with my damn yoga blocks."

A grumbly voice had all of us turning, and Mateo already moving to help an older woman entering the gazebo with a couple tote bags. The two of them exchanged a few friendly words in Spanish and she let out a hearty laugh, handing everything over to Mateo.

"Pick a spot," she said, gesturing to the ground. "Put your mats down. Oh look, it's the hockey player."

"Hi," I said.

"Don't *hi* me. What are you, nine? Roll out your mat."

"Yes, ma'am."

It had been a long time since I tried yoga, and there was a goddamn reason for that. It was fucking hard. Trying to move my body to Lola's instructions was harder than most of the workouts I'd done in my entire life. Every part of my body ached and creaked like an unoiled machine, protesting as I tried to move into downward dog.

At least I wasn't the only one. Dallas, Austin, and Mateo struggled just as hard. June, Avery, and Evie looked like they'd been doing this their entire lives.

I was a little jealous.

Only because I love the idea of being able to flow with my body like that. It would take practice. Maybe if I added it to my PT routine in the mornings, I'd slowly become more flexible . . .

I was careful with my right shoulder, mindful of every movement. There were some poses I needed to adjust for, and some I straight up couldn't do.

By the end of the yoga class, I was covered in a layer of sweat, but my muscles were thankful for the stretches I'd done. And even though I certainly wasn't the best at it, and felt somewhat like an idiot, I felt a lot better than I had when I woke up this morning.

I sprawled out on my yoga mat as we stayed in savasana, staring up at the roof of the gazebo. I turned my head slightly, looking out at the park. I was supposed to be focusing inward, but this was the part of yoga practice I always had trouble with, so I always picked something else to focus on.

The park wasn't exactly green, not like one would expect. In fact, everything was dead and yellow. But the sky was bright blue, the clouds like puffs of whipped cream. And there was something familiar and wonderful about being back in the place I used to think of as home.

My gaze tugged up slightly, and I realized Mateo was looking right at me. We were lying so close to each other that it almost felt intimate.

The fucker winked at me.

I shook my head and looked away, but god damn it. I smiled like a fucking idiot.

"All right," Lola called. "Class is over."

I heard Avery snort and we all slowly sat up. I rolled my neck and adjusted my shoulder.

"How are you feeling?" Mateo asked softly. "Shoulder?"

I nodded solemnly. "It's okay. Or it will be. Hopefully."

Mateo nodded, but didn't press. The two of us sat on the ground as our five—*friends*? Could I even call them that?—started to chat and move about, helping Lola get everything picked up around the gazebo.

Avery occasionally glanced over at us, her cheeks turning red each time. My heart rate picked up.

Mateo sighed next to me, and I couldn't help it. I was going to be a little nosy. "What's wrong with you and Avery?"

He mumbled under his breath in Spanish. "*Estoy condenado a la soledad.*" He shook his head. "Is it that noticeable?"

I glanced up as Austin and Dallas started talking to their sister. Meanwhile, both June and Evie stole curious glances at the two of us before walking Lola down the park path.

My stomach did a slow flip. "I think it is to everyone but her brothers."

CHAPTER TWELVE

My eyes watered as I twisted further, moving my right shoulder gently. The resistance band stretched. I rolled through every motion, throat constricting, trying to force my body to relax. I could do this. I'd done much harder things to my body in the past.

God, recovery fucking sucked.

I was torn between feeling angry that I'd neglected myself to this point and frustrated that I couldn't handle what I used to be able to do. That I wasn't as strong anymore.

Then there was the sadness.

It wasn't something I'd given much thought to, but sometimes it came up, a tiny voice I could ignore most of the time.

Was I a failure for wanting to walk away from my career? The career I'd spent years training for? The amount of time and money I'd invested into being a hockey player was all going down the drain, and yet . . .

I winced as my shoulder twinged. My lungs dragged in a deep breath, my ribs stretching as I held it, forcing myself to release slowly. To exhale the sense of dread.

The good news was that yoga hadn't completely destroyed me this morning. I knew I was going to be a little bit sore, but

I'd still felt good enough to do all of my physical therapy today as well.

I was going to get there. One way or another, I was going to build up the strength again. The flexibility. I was going to treat my body better. I deserved it, right? After so many years of pushing myself, this was what I needed.

My phone rattled on the kitchen coffee table. I continued to do my reps, staring at it. I wasn't supposed to be afraid of my phone, that was ridiculous. But there was a small part of me that feared what would be on the screen every time the notification came through.

Avoiding everyone wasn't a good idea. I knew that. But I didn't have answers for any of the teammates or the coaches who texted me. I didn't know what to tell fans, didn't know how to handle shit. Robin had told me to stay offline, but she hadn't told me how to handle all of the people that knew how to reach me personally. She didn't tell me how to handle their concern— a concern that made me feel small.

I knew that everyone meant well by checking in on me, but it made me feel like a failure.

God, it was probably time for me to set up a therapy appointment. Not the physical kind, either. I had been going regularly for a bit, but fell out of habit . . .

I finished my reps and then released the resistance band, plopping down onto the soft couch. It creaked beneath me as sunlight slanted into the living room, warming my shoulders as if to tell me *good job*. I'd even done *yoga*. A full session, too.

I'd also witnessed firsthand the tension between Mateo and Avery.

Those two were always on my mind now, without fail. It was like clockwork through the day. One moment I'd be going through the motions, the next I'd be daydreaming about kissing one of them. *Both* of them.

What had happened between them? Had Austin finally caught wind of the romantic interest there and lost it?

I picked up the TV remote and flipped it on absent-mindedly.

The way Austin and Dallas were lingering over Avery's love life bothered me. She was more than capable of making her own decisions. Plus, Mateo clearly liked her. Loved her, even. He was a good man. An attractive, flirty, mustached firefighter who . . .

Needed to stop being in my thoughts so frequently.

Fucking mustache. Slutty glasses. He knew exactly what he was doing and owned it all the way. His confidence itself was a turn on.

My finger paused on the remote, my throat tightening as a sports channel flashed on the screen.

Hockey Star Done?

Replays from past games flashed on the screen as two sports journalists talked. I did my best to tune them out, but winced at the words *burned out, finished,* and *a waste of talent.*

The game they were showing replays from had been one of the hardest I'd ever played, but we'd pulled through. I'd blocked a shot that would have been one of the greatest of all time—if he'd made it.

I smiled to myself, remembering the roar of the arena.

It only took a few seconds to change a game completely.

The next clip burst my bubble. I exhaled slowly as a clip of my shoulder injury followed.

From the outside, it didn't even look like that significant of a collision. One of the other team's players had barreled toward me and made his shot, slipping on the way. I'd blocked the puck, but not before hitting the ground, then hitting him.

I blinked, realizing I'd never even watched the clip.

The fucking pain. It was seared in my mind, the way my

rotator cuff had ripped. The burners that followed from that injury were still an issue today. Some of the nerves were damaged, leaving me with sudden electric shocks, tingling, pins and needles, and occasional weakness in my arm. Sometimes shaking, although that'd lessened over time.

But I *had* healed some. It wasn't constant anymore.

I was healing. I would heal. I had to heal. If I ever wanted to go back, I had to . . .

Could I even go back? Probably next season, I could hit it hard. I'd need to get back into my old routine after leaving Whynot and keep in shape while my shoulder continued to get better.

None of it appealed to me.

I turned off the TV and sat in silence.

Sitting and doing nothing didn't appeal to me either.

I got up and headed to the front door, slipping on my boots. Eventually, I'd break these fuckers in. At least then I'd stop getting side looks from locals.

My camera bag hung from one of the jacket hooks. I slid it over my chest and stepped outside, wrinkling my nose at the heat. The sun was about to be hitting golden hour, though . . .

Which was the perfect time to snap some pictures.

Photography had been my own little secret for years. A hobby that kept me grounded amid all the bullshit. It was one of the few things I did for myself. I'd never be good at fumage or any sort of art like Avery did, but a camera? It worked for me. It made me happy. Capturing small moments, playing with lighting—photography brought me peace.

I stood on my porch and unzipped the camera bag, pulling mine out carefully. I turned it on, setting everything up.

The sound of a door slamming shut echoed down the street. I looked up right as Avery stepped out of her little house, her head tipping to the side when she spotted me.

I felt as though I'd been caught with my hand in the cookie jar. I immediately put my camera away, blush creeping up the back of my neck as she waved at me and crossed the street.

God, she was gorgeous. I swallowed hard, all my words disappearing like I was an idiot as the sunlight hit her. The blue at the ends of her hair lit up, her eyelashes long, freckles cute.

She slowed at the bottom of my step, her hands going behind her back. She'd changed out of the yoga clothes and was wearing what I'd determined to be her favorite overalls. All the paint stains only contributed more evidence.

"Hey," she said. "How was yoga?"

I cleared my throat. "It was good."

Fuck, I was bad at this. I was really bad at this. Why did I feel so nervous? Why were my hands so clammy? Why was I such an idiot around her?

"Good. I like her yoga classes. It's nice to get moving so early in the mornings. I think without it, I'd turn into a shrimp."

I raised a brow. "A shrimp?"

"Yeah. I'm always hunched over while painting." Avery grinned. "What's in your bag? You going out?"

"Oh, it's nothing," I said. "I'm just taking a walk. Not sure what else to do with my evening."

"Bored of Whynot already?"

Her teasing did something to me. My stomach twisted into a thousand butterflies, the warmth rolling up my spine getting hotter. "Never. I love it here. I think I've missed it."

Avery's smile softened. "I guess I can see why. It does have a certain charm about it. I love painting landscapes around here, too."

"Where's your favorite spot?"

Her eyes lit up. "Are you gonna walk there?"

"Yeah," I said, unable to stop myself from smiling back at

her. "Seems like it would be a good way to spend my evening, unless I can't get there."

"You can," she said. "I already know Mateo won't mind, but behind his backyard there's a spot where you can see the Davis Mountains in the distance. He's just a couple blocks over, but there aren't any houses close by, so it's just a lovely view. If you're wanting something more modern looking, I'd check out the hotel. The courtyard is really cute."

"Austin did a good job on it," I said.

"He did. Worth him breaking his finger on the fountain."

I laughed. "He flipped me off while showing the break."

"His favorite thing to do," she laughed with me. "Want me to give you a ride anywhere? Since your car is still out next to the cactus."

"I'm okay," I said. "I'll find my way. Are you going out for the evening?"

"I wish." Her shoulders deflated slightly. "I have Sunday night dinner."

The way she said that told me she didn't want to go. "With who?"

"Dallas, Austin, and my mom. She's just . . . We have a tough relationship."

"I'm sorry," I said gently. "I know how that can be."

"It's okay," she dismissed. "Don't suppose you want company for whatever it is you're doing? I could text them and tell them you needed help with something."

Every part of me screamed *yes*. Having Avery take a walk with me, while it might be the simplest thing in the world, would automatically brighten up my day. Plus, the photos I could take of her . . .

But, I didn't need Austin realizing I definitely had a thing for his sister.

"It's more of a solo thing," I finally said.

"Oh. Got it." Avery sighed and glanced up at the sky. "I gotta get going, Levi. I'll see you this week? Maybe at my art class?"

"You really want me back after I lit your hair on fire?"

Avery's laugh was everything I needed to hear. "I always want you. I mean, uh, I want you in class. Always." Her cheeks were as red as mine were now. "Okay, um, I'm gonna disappear into nothing now. See you later."

I want you back. The words were on the tip of my tongue but I watched in stunned silence as she darted across the street and climbed into her big truck.

She drove off and I shook my head, clearing the fog of stupor.

There was just something about Avery Whynot that left me tongue tied.

CHAPTER THIRTEEN

This was a bad fucking idea. *Bad idea, bad idea, bad idea.*

I couldn't do nothing, though. Not after seeing how Avery looked at Levi at yoga.

I knocked on the front doors to Evie's bakery and waited patiently. The sky was still dark, the sun not even close to rising.

Evie's familiar face appeared on the other side. Usually her expression was a slice of sunshine, but today she scowled at me as she unlocked the door. "What are you doing here so early?"

"I want fresh conchas and a coffee, please," I said. "I'll do anything for them."

"Aren't you supposed to be at the fire department?"

"Not yet," I said. "And I'm on call. Don't worry, our town is safe."

She crossed her arms. "Can't you get them when I open?"

"No. *Pleaseeee*, Evie. I'll owe you one."

Evie pressed her red lips into a thin line and regarded me with a look that had my insides shriveling. Even though the bakery wasn't open yet, she was already dressed to conquer the day. She wore a bright blue dress with an apron over it, her pastel pink tennis shoes squeaking against the checkered floors as she took a step back to let me in.

"Who's the special someone?"

"You already know."

Evie's brows shot up. She stared at me for a moment and then let out a long hum.

"But you're not gonna say anything to anyone."

She tipped her chin up. "I never agreed to that."

"You will if you want me to keep your secret."

Her mouth dropped. "And what fucking secret is that, Jimenez?"

I wasn't going to say it aloud, because I didn't need to. She knew exactly what I was talking about, because just like she kept my secret—I kept hers.

Right when Avery had moved back to Whynot, it'd been pretty clear I was pining for her. Our group had gotten together for an event, ended up drinking too much, and Evie and I had confided in each other.

For two years, Evie had known how I felt about Avery.

Just like for two years, I knew how she felt about Austin Whynot.

"All right, fine. I'll make her coffee exactly how she likes it. But why now, Mateo?"

"*Why not?*"

"Oh my god." She sighed, waving her hand to follow her. "What am I going to do with you?"

"Rescue me. Help me win the girl."

Evie shook her head as she led me behind the counter. Even this early in the day, everything in her shop was organized and perfect. The scent of pastries warmed the kitchen, a rack full of them waiting to be picked clean by everyone in Whynot.

"I have so many questions." Evie grabbed a set of tongs and

pulled two pink conchas off a tray and put them in a bag. "But I'll ask them later. I'm on a tight schedule."

"I can make the coffee," I offered.

"Nope. I've been making her coffee for years. And for better or worse, I'm invested in the two of you."

"You're an angel," I sighed.

"You say that now, but if you break my girl's heart, I'll crush your nuts with my rolling pin."

I winced at that vivid imagery as Evie handed me the bag. The coffee here wasn't fancy like it was at the other shop in town, but it was good. I leaned against the counter as I watched her whip up Avery's to-go cup, making mental notes.

Black coffee, a few dashes of creamer, three packs of raw sugar. Avery liked it sweet.

"You're the best," I said as she put a lid on it.

"I sure am. I expect full details later."

"Only if you're not saying anything to anyone."

Evie handed me the cup and gave me a flat look. "Avery is one of my best friends, but I've kept your secret."

"Austin is one of mine, but I've kept yours."

The corner of her mouth tugged. "Except now you're branching out. Breaking the rules. Taking her coffee and breakfast before the sun even rises."

"I just need to talk to her."

"Right. Talk to her. And this has nothing to do with the texts she showed me and June in the chat yesterday?"

I closed my eyes for a second. Of course she'd shown June and Evie our texts.

"Or the fact that you made a half-assed move because you're *jealous*?"

"I'm not jealous," I argued.

"*Sure* you're not. You should have seen how the three of y'all fucking acted yesterday at yoga. I know that man has his eyes on her. He can barely pay attention to anything else. The only reason Austin and Dallas didn't notice is because, despite their plan to ruin Avery's dating life, they're still guys." She shrugged. "Jealous or not, whatever gets you to make a move, I guess."

"I like Levi, too." My cheeks turned hot as the admission slipped out. Not because Levi was a man—everyone in our close friend group knew I was bisexual, just like I knew about their sexualities too. But because, well, I liked Levi *and* Avery.

Evie's brows arched. "Oh?" She planted her hands on her hips and stared for a moment as the implication sank in. "Oh."

"*Oh* is right. Now, I gotta go."

"All right. Stay out of trouble. Text me later."

"Will do."

CHAPTER FOURTEEN

I slowed my truck as I turned onto Armadillo Lane, parking right behind Avery's in her drive. I could almost still feel Evie's hawk eyes on me as I jumped out, snatching the conchas and coffee, and sending up a silent prayer that I wasn't making a mistake.

The little house Levi was staying in was across the street. The living room light was on, which meant he was up. Must have been an early riser, too. Hell, there was a very real part of me that wished I was bringing him breakfast. But not yet.

I needed to make things right with Avery first.

Something had shifted between us. Maybe I'd been thinking too much about being with her, or maybe it was the way I'd seen him look at her.

Or the way he'd looked at me.

Regardless, Avery left me on read after my text to her, and I'd barely slept a wink since then. Seeing her at yoga had been torture. Working all weekend didn't even make me tired. I'd gone home and tossed and turned while thinking—*what if?*

Keeping secrets from Austin and Dallas was a bad idea. I knew that, and yet, the temptation to finally explore what I'd felt for Avery for so long was too great.

Especially now that I knew she might be interested too.

That was the real problem. I'd done a great job of lying to myself. Convincing myself that Avery would never be interested in me. That she thought of me as nothing more than a family friend.

I walked up the little sidewalk, pressed the doorbell, and waited. Avery's front porch was decorated with the same brightness as her gallery. She had a welcome mat with a rainbow on it, a few plants in painted pots. Everything in Avery's world was always vibrant and beautiful, and I just wanted to be part of it.

Already prepared for Avery to be cussing up a storm the moment she tore the door open, I held up the bag of pastries. "Can I come in?"

"It's not even six yet. Have you lost your mind?" Avery's cheeks were bright red. She wore nothing but shorts and a tank top. I swallowed hard, trying to keep my gaze strictly on her face.

"Please," I whispered.

She pressed her lips together, but then she stepped to the side, letting me through the doorway. Avery let the door fall shut, scrutinizing me as I kicked off my boots next to hers.

"You haven't woken me up this early in ages."

"Well, I've had a lot to think about," I said.

"Oh? I thought we were just going to ignore everything and keep playing pretend."

My shoulders tensed and I turned to face her, using the coffee and conchas as a shield. "I don't want to let things sit. So I decided to bring you breakfast."

Her gaze raked me up and down.

I held up the coffee. "I brought you caffeine."

Her teeth sank into her bottom lip, her expression softening slightly. "Well, can't say no to that. Come sit."

Avery's house always smelled like her. I inhaled the sweet scent as I followed her to her living room, taking a seat on her couch as she turned on a couple of lamps and then settled down next to me. She swept her hair back and I realized the ends were blue.

"You changed your hair."

Avery picked up one of the ends, twisting the blue between her fingers. "I did a few days ago. June helped me."

"It looks really good," I murmured.

Her lips twisted with a sly smile and she took the coffee from me, taking a slow sip. A soft moan left her. Fuck. My stomach slowly flipped, my blood rushing in my ears. Just that perfect little sound had me wondering how to have her making it again.

For two years, I'd thought about what it would be like for us to be together. For two years, I'd told myself we never could be. It'd been easy to convince myself that she didn't want to date or that we were too busy.

After the exchange in her studio, I couldn't just let things go. The truth was, we *were* friends. The desire simmering in me was just the tip of the iceberg. She'd been part of my life for so long now, that the idea of putting our friendship at risk scared the hell out of me.

But because we were friends, I wasn't going to just let this sit without addressing it.

Avery took another sip of coffee. "So . . . Are we gonna sit here or are we going to talk?"

I was sweating. I adjusted myself on the couch, trying to find the words. "I shouldn't have said anything."

Her brows pinched and she shook her head, immediately stiffening. "No. We're not going to ignore this, Mateo. Unless I'm wrong about what I think you were trying to say. And if I am, then please go ahead and bury me in the Whynot Cemetery, because I don't think my ego will recover."

"You didn't misunderstand me. But your brothers are my best friends. We live in a small town. Everyone knows everything about us."

"This isn't about them, though," she said. "If there's some sort of tension between us, then I want to explore it. I deserve the chance to be with you, Mateo. Only if you want to be with me too, though. If you tell me here and now that you don't feel any of this and just want to be friends, then we'll be friends."

"I do feel it. I've felt it since you moved back, Avery."

"*Since I moved back?*"

"Yes," I rasped. "Two years. I've wanted you for two years."

I leaned forward and sat the bag of pastries on her coffee table, and then slowly slid to the floor, kneeling in front of her so that we were at the same eye level. She leaned past me and put her coffee down, and then stayed perched forward, her eyes searching mine.

"What has taken you so long?" she whispered. "I've been losing it, Mateo. For so long. I swore you only thought of me as—"

"Avery, you are my friend. But, I do not think of you as *just* a friend," I said. "Or a sister. Nothing like that. I've never felt that way. But Austin and Dallas being so overprotective always made me worried that if I tried something and it didn't work out, it would make our lives harder."

"It would."

I swallowed hard, searching her eyes. Her lashes were so long they cast shadows down her soft cheeks. I traced the curves of her face with my gaze, drinking her in for the first time without hiding it.

"Mateo," she whispered. "Is *this* how you've been looking at me?"

I nodded. "Every time you're lookin' the other way."

"*Oh*." Her eyes dropped to my lips. "I think I want to have the rest of this conversation later."

Oof. My heart dropped and I started to get up, but her fingers curled into my shirt.

"I didn't mean for you to get up," she said. "I just meant that I want to do more than talk."

It took a second for my brain to catch up with what she meant. I stared for a moment, and then my gaze dropped to her lips. "If I kiss you . . ."

"Then there's no going back."

Was I really going to do this? I'd dreamt about it for so long that this moment felt surreal.

Fuck it.

I slowly stood up and held out my hand. Her palm was soft against mine as I pulled her to her feet, and led her around the couch.

"What are you doing—"

I tangled my fingers in her hair and backed her against the wall, my cock straining against my jeans. Avery whimpered as her head tipped back, her lips parting as I leaned in. A breath of space stood between us, my entire body craving her.

"I've been thinking about kissing you for so long," I whispered. "So fucking long, Avery."

"I've thought about it so many times I've lost count," she rasped. "Kiss me. *Please*."

I tightened my grip on her hair just enough to keep her from closing the gap. Slowly, I leaned in and brushed my mouth against hers.

God, she was sweet. Just as sweet as I'd imagined. Her arms wound around my neck, a soft grunt leaving me as our kiss deepened. I nudged my knee between her legs, parting them as our tongues met.

My head spun as her palms cupped my face. We broke the kiss, my eyes shuttering as I inhaled her scent.

"Come to my room," she murmured, rubbing gentle circles with her thumbs along my cheeks. "To my bed."

"The sun is almost up," I murmured. "My truck is in your driveway."

"Then let's go ditch it at your place and I'll bring you back. I want you. All morning, every morning."

I kissed her again and smiled, breathless as I pulled away. "Every day?"

"Every afternoon."

"Every night."

Avery's smile melted my heart. "Every night, hotshot."

I pressed my forehead to hers, thinking about the truck out front. No one would guess what we were doing, right? No one would know.

"What if we continued what we've started and deal with the truck later?" I asked.

"That sounds like a perfect idea to me."

CHAPTER FIFTEEN

I couldn't stop kissing him.

After dreaming about this moment for so damn long, it was even sweeter than I'd imagined. Hotter too.

My hands slid down his muscled chest and I grabbed the hem of his shirt, giving it a tug.

Mateo smirked. "Need something, Blue?"

"Shut up," I hissed, pulling it over his head.

Damn. I'd seen Mateo shirtless before. So many times in the summer over the last couple years, our group would end up around a pool drinking beers and trying to stay cool. But there was something different about having him shirtless right in front of me, *just* for me.

I was going to implode. My heart pounded as he gently took my wrists and lifted them, pinning them above my head to the wall behind me. His mouth brushed mine and I parted my lips, hungry for more.

He was a damn good kisser.

A soft moan slipped out and he responded by tightening his grip on my wrists.

"You keep making the prettiest fucking sounds, *mi cielo*."

Heat pooled at my core. His mustache was soft against my

skin as he leaned down and trailed kisses over my neck, brushing this spot that made me shiver involuntarily. Pleasure sparked everywhere he touched or kissed until I was moving my hips.

"I'm desperate," I moaned.

"I'm going to take care of you. I promise."

He released my wrists and looped his fingers in the band of my shorts. My mouth dropped as he tugged them down and knelt as they hit the floor. He pushed my thighs apart and I became all too aware of the fact that I was almost naked in front of Mateo.

Mateo.

He looked up at me and gave my tank top a tug. "I want you to take this off. I want to see you naked and needy while I make you come on my tongue for breakfast."

"Oh god," I rasped.

I did as he said, though, and took my top off. I wasn't wearing anything underneath it. Goosebumps pricked my skin as he looked up at me, his eyes warm with adoration. His gaze made me want to melt into the floor and hide.

His palm slid up and down the side of my thigh, tracing lines with his fingertips. "What is it?"

"I haven't done this in so long. I'm nervous you'll not . . ."

His brows raised. "That I'll what?"

"I don't know," I said quickly, my cheeks flaming. "Not be attracted to me? I—"

"*Avery.*"

He was quick. I squeaked as he stood up, grabbed hold of my hips, and spun me around against the wall. *Fuck.* The denim of his jeans brushed my ass as he pressed himself against me, his words firm in my ear.

"Can you feel how hard I am for you right now?"

I could. Without a doubt, I felt the outline of his cock

straining against *me*. My eyes closed and I whimpered, my head spinning.

"*Avery.*"

The way he said my name was a demand. "*Yes.* I can feel you."

"How on earth could you doubt for a moment that I want you? I think you're gorgeous." His hand slid down to my pussy as he continued to talk deep and softly to me. "I've wanted you ever since you came back to Whynot. I've wanted you since the moment I laid eyes on you. I've come so many times alone in my bed while dreaming about you being there with me. I've thought about touching you, *worshipping* you, every day and night for years. I want you, Avery. Never doubt that. Okay?"

"Okay." It was the only word I could form. I was so turned on while feeling vulnerable and a little silly too, my thoughts were muddled. But, I knew one thing. "I want you too. Now. More than anything else."

Two fingers slid against my clit. I gasped, my head falling back against his shoulder as his other arm wrapped around me firmly. Mateo held me in place as his fingers met my wetness.

He groaned. "Fuck. I love how wet you are for me right now."

My hips rocked as he circled my clit slowly. Shockwaves rolled through my body. Every part of me was crying for release and it was impossible to think of anything aside from the feel of his body against mine. The strength in his grip, the easy circles his fingers were making on my clit.

A curse left me and I clamped a hand down on his forearm, holding onto him as he kept teasing me. He was taking his time. There was no rush in the way he was touching me, and that was driving me insane.

"Don't you want to head to the bedroom?" I asked.

"Not yet."

Fuck. His patience would be the death of me.

"Please," I whined.

Mateo chuckled and started to rub my clit a little faster. "We're not going to the bedroom until you come for me."

I sucked in a breath as he pulled his fingers away and turned me back around. My back pressed into the wall as he kissed my lips first, then trailed them down my neck and to my breasts. A moan caught in my throat as he took one of my nipples into his mouth and sucked, his thumb gliding over the other.

God, I was going to combust. I rolled my hips as he continued back down to his knees again, lifting my leg and draping it over his shoulder. I buried my fingers in his hair to steady myself right as he pressed his tongue against my clit.

Fireworks popped in my veins. Every touch felt so fucking good.

Mateo wasn't shy about eating me out. I stifled a cry as he buried his mouth against my pussy right as he gently slid two fingers inside me. His mustache felt so damn good. I gasped, rocking my hips faster, riding his face. He created a rhythm with his tongue and fingers that had me melting and crying and moaning until I was a mess for him.

I was so fucking close. Riding the edge closer and closer—

My voice rang through the house as his fingers curled against a spot that pushed me over the edge. I came hard, pleasure tearing through me as his tongue continued to work magic, lapping up every second of my orgasm.

Holy shit. I panted as I sank back against the wall. I looked down, everything hazy as Mateo sat back and licked his lips, bringing the fingers he'd just made me come with to his mouth. It was such an erotic sight watching him lick me off his hand that my breath caught, my mouth dropping.

And then he winked.

He fucking winked.

"You're impossible." That earned a smirk from him.

My gaze fell to the outline of his erection. I dragged my tongue over my bottom lip.

"I think it's my turn," I said.

"I think—"

Knock, knock, knock.

Fuck.

Mateo's eyes shut, his expression twisting with a mix of frustration and dread—exactly what I felt too. He was still hard and there was absolutely no fucking way he could answer the door like that.

"Godammit," I whispered.

The knock came again, a little more insistent. I quickly snatched my shorts and tank top up and put them on.

"Fuck. We're getting caught," Mateo whispered. "You look ravaged."

"I *have* been ravaged," I hissed. "Fuck. I'll just say I was working out. But you need to go work *that* out ."

Mateo looked down at his jeans and made a face.

I swept my hair back behind my shoulders and tried to gain some sense of composure. Whoever the fuck was at my door, I was going to be kicking them off my step.

Unless it was one of my brothers.

Jesus Christ, I really hoped it wasn't one of my brothers.

I rushed to the door, looked through the peephole, and blanched. *Oh god.* I unlocked and yanked it open.

Levi stood on the other side, scratching the back of his head. He turned to face me, and his eyes popped wide.

"What do you want?" I asked.

My cheeks were the color of a ripe tomato. It was probably for the best that out of all people, Levi was the one to interrupt us, but I still felt the heat of embarrassment.

His nostrils flared. "Uh . . ."

I looked down at myself. My nipples were still hard. My skin was flushed. I probably smelled like sex. *Like Mateo.*

"I've forgotten how words work," he mumbled.

Levi blushing could have been a new kink for me. The way he'd blushed while standing on his porch the other night had made me run away, but I couldn't run now. I stared at him for a moment and then raked my fingers through my hair.

"Are you okay?" I asked.

"Yeah. Yes. Of course. I came over to ask if you have any baking soda."

"Baking soda?"

"Yes."

What the fuck does he need that for?

I heard footsteps behind me and turned right as Mateo filled the doorway with a stupid, flirty grin.

He was still shirtless.

"Morning, Levi," he said.

He leaned against the doorway as I gave him a devilish glare. "Someone is gonna see you."

"Only Levi will," Mateo said.

Levi made a noise that was somewhere between a groan and grunt. "Sorry. I interrupted something."

"No," I said quickly. "It's not what it looks like."

"It is what it looks like. You could join us," Mateo offered.

My god, kill me now. I turned around to give Mateo a wide-eyed look, but he kept that easy smile, his attention fully on Levi.

Although . . .

My brain short-circuited at the thought of the two of them doing *things* to me. With me. Kissing me, touching me—

"I have to go," Levi said shortly.

I turned back around. Levi was already off the front porch,

his shoulders stiff as he crossed the street and headed straight for his front door.

Well, great.

I turned around and shoved Mateo back inside, scowling as I shut the door.

"What the hell was that?" I asked.

"He wants you," Mateo said simply. "It's pretty clear."

I didn't know what to say to that. I opened my mouth to speak, but no words came out.

Mateo raised a brow. "Are you interested in him too?"

I felt like I was about to ruin everything by being honest. But then again, this was Mateo. I knew I could tell him anything, even if it wasn't what he wanted to hear.

"Yes. I am interested in Levi. I doubt he's interested in me, though. I don't even know if he likes me."

"Oh, I think he does." Mateo crossed his arms and leaned against the wall. "What if I told you I'm interested in him too?"

My mouth dropped. I stared at him for a moment, and then let out an incomprehensible noise. "Well," I squeaked. "You have told me before you don't mind sharing."

"I don't mind with the right person." His mustache lifted as he offered me a shy smile. "I don't know, Avery. There's a certain kind of tension between the three of us when we're together. Clearly."

"There is."

We were both silent for a moment. Oh god. It hit me that Levi had just caught us in the middle of sex. I let out a soft giggle.

"*Qué?*"

"Nothing. If that were anyone else, we would have been in trouble. Also, I think I'm being greedy by liking the idea of having two boyfriends."

Mateo stepped closer and planted an easy kiss on my lips. "Then I'm greedy by wanting a girlfriend and a boyfriend."

"Is it greedy? In this economy?"

He laughed as he pinned me against the wall. His fingers curled into my hair and he gave me a gentle tug, the feeling of it going straight to my pussy.

A soft moan left me. I arched slightly, all of the bubbly excited energy between us melting into something hotter, needier.

"Do you like the idea of him fucking you with me?" Mateo whispered in my ear.

"Yes," I gasped.

Fuck. I liked that more than I cared to admit.

"He may not even be interested in me," Mateo murmured. "Although, I know he wants you."

"Why do you think that?"

I sucked in another breath as I felt his cock hardening against me. I reached down between us and slid my hand into his jeans, closing my hand around him.

"Fuck," he grunted. "I've seen the way he looks at you."

I was holding his cock. He was so hard. Thick and long and I *needed* him in my mouth. Heat skated through my veins, every part of me craving more with him. I tilted my head back, biting his bottom lip.

Mateo grunted, letting out a soft growl as he continued to hold me in place. "This will be our secret. And we'll see what happens with Levi. I think we should seduce him."

"We?" I snorted. "You're the sexy one here."

He bit my bottom lip back. I squeaked as the brief pain made me even hornier.

"We're both sexy. Or do I need to show you?"

I held his gaze and then slowly smiled. "How about I get on

my knees and show you how sexy you are? And you can show me after that . . ."

Mateo swallowed hard. "I do like that idea."

I realized I'd never wanted to suck a cock so badly. I swept my hair back into my grip. "Hold this up for me, please."

He replaced my hand with his, giving me a tug until I was looking up at him again. Mateo raised a brow. "You're only sucking my cock until I'm ready to bend you over your bed and fuck you."

I smirked. "We'll see."

CHAPTER SIXTEEN

I wasn't sure exactly what the hell I'd interrupted, though my mind was certainly coming up with a hundred vivid explanations. Now, all I could think about as I speed-walked across the street back to my front door was—*fuck, I wanted them.*

Not just Avery. Not just Mateo.

The two of them. *Together.*

I burst through my front door and slammed it shut behind me. The walls rattled as I twisted the top lock, my cock straining against my jeans.

Holy fuck.

My loyalty to my friend and plan to stay away from his sister failed as I planted my hand on the wall.

Had I really just interrupted them fucking? I'd heard Mateo's truck rumble up the street earlier, and yes, I'd peeked out my front window like one of *those* neighbors.

Genuinely, I'd wanted baking soda. I was trying to cook some healthy muffins to freeze so I stopped ordering food. But had I also been aware of the fact that Mateo had showed up on her doorstep at the ass crack of dawn?

Yes.

Had I also walked over there to ask because maybe I sort of

hoped I'd interrupt them? Because I was maybe a smidge desperate?

I wasn't answering that.

I rushed down the hall to my bedroom, shaking my head at myself. My fingertips brushed my belt buckle and I undid it quickly, needing to get the fuck out of my clothes before I made a mess just from thinking about them. I kicked my jeans and briefs off into a pile on the floor.

God, the look on Avery's face . . .

Fuck.

My shirt was next. I yanked my blankets back and rolled onto the bed. *What is wrong with me?* I felt like I was in fucking heat. A whimper left me as my cock throbbed, begging to be stroked while I thought about Avery's just-kissed lips.

There was no doubt about it. The way her skin was flushed, her nipples hard and wanting to be sucked. *Goddamn.*

The way Mateo looked at me when he'd come up behind Avery stuck in my head. He looked too damn good shirtless.

And his fucking smirk.

The way he flirted never failed to turn me on and make me panic. There was something so effortless about it. A little slutty. Like his glasses. He knew he was hot, he knew what he wanted, and I loved that.

He was probably just teasing me. I was probably just reading too much into it all.

But dammit, a man could dream, right? A man could dream about a hot boyfriend and a hot girlfriend. There was nothing wrong with that, right?

Avery had looked at me like I caught them with their hands in the cookie jar. I knew that there was *something* there. I'd seen it the first day I'd run into both of them. Mateo told me there was nothing going on between them, but his words didn't match the way they looked at each other when the other wasn't watching.

I closed my hand around my cock. A soft groan split my lips, my head falling back. God, this was wrong. Avery was supposed to be off-limits. I was supposed to hold onto some shred of respect for Austin and stay far away from his little sister.

And yet here I was thinking about getting on my knees and tasting her sweet pussy while fucking my hand.

Mateo came back to mind. There was just something about the two of them together. The thought of them with me. It had gotten underneath my skin since I'd come to Whynot.

Maybe it was because I'd walked away from everything, or maybe it was because it'd been a long time since I'd been with someone who didn't want me for my career—not that I knew whether Avery or Mateo even wanted me. Even with his flirty invitation . . .

Pleasure jerked through me as I stroked myself faster. Up and down, thinking about her pussy milking me as she rode me. *Fuck.* Just knowing I wasn't supposed to be doing this made it all the hotter.

Alone in this room, all my fantasies let loose. My head tipped back against the pillow, my hips pumping as I moved my hand, needing to come so fucking bad.

The thought of taking Avery at the same time as Mateo crossed my mind, and every nerve in my body lit up with lust. God, I wanted them. I couldn't have them, but I wanted them so fucking bad. My cock pulsed against my palm, my strokes faster. My breath hitched, and I moved my hips, imagining thrusting in and out of her. Feeling his cock rub against mine. Pulling her hair, or even his hair. Getting on my knees and eating her out after the two of us came inside her.

There were so many different things that we could do together, so many positions, so many kinks to explore.

I was desperate for that release. Hungry to try new things.

It's not gonna happen. Even reminding myself of that didn't stop the thoughts from spinning.

I was always bad at relationships. Things never worked out. Which was *exactly* why I shouldn't have anything to do with the two of them. But if the chance offered itself to be with them in the bedroom again, I'd be stupid to walk away from that.

In the bedroom, I was always expected to be the Dom. Most of the time, that's what I preferred to be. But on the occasion that I wanted to submit, I craved it so fucking badly. Yes, I was big and strong. Yes, I could put someone on their knees and make them beg for my cock. I loved playing with rope and paddles and blindfolds and ball gags. I loved coming up with predicaments that made my submissive wonder if they'd be able to make it out of their position, while knowing they could trust me explicitly.

I loved all of those things, but . . .

Sometimes I just wanted to be a good boy.

And I really wanted to be good for Mateo and Avery.

That was the thought that pushed me closer to the edge. The idea of kneeling before them. Looking up at Mateo with the same sort of reverence I wanted to look at Avery with.

My eyes closed, my breath catching. Fuck, I was close. The blush on Avery's cheeks and smirk on Mateo's face came back to mind, and I groaned.

What were they doing now?

I'd definitely interrupted something.

Something.

Fuck. I was so close to coming. Hell, if I would've stayed around longer for the tension between those two, I might've just come on her doorstep like some sort of desperate perv.

That would have gotten me kicked out of Whynot for sure.

"Fuck," I groaned.

I was so close. So fucking—

I gasped as my orgasm hit me, my entire body feeling the rush of pleasure as cum burst from the head of my cock. It shot onto my hand in spurts, dripping down as I finished, my moans collapsing into heavy breaths.

Every bone in my body relaxed. I stared at the ceiling, the fan doing lazy laps as I thought—*what the fuck am I getting myself into?*

CHAPTER SEVENTEEN

Mateo gripped my hair as I knelt down and pulled his jeans to his ankles. His cock sprang free, precum dripping from the tip. I held his gaze as I leaned forward, swirled my tongue and tasted him.

His grip tightened, his head tipping back as I took him deeper. It'd been so long since I'd done this, but it felt right with him. Every moan I drew out pleased me. I wrapped my hand around the base, stroking as I bobbed my head, all while watching lust dance across his face.

"Fuck," Mateo moaned.

I raked my nails down the front of his thighs, earning a hiss between his teeth. He pulled my head back and leaned down, brushing his mouth against mine.

"I want to keep sucking you," I gasped.

"If you do, then I'll come. And I want to hold out as long as I can. Stand up."

He pulled me to my feet and I squealed as he lifted me, throwing me over his shoulder with ease.

"Oh my god," I gasped. "How in the hell did you do that?"

He patted my ass as he carried me toward my bedroom.

"Those firefighter muscles, baby. I train to save people just like you."

"Just like me, huh?"

I laughed as he stepped into my bedroom and tossed me down onto the center of my bed. "Stay there," he said.

I raised a brow as he left the bedroom. I heard him rummaging through what sounded like his jeans for a moment and then he returned with a condom.

"You just keep those on hand, huh?" I teased. "Who have you been seeing in Whynot?"

"I've only had eyes for you. I keep one in my wallet though, because you never know."

I fought a smile. "Or maybe you planned to seduce me."

"I hoped to. Been thinking about it for so fucking long, this feels like a dream."

I propped myself up on my elbows, my stomach flipping as he knelt on the edge of the bed. His cock was hard, his eyes trained on me. I drank in the sight of him naked. Light from my bedroom lamps bronzed his skin, turning just the edges of his curls golden brown. But it wasn't just how hot he was that did it for me—it was the way the corner of his eyes crinkled when he smiled. The way his eyes softened when he looked at me. The way his mustache tipped up like a sexy villain when he smirked.

The firefighter calendar models had nothing on Mateo.

"We'll take it slow," he said.

"I don't want to take it slow."

He raised a brow as he tore open the foil pack. I slid my hand down to my pussy as I watched him roll the condom over his cock. My fingers brushed over my clit and then pushed inside myself. Fuck, I was soaked. Aching to be filled by him.

"Look at you," he murmured. "You're so beautiful, Avery. Are you sure you want to do this?"

"I'm sure. I'm more than sure." I had no doubts in my mind. Did I tell him about all the sexy dreams that had woken me up over the last couple years? Did I tell him that I'd definitely made myself come while thinking about riding that damn mustache? "I need you. I want you. I'm so fucking wet for you, Mateo. I need you inside me, to feel you. And there's so many things I want to . . ."

I trailed off. I knew Mateo was kinky, and he knew I was. Only because it'd come up casually one time while we were talking a few months ago, and since then, it'd lived rent-free in my mind.

"Tell me," he said as he crawled toward me. "Tell me what you want to do."

My brain short-circuited as Mateo grabbed hold of my ankles. He pushed my legs apart as he moved on top of me, settling his weight on top of mine.

"Tell me what you want, Avery. I want to hear it all."

He kissed me, his touch gentle as he pressed his lips to my forehead.

"I want this." My cheeks flamed. "You know I'm kinky. Or well, I would be if I dated anyone here."

"I do," he said. "We've never talked about it in depth. You know I am too."

I swallowed hard. I was nervous but I felt comfortable with him. The thing about Mateo was that I already trusted him. I *knew* him.

"I just want to be careful," he said. "I . . ."

I pressed my lips together. I knew what he was asking—could I be kinky again? The last person I dated had shattered my entire life to pieces, and then my dad died. When I first came to Whynot, I'd been such a fucking mess.

But I'd taken the time to heal. I'd gone to therapy. And while there had been things in the sexual part of our relationship that had been manipulative and harmful, I didn't think that would influence what I wanted to do with Mateo.

"We don't need to jump into anything today," I said. "But I want to explore our kinks together, Mateo. And I need you to trust that I would tell you if something goes too far or if it brings up feelings from the past."

Mateo nodded. "I trust you, Avery. I just would never want to do anything to hurt you."

"I know."

"I want to do this again. I want to do this over and over. I don't think I'll ever be able to walk away from you after today."

He closed his eyes, his forehead still resting against mine. There were some insecurities between us. I knew we were both wondering if we were making a mistake. What if someone found out and tried to ruin things? What if my brothers found out and stopped being his friend or tried to make things a bigger deal than they were?

What if I fell in love with him but he didn't love me back?

This was the kind of relationship that would ruin me if it didn't work out. Maybe even more so than the last.

There were so many questions, but no answers.

We were taking a risk. But I couldn't stop myself from doing so. I'd wanted him for so fucking long and now that I knew he wanted me back—I needed to see what this could be like.

His mustache twitched with a sly smile. "I want to know what sort of kinky things you want to do with me."

"I'll tell you all about it after you fuck me senseless."

Another stupid grin. I wound my arms around his neck, hugging him. Given how horny we were, it was something that was so innocent, but it was needed. Because even if we crossed this line, he was my friend. He would always be my friend.

At least, I hoped that was the case.

"Please," I whispered.

Mateo let out a long groan. We couldn't wait anymore.

He sucked in a breath and sat back as he grabbed hold of his erection. I swallowed hard, lifting my hips to meet the head of his cock. He rubbed the thick tip against my entrance, his gaze falling on my pussy. I watched his face as he watched me, moaning as he teased. I bucked my hips, begging for more. God, I wanted him. I wanted him so fucking bad.

He planted one hand to the side of my head, and I brought my legs up, spreading for him.

"I'll take it easy," he rasped.

"No," I groaned. "I want this hard and fast."

He shook his head. "You're killing me, Blue."

Mateo thrust forward slowly, even with my begging for it to be faster. Inch by inch, his cock filled me, all while I whimpered and gasped, stretching around him. My nails raked down his back as I gripped him tighter, the weight of his body perfect against mine.

"I can feel you milking me," he gasped. "*Fuck, you feel so good.* You feel so fucking good."

I couldn't even form words anymore. All I needed was him to fuck me senseless.

I moved my hips and he met my movement with his own. He thrusted, taking it slow at first, his gaze locking with mine. Between gasps and moans, he never looked away as he started to pump his hips.

There was something between us. Something I've never experienced before with a lover. A connection full of passion and need and lust.

His movements quickened, his cock driving in and out of me. I tightened my grip around him, whimpering as he fucked me harder, the bed squeaking beneath our movements. The full-body relief that came from not only being fucked, but being fucked by *him*, was so incredibly fulfilling.

I gasped his name over and over, chanting it. My legs locked around his hips, my fingers gripping his hair and dragging him into another full kiss. His tongue danced with mine, the heat between our bodies creating a layer of slick sweat.

"Fuck," I gasped. "I need you from behind. The angle—"

I squealed as he pulled out and rolled me over. He snatched a pillow from the top of my bed, wedged it beneath me, and thrust back into me so quickly my head was spinning. He tugged a fistful of my hair, holding onto it as his other hand settled on my hips and he thrust deep.

This was the angle that was going to ruin me. My fingers gripped the blankets, my face burying into the pillow as he set a rhythm that drove me wild. My cries were muffled as he fucked me harder, moans leaving me as his cock hit just the right spot.

He let out a string of curses in Spanish and I caught most of them, blushing as he maintained the same brutal rhythm.

"I'm going to come," I gasped.

"Come on my cock for me, baby," he grunted. "You look so goddamn good taking my cock like this."

Fuck. No one had ever dirty talked to me before, not like this. Not in the way I'd always craved.

"Fuck," he moaned. "I can feel you squeezing me."

"You're so deep."

My words were breathy and muffled from the bed. I was drooling straight into my sheets, the feeling of his body pounding against mine putting me in some sort of trance. I moaned as I felt the edge of my orgasm so close. So fucking close.

Fireworks sparked in every nerve. My orgasm crashed into me and I cried out, tensing as the waves of pleasure took over.

"There we go," he hummed. "Good girl. Good fucking girl.

God, you're taking me so well, baby. You're doing so good coming on my cock like this. I love the way you feel."

His words did me in further, my orgasm stretching out as more pleasure battered me. I panted as I melted into the bed beneath him, feeling his hands grip my hips as he pumped a few more times and then groaned.

He collapsed against me, his breaths as labored as mine. He leaned his forehead against my back, our bodies melded together as we came down from the high of orgasming so damn hard.

"Fuck," I mumbled.

Mateo chuckled and kissed down my spine, slowly easing out of me. He rolled to the side and left the bed for a moment to throw his condom away. He returned in a blink, settling down next to me and pulling me close.

Our legs tangled together. I pressed my face against his chest, breathing in his scent.

"That was . . ." he trailed off.

"Magical?"

"Life changing."

I smiled against him. "Agreed."

"I wanna tell the whole world, Avery."

I wrinkled my nose. I hated keeping secrets, but I knew we needed to for now. The last thing we needed was everyone up our ass about a relationship. "We have to keep this secret. At least for now, while we figure out what we want."

"What about your friends?"

I didn't want to lie to June or Evie. They'd figure it out quickly, though.

"I'll tell them," I said. "But they won't tell anyone else. I trust them."

"I do too. Evie has known I've wanted you for years."

I gasped. "*What?*"

Mateo's smirk told all. "Yeah."

"I can't believe she never told me. What a traitor."

"It's okay. Worth the wait." Mateo hummed. "We should definitely seduce Levi."

The way my pussy reacted to that told me that my entire body agreed. "I'd like that."

I smiled as Mateo pressed a kiss to the top of my head. I leaned against him, thinking about how right this felt.

"I need to go," he whispered. "I don't want to move, though. I want to stay with you like this all day. But the sun is well up and my truck is in your driveway. And if someone knocked on the door right now . . ."

My heart skipped a beat. "Give me two more minutes."

"I'll give you the rest of my life."

My brows shot up and I tipped my head back to look at him. He planted a kiss on my lips before I said anything, his arms tightening around me until we were as snug as possible.

"Two more minutes," he said softly.

I was going to soak up every second of them.

CHAPTER EIGHTEEN

The only thing that was keeping me sane at this point was my camera.

Avery and Mateo were gonna be the death of me. I hadn't seen them since I'd interrupted them, but that was probably for the best. I wasn't sure I'd be able to say a damn thing without thinking back to how flushed they'd both been.

I knelt down as I took a couple of photos in the courtyard at Whynot Stay, listening to the trickle of water from the fountain behind me. It was quieter during the week, although there were still a few guests here.

My finger pressed the button a few times, every photo only slightly different. I stilled as a butterfly drifted down onto a cactus flower, its wings winking brilliant colors at me.

"How's it going?"

"*Fuck.*" I jumped up, startled to see Mateo leaning over the courtyard fence and watching me.

He winced apologetically, pushing his glasses up the bridge of his nose. "Sorry. I didn't mean to scare you."

"You scared the butterfly more than me," I grumbled.

Although that wasn't true. The butterfly was still on the

flower, not giving a shit about the beautiful firefighter next to us.

Mateo was wearing firefighter pants with suspenders over a navy T-shirt. His muscles bulged, even when he was relaxed.

"Taking pictures?" he asked.

"Yeah."

"What for?"

"Fun."

Mateo smirked. "A man of many words today."

His teasing made me smile back and I shook my head. "I've been called worse."

"Hmm. I can't see why anyone would call you anything bad."

"Well, you've never had your ass beat in the rink by me."

Mateo's laugh rang through the courtyard. I slipped my camera strap around my neck and stepped up to the fence, leaning next to him and meeting his warm gaze. I swore Mateo had the prettiest eyes. Dark lashes, brown irises that swallowed me right up, light wrinkles at the corner from smiling so much.

I was pretty sure any wrinkles of mine were from scowling.

Maybe I could change that one day.

"I can't play hockey," Mateo said. "I don't think I've ever seen a hockey stick in real life."

"I don't know why you ever would out here," I said. "The only reason I ended up playing was because I also grew up in Minnesota. Have you ever visited?"

"Minnesota? Nope."

Mateo leaned in a little closer, his face close to mine. Close enough that my eyes kept dipping to his mouth, to his mustache, to the way I wanted to kiss him. I could kiss him right here and now. *Fuck.*

"At some point I want to do a road trip and hit all the

states," he continued. "Would be fun to do with another person, though. Maybe even two people."

His insinuation didn't miss me, although I wondered if he was serious. Did he really mean Avery *and* me? Was I being presumptuous?

"I've done some small trips," I said, my throat suddenly parched.

"With a partner?"

I shook my head slowly, gaze back on his mouth again. "Never. Most of my trips have been for work the last few years. So usually with a group of grown men who just want to drink and get laid."

"Does that mean you stayed on the bus knitting blankets for kittens?"

I barked out a laugh. "No. It does not."

"Didn't think so." He flashed a knowing grin. "Can't see you being a nun, exactly."

"I'm the furthest thing from it."

"Oh really? I have my doubts."

I scowled at him. "You'd be surprised by what I'm into."

"I'm sure I would not be. But let me guess—rolling around in bed with an artist and firefighter?"

Fuck. My thoughts evaporated. I opened my mouth to speak, but wasn't even sure what to say. The idea of being between whatever was happening the other day at Avery's hit me, and I bit back a groan, looking away.

"I'm sure the two of you are doing just fine," I muttered.

"Well, you won't know until you see for yourself."

I was a goner. Mateo was going to make me implode. My cock hardened just enough to press against my jeans, all my blood roaring in my veins.

Why did he have to be so hot?

How was I even supposed to respond to him?

Yeah, I'd really like to join both of you and roll around in bed until the three of us are hot little messes—

But, there were three problems.

Avery was Austin and Dallas' sister.

Mateo was their friend.

And I was leaving Whynot. *Soon.*

He winked at me and leaned back, straightening his back. His smile faltered slightly, his expression growing more serious. "I feel like I have things I want to say, but—"

"Mateo, come in. Mateo."

A radio attached to his belt interrupted us. Our eyes locked for a split second.

"Sorry," he whispered.

"It's okay. We..."

"We'll talk another time, okay?"

I nodded as he picked the radio up and pressed the button on the side. "What's up?"

"Those kids are at it again. They're popping fireworks in the park, and someone called it in because they saw smoke."

"Fucking, of course." He rubbed his face as he pressed the button again to speak. "I'll head over."

He clipped the radio.

"Need any help?" I asked. Why I was offering, though, I had no idea. I wasn't a firefighter. It wasn't like I'd even know what to do except bodycheck someone.

"I'm okay," he chuckled. "There's a couple of teenage boys that have been doing some dumb shit. The second they see me, they'll be out of the park in a blink. I just need to make sure nothing actually catches."

"I'll see you around then."

Mateo nodded. "Don't be a stranger. Let's get lunch soon."

"O-okay."

My voice shook just a little bit. Mateo headed to his truck

and I held up my camera, thinking about grabbing a picture of his broad back, his muscles, the waves of heroic energy falling off him in waves.

But a moment like this, I didn't want to watch through a screen.

Even though I was a photographer, there was not a single photo that could be taken that would do that man justice.

He was just too damn hot.

CHAPTER NINETEEN
 *Mateo*

I was on cloud nine for the rest of the week. Ever since Avery and I had been with each other, we'd been texting non-stop like two goofy lovestruck teenagers.

I walked through the fire station's break room to the microwave, ramen in one hand and phone in the other.

> What are you up to tonight?

Dots popped up under Avery's name.

> Family dinner tonight. What, are you lonely at the station with your ramen?

> Sure am . . . what if you came by? I can show you my fire pole ;)

> Absolutely NOT. We're keeping everything a secret, remember?

> How about you go keep Levi company?

I raised a brow as I put my ramen in the microwave. She had a point, though. My shift would end in about an hour, one of our volunteer guys would take over, and I'd be free unless there was an emergency.

I already knew Levi was at home. What else was there to do in Whynot on a Sunday night?

> Good idea. I'll show him my fire pole

Oh my god

> Remind me to show you all the kink equipment I have when we see each other Wednesday . . .

Oh I will. I've been thinking about it non stop.

I grinned like a damn idiot. Since Friday, I'd done a little online shopping too. Maybe I was being overly ambitious, but giving gifts was one of my favorite things to do. And kinky gifts? Even better.

Had I dropped five hundred dollars on a new leather flogger, a new riding crop, a new ball gag, and a couple collars?

Yes.

Had I dropped even more on a midnight blue lace bodysuit that I thought would look really damn good on her?

Yes.

Should I have waited to see if Avery and maybe Levi were even interested in those things?

Also yes.

But what was the point of having adult money if I didn't spend it on adult things sometimes? I already had a paddle and other kinky items, but I wanted stuff for *us*.

I opened a leftover container of birria as the microwave beeped and swapped the ramen with it. A minute later, I added the meat to my ramen and carried my soup to the break table, glancing out the window that overlooked the street.

The station was a small one. It was outdated too, for the most part, although we did in fact have a pole.

My ramen was going to take a minute to cool down, so . . .

I pulled out my phone again and found Levi's name. Austin had given me his number, although we'd yet to text.

> Hey, it's Mateo. Are you busy tonight?

Read. My heart pounded in my chest as I waited to see if he'd even text back. God, my hands felt clammy. My entire body felt clammy, actually.

> Not busy. You?

Hell yeah.

> I get off work in an hour. Want some company?

I was met with silence. Fuck. Maybe I was wrong—

> Sure. Come over after. I have muffins that need to be eaten

Muffins? I was sure he didn't mean his ass, right? I mean, either way . . .

> Sounds good. See you in a bit

The next hour was the longest hour known to man. By the time Tommy sailed through the front doors to the station, my boot was hitting the sidewalk. I beelined for my truck and started it up, my pulse racing as I drove down the street toward Levi's.

Flirting had always come naturally to me. I loved flirting. I loved making people blush. I loved a good challenge, too.

Levi felt like a challenge. A really hot, hard, muscled challenge.

I was really doing this. I thought about Levi's expression when he saw me and Avery. The heat in his pretty eyes, the blush that crept into his tan cheeks. He'd looked like he was ready to get on his knees right then and there.

Or maybe I just wished he had.

I slowed as I turned onto Armadillo Lane. I pulled into the drive and hopped out, glancing across the street at Avery's little house. She'd really turned that place into a home since moving in. I remembered when I first came to Whynot and it was just a sad house that'd been on the market for who knew how long.

The house Levi was renting while he was here was an Airbnb that'd been flipped by a couple who'd moved to Colorado. They'd made it nice, though, and I was constantly surprised at how many people rented it to visit our dusty corner of the world.

I didn't bother locking my truck and headed to Levi's doorstep. The door was painted bright yellow and there were a couple of pink pots with dead plants in them. I raised my hand to knock, but the door swung open, Levi filling up the frame with his massive shoulders.

I opened my mouth to speak, but found myself at a loss for words.

Levi was shirtless and in jeans. But over his bare chest and denim was a pastel pink apron with lacy frills and hearts.

"I have so many questions," I finally said.

Levi grunted and stepped to the side to let me in. Heat crawled up my spine as I passed him, the two of us squeezing into the foyer as he closed the door. He twisted the lock and planted his hand on his hips.

"So my muffins are failing," he sighed. "I bought baking soda instead of powder, and didn't realize it until now. You'd think for someone who has a fucking degree in math and keeps about twenty different spreadsheets, I'd be able to bake."

The scent of blueberries filled the house. I kicked off my shoes next to his boots. "Did you say you have a degree in math?"

"Yep. Shocking, huh?"

"A little. And spreadsheets?"

Levi smirked. "I love them more than anything else. They keep me organized."

"Uh-huh. I see." *Interesting.* It was probably too much that the first thought that crossed my mind with that new information was *I bet he has a kink spreadsheet.* "I can't say I'm much of a baker, either. But I'll still happily try your muffins."

"The thing is that they're protein muffins. I've been trying to avoid completely derailing how I eat. I used to get some from a little bakery down the street from my apartment, and this was my half-assed attempt to bake them here."

Now, I made a face. "Like healthy muffins?"

"Yep. I tried. I don't think they'll be very good."

"I'll still try them." Although I was growing less and less enthusiastic about the muffins.

Levi led me from the hall through the living room at the front and to the kitchen. He felt very out of place in this house, like a giant living among glass breakables. I wondered what his apartment back in Minnesota looked like as we entered the kitchen, and then all thoughts blanked as I was presented with a blueberry muffin mishap.

I clapped my hand over my mouth, stifling a laugh. I wasn't sure if this was really just a baking soda issue or whatever the fuck he'd said. The muffins had blown up into a gooey disaster all over the pan, blueberries leaking out, protein powder scattered across the tiled counter.

All I could say was, "You made quite the mess."

"I did," he groaned. "You're laughing at me."

"I am . . . *not*," I choked out. Levi crossed his arms and stared at the muffin pan like it was the most disappointing thing in existence. I fought another laugh, doing my best to keep it in check. "Those look pretty bad."

"Want to taste one?"

"Not really. I think those might possibly be the worst muffins ever."

"Don't judge a book by its cover."

I was barely holding in my laugh. "I do have a suggestion."

He slowly turned to face me and raised a brow, serious aside from the fact that his eyes danced with amusement.

"Maybe make an alliance with Evie. You met her last week at yoga. She owns the bakery. I'm sure she'd make you some protein muffins that won't be . . ."

"A disaster?" he asked flatly.

"Um . . . Yes."

Levi chuckled and shook his head, turning his attention back to them. "How the fuck am I going to clean this up?"

"I have no idea. I'd throw the whole pan away."

"The whole pan? Absolutely not." Now, his laugh was a little heartier. "I'll deal with it in the morning. Want a THC drink? It's light, like a beer. I like it a lot more than alcohol."

My brows shot up. "Hell yeah, Minnesota. I'll take one."

Levi opened the little blue fridge that looked like something straight out of a 1950s trad wife magazine and handed me a drink. We both cracked open our cans and I took a sip, watching him a little too closely.

Levi's eyes widened and he frowned. "Forgot I was wearing

this thing." He looked down at the apron and put his drink on the counter, mumbling under his breath. "I'll be back."

"You don't need to take that off on my account."

He shook his head. "You're welcome to wear it instead."

"Shirtless or fully naked?"

"Dealer's choice." He chuckled, then cleared his throat. "I'll be back."

"I'll wait for you outside?" I needed some fresh air, especially with the way my cock was already reacting to him. My blood was hot and I needed to ice out the sexy thoughts before they burned me.

"Sure. I'll be there in a moment."

CHAPTER TWENTY

Fireflies winked at me as I stood in Levi's backyard—*waiting*. I craned my head back, looking up at the stars and feeling nerves hit me in full force.

I was really here. I was really doing this. I wasn't even sure it'd go anywhere.

The screen door snapped shut and I turned as Levi came out. He'd put on a soft stonewashed gray T-shirt and jeans. I wanted to take them right back off.

Levi held my gaze as he took a sip. "Want to sit with me?"

"Sure," I said. "Why not?"

He groaned. "That joke is killing me."

"It never gets old," I teased as I bounded up the steps to his porch.

He sat down on the porch swing, sliding all the way to the right. I hesitated for a moment and then decided—fuck it. I was going to join him. I sat down on the left side, an awkward amount of space between us.

Selfishly, I wished we were sitting hip to hip. Holding hands even. *Something* aside from dancing around whatever this feeling was.

What was I even doing? The tension between us was so

thick I could cut it with a knife. A fire burning so hot, I felt the need to douse us with a hose.

"Can I be honest?" I asked him.

Levi drew in a sharp breath, keeping his gaze on the backyard even though there was nothing interesting there except for dead grass and some rocks. Occasionally, a firefly would blink at us, so maybe that's what he was looking at.

Or maybe he just couldn't look at me.

"Yes," he finally said. "I'd like for you to be."

Nerves fired up in my belly. I felt like I was going to throw up. It didn't matter how easy it was to flirt, telling someone the truth like this always made me anxious. "I want you. I've wanted you since I saw you standing outside Avery's gallery. I think you're hot. I think you're interesting. And I feel like there's something here."

He was silent for a moment, his muscles tense. I swallowed hard, wondering if I was misreading everything. What if he actually wasn't into men? What if there hadn't been any vibes between us, and I'd just been making it up?

Oh god. That would be awful.

I didn't even want to think about the fact that I was flirting with my best friend's *other* best friend *and* his sister. If Austin ever found out, I wasn't sure he'd forgive me.

Then again, it wasn't any of his business. We were all adults.

Still . . .

Levi cleared his throat. "What about Avery?"

"I want her too. I suspect you do as well."

I caught a hint of amusement in his half smile. Light shined on the side of his face from the backdoor, shadows swallowing the rest of him.

"When you flirt with me, it makes my heart stop," he whispered.

"I hope in a good way," I murmured, clutching my drink. "And not in a 'I want to punch this guy' way."

Levi didn't say anything. But, his hand slowly moved across the wooden slats of the swing, closing the gap between the two of us until his fingers entangled with mine.

Was it silly to feel this excited about holding someone's hand? Maybe. But Levi's hand was large and rough and full of so much strength and gentleness at the same time, and I was melting into a puddle on the inside.

"It's in a good way," he whispered. "I'm bisexual too, Mateo. Well, I mean, I'm assuming—"

"Yes," I breathed out. "I am. And you are."

He nodded. "Yes. But I'm not very good at stuff like this. I mean, maybe in the bedroom. At least that's what I've heard. But with relationships and romance, I'm bad. So I don't think I can promise anything more than a physical connection, especially if I leave in a few weeks."

My chest squeezed. While I wasn't looking for a promise of forever, I did like Levi beyond the physical attraction.

But, I wasn't going to walk away from a chance to be with him in whatever way I could.

"I understand," I said. "Although, I doubt you're bad at relationships."

"My track record disagrees. Also, to be clear, I want Avery too. But her brothers would murder me. You too, probably. And all three of us together? I think Austin would have a heart attack."

"Avery and I have been dancing around each other for years, but we decided to give this a chance as of last week. You kind of walked in on us finally giving things a chance. And over the last week, we've been texting and talking and planning. Honestly, your arrival was what made me finally do something. But we're keeping things secret from everyone but June and

Evie, because they're Avery's best friends and we don't want to hide from them. Plus, they'll keep their mouths shut."

He let out a soft hum. "I have to wonder why they got so over-protective."

"Who? Her brothers?"

"Yeah. Austin has kept a lot from me over the years, so I feel like I'm missing information."

"I know part of the reason why," I said vaguely. "But it's not my story to tell. All I will say is that she dated someone that used to be friends with Dallas and Austin, and he hurt her."

Levi's grip tightened. "Physically?"

"I'm not entirely sure." Even I didn't know everything. "I think it was more mental manipulation. But no one has told me the whole story, and I've never pried."

"Mental abuse can be just as bad."

"It can be in a lot of ways." I swallowed the flame in my chest. The idea of anyone harming Avery made me want to commit homicide. "I think Austin and Dallas watched her break apart. Then their dad passed away literally on their drive home, and she moved back here, and since then—they do everything they can to protect her. I get it. I really do. And I've sat on the sidelines just telling myself I could never have her."

"I'd never want to hurt her."

"Me neither."

"I'm not sure if it's a good idea to get involved then."

"The thing is, Levi—we're all adults. If you want her and she wants you, then there's no reason not to go after that feeling."

"You better not say 'why not' to me right now."

I chuckled, giving his hand a gentle squeeze. "All I'm saying is that Avery is worth taking the chance on. And as someone who's waited two years to start showing her how much I care for her—don't wait."

Levi hummed, finally turning his head to look at me. I met his gaze and everything in the world seemed to slow.

"What about us?" he asked.

"Well, I told you I want you."

"And if I said I want you too?"

My heart slammed against my ribcage. "I'd ask what are we still doing holding hands on your back porch?"

"And then I'd get up and lead you to my bedroom."

"And I'd get on my knees and suck your cock."

Levi pulled my hand toward his lap. My palm smoothed over the denim, and his hard cock strained against his zipper. Jesus Christ, he was fucking huge.

"Maybe we should kiss first," he said.

"Maybe we should."

We put our drinks down on the porch. Then, he dragged me forward. The porch swing squeaked beneath us as he pulled me into his lap, lifting me with an ease that made my head spin. It wasn't like I was a light guy, but the way he manhandled me made me feel like a goddamn princess.

And I fucking liked it. Even knowing that I was going to dominate him, I liked it.

No, I *loved* it.

My knees settled on either side of his hips. My cock hardened, rubbing against the outline of his erection as I rocked my body against his. His fingers knotted in my short curls and he tugged my mouth to his. His mouth was hot and needy, but so was mine. Our kiss was rough. Hungry. Desperate to satiate this thirst I'd had for the hockey player ever since he dusted our town with his expensive unworn boots.

"Fuck," he grunted.

Fuck was right. I drew back, holding his gaze for a second. Something unspoken passed between us and in one easy motion, my legs wrapped around his waist as he stood up, holding me to him as he carried me through the backdoor.

It slammed behind us, echoing through the house as he shoved me against the wall. Our kisses consumed us, every part of my body on fire for him.

"I hope you have lube and condoms," I gasped.

"I do. Thank fucking god." He paused for a moment, cocking his head. "Am I fucking you or are you fucking me?"

I raised a brow. "Do you want me to fuck you, Levi?"

He swallowed hard enough his throat bobbed. Pink blossomed in his cheeks, turning his face scarlet.

"We can do both," I offered. "I got all night. I'm off the clock unless Whynot catches on fire."

Levi grinned, and I realized it was maybe the first time I'd seen him truly smile. There was nothing fake about it. And dammit, he was fucking gorgeous when he smiled.

I cupped his jaw, running my fingers through his beard. "Carry me to your bed. Now."

"So you're the demanding one."

"I sure am," I said. "But I'll take care of you."

With that promise in mind, heat warmed his gaze and he held me close, taking me through the dining room, down the hall, and straight to his bedroom. I reached behind him to flip on the light as he kicked the door shut behind us.

"I'll turn on a lamp," he grumbled.

"Not a big light guy?" I teased.

He tossed me onto the bed and I laughed, leaning over to turn on the lamp as he flipped the switch off again.

"I hate big lights," he said. "And this one is especially egregious. All the lights in my apartment back in Minnesota are a certain kind that don't feel like god is staring down at you when they're turned on."

I snorted as I sat up, ripping my shirt off as I watched him. I hadn't even thought about the fact that his home was some- where else. "I forget you have an apartment."

"Yeah," he said. "Right around the corner from where we practice, so I just walk to work."

"So your life revolves around hockey."

"It did." He tugged his shirt overhead, revealing a muscled set of shoulders and chest, along with abs that had softened slightly over the last few weeks. "Not anymore, though."

My smile softened and I tilted my head, regarding him thoughtfully. He held my gaze as he tugged on his belt buckle, standing at the edge of the bed and watching me. The metal clinked as he took it off, the leather zipping against the denim as he tossed it to the floor. Before he could undo the top button, I held up my hand, sitting forward.

"I'm doing that," I said.

His hand stilled as I moved to the edge of the bed. I sat with my thighs straddling either side of him and tilted my head back. I loved looking into his eyes as my fingers tugged at the cool button, snapping his jeans open. I slowly undid the zipper, only pulling my gaze from his to look at this cock. He was so unbe- lievably hard. I tugged his jeans down, taking his briefs with them until his cock sprang free.

Holy shit. My mind ran blank as I stared at his cock. He was thick and long, veins bulging along the shaft. I took in the sight of his balls, the V of his hips, the magnificence of *him*.

Levi was one of the sexiest men I'd ever seen. Certainly the sexiest man I'd ever been with.

Sucking his cock was going to be difficult.

But I liked a challenge.

"If I'm too much—"

"Don't even go there," I interrupted. "You have a damn fine cock."

I looked up, and the man was blushing. *Blushing.*

147

"I'm going to suck you until you're begging for more," I promised. "And then I'm going to fuck you until you're screaming my name."

He opened his mouth to speak, but words died as I closed my hand around him, guiding the tip to my mouth. The salty taste of precum hit my tongue and my own body responded.

Feeling the weight of his cock in my mouth as I took him deeper turned me on in a primal way.

Levi's groan was music to my ears. His breath hitched as I took him deeper, all the way until the head of his cock hit the back of my throat. I closed my hand around the base of his shaft, stroking him slowly as I found a rhythm that had his hips bucking with need.

"Fuck," he grunted. "*Mateo.*"

Oh yeah. Hearing him rasp my name like that? Every nerve in my body lit up with lust.

I pulled my mouth off his cock right as his movements became hurried. He blew out a breath as I closed my hand firmly around his cock, his gaze locking with mine.

"You're going to be a good boy for me, aren't you?" I asked.

"*Yes.*"

His answer came without hesitation.

"Please," he whispered. "Please fuck me. *Please.*"

CHAPTER TWENTY-ONE

Bending over my bed on all fours for a flirty firefighter hadn't been on my Escape to West Texas to-do list, and yet here I was.

My thoughts ran non-stop as I adjusted myself. Lust pumped through, every part of my body *needing* more from him.

The mattress shifted as Mateo knelt behind me. His hands worked down my back, down my sides. I stiffened as he neared my shoulder, but he paused.

Mateo let out a soft hum, his fingers turning gentle. "If this position hurts you, we can adjust. We can use pillows. We can do whatever you need to feel comfortable."

I didn't like showing weakness, but I also didn't want to deal with a fucked up shoulder this week. "All right," I mumbled. Reluctantly, I grabbed a couple pillows, putting one beneath my chest, and using the edge of the other to cushion my right side.

I cleared my throat. "Sorry. Lot of injuries from games."

He tsked. "Don't be sorry." His mustache brushed my skin as he peppered kisses down my spine. "I want you to feel good. Are you comfortable?"

My heart pounded as I adjusted my body a bit more. My

shoulder didn't feel any strain and while I was tense, that was from anticipation, not my body struggling to stay in this position.

"Yes," I said.

"Good."

Slowly, I sank into the idea of submitting to him. There was something about him that made me feel safe, which had always been hard to find in a partner.

The part of me that wanted to do this exact thing to him was also thoroughly enjoying being the one on my knees.

"Relax," he murmured.

"I'm trying."

Mateo chuckled and continued to rub my muscles, all while my cock raged. I was so fucking hard from being edged by him. Ever since I'd come to Whynot, I'd thought about what this would feel like.

Mateo made my heart skip beats and my mind run blank. In the short time I'd known him, I already knew he was the kind of person that made me feel whole.

And that scared the shit out of me.

"Tell me what you like," he said.

"Do you mean kink—" My words cut off as he leaned forward and closed his hand around my cock. I sucked in a breath, everything melting into a moan. "Fuck."

"Yes," Mateo whispered. "I *do* mean kink. Tell me what you like."

"But I can barely think," I protested, rocking my hips.

He started to stroke me. "I believe in your ability to focus, Mr. Math Degree."

Fuck. It was impossible to form any full thoughts. Pleasure shot through my body as he stroked me slowly, his hand moving up and down at a pace that made every muscle in my body tense.

"I'm a switch," I huffed. "Most of the time I've been expected to Dom. And I love it, don't get me wrong."

"But you crave submission."

"Yes," I rasped. Holy fuck, this was hot. I felt his cock hardening against my ass, his body molded against mine as he continued to stroke me. "I haven't explored kink too much as a submissive. But, I think I know what I like. Bondage of any sort. Rope, especially. I like having my hair pulled. I like spreader bars and hand cuffs. Floggers, spanking, some light impact. I love sensory deprivation. Not being able to see or hear and knowing something is about to happen . . ."

I trailed off as he pumped my cock faster.

"I like being used. I want to be used. I want to please you. *Fuck.*"

Mateo was turning me into a pathetic fucking mess.

"What else?" he asked.

"I want . . . I want to be a good boy. I fucking love being called that. I don't know. As far as pain goes, I like a little bit. But not a lot. Just enough to give pleasure an edge."

I felt him nod. "I understand."

"I'm not used to being on this end of things."

I felt him smile against my back. "I'm excited to see how you are when you switch. But seeing you so submissive and needy right now . . ." He thrust his hips against me, grinding his cock against my ass cheeks. "It turns me on. Every part of me just wants to fuck you right now, but I want to savor it. I want to take my time with this perfect ass."

I shivered as he released my cock and sat back. I could feel him looking at me. My cock jerked as he grabbed my cheeks and spread them.

Fuck. I wasn't used to being looked at like this either. My blood pumped, my face pressing into the pillow as my cheeks burned.

"Are you embarrassed?" Mateo murmured.

"Maybe a little. The guys I've been with, it's always been quick. And usually me on top." Hell, I couldn't think of a time I'd ever really submitted for anyone.

"I bet people see you and think you have to be dominant. As a hockey player with so many muscles. You're so fucking strong and tall and handsome."

"Yes," I whispered.

"But I see you and I think I want to put you on your fucking knees."

Shit.

"I remember driving up and seeing you on the side of the road . . ."

His hand closed around my cock again.

"And thinking you have such a fine ass in denim. And wondering what it would be like to have this moment. Feeling you beneath me. Seeing how goddamn good you look submitting to me."

I grunted as he leaned forward, and I felt the tip of his tongue against my ass, circling me slowly, teasing my hole and sending shockwaves of lust through me. I didn't think my cock could get any harder, but I was wrong. The roughness of his mustache and the softness of his tongue turned me on even more, my body so desperate to be fucked.

"That's it," he murmured between licks. "Take it like a good boy."

A wave of pleasure rushed through me as he kept jerking my cock while his tongue explored me. All of the tension left me as I sank further into the feeling of being with him.

The thing about Mateo was that he made me feel safe in this headspace. And that made me want to give in even more.

I whimpered, moving my hips involuntarily. I was so close to the edge already, and decided I wasn't going to stop myself from coming. I wasn't going to hold back. If he wanted to make me come, then I'd come for him.

Mateo's tongue prodded deeper, but then he drew back and replaced it with two fingers. "Where's the lube?"

"Top drawer."

The bed shifted as he leaned over and yanked the drawer open, pulling out the bottle and a condom. He uncapped it and poured lube onto his fingers. I looked back over my shoulder as he worked it around my ass, then slowly, carefully—pushed two fingers inside me. I moaned as he worked them in, taking his time.

He was going to force me to appreciate the torture of anticipation.

"Look at you. Fuck, you look good like this." He pushed his fingers right up against my prostate, and I gasped, pleasure shooting through me. "I'm not giving you this cock until you beg for it."

"Please," I immediately gasped. "Please. I need you inside me. I need to feel you fucking me."

He pumped his fingers in and out at a steady pace. "I remain unconvinced."

Fuck me. I groaned into the pillow, pushing my ass back to meet each movement. "Mateo, please. Please fuck me. I've been thinking about this all weekend. All week. I don't just want your cock, I *need* it."

I did nothing to fight the desperation in my voice. Mateo gave my ass a light slap and then released my cock and pulled his fingers free. A streak of excitement ran through me as he leaned down and kissed my back again. He lined himself up behind me, the sound of the condom foil ripping building the tension. Fuck, I was already close to coming.

My heart hammered as the head of his cock nudged me.

"Please," I whispered.

"I know, baby," he murmured. "You need my cock."

"I need it."

"And I'm going to give it to you."

He pushed his hips forward, entering me slowly. I groaned as I took him, realizing just how thick he was as he stretched me around him. He paused to pour more lube on my hole, working it until he was able to thrust, filling me completely.

"Fuck," I groaned. "Fuck. That's so much."

"That's only half."

Only half?

I thought he was all the way in, but I'd thought wrong. I groaned as he gave me more until he was finally fully inside me.

He reached around and grabbed hold of my cock again. My eyes closed and I realized I was already drooling as he started to drive his cock in and out, matching the same rhythm he was stroking mine to. My moans filled the room along with the sound of our skin slapping together.

"Fuck," he mumbled.

A string of curses followed and I grinned, blinded by the pleasure bursting in every cell, thrilled that he was coming undone just as quickly as I was.

"I'm so close." My voice was muffled by the pillow, grunts and groans between my words. "Please. Please let me come."

Mateo's chuckle was lost as he thrust harder, pounding me into the pillows, into the mattress. Lust clawed at my spine, pleasure spearing through me and pushing me closer and closer. All the times I'd imagined him fucking me didn't do justice to the real thing.

"I'm gonna come," I rasped. "I'm so close."

Mateo groaned and drove into me, every movement taking me there. I squeezed my eyes shut, my voice ringing as my orgasm hit me, my cock jerking as I came. His hips stilled as he buried himself deep inside me, his voice joining mine.

Fuck, he was coming with me.

"You feel so fucking good." His hands held my hips in place as more cum spurted from my cock, wetting the blankets beneath me. I was making a goddamn mess, but I didn't care.

Mateo collapsed forward, his weight comfortable on top of mine. "Good boy," he murmured, kissing my shoulder. One of his hands slid up, his fingers ruffling my hair in a way I enjoyed more than I thought possible.

I sank against the mattress, letting both of our bodies meld into it.

"Fuck," I mumbled. "That was . . ."

"That was really fucking good."

All I could do was nod as he continued to rub my head in gentle circles.

I was comfortable.

I didn't want him to leave. I could stay like this all night.

Hell, I wanted him to be in my bed all night.

There may have been rules and secrets when it came to dating Avery, but there weren't any when it came to the two of us. Right?

"Do you want to stay?" I whispered.

Mateo nuzzled my neck and gave me a soft kiss. "I want to, but I have to be at work early—like, five in the morning early."

I groaned. "Stay anyway."

He smiled against me. "That's early, Minnesota. Are you sure?"

I lifted up slightly, turning just enough so I could look into his eyes. "I want you in my bed," I said. "If you want to, of course. If not, I understand."

He sat up slightly and pulled out, then surprised me by

rolling me onto my back. I sucked in a breath as he pinned me beneath him, his face hovering above mine.

"You want me in your bed, huh?"

God, he was such a cocky bastard.

"I do." I fought with a smile and lost. "I want you in my bed."

"I'll have to leave early. Maybe before you wake up."

"I don't care."

"I thought you didn't want to date. You've got a cactus heart. Prickly. Grumpy."

"I said I want you in my *bed*," I said. "Not that I want to date. Not that I don't want to date, it's just . . . It's complicated."

"Mm-hmm. How about you get me into your shower? And then you can get me into your bed."

"You've got yourself a deal."

CHAPTER TWENTY-TWO

This was going to suck.

I drummed my fingers on the steering wheel, anxiety corroding my mental state like battery acid. Mom's house was just a few minutes outside of town. The driveway was long and rocky, my truck wobbling as I pulled between my brothers' trucks.

I turned off the engine and sat still for a moment.

My childhood house wasn't home anymore.

It had felt like home my entire life until Dad died. A four bedroom, two bath, with brick walls and a large flagstone wrap-around porch I'd spend countless days playing on. I used to spend hours drawing with chalk, creating art my dad would croon over and my mom would wash off later.

This house held a lot of good memories. A lot of frustrating ones. Some bad ones. And then there was the sadness that had bled its way into every nook and cranny.

I always knew losing someone would be hard. Everyone *knows* that. But when it actually happens, the grief is an all-consuming leech on life. All of the knowing could never have prepared me for how fucking hard life would be without the man who raised me.

I hoped I would make him proud. I tried my best with the studio and helping out where I could around town. It wasn't necessarily the glamorous life I'd imagined for myself, but I still got to do what I loved.

Evie and June were going to kill me. I was tempted to text them now to fill them in on everything that had happened with Mateo, but I'd kept it all to myself over the last few days. Texting him, openly flirting with him, staying up late in the night talking on the phone. I hadn't felt this sort of giddy happiness in so long, and I didn't like keeping it a secret.

Not from them, of course. I'd fill them in soon. But, I knew it would be a four-hour conversation over cheap margaritas, a bag of chips, and bad 80s hair band music.

I glanced at my phone, wondering if Mateo's seduction plan was working.

Ugh. I needed to put all of that out of my mind and ready myself for dinner.

I hated that I always felt the need to put guards up when I was around my mom. I did love her, but that didn't change the fact that my relationship with her was far different than she had with my brothers.

My blood pressure was skyrocketing just from sitting in the driveway. I did what my therapist had suggested and drew in a slow, deliberate breath. I held it, released it, and reminded myself that this would be fine.

I did dinner every Sunday and was fine. Right? And if things went sideways, I'd remove myself from the situation. I'd hold my boundaries. I'd make sure that if she said anything mean or completely rude, I'd leave.

"You coming inside?"

Austin's muffled yell from the front door was the end of my peace. I grabbed my bag and hopped out of the truck. I headed down the sidewalk and plastered on a smile, but who was I kidding? Austin had the same forced smile on his face.

I raised a brow. "Anything I should know?"

"Well, she's asking Dallas and I when we're going to give her grandchildren," he said lightly. "So I'm happy you're here. You can take some of the heat."

"Oh joy. Great. Wonderful."

Austin held the door open for me and I stepped inside, immediately met with the familiar scent of meatloaf, mashed potatoes, and roasted veggies. I kicked my shoes off and hung my bag, rolling my shoulders and bracing myself for whatever mess this was going to be.

"Hi," I called, heading straight to the kitchen.

I rounded the corner and wasn't surprised to see Mom pulling a pan out of the oven. My smile faltered as she stood up. She'd lost some weight and that concerned me, since I'd seen her only last week. Her hair was pulled back into a bun and I noticed more gray than usual. She turned, the angle showing me her face, and . . . damn. Maybe Dallas was right to be worried. She wasn't wearing any makeup.

My entire life, this woman got up before dawn to put her face on. It's just how she was. In fact, I couldn't remember a day where she didn't have makeup on before eight in the morning—including the day of my father's funeral.

"Avery," she said without glancing at me. "Glad you made it on time."

Just a little slap. "Just a couple minutes late. Where's Dallas?"

"He's hanging up some pictures of Dad for me."

Well, fuck. Great. My stomach did a slow flip, but I kept that smile plastered on as I stepped up to the sink to wash my hands. "Want some help?"

She snorted. "Since when do you help in the kitchen?"

"Almost every Sunday," I said. "Would you like some help?"

If I didn't help, she'd grumble about it the rest of dinner.

Mom sighed. "Set the table. Use the green dishes. I'm tired of the blue ones."

"All right," I said.

The dining room was right across from the kitchen. It was large and good for parties. A wooden hutch with glass doors sat against the wall, full of different dish sets that'd been in the family forever. I opened it, carefully pulling four plates from the green section. My gaze lingered on the fifth plate, but I let the door close and carried them to the table, setting everything quickly.

My spine stiffened as she slammed some of the cabinets, grumbling to herself under her breath. I was pretty sure I caught the words "ungrateful" and "always doing all the work," but decided to tune her out.

For a while there, I thought it was going better. After Dad died, she'd been a lot nicer. She'd clung to me in a way that made me feel wanted. But now, I was pretty sure she'd completely swung the other way and wanted *nothing* to do with me.

I ignored the ache in my chest and returned to the kitchen, opening the silverware drawer. We didn't say a word to each other until Austin came back into the kitchen.

"Can I help?" he asked.

"We've got it," Mom chimed. "You can take a seat, if you want."

I pressed my lips together and finished setting out linen napkins with forks and knives.

"I'll put the food out," Austin said, grabbing dishes off the counter.

He could ignore her like that without getting scolded.

Dallas walked into the room with a hammer in hand. He dropped the tool in the drawer next to the sink, then gave me a big hug. Tension radiated through him as he kissed the top of my head.

"How's it going?" he asked.

"Good," I lied. "Got the pictures up?"

Dallas nodded, but didn't smile. Of the three of us, he didn't pretend as much. His eyes were a little glassy, his jaw set. None of us were happy about the photos going up, because it would just be a knife to the heart every time we saw them.

"Where'd you hang them?" I asked.

"In the hallway going upstairs," Mom answered.

Great, so they were unavoidable. "That's nice," I said.

"I think we're all ready," she said as she grabbed a pitcher of sweet tea and carried it to the table.

We all dragged out our chairs and took our designated seats, ignoring the empty one where Dad used to sit. I wished that she would just get rid of the chair. Hell, I wished I could break it apart. But, instead it sat there, solemn and dusty like a headstone.

"Thanks for cooking," Dallas said. "This all looks good."

"Of course," she said.

"Maybe next Sunday we could do pizza," I said. "So you don't have to cook every week."

"What—do you suddenly not like my cooking?" Her words dripped with accusation.

Here we go. "No," I said as I piled my plate. "Clearly I like your cooking. I've been eating your food my entire life, Mom."

"It's a good idea," Austin backed me up as he piled his plate with food. "Just to do something easy. How has your week been? What have you been up to?"

"No different than last week," she said with a shrug. "Did

some work around the house. Watched a show. I saw some video about a politician that was caught in a sex club."

"That was fake, Mom," Dallas sighed like he'd gone over this fifty times already. He probably had. "Some of that AI bull-shit. It's called a deep fake."

"Oh. Well I guess that's good news," she said. "Computers can really do that now?"

"Unfortunately," Dallas said. "You know not to watch the news unless it's from the sites I gave you."

She smiled and it *almost* reached her eyes. "It was on Face-book. One of the ladies I used to get lunch with shared it."

"Speaking of," I said. "Have you gone out for lunch with any friends recently?"

Mom narrowed her eyes on me, the mood shifting. "No. Why?"

"Seems like it would be good to," Austin said. "You used to go out three times a week."

"Used to," she said. "Just trying to save money."

"Mom, you know you have plenty of money to spend on getting lunch with friends a couple times a week," Dallas said. "We're just worried about you staying in too much."

"I'm doing just fine, darling."

Fine. God, that word was fucking cursed. Everyone at this table was *fine*, but none of us actually were.

It was always me that had to rip the bandaid off. "We think you need to see a therapist," I blurted out.

The table fell silent and our mom stared at me like I'd grown two heads. Dallas leaned back in his chair, rubbing his stubble in a very stressed out way. Austin's brows shot up as his expression hit the *oh shit, Avery went there* face.

"Excuse me?" she asked.

"We think you need therapy," I said firmly. "It's a good thing. It's healing. I go to therapy and—"

"Well you go because you've got problems up there," she said, making a gesture toward my head.

"Jesus. *Mom*," Dallas interjected. "That's not an okay way to say that. And therapy is healthy, especially after loss—"

She sat her fork down, the metal clinking against her plate like a sharp exclamation point. "I'm not going. I'm doing just fine."

"You're not though," I said. "You're not wearing any makeup. You've lost weight. We know you're not going out like you used to—"

"I'm saving money." She tipped her chin up defiantly, and I got a glimpse at where my fucking stubbornness from. "None of you need to worry about me."

"But, we *are* worried," Austin said. "We all think you need to do this."

"And I said no. End of discussion."

"It's not the end of discussion," I said. "We're not children anymore, and you can't just shut us down."

Her eyes narrowed on me. "Why do you always have to pick a fight with me, Avery? What did I ever do to you except give you a roof over your head?"

"Oh, I'm sorry. I didn't realize that was a hard thing to do, since you're the one that chose to have me," I seethed.

"Avery," Austin said softly.

"No, really," I said. "It's not even that I'm picking a fight with you. I'm just not rolling over and doing exactly what you say anymore. You do need therapy. Half of the money I pay my therapist has literally gone to me trying to fix my relationship with you."

"Well, they've done a shit job."

Ouch. My eyes stung. "I'm trying harder than you are."

"Are you? You never come see me. Never call me. Never do anything with me."

"You don't see me, call me, or do anything with me either. It goes both ways. I shouldn't always have to be the one to reach out."

"And I should be?"

"At least *sometimes*," I said, exasperated.

She scoffed. "Well, I'm sorry I'm not your father. He always had a way of getting through your bullshit. I have no idea how, though, and never will."

I stared at her for a moment and then pushed my chair back.

"Avery," Dallas pleaded.

I stood up and grabbed my plate, taking it to the kitchen. My spine stiffened as my mom sighed.

"Avery, I take it back," she said. She clearly didn't fucking mean it. "Stop being dramatic."

"Mom, you're not being nice right now," Austin said, his words stiff. "We're trying to help you, and you're not listening to us."

"What? I'm not the one stomping around and being a bitch about it. She is."

"*Mom*," Dallas snapped. "What is *wrong* with you?"

I cleared my plate and put it in the sink. My eyes continued to burn as I swallowed back tears. I needed to get the fuck out of here, but I paused to look at the three of them. She twisted in her chair to give me an exasperated look. Austin was clearly angry, and Dallas was in shock.

I just couldn't keep doing this. I couldn't keep pretending our family was fine.

My words were calm and measured. "I'm not doing this anymore. I won't be back next week. Until you go to therapy and start working out your issues and why you hate me, I will not step foot back in this house again."

"Avery, I take it back," she said again. "Your dad always understood you."

"Because he tried to, and you never have."

"Well, sorry he's not here to mediate."

"Me too."

My mother scoffed as I fled. Dallas stood up to follow me as I headed straight for the door.

"Avery," he said softly. "We need to—"

I spun around to look up at him and his expression died when he saw mine. His eyes shone as he dragged me into a full hug.

"I'm sorry," he whispered. "I'm so sorry she's like this. You don't deserve it."

"I don't." A sob loosed in my chest. "I need to go."

He gave me another squeeze and then released me. "Want me to text Mateo? I'm sure he could pick you up."

"No," I said quickly. *Mateo is hopefully having mind blowing sex with your friend right now.* "I'll go to June or Evie's."

"Okay. Are you okay to drive?"

"I'm fine." I wiped my eyes quickly and slid on my shoes. "I can't keep doing this, Dallas. I'm sorry."

"She went too far. Austin and I will talk to her."

"Good luck."

Voices echoed from the kitchen and Dallas turned slightly, making a face. "Fuck, man. I'm so tired of this."

"I know. Call me if you need me," I said. "I'm sorry I can't stay. I can't keep doing this. We can't keep acting like everything is fine. And until she starts to work on herself, I can't keep putting myself in this position. Every single week, I have to jump through hoops to make myself feel okay. I can't."

"It's okay," he said softly. He genuinely meant it, too.

"Thank you for trying. I love you and I'll see you this week. We'll make our own dinner plans, okay?"

The tension melted just a little. "Okay."

"I'll text in a bit."

I nodded and drifted outside like a ghost, pulling my phone out of my pocket as I headed to my truck. I pressed June's name to call as I got in and backed out of the drive, tears streaming.

"What's up, buttercup?" June answered.

"My mom is a bitch," I sobbed.

"Oh no. Need to come over?"

"Yes," I sniffled. "Can you call Evie?"

"That bad?"

"Yeah. I'm not going to family dinners anymore."

"Well, shit. All right. I'll see you in a few. Did you even eat?"

"Not really."

"I've got leftovers and Evie can bring us stale bakery goods. And once you feel better, you can tell us about Mateo's little morning coffee concha run you've been keeping to yourself this last week."

It was a gross, snotty laugh—but I still laughed. "I'll be there soon."

CHAPTER TWENTY-THREE

June's house was ten minutes from mine, and five from Evie's. I barreled through June's front door, kicked off my shoes, ran straight to the living room, and threw myself on June's couch between the two of them to sob.

"Oh honey," Evie said, rubbing my back. "What in the hell happened tonight?"

I couldn't form the words to explain yet. I just needed to cry it out. They were patient with me, holding me between them as I cried. I was an ugly crier too—one of the ugliest—but they didn't care. They just loved me the way my mom should have.

June got up and left for a couple minutes, then returned with three plates full of pasta and garlic bread. I sat up slightly, sniffling as I took my plate, clearing my throat.

"Sorry," I sighed. "It was bad."

"Whatever she said clearly hit something," Evie said.

The three of us settled on the couch and dug into our food. Despite the fact I couldn't breathe through my nose, the pasta and bread cut straight through the sadness like a soothing carb balm.

"She's depressed," I finally said. "She's not going out

anymore. She's lost weight. I think the first year, we expected her to be grieving, but it's been a lot longer than that now. And I think she's gotten worse. Dallas came over on Friday for dinner and Austin stopped by too. We decided we wanted to talk to her tonight about going to therapy."

June let out an abrupt laugh and covered her mouth. "Sorry. I just know that didn't go over well."

"It did not," I said.

Evie sighed. "I do not envy either of you. My mom will be your mom too."

"She is," June chuckled. "I'm tempted to call her up just so Avery can have a hug without strings attached."

I chuckled and took another bite of fettuccine, thinking about Evie's family. Out of the three of us, her relationship with her parents was by far the healthiest. They were both happy and good and loved her. They were so fucking proud of her. And June and I had *definitely not* spent hours at this point in our friendship with Evie talking about how much we wished our moms were like hers.

"I think being an only child helps," Evie said. "I got all their love."

"There should be plenty to spread around," June said. "I think you just have good parents, Evie. They're balanced people."

I nodded in agreement. "So true."

"Well, they love when you come over. Their door is always open, too. But maybe knock first."

I grinned and laid my head on her shoulder, stretching my legs out. June's couch was large and comfortable. We called it the "Breakdown Couch," because if one of us needed to cry, we always convened here. The cushions were permanently stained with our tears.

"The kicker was that she said my dad always understood

me," I said. "And she said she was sorry she wasn't him, but in that sarcastic, condescending tone. And it just sent me over the edge."

"Damn," Evie muttered. "That's low. Even for her. Your mom has her issues, but she's not usually mean like that."

"Yeah," I whispered. "So I'm done. Dallas walked me out."

"I bet he was worried," June said.

"He was. And Austin started arguing with her. I didn't hear what they said, but I could hear his tone on the way out."

"Good," Evie said. "Maybe she'll listen to them."

"I hope so," I said. "I do want her to be better, you know? I'm hurt and angry, but I don't want her to be depressed. I want her to be happy. I want her to want to know me."

At this point, that felt like a pipe dream.

"It's her loss," Evie said gently.

"Agreed."

June tucked her legs against her body and balanced her plate on her knee. I could feel them both looking at me now—despite the upsetting dinner, I smiled.

"All right," I said. "I've cried it all out. Life sucks, so does family. We can move on to other things."

"*Mateo* things? *Levi* things?" June chimed.

"Yep."

"Thank god," Evie said. "I've been dying to know. *Dying.*"

"Oh," I said, sitting up slightly. I pointed my fork at her. "You're a bitch, by the way. Mateo told me you've known he's liked me for *years*."

"That son of a bitch," Evie groaned.

June let out a soft giggle. "I've known too."

"What?!"

"Girl, we have *eyes*." Evie gave me a half amused, half exasperated look. "Why do you think we encouraged you to make a move?"

"*Okay*," I said. "Well, *maybe*, both of you could have been like 'Hey, Avery, we *know* Mateo likes you,' because that would have made me make a move faster."

"We did say that," Evie said.

"We certainly did." June raised a brow. "We have texts to prove it."

I made a face and bit into my garlic bread. "Okay, well. I don't know what to say to that."

"What you can *say* is all the details of what happened. And how Levi fits into all this too," Evie prodded.

"Okay, so . . ." I trailed off and fought a smile. "Mateo is really fucking good in bed."

Evie and June screeched and I gripped my plate like a shield so my pasta didn't fly everywhere from their excitement.

"I fucking knew it!" Evie yelled.

"I knew it! Oh god, I bet he's got a big dick," June exclaimed.

They both fell silent and stared at me.

"He does," I confirmed.

They screeched again and Evie held up her hand. "Not that size matters. He has know how to use it."

"We all know that flirty bastard knows how," June said with a grin. "Oh my god. I want all the details. Every single one."

I smirked and took another bite of pasta before spilling everything to them. Did I spare any details? No. I even told them about Levi interrupting us for baking soda, and how Mateo suggested he join us. I told them about our texts and late night calls over the last week, and how good it felt to be talking to him like this.

"You're going to get railed by both of them," Evie said smugly. "I just know it."

"I don't know," I snorted. "I mean, maybe? Maybe not?"

"It's not a *maybe*," June said. "I give it a week, tops. Your birth control better be up to date."

I barked out a laugh. "IUD, baby. This uterus is locked down like Alcatraz."

"Good, because I foresee double cream pies in your future," Evie said.

The three of us laughed until we couldn't breathe, and I felt a weight lift off my shoulders. I finished telling them about the rest of our time together and then relaxed into the couch with a big, silly smile.

"Damn," June sighed. "Well, now I'm jealous. But also proud. Good job."

"Thanks, I tried so hard."

"And now he's seducing Levi?" Evie asked.

"Yeah, but who knows if that's actually happening," I said. "Levi is a little tough. I'm not quite sure he'd be open to being together, or the three of us being together."

"And what about you? What do you think? I don't think you've ever dated two people at the same time," June said.

"I haven't," I said. "It feels like it could be right, though? I knew a few polyamorous people when I lived in Austin, and they made it work. Although, again, I'm not sure if Levi would actually want to date, considering I don't think he's staying here."

"Well, only one way to find out," Evie said.

"True." June let out a soft hum. "See, I could get on board with having a girlfriend *and* a boyfriend."

Evie laughed. "At this point, I feel like I need to be in a pack dynamic, like one of those omegaverse books. I just want to be pampered like a princess."

I grinned. "I could see that for both of you."

"Our little omega," June teased Evie. "I would not want to live in a house with multiple men, though."

Evie smirked. "The trick is having one of them into being our sexy maid."

My brows shot up. "Damn, Evie."

"What? Don't give me shit about my latex maid fantasies, Avery. We all know what you're into."

My grin was downright evil. "You have a point."

And now, all I could think about was what it would be like to be kinky with Levi *and* Mateo. I'd probably melt right into the floor between them.

"We require updates about this next week," June said. "And right after it happens. None of this waiting until days after bullshit."

"Yep," Evie said. "I want to hear everything."

"I'll keep you updated," I said. "If there's even anything to update about."

They both rolled their eyes, because we all knew there would be *something*.

CHAPTER TWENTY-FOUR

Sweat broke out across my forehead and back as I did my final rep, lifting my weights overhead to place them on the rack. The metal clinked as I groaned and melted onto the bench, staring at the ceiling.

I'd been working out for two hours, trying to chase the horny demons out of my system, but it wasn't working. I sat up and snatched my water bottle off the floor, using the hem of my Whynot Fire Department shirt to swipe my forehead.

After last night with Levi, I slept like I was dead for five hours in his bed, woke up, and snuck out of his house with my mind all over the place. I got to the station around 5:00 a.m. to relieve David, one of our volunteer firefighters, and took over for the day.

With it being Monday, I was going to do hydrant checks, equipment checks, and then be on call for any emergencies.

Fingers crossed there weren't any. My muscles burned as I stood up and stretched side to side, my thoughts bouncing all over the place. From work to Avery, work to Levi, work to *fucking the two of them until they were whimpering messes*, work to *how in the fuck had I ended up being the leader of a whole-ass station*, work to *how do I set up a three way date . . .*

Basically, my mind was a hamster on a wheel and it wasn't going to stop spinning all day, no matter how much I pushed my body physically.

The station was quiet as I left our dedicated gym area and headed to the kitchen. One of the guys had stocked it over the weekend, and there were some fresh bread loaves on the counter. Evie must have dropped off a couple for us.

The thing about having a fire department in a town this small was that it was mostly community organized. The fact that I was able to do this and be paid for it was lucky in a way, but the town had pushed to keep me here. Honestly, that was Austin's doing. I knew he'd fought as hard as he could for that.

A lot of small towns were only run with volunteers, and Whynot wasn't much different. In total, we had fifteen volunteer firefighters, including Austin and Dallas, and then me. I had the station alone for another hour or so, and then one of the guys would join me for about four hours while we did the equipment checks.

Which meant I had another hour to keep thinking about Levi and Avery.

What we needed was a date. A date without drawing attention from Dallas or Austin, because otherwise, there'd be hell to pay. There would be eventually when they found out, but I agreed with Avery on taking our time in secret.

I pulled out two pieces of bread and tossed them on a plate, making a turkey sandwich quickly. It wasn't exactly breakfast food, but I didn't care. I piled the turkey and cheese high, my stomach grumbling in anticipation.

Between the sex and two hours in the gym, I was tempted to eat two sandwiches. I took a bite and groaned, my eyes fluttering. Yep, I'd needed food.

I also needed to see Levi fuck Avery.

Dammit. I just couldn't keep my mind off the two of them.

The biggest question in all of this was Levi. He was going to keep us at arm's length, and I worried about that hurting Avery. But I also had to trust that if the two of them got involved together, they'd be able to handle themselves the same way Levi and I could.

I wanted to know more about him. I knew almost everything about Avery. Over the last couple of years, we'd become close. As close as you could become to someone without dating them. Whenever she needed something, I was usually the first person she called after June or Evie. Oftentimes, she called me before she called her brothers, which I'd always felt pretty damn proud of.

I wanted her to rely on me. I wanted her to always know that I would be there for her, no matter the time of day or night.

Could I ever get to that point with Levi? Could I ever be the one that he'd call if he needed something? There was a sharp little splinter in my heart when I thought about the fact that he'd be leaving so soon. I knew it was a bad idea to get involved with him, but I just couldn't stop myself.

There was something about him that pulled me in, something I just wanted so desperately.

I'd seen that same desire in Avery. She wanted him, the same way I wanted him too.

Now we just had to figure out where to go from here.

I polished off my plate, washed it in the sink and set it on the dish rack to dry. It took a couple minutes to clean up the kitchen, but once I had everything tidy, I headed straight out to the garage.

Whynot Fire Department blazed on the side of the crimson fire engine. It wasn't the most pristine fire truck I'd ever seen, that was for damn sure. I'd been pushing to get a new truck, but it was a matter of funding. That was the other thing about small towns, money was always an issue. It didn't matter that we had a festival that brought in thousands of people every year, or the fact that we were next to a national park that brought in visitors every summer.

I pressed the button on the garage opener and watched as the door slowly slid up, humming as it gave me a view of the street. The air was still today, not a breeze to be felt. It was going to be a scorcher. I was already covered in sweat, and didn't bat an eye as I crossed to our giant fan and turned it on. I'd keep it going as I scrolled through my checklist.

Once a month, I checked all of the suits, every part of our fire truck, and all of the other equipment that we had on hand. In a city, I would've been doing these checks much more often. But, thankfully, a lot of the time this equipment didn't get much use. That was a good thing, I reminded myself. I didn't want there to be emergencies, but I also wanted to make sure I was always ready to go if there was one.

Last year, there'd been a fire at the old bank on Main Street. If it weren't for our fast response time, it might've taken a couple other buildings down with it. One of the managers had lit a candle in the office and forgotten all about it. It was always candles. I hated them.

I was into some very kinky things, but there were a couple kinks that were off the table for me because of what I'd seen in my line of work. Wax play made me anxious because a good portion of the devastation I'd seen in my line of work had come from candles. Whips, riding crops, and canes were also off the table because of a situation I'd had my first year as a firefighter. We'd been called to a scene that I never let myself fully think about, but it had stuck with me nonetheless.

In Whynot, most of the emergencies I saw were people overheating. Occasionally there were fires or car accidents. A lot of the time, I was responding to calls from elderly people who'd fallen.

"Morning."

I jumped and spun around, cursing under my breath as Dallas walked up to me wearing his navy blue volunteer shirt.

"What the fuck, Dallas. Don't scare me like that," I snapped, earning a wide grin from him.

The asshole raked his fingers through his dark hair and leaned against the truck. "Sorry. How's it going? You look like you've been working hard."

I looked down at myself. A line of sweat trailed down my chest and I realized I needed to change shirts. I probably reeked, too.

"Worked out for a while." Dammit, did this mean Dallas was who I'd be working with today? I couldn't think about Avery with him around. Or if I did, that had to be some sort of sin. I wasn't even religious, but it just felt wrong. "Are you my volunteer today? On a Monday?"

He nodded. "Yep. I know it's unusual, but I was asked to switch in our chat and didn't have any work to do this morning, so I agreed to it."

"Oh."

Dallas narrowed his eyes on me. "I can see you're thrilled. What'd I ever do to you?"

"I am thrilled," I snorted. "Just unexpected, is all."

"Uh-huh. How come you never bring me lunch like you do for Austin?"

"Hey," I said, holding up my hands. "He brings *me* lunch. Don't be jealous."

He shrugged, but held his smile. "Just giving you shit. It'll be good to catch up, though."

"It will be. How has everything been going? How's your mom?"

His gaze darkened and he sighed, pulling his gaze away. "Avery isn't talking to her now. And family dinners won't be happening anymore."

All the alarm bells rang in my mind. Avery hadn't texted me about it, and that . . .

Hurt? Maybe that wasn't the right word.

I resisted the urge to pull my phone out and text her. "What happened?" I asked.

"Dinner was bad last night, man," Dallas said. "We were trying to talk Mom into going to therapy, but she took it out on Avery. And this was all after her grilling Austin and I on having children. And also after her handing me a stack of framed photos of Dad for me to hang up in the stairwell."

"Fuck," I muttered, crossing my arms. I leaned back against the railing, frowning as I studied him. "That's a lot. Are you okay? Is Avery okay?"

"I'm okay. Avery, I don't know," he said. "She told me she would be. June and Evie were there for her last night. Has she said anything to you yet?"

My spine stiffened slightly, but I reminded myself that Dallas and Austin knew Avery was close with me.

Just not how close we were now . . .

"Not yet," I said. "I'll check in on her, though."

"Thanks. Yeah, at this point, I'm not sure what we're supposed to do. Mom's gotten worse. Not going out, not eating well, not keeping up with her friends. It's been two years."

I swallowed hard as silence fell between us. The day his dad had died had been one of the worst days of my life. I'd gotten the call that Mr. Whynot had fallen and was unresponsive. I'd never driven so fucking fast in my life.

I did everything I could to revive him. And I had him. For a moment, I had him.

And then I didn't.

His death haunted me ever since. Not only because his children were my best friends, but because he'd always been kind to me. He'd made sure I'd felt at home in Whynot, just like he did for everyone here.

"Mateo," Dallas said softly. "Every time I mention my dad, you get that look on your face as if it's your fault what happened. And it's not. He died early. It was a heart attack. None of us saw it coming."

"It still feels like I failed," I said grimly. "He's the only person in Whynot that has ever died in my arms."

"Good place to go," he said. "You did everything you could."

My eyes pricked with tears and I swallowed hard, turning my gaze to the concrete floor and picking *something*—literally *anything* else—to focus on. "Maybe I should stop by and talk to your mom. She's always had a soft spot for me."

"She sure fucking has," Dallas snorted, breaking the tension. "Austin and I thought we should have brought you along last night, but Avery vetoed us. Maybe you can come this Sunday."

I raised a brow. "I said she has a soft spot for me, but I'm not sure that means she'll listen to me about therapy."

"Well, she's gotta do something. I've never heard Austin yell at her like that. Hell, I've never been that upset by something she's said."

"What did she even say?"

Dallas made a face, but then recounted last night's conversation. By the time he finished, my worries about Avery had skyrocketed. "Fuck," I muttered, shaking my head.

I pulled out my phone and shot Avery a text.

> Are you okay? Dallas is at the station with me today and told me about dinner

Her response was quick.

> Avery: I'm okay. I mean, I'm not, but I am. But June and Evie comforted me
>
> The only reason I didn't text you was because I knew you were with Levi and didn't want to interrupt
>
> . . . and how did that go???

> Mateo: I'll fill you in later. Promise

"What'd she say?" Dallas asked, creeping closer.

I shielded my phone from him before he saw what she'd said, my heart thumping in my chest. I became all too aware of the fact that I could have been caught just now. That Dallas could have looked through our texts and found out the truth.

Fuck.

I cleared my throat. "She said she's okay. Well, that she isn't, but she is."

Dallas nodded. "Good. Thought that'd be the case. Well, I told her we can start our own family dinners. Maybe we should round up June and Evie too. Make it a group thing."

"That sounds good to me," I said. It actually sounded like a fucking disaster, given that Avery and I were sneaking around. And technically Levi and I were now too. "Could be good for all of us."

"I'll text our chat. It's time we dusted it off," he said.

I raised a brow at him. "You're going to be the one to text? What happened to you being all quiet and broody? You're never the one to organize shit like this."

His cheeks reddened and he shrugged his shoulders, although it was a forced shrug. "Just think it would be good for everyone to spend time together, is all."

Now, it was my turn to narrow my eyes on him. "*Who* are you wanting to spend time with, Whynot?"

"Everyone, of course."

I wasn't buying that. "Sure."

He tipped his chin up. "How about you keep your secrets, and I'll keep mine?"

Now, what in the actual fuck did he mean by that? I raised a brow, but decided not to push any further.

"Fine," I said. "We got equipment checks and hydrant checks on our list today."

"All right, boss," he said. "Tell me where you want me."

CHAPTER TWENTY-FIVE

 *Levi*

I turned on my phone and sighed.

The amount of messages was slowly becoming more manageable. But only slightly. I scrolled through all the texts and then cleared all of them with a click, rolling my shoulders back as I sipped my coffee.

All of my teammates were still concerned. I was appreciative of their check-ins and did my best to respond, but none of them were really my friends.

It was a reflection on me more than anyone else that I didn't have any close friends. It was something I wanted to work on. Thinking of Austin as my closest friend was probably not the healthiest, considering how much we'd omitted in our talks.

And I knew he'd hate me if he found out about the thoughts I had for Avery. Or hell, about Mateo, too.

I shifted in my chair as I thought about Sunday night. It was Tuesday and I'd spent yesterday jacking off thinking about Mateo fucking me again. In my weekly spreadsheet, Monday had three things on it. *Jacked off. Made better muffins. Jacked off again.* I'd wasted an entire day just being horny and wanting *more*. Thinking about everything we'd discussed about Avery.

Wondering what it would be like for the three of us to be together.

He'd tried to sneak out yesterday morning. He was quiet, but the truth was, I'd been awake before he left, thinking about him. Thinking about how good it felt to have him in my bed.

Even now, my cock perked up at the thought of waking up next to him again. I took a deep breath and tried to refocus on my messages. I clicked on the messages from Robin.

> Robin: Hello from your underpaid agent.
>
> Just kidding, I'm not underpaid. Everything is going fine and I've put out all the fires. Everyone is desperate for you to return back to the team, though. How's your time in Texas?

I smiled. This was, in fact, why I paid her so much.

> So far, so good. Sorry I've been offline a lot. It's been good for me though
>
> Robin: Don't be sorry, I'm glad you're taking your time. How's your body feeling?
>
> Right shoulder is still giving me trouble. I've been doing PT every morning and I did yoga on Sunday
>
> Robin: WOW. Levi Rayburn in yoga? Never thought I'd see it.
>
> Take care of yourself. Get plenty of rest
>
> I will. Thanks for handling everything
>
> Robin: Of course!
>
> I will be dragging you back to Minnesota in 3 weeks though. Texas can't have you for too long

My stomach did a slow flop.

Did I even want to go back to Minnesota? That was where my life was. Not here. I had my apartment and all my belongings and my career up there. Everything I'd spent years building toward.

And yet, all I could think about was Avery and Mateo.

Another text popped up, stealing my full interest. It was as if Mateo had heard my thoughts.

> Mateo: Avery, this is Levi's number. Levi, this is Avery's number
>
> We should go on a secret triple date ;)
>
> I'm free tomorrow night. Well, really any night, unless Whynot catches on fire.
>
> What I'm saying is—I want both of you. Badly. Terribly. And I think you both want each other and me too

I rubbed my chest. Was it hot in here? Why was there suddenly sweat dripping down my back?

Avery's texts came in next.

> Avery: Oh god. Hi. Good morning.
>
> I'm free tomorrow night too. If we do anything, I really don't want my brothers finding out. At least for now

I chuckled and responded.

> None of us want them to find out. Secret is safe with me. I'm also free tomorrow night.
>
> I'm not very good with words, but I also want both of you
>
> Mateo: Let's meet at 7p?

> Avery: Come to my place, easy walk. And my bed is comfy

> Mateo: Already inviting us to your bed, I see

> Avery: Sure am

Fuck me.

> The two of you are trouble. I'll see you tomorrow

> Mateo, I wouldn't mind if you brought the kink equipment you mentioned

> Just in case . . .

> Mateo: Was already planning on it. Just in case

> Avery: I have some lingerie I haven't worn before, so I'll dust them off.

> Avery: Just in case

"Jesus Christ," I whispered. "Fuck me."

How in the hell was I going to make it to tomorrow? It felt too long from now.

> I'm trying to focus, but don't think I'll be able to until tomorrow

> Mateo: Same. I'm home for another hour so I'm going to go pick out some stuff for my kink bag . . . and think about Avery's lingerie

I was so tempted to ask him if he wanted company. With a groan, I pushed back from the table, my cock fully hard in my briefs. I stood up and headed straight for the bathroom, stropping and flipping on the shower.

I stepped under the hot water and planted my hand against

the tiled wall, huffing as I closed my hand around myself. Goddamn, I was hard.

"Fuck," I moaned. "*Avery.*"

Her lips felt so damn sweet on my lips. The thought of her wrapped in black lace, or even a corset, was already pushing me to the edge.

I wanted to share her with Mateo. After Sunday night together, I knew it would be fucking good. Especially him Domming us. Telling us what to do, how to be good for him.

I stroked my cock faster, whimpering as I imagined thrusting into Avery while Mateo thrusted into me.

Knock, knock, knock.

I paused, releasing my cock to listen.

Surely someone wasn't knocking at my fucking door.

The sound came again. More insistent. More annoying this time. Jesus Christ, I was clearly busy. Right? Couldn't they see that?

I ignored the knocking and grabbed hold of my cock again, pushing myself closer to the edge.

Knock, knock, knock.

"Fuck me," I growled.

I turned off the shower and yanked open the curtain. I was gonna lose it. Whoever the fuck was at my front door was about to get an earful. In fact, I'd probably be the talk of the town, because I wasn't going to do anything to hide the fact that I was in the shower.

Snatching my towel off the rack, I pulled it around my waist and stepped out, going down the hall. That knocking came again, and I unlocked the door quickly, a growl leaving me as I damn near pulled the fucker off the hinges.

"Hey, neighbor. *Oh my god.*"

All my anger vanished into smoke and my mouth fell open as I came face to face with Avery.

"What are you doing?" I rasped.

Her cheeks turned scarlet and she planted her hand against my chest, shoving me back into the house. "Someone is gonna see you, Levi Rayburn. You fucking idiot."

"I'm the idiot?" I rasped as the door shut behind her. "Why were you knocking on my door?"

"Because I wanted to see you."

Oh. My mouth ran dry. I became all too aware of the fact that I was only wearing a towel.

And Avery . . .

God, she was wearing a sundress.

"Avery," I choked out. "You should go."

She raised a brow. "Do you want me to?"

No. No, I wanted her to stay. "I . . ."

She leaned up on her tiptoes, but still wasn't tall enough to kiss me. Her fingers looped around the towel, and with a gentle tug, it fell to the floor.

"Woman," I whispered. "I was in the shower, about to come while thinking about fucking you. And now you're here."

"And now I'm here," she murmured, her eyes drifting down to my cock. Her eyes widened. "Oh my god. You're . . ."

"Hard."

"Very hard." She swallowed, her gaze meeting mine. "I have a thought. Well, a proposition."

I was standing buck-ass naked in the foyer, and she had a proposition?

"Avery . . ."

"So, here's the thing. I want you. Really bad."

Fuck.

"And we have a date with Mateo tomorrow night. But I've been with Mateo. And so have you. Right?"

I nodded, trying to make my mind work. All my blood was

in my damn cock. *Sixty-nine squared is four thousand seven hundred and sixty-one—oh god, sixty nine—*

"And I think you want me," she said quickly. "I mean, I'm not entirely sure—"

"Look down again and try to tell me you're not sure I want you." Her eyes slid back to my cock, and it perked in response. "I *want* you, Avery."

Avery's throat worked as she swallowed hard. "I really want you too. And I just think maybe we should see how we are together, one-on-one, before doing something with Mateo. Because I don't think we're just going to have a date tomorrow night."

"I don't either."

"Right. Well, you're naked. So."

She grabbed the hem of her sundress and started to lift it, but I grabbed her wrist, stopping her before she pulled it all the way off. "Stop. Hold on. Jesus Christ, Avery."

She froze, her eyes widening further as she looked up at me. I could see the doubt start to creep in and lifted her before she tried to run away, scooping her into my arms. She squeaked, her arm looping around my neck.

"Do you have plans today?" I asked her.

"No," she whispered. "I'm sorry. I feel like an idiot now, I didn't mean to just come over and—"

"*Avery.*" My nostrils flared as I held her against my chest and turned the lock on my door. "One more word like that, and I'm gonna have to bend you over my knee."

Her expression turned to shock, and then melted into something else. Something full of desire and lust and—*fuck me.* The way she was looking at me right now was almost enough to make me come.

I carried her down the hall and straight to my bedroom. Right to the bed I'd gotten destroyed in two nights ago.

Maybe Avery was right for coming over, because the way I felt with her was completely different from how I felt with Mateo. The dominant part of me craved her so badly. My head was full of a thousand wicked things I could do to her.

"I can't believe you just marched across the street and knocked on my door until I answered," I said as I sat down on the edge of the bed.

I adjusted her position until she was straddling me, the skirt of her dress hiking up. I tipped her chin up with my finger as her hands settled on my shoulders.

Finally. I had her exactly where I wanted her. I smiled. "And I can't believe you think I'm just going to fuck you without even kissing you first."

CHAPTER TWENTY-SIX
Avery

Levi's hands were rough against my skin, and that felt really fucking good.

I felt like an idiot. Just a little bit. After those texts, I'd looked out my window, saw Levi's car, and got it in my head that it would be best for me to make a move. I'd march on over across the street, have mind blowing sex, and then go about my day.

The thing was, Levi wasn't just a quick fuck to me. And not only that, I hadn't expected him to open the door wearing nothing but a towel and looking so angry.

Then seeing all the anger evaporate the second he laid eyes on me . . .

"Levi," I gasped as he seated me in his lap.

His eyes widened. "Are you not . . . Are you not wearing panties?"

I wasn't. I blushed as a wave of embarrassment hit me. God, I'd really just thrown myself at him. "Sorry," I rasped. "I went a little far. I promise I'm not just a . . . what are they called? Puck bunnies? I don't even know what I'm saying anymore actually, I feel like an idiot. This was silly of me—"

He cupped his hand over my mouth.

"Baby, if you say one more thing about being an idiot, I'm gonna have to give your mouth something to do so you don't talk negatively about yourself."

Heat skated over my skin as he lowered his hand, his mouth only inches from mine. More than anything, I wanted to kiss him.

"Levi," I whispered. "You drive me a little bonkers."

"*Bonkers?*" He snorted.

"What?"

"Just a funny word."

"It's a normal word. A good, normal word."

"It's a ridiculous one."

"It's an effective one, Levi Rayburn. Because *you* drive me *bonkers.*"

"I see." He leaned forward, his green eyes searching me for a moment.

Then his lips pressed against mine.

All of that wildness between us spun out into something primal, something hot and heavy and hungry. I moved my hips against his lap, enjoying his pained groan as my bare pussy rubbed against his cock. The desire between us snapped from ember to flame, our tongues meeting as he deepened our first kiss, his fingers knotting in my hair.

"Fuck," he groaned. "You taste like sugar. So fucking sweet."

"You got your kiss," I gasped, rocking my body against his again. "I want more."

"Say please."

I narrowed my eyes, but leaned forward, giving his forehead the gentlest kiss.

"*Please*, Levi. Please fuck my pussy."

"Dammit, Avery." He grabbed hold of my hips and spun me onto the bed, pinning me down on my back with his entire body. My hair splayed out, the skirt of my dress pushing up as he gripped my thighs.

Levi sat back for a moment, his gaze falling to my pussy. I started to put my knees together, but he stopped them. "I want to see you," he whispered, pushing them further apart.

My heart thundered as his eyes darkened.

"Fucking gorgeous," he murmured. "Look at how wet you are. Is that all for me?"

"Yes," I squeaked.

"Good girl."

My muscles quivered as I tried to put my legs together again, but there was no stopping him. I didn't want to stop him, either. Levi grunted softly as he kept them splayed and leaned down, his gaze locking with mine at his mouth met my pussy.

"Oh god," I rasped, my head falling back.

Levi Rayburn knew how to make me feel good. I groaned as his tongue circled against my clit, his thick fingers digging into my thighs as he kept my legs pried apart, the firmness of his grip making me even wetter. He had me pinned *exactly* how he wanted me.

I gripped his hair and rolled my hips, moaning as he buried his face against me. His tongue worked magic as he carefully pushed a finger inside me, followed by a second.

For the last two weeks, my fantasies about Levi had been over the top. I'd wondered what it would feel like to be beneath him, to be wrapped in his muscles, to feel the weight of his body on top of mine. But nothing prepared me, for the fact that he was even hotter in person than he was in my head.

I moaned as he continued to fuck me with his fingers and mouth, his tongue lavishing upon me, worshiping me.

I tightened my grip on his hair and gave him a tug. "Kiss me," I rasped. "I want a kiss. Please."

He immediately kissed up my body, his mouth against mine

in a blink. He kept thrusting his fingers in and out of me in a way that wasn't too rough, but also wasn't too gentle. The taste of me on his mouth made me whimper.

I just wanted more. Maybe I was greedy now. Greedy for wanting two boyfriends. Greedy for wanting my boyfriends to be boyfriends, too. But I didn't care if I was at this point. Fuck it all, I was going to be as greedy as I could be.

Our lips broke apart and I kissed down the side of his neck, sinking my teeth into his hard muscle. He growled, his breath catching in his throat as I released him and looked at the mark I left.

Fuck, I hadn't even asked him if I could bite him. I started to apologize, but I did didn't get the words out before he huffed—

"Do it again. Mark me. Make me yours."

I swallowed hard. I kissed over the mark I'd left before sinking my teeth in him again like a hungry little vampire. Levi's groan went straight to my pussy. He moved his hips against me, his cock grinding against my thigh, hard and dripping.

"Again," he demanded. "All over."

I switched to his other shoulder and bit him even harder. He kept grinding his cock against me, his moans feeding my muse. The thought of him sitting and stroking his cock while I painted him came to mind and I reeled back, staring at him with wide eyes.

"What is it?" he asked.

"Nothing, I just . . . Well, I want to paint you."

The corner of his mouth lifted. "You want to *paint* me?"

The amount of times this man was making me blush should have been a crime. "Maybe."

"Maybe *yes*," he teased, cupping my breast through my dress. "You can paint me any time. I'll sit as long as you want. But right now, I need you to take this dress off for me, Avery."

"Yes, Sir."

His expression turned stormy as I pulled the dress off and tossed it to the side, now completely naked. His gaze raked over me hungrily, setting every part of my body on fire. My nipples hardened, the blush creeping across my chest.

"You're a fucking angel," he whispered, gripping his cock as he looked down at me. "God help me. Your brothers are gonna murder me, Avery. They're gonna fucking murder me and have every right to. And I don't even give a fuck. I need this pussy on my cock."

"Please," I whimpered, sliding my hand down between my legs.

I was so fucking wet. My eyes widened in shock as I realized just how turned on I was. I turned my attention from myself back to Levi. Bite marks peppered his shoulder muscles, his lips still glistening with *me*.

"Stay there," he said, getting off the bed quickly.

As if I was going anywhere. My eyes fluttered as I slid my fingers inside myself, using my wetness to circle my clit. I moaned as Levi hurriedly opened the top drawer on the oak side table and pulled out a condom, tearing it open. I pushed my brown and blue waves back behind my shoulders as he put the condom on, the mattress shifting as he knelt between my legs.

He grabbed hold of my thighs and dragged me toward him.

"Oh," I gasped, surprised by his strength.

I shouldn't have been, but still. He moved me with such ease.

Being manhandled by a hot hockey player was maybe my new kink.

Levi guided the head of his cock against my pussy. I

propped up slightly, watching as he paused, hovering just at my entrance.

"Please. I want this so badly."

"I know you do." His voice was gruff. "I want you just as bad, but I want to remember this forever."

Levi stared for a few moments longer, settling his palm right above my pussy, resting his thumb over my clit. I gasped as he slowly moved his thumb as he pushed his cock inside me.

I groaned, a full body wave of pleasure rolling through me as my pussy stretched around his thickness. He took it slow, giving me time to adjust to the size of him. My fingers gripped the sheets, every sound coming out of me involuntary.

"Fuck." Levi paused, gritting his teeth. "You feel too fucking good."

"I can take it all. I want it all."

He shook his head, concentrating as he slowly gave me another inch. His brows drew together, his muscles tensing as he controlled every movement. I started to reach for his hand on my pussy, but he shoved it away.

"Cover your pretty little mouth if you need something to do with your hands."

"Why?" I rasped.

"So the neighbors don't hear you screaming my name."

Levi thrust forward, giving me the rest of his cock. I cried out, slapping my hand over my mouth as pleasure battered me. He dragged his hips back and then thrusted again, grunting as he leaned forward, his hand planting into the blankets and mouth meeting mine in a fevered kiss.

I wrapped my legs around his hips, gasping as he started to pump in and out. Little lightening bolts struck every nerve ending, pleasure bursting through me like fireworks as he fucked me.

It felt so right, being with him. I moaned between kisses, winding my body around him like a vice.

The bed squeaked beneath us, heat filling the room. Between the summer sun and the friction between our bodies, we were both covered in a layer of sweat.

Levi drove into me in a rhythm that was harsh and full of unbridled desire, the two of us moving against each other. I couldn't get enough of him. *Fuck.* His cock glided in and out of me, my hand still muffling all of the sounds I was making. Because dammit, he was right. The neighbors *would* hear us at this rate.

Hell, it was reckless, but I kind of wanted them to.

"*Levi.*"

I moaned his name in his ear. I swore his thrusts got harder the moment I did, my eyes glazing over. I couldn't think. I could barely even see. All I could focus on was the feeling of his cock inside me, and the way our bodies fit so damn perfect together.

He knotted his fingers in my hair, pulling my head forward and kissing me again, our tongues dancing as he fucked me harder. He kept the same rhythm until he suddenly pulled back, pulling out of me.

"What?" I gasped. "What's—"

Without missing a beat, he pulled me against his body and rolled onto his back, seating me on top of him. I squealed as he lifted my hips, placing me over his cock and thrusting up inside me again.

Holy fuck. My eyes rolled back. I gasped, planting my hands on his chest, my head tipping and hair tumbling down my shoulders. Taking him this way was even more intense. There was something about this angle, about sitting on him. Gravity was doing all the work, and his cock was so fully deep inside me, I swore I'd be feeling him for days.

"Oh my god," I gasped.

"You're fucking gorgeous. You look like a goddess right now."

I felt like a goddess. I put all of my weight into my hands, lifting my hips up slightly before going back down, setting my own rhythm now that I was on top. Levi's calloused hands ran up and down my sides, cupping my face, tugging my hair. Pleasure shot through me as I moved, our bodies dancing together. The sound of our skin meeting, our breaths melding, our bodies becoming one—all of it was pushing me closer to coming.

Fuck. That hungry desperation reared its head as I rode him. I raked my nails down his chest, earning a hiss between his teeth. I hadn't even meant to do it, but he grabbed hold of my wrist, keeping my nails against his skin and nodding.

"Again. I want to see you all over me when I wake up in the morning. I want Mateo to see it tomorrow on our date."

That alone made my hips move faster. I scratched him again, leaving angry red marks over his chest. There was something so incredibly erotic about knowing it turned him on. I *liked* marking him. I liked knowing that he wanted to see me on him later.

I wanted that too, I realized.

"I want you to bite me. Mark me. I want the same thing," I rasped. "Spank me. Bite me. *Something.*"

Levi groaned, his hips lifting up and down with every movement. "I'll spank you later. I promise. I'm too close to coming right now."

I was too close too. All I could do was nod breathlessly, bouncing up and down and chasing the orgasm that was so, so close. I tipped my head back, my eyes shutting as I let the euphoria overtake me.

"That's right. I can feel you milking my cock. I want to feel you come around me. I want to feel you squeezing me."

He talked me through every feeling, his voice low and raspy.

"You're doing so good for me. Fuck, you feel so fucking good."

I whimpered, sucking in a breath the moment I found the right spot. His cock was hitting me just right, our bodies moving at a tempo that was perfect.

"I'm so close. I'm so close."

"Fuck, that's good. That's really fucking good. Use my cock, baby. It's all yours. Every fucking inch."

I leaned forward, crying out as every muscle tensed and my orgasm shattered me. Everything disappeared around me, the connection between us grounding me as I came. I lost track of time, of where I was, of everything.

All I could focus on was riding out the pleasure, and Levi's voice. Still talking low. Soft.

"That's my girl. You're so beautiful when you come. You're so fucking gorgeous, Avery. I'm lucky to be here with you. *Good girl.*"

I melted against him, collapsing forward with a soft sigh. He moved his hips, still thrusting into me until his body still and he grunted, his grip tightening as he came.

Part of me wished his condom was off so I could feel his cum inside me. That thought danced in my mind as our bodies relaxed and I laid completely on top of him. *I could stay here forever.*

CHAPTER TWENTY-SEVEN

It took a few minutes before either of our brains started working again. I lifted her hips, my cock sliding out of her as she shifted to the side and settled next to me.

The moment my mind started working again, all I could think was—*what the hell was I doing?*

There was something different about this with Avery and Mateo. It wasn't like anything I'd ever experienced with other people before. That scary feeling I had with Mateo came roaring back as Avery sprawled out on top of me.

"You're thinking about something," she murmured. "What is it? What's wrong?"

"There's nothing wrong with this or us," I said quickly. "I just . . ."

I trailed off. Maybe this wasn't the right time to get deep.

"Tell me. I want to know. Talk to me," she urged.

I blew out a slow breath. "I just don't know where I fit in anymore. I don't know what I want exactly. So many people have told me I'm at the height of my career, and yet I just want to walk away from it all. I woke up one day and asked myself if I was happy—and I wasn't."

Avery let out a soft hum and wrapped her arms around my

chest, resting her head at the center. "So that's why you came to Whynot? But aren't you planning on going back in a few weeks?"

I didn't even want to think about that now. It was hard to imagine leaving Whynot while Avery was in my arms.

"I'll need to decide by then if I'm going back or not. Regardless, I'm off for the season. I've pissed a lot of people off, I'm sure. I'm not really sure what's going to happen with my career. But there's a part of me that doesn't care."

"Is it that you don't care or is it that you're avoiding confrontation?"

I wrinkled my nose, sliding my gaze down to the top of her head. She smiled against my chest without looking up.

"I've been there," she said. "I know how it feels. I also know how it feels to wonder where you fit in with what you do. Being an artist, everything I do is dependent on how I feel. I have to be in the right headspace to create art, and if I'm not, I can't even pick up a paintbrush. Everything in the world feels bleak and I'm left wondering if I'll ever make art again. That's how it was when my dad died."

My hand settled on her side and I rubbed her gently up and down. "What changed? All the art I've seen from you is beautiful."

"Well, when he died, there were a lot of life changes that happened for me at once. I moved back to the town I swore I'd never live in. I took over his gallery and the expectation to know how to run a business fell on my shoulders. My brothers got a lot thrown their way too. And on top of it, my mom lost it. She still isn't whole. I don't think she ever will be. She never imagined a world without my dad in it. Hell, I didn't either."

She drew in a shaky breath, her arms tightening around me.

"I couldn't create anything for the first two months. All I

had room for was action. To learn how to take over things, to be there for my family, to move into a new place. I wasn't sure I'd ever actually be an artist again. I thought I'd lost my spark."

"I can't ever imagine you not painting."

"I didn't either until then. I wondered if I'd been lying to myself about being an artist. I went to school for it, which felt silly, but I reached for my dreams because of my dad. I'd sold a few pieces by then, but I convinced myself I was a fake."

A soft hum filled my throat. Whenever I recalled my summers visiting Whynot, if I thought about Avery, it was remembering her always creating something. Drawing, painting, making pottery out of mud. The need to create had always been there for her.

"It was a dark time. But then, I had a day with nothing to do. Nothing. I sat on the floor in my living room and stared at the clock my dad gave me years ago when I said I wanted to become an artist, and I finally cried. It was like a dam broke, and all of my pain and sadness and anger and frustration rushed out. I had to do something with it. I couldn't just sit there anymore. And this pressure I'd put on myself to be something I wasn't disappeared. I didn't have the strength to keep feeling like a fraud anymore, so I let it go. I picked up a paintbrush."

"And you made art again."

"I did." She tilted her head and looked up at me. "Everything ebbs and flows. Sometimes your passion for something disappears. Sometimes it needs to so that when it comes back, you're reminded why you loved it in the first place. The art I created after my dad passed away made enough money so I could rebuild parts of the gallery and studio. I was able to fund community classes and discovered I had a love for teaching. That collection ended up in a few magazines and on the walls of people with way more money than I could ever dream of. So even though he was gone, he was still there for me. My art was still there for me. I never lost it. It just needed rest. My heart needed space for grief. It still needs space for grief."

I swallowed hard and looked up at the ceiling. "The thing is —hockey was never that for me. I do love it. I'm good at it. I got really damn lucky with how my career ended up. But it's never fulfilled me the way your art fulfills you."

"What does fulfill you then? What brings you joy?"

My heart skipped a beat. I knew what brought me joy, but it wasn't anything more than a silly hobby.

Avery sat up slightly, smoothing her hand up my chest. "I just felt every muscle in your body tense."

I blew out a breath, trying to relax. She was far too observant for her own good. I had a feeling I'd never be able to hide from Avery. Not really, anyway.

"What is it?" she murmured.

"It's just silly."

"I'm sure it's not."

I pressed my lips together, trying to decide if I was actually going to show her.

I hadn't shown anyone this. Not a single soul.

Avery swung her leg over my hips and settled on top of me, planting her hands on my chest. Waves of blue shifted forward as she looked down at me, her brow raising.

"Spill," she said. "Tell me your secrets, my darling brooding man."

I snorted, but an ease rushed over me that I hadn't felt in a long time. I realized I was comfortable with her. Although the idea of showing her something I enjoyed—something I'd kept a secret for so long—made me nervous.

"When I used to visit in the summers, it was hard, because my dad and I never got along," I said. "I think everyone in Whynot was aware of our problems. He was a mean bastard."

"I'm sorry," she said.

"It's okay. I've worked through my grief with him. A lot of therapy and a lot of time away. But here's the thing, Avery. When I was here, your dad stepped in, and your family always gave me a second home. There was one summer when I was fifteen, and Austin and I had started getting into trouble here and there. The night before, we'd gone around town and hit people's mailboxes."

"Oh my god, I remember that," she said. "Austin got grounded."

"He got grounded and I was so fucking scared my dad was going to hear about it from yours. But instead, your dad took me outside and gave me a stern talking to. My ears were fucking red by the time he finished. Then he gave me a camera and told me 'do something useful and go take pictures of a cactus heart. I need it for a reference.'"

Avery grinned. "That was a pretty good impersonation."

I smiled as I thought about how mad I'd been. Mr. Whynot had been so blunt and direct, and the thought of taking pictures had felt so stupid at the time.

"I was such an angry teen. I told him he was being a dick. Taking pictures was stupid. No one wanted photographs of anything. His art was stupid. I said so many mean things, and he didn't bat an eye. He shoved the camera in my hands and told me to take a walk. Never threatened to tell my dad on me. Never threatened to kick me out. He was stern, but he was never mean. I don't think that man had a mean bone in his body."

My throat burned and Avery's expression softened, her eyes glossing with tears.

"I ended up staying outside until the sun set. I took so many pictures. They were all bad, I'm sure. I took pictures of cacti and lizards and the sky and random shit all around town. I can't paint or draw to save my life, but photography makes me happy. Your dad changed my life that day."

I swallowed down the sadness I felt in knowing he was gone.

"Part of the reason I wanted to visit him when I got in town was because photography became my hobby over the years. I don't know if I'm any good, but I wanted to thank him. It's something I never talk about or show people because it's always been just for me, but it's kept me grounded amid all the other career stuff. Being in the hockey world has changed my life for the better in so many ways, but I think having this for myself kept me from turning into too much of an ass. I've seen it happen to so many guys—it all goes to their head, and then they ruin their lives." I paused, mulling over the fact that I'd literally just walked out the door on my career. "Well, maybe I have ruined my life now, I don't know. But what I do know is that your dad changed me. And I'll be forever grateful to him."

Avery sniffled and I reached up, thumbing away a tear as it fell.

"That's how he was," she whispered. "Always helping people. Always bringing them together. And don't get me wrong, he wasn't perfect. Austin, Dallas, and I have spent the last two years cleaning up some of the financial messes he left behind. But he's part of the reason I'm an artist."

"He's part of the reason Whynot felt like a home to me," I murmured.

But now, Mateo and Avery were starting to make it feel that way too.

Avery grabbed hold of my wrist and brought my hand to her lips, kissing the inside of my palm with a gentleness that made everything in my world turn upside down.

There was something different about me when I was with her.

Content.

She made me feel content.

She settled all the wild storms in my heart and quieted the rush of thoughts. She made me forget about all of my worries and the weight on my shoulders that held me down.

Avery wiped her eyes and shook her head. "All right. No more tears. I just had some of the best sex I've ever had, and don't want to be digging into big feelings."

I raised a brow. "Best sex, huh?"

"Some of the best sex," she said with a smirk.

"I bet Mateo is right up there too, huh?"

"He sure is. So, are you going to show me your pictures or what?"

My hands fell to her hips and I held her in place as I sat up, stealing a thousand little kisses that had her giggling. Her arms wound around my neck, her legs around my waist as I peppered more on her cheeks.

"*Oh*," she laughed. God, her laugh was a gift. "You monster."

"A kissing monster."

She grabbed hold of my face and moved hers just in time so that our lips met. I smiled against her, reveling in the taste of her, the feeling of her body against mine. I caught her whimper in my mouth as our kiss deepened, her sweetness changing to something hotter, something needier.

"Levi," she rasped. "You're supposed to show me your pictures."

"Do I have to?" I sighed.

"Yes," she giggled, drawing back from me. "I want to see them. Oh, I just realized." She narrowed her eyes on me as if she'd made a discovery. "The camera was what was in your bag the other night on the porch."

"It was," I chuckled.

"Did you go to any of the places I recommended?"

"I walked down main street," I said. "I did go through the courtyard at the hotel. You were right. It was perfect."

"I want to see them. Because if we get distracted again, I know I won't."

She had a point.

I wrinkled my nose and sat up in bed, groaning as my feet hit the floor. "They're not even that good."

"I'm sure they are."

Now I was nervous about showing them to her. What if they were complete trash? I slowly stepped up to my dresser and pulled open the top drawer, pausing when I saw what was on top.

My jersey.

I'd forgotten all about it over the last couple weeks. I stared at the number ninety on the front, our team's purple bear logo printed on soft silver mesh material. I brushed my fingertips over it and smiled.

"You know what? I'll show you. *If* you wear this." I pulled the jersey from my drawer. Was I being a little possessive? Yes. Was this kind of like a cowboy marking his territory by having his partner wear his hat? Also yes.

But I really wanted to see her in my jersey.

Avery smirked. "Deal."

CHAPTER TWENTY-EIGHT

I was throughly fucked.

In the best way possible.

Not only that, I was wearing Levi's jersey.

There was something primal about wearing a man's shirt after sex. I pressed my nose against my shoulder and took a deep breath, not surprised that it smelled like him. Woody vanilla with a ginger zing that made me wonder what his body wash was and if I could steal some for myself.

I looked at myself in the mirror on the back of the door as he pulled on his briefs. Neither of us could stop smiling.

Between Mateo and Levi, I had to be the luckiest girl in Whynot. Probably even Texas. Maybe even the world.

"How about some lunch?" he asked. "And maybe we should text Mateo."

"I know what to send him. I left my phone at my house, though."

"Good thing I have mine." He picked his up from the side table and unlocked the screen, handing it to me.

I flipped to his camera and turned it around to take a selfie. My cheeks were rosy, my hair mused. His silver and purple jersey swamped me like a mini dress, but I really wanted Mateo to see it on me.

I snapped a picture and put it in our group chat with a wink.

Levi loomed behind me, then wrapped his arms around me and tugged me close. His chin settled on my shoulder as we watched the typing bubbles appear.

> Mateo: Fuck. I'm at work

> Mateo: And now my cock is hard and I'm jealous

>> We'll see each other tomorrow ;)

> Mateo: Avery, did you steal his phone? Levi doesn't use wink emojis

I grinned and Levi snorted. "Tell him," he murmured, kissing the side of my neck.

>> I did. I'll text you later :P

> Mateo: Send me more pictures.

> Of BOTH of you.

"Mmm." I turned around and looked up at Levi, raising a brow. "Can I take a picture of you? You can lay back on the bed with your briefs on."

Levi pressed his lips together. "He doesn't want to see me."

"He definitely does."

Levi's phone rattled in my hand and we both looked down at the message. I gasped as a picture of Mateo's bulge came through. The two of us drooled over the sight of him hard in his firefighter pants and suspenders.

He was *really* hard.

"Fuck," Levi groaned. "You know what? Come here."

He pulled me close and lifted me, my legs wrapping around his waist. I held onto him as he took the phone and opened the camera, using the mirror to take a picture of him holding me, the jersey hiked up above my waist.

Which meant Mateo would be able to see my ass.

And the hard-on growing in Levi's underwear.

"You're trouble," he mumbled. "You know that? Can I send him this picture?"

He showed it to me and I nodded immediately. This was turning me on all over again. "See," I rasped. "I knew the pictures you took would be good."

"Fuck, Avery. I'm fucking hard. I don't think we're gonna make it to the kitchen to show you my photos."

He was right. There was no fucking way.

"Send him the picture. And then I want you on top of me again. Coming inside me again. Maybe even . . ."

I trailed off and his muscles tensed. Shit. Had I said too much?

"Hold on. Pause," he said seriously. He held up the phone and sent the picture, then tossed it down on the bed, giving me his full attention. "Do you want me to come inside you? Without a condom?"

"Yes," I answered immediately. "But there's no pressure to. I am on birth control and it's something I enjoy. Although, maybe we should talk to Mateo too."

Levi nodded earnestly, tightening his arms around me. "That's a good idea. I want to come inside you. The thought alone turns me on. I'd be a liar if I said that didn't do it for me. But let's wait until we talk with Mateo tomorrow. Let's see where the three of us are at. I've tested recently and came back negative, but I still rather check in with him first."

"Me too," I said with a smile. "It's good to have something to look forward to."

"It is," he agreed.

"Which means . . . one more round, then you have to show me your photos. It's a requirement."

"A requirement, eh?"

He backed me toward the bed and dropped me in the center, his cock raging hard, throbbing and begging to fill me up. My hand slid down to my pussy, my eyes popping wide as I realized how wet I was.

"Fuck," he grunted, feasting his gaze on my fingers sliding in and out of myself.

"Levi, *please*."

Precum beaded at the head of his cock. The very thought of him coming inside me again sent little shock waves through my body, even with a condom on. My teeth sank into my lower lip as I drank every part of him in. His chest hair, the V line at his hips, the veins that traced his cock.

Fuck. *Lucky.* I was damn lucky.

His breath huffed as he grabbed a condom and rolled it on. The bed shifted as he joined me, his arms wrapping around my waist and rolling me over onto all fours. I squeaked as he drew my hips back and pushed my chest into the blankets.

Levi leaned past me and snatched a pillow, quickly wedging it beneath my stomach for comfort. *Damn*, what a man. I looked back over my shoulder at him, my mind glazing over with lust as I slid my hand down between myself and the pillow. I was wet and needy and desperate for him to fuck me again.

My fingers settled against my clit and I whimpered as I circled it.

"You're so fucking hot," he rasped. "Damn, Avery. Look at you."

"*I need you.*"

Levi became motionless for just a second and looked dumbstruck. The power of being desired thrummed through me. He shook his head, sucking in a breath as he positioned himself against me, guiding his cock against my pussy.

The moment he pushed into me, we groaned together, his cock spearing me with heat.

"Fuck," he gasped. "Fuck, Avery."

"*Fuck me,*" was all I could say.

He gripped my hips hard, holding me in place as I buried my face into the blankets. Our moans filled the bedroom, music to my ears as he drove into me. *Fuck.* My eyes rolled back, my fingers gripping the blanket. I swore, he was going to make me drool. The sounds of our skin slapping together followed as he fucked me harder.

It felt so fucking good to be bent over like this for him, every thought getting railed out of me.

"You take me so well," he growled. "You look so good like this, baby. *Fuck.*"

I pushed my hips back to meet each thrust, taking his cock deeper with every movement. I cried out, my face pressing into the blankets and muffling every little noise I made for him.

"*Levi,*" I gasped. "Please don't stop. Please. Fuck. *Right there. Right there.*"

He kept the rhythm, hitting the same sweet spot that was driving me wild. My back muscles tensed as I gripped the sheets harder, his thrusts sending a rush of euphoric lust through me. His cock was so fucking hard and I was so close to the edge, fighting the need to come as I heard his breaths shorten, his movements turning jerky as he got closer and closer to orgasming.

It was as if he *needed* to make me come. Even though he was right on the edge, he was holding out to make sure I came first. I twisted slightly, looking over my shoulder at him before my eyes shut, a gasp tearing from me.

Every thrust was harder, deeper. He leaned forward, sliding his hand beneath me and pressing his fingers against my clit. I whimpered as he started to circle me quickly, still fucking me with the same brutal rhythm.

"Fuck," I cried. "Oh god."

I bucked against him, fighting the pleasure. His muscles strained as he held me in place, circling my clit until I started to quake. My voice pierced the room as I arched, my pussy milking him.

"I'm so close," I gasped.

"I know, baby. I can feel it. Give it to me. I want to feel you shaking around my cock like a good girl."

I groaned as he maintained the steady pump of his cock.

"*Levi.*"

I chanted his name over and over until my back arched and my muscles tensed, every part of me going rigid as my orgasm crashed into me.

"Good girl," he praised, still fucking me as I collapsed beneath him, my breaths uneven. "You did so good for me, baby."

"*Fuck.*"

Every part of me was limp. Every part of me was satiated. Levi's hold on me tightened and he grunted, giving one final thrust right as he came, burying his cock deep as he filled me. More pleasure zipped through me like lightning, every part of me feeling the deep tug of satisfaction.

He melted against me as the last drop of cum filled the condom. I shivered, thinking about how hot it would be when that condom came off. Levi kissed down my spine, sighing happily as he pulled out.

I collapsed completely and he rolled to the side, pulling me against his hard body. My hair was messy, sticking to my forehead. I still wore his jersey proudly, the fabric pushed up, soft against my skin.

"I'm taking a picture of you," he murmured. "But in my head. For my eyes only."

I smiled against his chest. "Speaking of . . . you owe me photos. Show me your photos."

He groaned, but I gave his chest a light tap.

"You're not getting out of it, sir. I want to see them," I said.

Levi stole a few more kisses until I was giggling. Finally, I gave him a shove, urging him to get out of bed.

"Show me," I said. "Pretty please."

"Fine," he chuckled. "If you insist. Just keep in mind, they're not very good. It's just a hobby. I'm not a professional."

I rolled my eyes as I got out of bed. Even if they weren't good, I didn't care. I just wanted to see what he'd created. What brought him joy.

Seeing that little sliver of him would mean more to me than the quality of the actual photos.

I followed Levi to the kitchen, looking around the house. I'd never been inside, despite living across the street for a couple years. Clearly, the couple who'd changed it into a rental had done a good job. It was quaint, but nicely decorated. Cozy and very *Texas*.

"All right," Levi mumbled.

He grabbed a stack of prints from the table, then hesitated for a moment.

His muscles stiffened as he looked up at me. "I've never shown anyone."

"I'm honored," I said, sliding up next to him. "Show me."

Levi spread the photos out on the tabletop and my mouth dropped. When he'd mentioned this being his hobby, I'd really expected it to look amateur. But his photography was amazing. I ran my fingertips over the edge of one of the photos, recognizing some of the spots around Whynot, including the court-yard at the hotel. All of the photos were in black and white, and the angles he shot from were interesting. They told a story, too, which was hard to do with photography.

I lingered on a picture of my studio. *Whynot Paint.* There was something so bright about it, even with all the color pulled away, and that made me happy.

Levi cleared his throat. "I've been kind of doing this in my spare time. Which I've had a lot of lately. And since I don't have my car back yet, I've been walking around and taking photos of the town. I don't know, they're not very good, but—"

"Levi, they're *really* good," I said.

I wasn't sure how to really tell him how fucking good they were. I'd seen photographers come and go through our town, but they always missed something about our corner of the world.

But not his.

"Do you have more?" I asked.

His eyes brightened and he nodded. A black bag sat on the table and he unzipped it, pulling out his camera. He turned it on and came around to my chair, leaning down behind me and showing me how to flip through the photos.

Damn, the ones he hadn't printed yet were even better. There were a lot of landscape shots that made me think we needed to get up to the mountains.

"We should have a picnic at the state park," I said. "And I can bring my art supplies and paint while you take pictures."

Levi was quiet for a moment and then I felt his lips press against the top of my head. "That sounds like the perfect date to me."

"It would be," I said excitedly.

"Mateo can come along and look pretty."

I laughed and craned my head back to look up at him. Levi

smiled as he kissed me on the mouth again, an ease settling between us that surprised me.

"You know, for someone that made me want to pull my hair out when you rolled into town, you sure are wonderful," I said.

He chuckled and straightened, rolling his shoulders carefully. I frowned when I noticed his wince.

"You okay?"

"Yeah," he said. "Just my right shoulder. It bothers me sometimes."

"Want me to give you a massage?"

"I won't say no to that." He settled into the other chair and propped his chin up in his hand. "I'm also thinking about going back to Sunday yoga."

"Oh yeah. That would be good. I don't go every week, but I'll go again this Sunday if you want. " I studied him for a moment. "Listen, I'm all for yoga and massages, but have you gone to a doctor for it?"

Levi groaned and put his head down on the table. I snorted, raising a brow at this little dramatic show.

"Do you know how many times I've gone to the doctor in my career? I've lost count. And I know I should probably go for this, but my hope was that it'd work itself out. It has been feeling better, it just hurts sometimes. I've felt better since being in Whynot, though. I think I was pushing myself too hard."

I reached across the table and slid my hand into his. "It seems like you needed this break."

I wish you would stay.

Those words almost came out of my mouth, but I swallowed them down. What the hell was I supposed to say to him? Leave your career completely behind and move to Whynot? What was a small Texas town compared to a city like Minneapolis?

The first little tear in my paper heart hurt. Because as special as it felt being with Levi, I knew this was fleeting. I knew he would go back home and forget all about me.

"I definitely needed a change. I feel guilty for taking it. Everyone is saying that I was at the height of my career, and this is a huge failing on my part. But there's a part of me that's gone numb to all that." Levi shrugged. "I would rather be here with you. I am more excited about our date night tomorrow than I've felt about anything in a long, long time. So, thank you for that. And thank you for giving me a chance."

I reached across the table and slid my hand into his, saying the cheesiest thing I could think of to break the tension between us. *"Why not?"*

Levi sighed, his eyes fluttering into a flat expression. "Fucking kill me."

"You gotta lean into it," I teased. "You're in Whynot now."

So why not stay? Why not fall in love? Why not break my heart again?

CHAPTER TWENTY-NINE

It'd been two weeks since I met Levi.

That little fact hit me out of the blue as I walked down the sidewalk to Avery's house. The sunset splashed across the sky, reminding me of one of her paintings I'd snagged for myself a year ago. It hung in my bedroom, and while it was just a landscape, I'd stared at it countless times while wondering if I'd ever get the chance to love her.

And now that chance was here. It felt fitting that the sky looked like her.

First date nerves were making me feel jumpy, but I drew in three deep breaths, centering myself as my boot met her doorstep.

I couldn't believe this was my first official date with Avery.

Or that it was also my first official date with Levi.

Two weeks since he'd shown up in Whynot, and he'd turned our lives upside down in the best way possible. I wasn't exactly sure what would happen between the three of us in the long run, but I knew what was going to happen tonight.

I tightened my grip on the leather bag I carried. Her little house was my favorite. She'd gone out of her way to spruce it up, a drop of rainbow in the dull beige of the rest of the street.

I took another steady breath. My heart was beating out of my damn chest. The photos that Levi and Avery sent me yesterday had been on my mind for the last twenty-four hours. Non-stop. Hell, getting through work today had been torture, just knowing that I had to wait until tonight to touch either one of them.

I'd packed a few things in my bag. Not that I needed them to dominate Avery and Levi, but I had a feeling we'd all enjoy what I brought. *If* we got that far.

I held up my hand to knock on the door, but it swung open. Levi's rugged face greeted me, his brows lifting as his eyes darted to the bag.

God, I loved making this man blush. He *knew* there were kinky items in here, and there was already a little bit of power in that—in knowing that my presence alone got him wondering what our evening would be like.

"Hi," he rasped.

"Hi," I said, stepping into the doorway. I kicked it shut behind me, all of my nerves vanishing. "Where's Avery?"

"I was helping her . . . uh . . . cook. She's in the kitchen." He was flustered, and that was really cute.

"Great. Kiss me."

It wasn't an ask, it was a demand. His breath whooshed out of him as he backed me against the door, swooping his mouth down to meet mine. He tasted like sweet tea and lemon and like a man who was going to be kneeling for me later tonight.

Levi drew back, clearly rattled. I was rattled too. I hadn't felt this sort of connection to someone before.

It just felt *different*.

A throat cleared and we both looked down the hall. Avery stood there with a smirk.

Wearing a blue paisley apron.

And a black sleeveless latex bodysuit.

Her hair was drawn back into a bun, her lips painted dark red. My knees felt weak. I suddenly understood why Levi was so damn flustered. The latex hugged her body in a way that had me drooling, shiny and reflecting everything around us. There was a ring at the zipper, begging to be tugged all the way down between her breasts.

"I know it's a first date, but . . ." she trailed off. "Am I too much?"

"Fuck no. You're never too much."

I dropped the bag to the floor and strode down the hall straight to her. Avery squeaked as I lifted her, pulling her against my body and kissing her hard. Her arms wound around my neck as I poured all of my hunger into our kiss. My hands glided over the smooth latex to her ass, and then further.

And I paused.

"It has a hole," she murmured.

I felt Levi's hand on my back and looked up at him, eyes wide. "It has a fucking hole."

"Are we even gonna make it to the bed?" he asked sincerely.

Were we? Jesus. I needed to think straight. We needed to have conversations about kink and about safety, about all of the adult-ing things that came along with being into BDSM.

"Yes," I finally said, leaning up to steal another kiss from our gentle giant. "We should have dinner and talk first. Although, if Avery is partially naked, I think it's only fair that we are too."

Levi smirked. "I think that's fair."

Avery winked at both of us as she twirled away, giving us the perfect view of her ass as she walked back toward the kitchen. The latex was so shiny, it reflected both of our awestruck expressions.

"I won't complain if you're both a little less dressed," she said.

"Goddamn," Levi whispered.

"Yep."

I swallowed hard. I was thirsty, but water certainly wasn't going to quench it. My hand fell to my belt and I undid it, the metal clanking as it unclasped. Leather slid over denim as I tossed it to the floor. Levi joined me, the two of us undressing down to our boxer briefs right there in the hall.

"Best first date I've ever had," Levi chuckled.

I grinned and my gaze stuck to him like glue. The outline of his cock was apparent, his slight erection making my mouth water.

All of the things we'd be able to do together . . .

Just the thought of having Avery suck him was enough to make me groan. "I need to get away from you before I drag you into Avery's bed."

Levi raked his fingers through his flaxen blond hair. "Same. I'll do the honors."

He slid past me, but not before his hand settled on my hip for a moment. Little sparks erupted as his fingertips grazed my skin.

"You dick," I mumbled as he headed to join Avery in the kitchen.

I leaned against the wall, watching the two of them. I pushed my glasses up the bridge of my nose and smiled to myself as the two of them bumbled around each other. A little awkward, a lot cute, and even more hot.

The way he looked at her made me *feel* things. For a man that looked so grumpy the first day he showed up in Whynot, when Avery was looking the other way, his gaze completely melted for her. His eyes turned to honey like she was the sweetest thing in existence. His posture softened, a smile tugging at his lips in a gentle, almost shy way.

He had it bad for her, and I loved that.

The apron and latex combo was going to be in my dreams for the rest of my life. The way it hugged Avery's body elicited a needy desire inside me to peel it all off.

But, I was getting ahead of myself. Aside from the raw sexual tension in the room, and the fact that I had brought an abundance of sexy things with me—I wanted to spend time with the two of them without pretending.

It was a weight off my shoulders to not have to act like I didn't want them both anymore.

"We made lasagna and a salad," Avery said. "Hopefully that's okay."

I finally left my voyeur spot for the bar. "That sounds great. Can I help with anything?"

A smile touched her red lips. "You can keep standing there looking like a hot professor."

My brows shot up. "A hot professor, huh? Is that what does it for you, Blue?"

Now she grinned. "No. A firefighter and hockey player do it for me."

Levi picked up the lasagna with oven mitts, chuckling as he carried it to her little table. They'd found a folding chair from somewhere and added it to the table, which was a good move, because otherwise one of us would be perched on the barstool.

I grabbed the salad bowl from the bar before she could and joined Levi in setting the table.

"How was work?" he asked. "Save any cats?"

"Not today," I said, glancing up at Avery as she brought cold water and tea to the table.

We all picked a seat and settled in, crunching together to fit at the table. She'd bought fresh flowers at some point and they sat on the windowsill. Or maybe June had dropped them off. I already knew she and Evie were in on our date, forever the best cheerleaders for Avery.

Just like Austin and Dallas were always pushing me, too.

I felt a flash of guilt for sitting here with their sister on a secret date. We never kept things from each other—especially when it came to dating. I'd been there for Austin more times than I could count, especially when he'd gotten his hopes up about someone or after a night he thought might turn into something more.

That was the thing about Austin Whynot. For someone who constantly sabotaged his sister's dating life, he was a romantic—maybe even more than Dallas. He just buried it beneath all the stress wrapped tight around his heart.

"How was your day?" I bounced back to them. "Did you even make it out of bed before noon?"

Avery laughed. "Only because I had classes to teach. I don't need the elderly population of Whynot knocking my door down."

"I don't know. I think they'd enjoy what they might see," I teased. "Levi looks damn good naked."

He wrinkled his nose, his cheeks rosy as he piled salad on his plate. "I don't need them seeing me like that. For your eyes only."

Avery snickered. I took a bite of lasagna and groaned, a little surprised. "Did you make this?"

"Yep. Me and the frozen section are in cahoots."

I laughed and took another bite. "Would never have known."

"You certainly did," she chided. "You know I don't cook like that."

"Yeah, you're right. I do know that." I knew a lot about

Avery, actually. In the back of my mind, there was this little part of me that'd been taking notes for two years.

Levi raised a brow, studying the two of us thoughtfully. His green eyes sparkled with amusement. "How in the hell have the two of you waited this long to get together?"

I opened my mouth to answer, but my words failed. Avery turned her attention to me and let out a soft hum.

"Well," she said. Her hand settled on top of his and she gave him a gentle squeeze before picking up her fork again. "I think there's a short answer and a long one. I think the short answer is maybe we were just waiting on you, Levi."

CHAPTER THIRTY

Levi's expression softened. "I don't think you need me."

"Hey. You told me if I talk about myself like that, you'd—what? Bend me over your knee and spank me?" she said. "So cut that out."

My brows shot up. "Did you spank her?"

"I wanted to," he said, holding her gaze. "Still want to."

"And I want *you* to," she answered.

"So do I," I said. "I think that may be important to make clear. I want you just as much as I want Avery, Levi. You're not an extra in this. And as far as why we waited for so long—I've been telling Avery for two years that we're just friends."

"Probably because of my brothers," she sighed. "They have their reasons for being overprotective, though. I dated someone who used to be their friend. His name was Kevin."

Levi scowled. "You dated *Kevin?*"

Avery made a face. "Right. I forget you lived here."

"Yeah, and I hated that fucker. He was always a dick to me."

Oops. Well, he was about to hate Kevin even more.

Avery sucked in a breath. "Okay, well. I moved to Austin to go to UT, and Kevin moved out there too. We reconnected and started dating, but our relationship didn't go well. Bad enough that Austin and Dallas came to bring me back to Whynot."

Levi was quiet for a moment, his gaze meeting mine. I was holding my tongue, and he knew that. This wasn't my story to tell, even though I wanted to blurt out just how fucking awful *Kevin* had been. But then again, I didn't know everything.

She pressed her lips together, going quiet for a moment.

"You don't need to tell us," I said gently. "We're here now. That's all that matters."

"Well, I actually think it might be good to tell you," she said. "I'm just embarrassed in some ways, I guess. Kevin did get physical with me. And I still have nightmares about him."

Jesus fucking Christ. I hadn't known that. I'd guessed. When Avery moved back, I'd had an inkling something like that had happened. There'd been times she'd shrink into herself if someone raised their voice, or if someone was fist fighting at a bar, she'd close her eyes and tune it all out. The protective streak in me had grown a mile wide around her, which was how we became friends.

No wonder Dallas and Austin were so protective.

Levi's face turned red and his body turned rigid, but he kept his words soft. "I'm sorry, Avery."

"I've worked through most of it," she said. "Really. I've gone to therapy. I've done the work and I'm proud of myself for that. I'm in a healthy spot in my life and I want to be in a relationship. But, I do still wake up sweating or crying sometimes. I can't help it. I hate it, but I can't help it."

"Well, we'll be there to hold you," I murmured. "Or be there to sit with you. Whatever you want, whatever you need, we'll be there."

Levi nodded. "Anytime, anywhere, whatever you need, baby."

Baby. I met his gaze again and smiled, warmth relaxing me

despite the fact I had half a mind to drive all the way to Austin, find Kevin, and break his nose.

Avery let out a sigh of relief. "Thanks. I feel better telling both of you. I guess we all probably have baggage, but mine feels heavy sometimes. I would understand if it's too much."

Levi shook his head. "It's not. Besides, Mateo and I are strong guys. We can handle it."

I raised my arm and flexed my bicep, earning a giggle from her. "See? Strong. Buff. Ready to carry your baggage and take care of you."

Avery shook her head, but I couldn't help but notice the way her dimples flashed. "You're ridiculous, you know. Both of you. Also, Levi, I don't think you're bad with words."

He shrugged his shoulders. "They just don't come easy at times. I'm better at showing how I feel."

I wiggled my brows. "Showing, huh? So your hard-on does indicate you're happy to see us?"

"*More* than happy." He shook his head at us and took a sip of tea to wash down a bite of lasagna. "So, what's in that bag, Mateo?"

"All good things," I teased. "I think talking about kink and sex is a good idea."

Avery clapped her hands together. "Absolutely a good idea. Levi and I almost didn't use a condom yesterday, but wanted to wait and talk with you first."

"Oooh." I leaned back in my seat, that thought going straight to my cock. And it was impossible to hide how much that impacted me. "Are you on birth control?"

"I am. And I've tested within the last six months, and was negative for everything." She gave me a cheeky smile. "I like cream pies."

"Oh yeah?" *Fuck me.* My cock throbbed and I tried to clear my head, focusing on literally anything else but the thought of our cum leaking out of her pussy. "I like them too. I'm glad you waited to talk to me about it, but I'm comfortable with it, if you both are. I have also tested negative in the last year, and . . . well, I haven't been with anyone except the two of you."

Levi nodded. "Same. I still brought condoms though."

"Good." I swallowed hard, trying to make my brain work. "You both know I'm kinky. I'm dominant. I like being the one in control. I like planning things. I've tried submission before, but it doesn't do it for me the same way dominance does."

"We all know I'm a sub," Avery said.

Levi leaned forward in his seat slightly, adjusting himself. "Well, I'm in the middle then. I'm a switch. But I think the dynamic feels natural to be submissive with Mateo, and dominant with Avery. And I think . . . I've wondered what it would be like to dominate Avery at your command."

"I like that idea," I said. I liked it *a lot*. "Avery, we've talked a little bit about kink in the past, but I don't really know what your experience level is. And Levi, same for you. Before I moved to Whynot, I was pretty active in the community. I'm a little bit of a slut . . ."

"We've noticed," Avery said, sticking her tongue out at me. "Flirty firefighter with an ego the size of his dick."

"Hey," I quipped. "I think my dick is bigger than my ego, actually."

"Uh-huh." She leaned back in her chair. "I haven't done too much. What I did with Kevin was unsafe. And it was always about him. Before we dated, I went to a kinky club in Austin a few times, but just watched people. I've always wanted to explore kink more, but obviously that's been off the table during the last two years."

We turned our attention to Levi and he cleared his throat.

"Well, I'm experienced. I have . . . I have spreadsheets. I brought them with me, actually."

"You brought homework?" Avery asked.

"I did."

"He also has a degree in math," I said, giving her a sly look. "He's secretly a lot nerdier than either of us know."

"He's also a damn good photographer."

"Is he?"

"Hey," Levi quipped. "Enough about me. I'll give you my spreadsheets. I'd love for you to fill them out, if you're interested."

"Of course," I said. "I used to have one saved on my laptop, but I need to update it."

"I'm sorry, hold on," Avery said. "What do you mean a spreadsheet?"

Levi and I exchanged knowing looks.

"Want to do the honors?" I asked.

"Yeah, actually." He got up from the table and disappeared down the hall for a moment, then returned with three folders.

They were color coded.

And labeled.

"So a lot of my experience has been on the top side," he said as he sat back down. "Even though I'm a switch, I'm usually expected to be the one in charge. And don't get me wrong, I love it. But it would be nice to explore submission, too."

He slid a folder with my name to me and another to Avery. She opened it up and her brows shot up.

"Oh," she said. "I see now. It's a list of everything."

"Everything I can find on the internet, along with yes, maybe, no, and a column for notes. It's something that's better updated online, but I printed them out just in case."

I nodded, thankful my brain was working again. "I'm glad you did this. And your list is about as comprehensive as it gets."

"What is *frotting*?"

Levi bit back a laugh. "It's when two men rub their cocks together, baby."

"*Oh.*" Her pretty brown eyes widened as she continued to scan the page. Or, *pages.*

I cleared my throat. "I like the stop light system for safe words. It's easy to use and concise. Green means yes, yellow means you need a check in, and red means stop. Red would end a scene."

"I've read that in one of my romance books before," Avery mumbled.

"Just what kind of romance books are you reading?" Levi asked.

"The good smutty kind. What else is there to do in Whynot? There's a love story between the library and my house."

Levi's laugh was easy. "Maybe you can show them to us. For research."

Her eyes lit up and I cocked my head, interested in her response to that. Something about that excited her.

"If you want," she said.

"We want," I assured her. "Always happy for fresh inspiration. Although, I do have some ideas of my own too."

"Oh really?" Levi chimed. "Share with the class."

"Can I get a please?"

"*Please, Sir.*"

The sarcasm dripping in his words would be burned into my memory for the night. I arched a brow. "I'll remember this later."

That sobered him some. "Pretty please. With an Avery on top."

She laughed as I rolled my eyes dramatically.

"If you insist," I said. "Where do I even start? I've been thinking about the two of you non-stop for the last two weeks. I brought a few tools in my kink bag, although none of them are things we have to use. I don't want either of you to push yourself or be uncomfortable. Can you promise me that?"

"Yes," Avery said.

Levi nodded. "Yes."

"Good." I blew out a slow, deliberate breath. Butterflies fluttered in my stomach as I did a mental inventory of everything in that leather bag, along with the countless fantasies that had been plaguing me night and day. "So, I've been thinking . . ."

"If you keep drawing the suspense out, I'm going to start masturbating," Avery quipped.

"No one is stopping you if you do that," I said. She narrowed her eyes on me, and I grinned broad. "I brought a flogger and a paddle. I also brought some rope. I brought some spreader bars. A couple blindfolds. I also may or may not have bought some new things online that will be here next week."

Both of their mouths fell open, but I kept going before they asked anything.

"As for what I'm thinking . . . I'm thinking I want to fuck both of you. I want to bend you, Avery, over the bed and spank your ass so you remember everything we do together for the next week. I want to put you, Levi, on your fucking knees and make you eat our girl out until she's screaming your name, all while I'm fucking you. I want to try every position possible with three bodies. I want to tie you both up in rope and tease you until you're both begging, cockhungry messes. I want to see if Avery can take both of our cocks. I want to give you both instructions for you to obey, and your reward will be to do anything to please me. And I want to make the two of you come so many times you forget your name, what town we're in, and the rest of your worries."

I exhaled and leaned back, drinking in their wide-eyed

expressions. I took a long sip of my water and set the cup back down.

"That's what I wanna do."

Levi let out a soft groan and looked away from us, his cheeks scarlet. "I wanna do that too."

Avery nodded and looked directly at me. "Where do we start?"

CHAPTER THIRTY-ONE

We started with homework.

I knew there were a lot of kinks out there. Truly, I did. And I had a lot of them. But my god, Levi had *four pages* worth for the three of us to work through.

"This counts as edging," I said as I continued to fill mine out.

"It definitely does," Mateo agreed.

Of the three of us, Levi was the most pleased with the spreadsheets. The more I got to know him, the more I saw a man made up of different parts. And the more parts I saw, the more I thought—*I'm gonna fall for him.*

Choking. Yes. *Bondage.* Yes. *Ball gags.* Yes. *Floggers.* Yes? I think? *Fisting.* That kind of scared me and turned me on at the same time.

Levi cleared his throat and closed his folder. "Mine is updated."

I looked up at him. We were in my living room, the three of us spread out—because if we sat too close, those sheets were never getting filled out.

"Mine is almost there, but we're in no rush," Mateo said.

His brows pulled together and he kept adjusting his seating, the same way Levi was.

Both of them were hard. I was wet. Drenched, actually.

Double penetration. I lingered on that one. Not because I didn't want it, but because the idea of them both being inside of me at the same time sounded hot.

I had a few NOs on here. Like degradation. That wasn't going to do it for me. Praise, while hard to hear at times, turned me on. I liked knowing I was doing a good job. I liked feeling safe in my desires.

I checked the last box and then added my sheets to the coffee table next to Levi's. Mateo peeked at the two of us over the top of his folder, raising a brow.

"Both of you are such good students."

See? *That* made me whimper and blush.

Mateo's pen marked the last box and he leaned forward, grabbing our sheets and lining them up so we could compare. I got to my knees on the floor, looking down at them and quickly scanning.

"We have a lot in common," Levi said softly.

"We do," I whispered.

Mateo nodded, quiet as he read through. "Levi, you like degradation? And Avery, you don't. That makes sense."

"I don't think I would," I said. "But it wouldn't bother me to be around it. Like if you wanted to do that with Levi while I'm here, I'd think it was hot. I just think my feelings would get hurt if it were directed toward me."

Levi dragged his chair as close to the coffee table as he could, our heads together. "I like it a lot," he said. "I like praise too. A mix of both turns me on."

Mateo nodded as he continued to scan. "Okay. This was very helpful, and I think we should make an online version too, so we can update it over time. But, this gives me a plan for tonight."

"It did?" Excitement made my heart leap.

"It did." His mustache tugged as he smirked. He leaned back on the couch and then patted his hand on the cushion. "Join me, both of you. Avery, I want you in the middle."

"Yes, Sir." I got up, my legs feeling like jelly. I'd been thinking about this moment for weeks, and now that it was happening, I was nervous and excited.

I shifted around the coffee table and sat down on the middle cushion. Levi joined us, taking the one to my right. I'd been wearing my latex body suit all evening, but suddenly I was a lot more *aware*.

Sitting between Levi and Mateo on the couch, every part of my body was fully conscious of every part of theirs. Aware of Levi's hand as it settled on my thigh, the way he squeezed me and how his touch bolted desire straight to my pussy. Aware of the way Mateo reached up to circle the side of my neck with his thumb, rubbing a spot I loved to have kissed.

My breath hitched and my cheeks burned like I was running a fever.

After Mateo's sexy little monologue, we'd cleaned up the kitchen fast. I'd taken a moment to text June and Evie to beg them to run interference if it looked like Dallas or Austin might try to stop by one of our places. And those two, being the best wingwomen alive, had somehow gotten those two knuckle-heads to turn on their locations so they could monitor them while I got my back broken by their best friends.

Jesus Christ. I'd have some explaining to do if—when—they found out about us.

But all of those worries whooshed out in a breath the moment Levi reached up slowly and crooked his finger beneath my chin. He tilted my head as he leaned down. *Oh my god, I'm going to kiss him.* Panic and excitement laced together as Mateo continued to draw those circles at the base of my neck.

Levi's lips pressed against mine. A soft groan left him, his grip on my thigh tightening. The pressure of his fingertips turned me on. There was something about being grabbed by him like this that made me desperate.

Fuck. A whimper caught in my throat as I parted my lips for him. His tongue swiped against mine, devouring me in a hungry kiss. He drew back right as Mateo tightened his grip on my neck and Levi turned my head toward him.

Mateo kissed me next. I sank between the two of them, my head spinning as they passed my kisses back and forth. Levi to Mateo to Levi until the taste of them blended together like a fine wine. I stole breaths between each heavy kiss, every thought blanking as I focused on the present. On kissing them. Being with them.

Levi kissed me once more but then knotted his fingers in my hair, holding me in place as his gaze landed on Mateo. I watched through a hooded gaze as Mateo swayed forward and they kissed next. *Fuck.*

Mateo looked at me. "Too much?"

"What?" I rasped.

"You made a sound."

Had I? I was so lost in watching them, I had no idea what sort of sounds I was making. "I'm so turned on right now I feel drunk."

"Me too," Levi said. "I don't want to rush things, but . . ."

"I do," I said simply. I was two seconds from ripping the damn apron and lingerie off and jumping them. "I want both of you. I want this."

"I do too," Mateo said, turning his gaze back to Levi.

He nodded. "Yes. A hundred percent yes. I should have brought lube and condoms over . . ."

"I have some," Mateo said. "Let's move to the bedroom. I'll go grab my bag."

"Are you going to spank me, Sir?" I asked

Mateo knotted his fingers in my hair and gave me a pull. I squeaked, that feeling like gasoline on a flame. "If you behave," he growled.

"More," I whispered, meeting his gaze.

I wanted him to pull harder.

"Dammit, Avery," he mumbled, standing up with a full hard-on in his boxer briefs. "Bedroom. Both of you. *Now.*"

"Yes, Sir," we said together.

CHAPTER THIRTY-TWO

Avery's bedroom was almost exactly how I imagined. Wood floors with three different rugs overlapping, each with different patterns and in different shapes and shades of pink. Her bed frame was a sturdy maple with a thousand pillows—okay that was an exaggeration, but there were a lot—and a pink duvet with a throw blanket draped across the end. Plants hung from the ceiling in the corner, and there were two side tables that matched her bed frame. Her room had an artist's flare that was so wholly *Avery*.

Was it weird that the thought that came to mind was *damn, I've never made my place feel like this*? Like a home. My apartment wasn't decorated. In fact, it was almost utilitarian. I did have a plant, but it was probably dead now since I'd left so suddenly without handing it off to my neighbor.

Avery picked up the throw blanket and folded it nervously as we waited, her attention on me as I looked around.

"I love your room," I said. "It's so bright and colorful and very you."

There was a board on the wall with a bunch of photos on it. I stepped closer, my chest squeezing.

There were none of her and her dad. She must have taken them down.

Avery followed me, her arm sliding around my waist. I pulled her closer and kissed the top of her head, breathing in the scent of her shampoo. She smelled like cinnamon and vanilla and a bit of citrus, a concoction that my brain would only attribute to her going forward.

"Do you think he's purposefully taking his time?" she whispered.

"Without a doubt."

I turned to face her, cupping her cheek and leaning down. She rose up on her tiptoes, her arms winding around my neck as she kissed me. It was gentle at first, but then that need came roaring back—sudden and all-consuming.

Fuck. I lifted her, pulling her legs around my waist. She whined in her throat as I carried her to her bed and sat her down on the edge, my knees hitting the floor as I pushed her thighs apart.

Funny how my body never protested when I was about to have sex. I'd maybe feel the aftermath tomorrow, but it would be worth it.

The sound of wood scraping had us both looking up at the doorway. Mateo came through carrying a dining room chair and his kink bag, his flirty and knowing smile making me wonder just what he had planned.

He placed the chair with enough space around it for movement.

"Levi," he said. "I want you to strip and sit in the chair."

My cock was already hard, but the firmness in his tone made me even more. I rose up, pausing to steal another kiss from Avery, and then stripped my boxers off. I took a seat in the chair, swallowing hard as I looked up at him.

"Good." Mateo carried the bag to the bed and unzipped it

slowly. Before Avery could even peek inside, he held up his hand. "I don't think so. Be a good girl and go suck Levi's cock while you wait."

"Can I have a kiss first?"

Mateo snorted and leaned forward, kissing her hard enough that when she pulled away, her head was spinning. She slid to the floor—more like melted—and then *crawled* to me.

"Fuck," I whispered as she knelt between my knees. "Look at you."

She preened under that. Avery reached back and tugged her hair free, then redid the bun so that it was tighter. Seeing her pull her hair back like that made me groan, precum dripping from the head of my cock.

The fucking latex. One thing the three of us happened to have in common was a love of latex. It looked so fucking good on her. Shiny and inky black and hugging every part of her, showing the outline of her nipples. I wanted to lean forward and tug the O-ring zipper down, but I'd wait.

I'd wait for Mateo's command.

Avery closed her hand around the base of my cock. I sucked in a breath, looking over at Mateo right as he pulled a ball gag and blindfold out of the bag.

He met my gaze right as Avery closed her mouth over my cock. *Fuck, fuck.* Pleasure prickled through every part of my body as she took me deeper and then drew back, her tongue swirling over me. She gripped the base, moving her hand as she moved her mouth, finding a rhythm that was bound to be my downfall.

"God damn it," I huffed, my head tipping back on a moan.

Mateo picked up the blindfold and came up behind the chair. I opened my eyes, looking up at him. His hand settled on my throat, not squeezing. But just the weight of his palm there was enough to make me feel submissive.

And safe.

Safe in that feeling of giving in. Safe in knowing that he was the one in control, and that he knew what I wanted. He knew what to give me, just like he knew what to give Avery.

"I'm going to blindfold you," he said as Avery took my cock deeper. "And then I'm going to put you in a collar. And our little artist is going to use your cock however I want her to."

"Yes," I rasped. "Please."

The collar was something I especially wanted.

"No one has collared me before," I said.

"I saw. I'm going to be the first."

And hopefully last.

I swallowed hard at that thought. It didn't belong in my head, but it was there nonetheless. Part of me wanted to believe this was it. That Avery and Mateo would be the ones for me. But that couldn't possibly work, right?

I didn't have a moment to keep thinking. Mateo brushed his mouth against mine like an incubus sealing my fate. Avery tightened her grip on my cock and my hips bucked, pleasure rushing through me. *Fuck*, I was hard.

"Good boy," he murmured.

He held up the collar and I straightened my head as he put it around my neck. It was thicker and heavier than I'd imagined.

"I may have gone a little extra with my adult purchases recently."

My brows shot up. "You bought this for me?"

"I did. I bought one for Avery too. Just in case."

"Just in case," I echoed, smiling as he kissed the top of my head.

The same gentleness he was giving me paired well with the euphoric waves of need battering me from Avery. I sucked in a breath as she hit a perfect spot and rhythm, and she fucking knew it.

"Good girl," Mateo said. "Keep that cock in your mouth. Let's see how long it takes until he comes."

"Yes—Sir," she gasped between sucking.

I looked down at her, tracing in the perfect sight of her on her knees for me. Her hair pulled back but messy. Her lips red and eyes glassy with lust, cheeks flushed.

Mateo placed the blindfold over my head, the silk soft against my skin. Avery disappeared from my view and darkness followed, but there was comfort in it. Not being able to see everything deepened my headspace. Every sound was heightened. Their scents. The feeling of Avery sucking me, teasing me, *using* me.

I listened to Mateo's soft hum and the sloppy wet sounds of Avery sucking me.

"She's looking right at me while she sucks your cock," Mateo said. "She's fucking gorgeous, isn't she?"

"Yes," I whispered. "She feels so good."

"I bet. Open up."

I opened my mouth for him. A smooth ball fit against my lips, keeping them parted. The leather straps were cool against my cheeks as he tightened around my head, clasping it into place.

It felt right. All of it just felt right. In the past, I'd put a ball gag on my sub, I'd collared them, I'd blindfolded them. But there was something completely different about being on the other side of this. It was vulnerable, like exposing all the raw gooey bits of my heart and leaving them out in the open to be studied.

But I was in Mateo's hands.

His very capable hands.

And I trusted him. I trusted Avery.

"You can still make sounds," Mateo said. "Try saying our safe word."

"*Re-d.*" It sounded messy and spit was definitely already starting to drip down my chin, but he was right. I could still get the word out. "*I'm good.*"

"Good. Avery, stand up."

I moaned as her hand and mouth left my cock. I listened as she stood up. She made a squeaking sound, breath hitching.

"She's looking right into my eyes," Mateo whispered. The sound of a zipper followed. Another moan, another gasp, another whimper. "She's so fucking wet for us. *Fuck.*"

Listening to him tell me what they were doing turned me on more than I ever expected. It was like listening to my own personal erotica, but it was *real* and happening right in front of me.

And I was sitting here.

Being good.

"Oh god," Avery whimpered. "Fuck."

I could hear him finger fucking her. My cock throbbed, begging for some relief. At no point had he told me I couldn't touch myself, so moved my hand around the base of my cock. I groaned, listening to the two of them intently as I stroked up and down, pleasure striking through me.

"Move your fucking hand, Levi."

"Fuck," I whined.

But I obeyed.

Mateo's chuckle was downright evil. "Turn around, Avery. Use his cock like a toy."

I gripped the seat of the chair as I felt her lower herself, hovering over me. Mateo leaned between us, guiding my cock against her entrance. A low groan left me as her pussy gripped me like a vice, hot velvet consuming me as she sat back. She cried out, taking every inch until she was fully seated, my cock completely inside her, stretching around me.

"Good girl," Mateo whispered. "You're doing so good taking every inch of him. I know he's a lot. Our man's got a big cock, doesn't he?"

"Yes," she whimpered. "He does."

"Sit back. Hold her up, Levi, if your shoulder feels good."

I nodded, my hands immediately moving to grab her hips. I lifted her with ease, still keeping my cock buried deep as she sat back, falling against my chest. My fingers met the smooth latex of her hips, and then the softness of her thighs as I held onto them, supporting her weight.

"God, look at you," Mateo groaned. "Spread and dripping for us. He's filling up every part of you, isn't he, Blue?"

"Yes, Sir." Her words were breathy, her muscles quivering.

"I want you to fuck her, Levi. She's going to hold my gaze the entire time while you take her and she's going to jerk me off."

My muscles tightened as I lifted her and then let her slide back down my cock. Spit dripped down my chin and into my beard, a groan leaving me as her pussy milked me. She felt so fucking good. All the sounds she made were so completely perfect, I wanted to remember them forever.

"Harder," Mateo commanded. "I know you can fuck her harder."

Fuck. I sucked in a breath through my nose, my mind spinning as every thrust turned deeper. Avery cried out, her head falling back against my shoulder.

"Good boy."

Fuck me. I'd be a liar if I said that didn't do it for me. Pleasure spread through my body, a shiver working up my spine as I got closer and closer to filling her up.

"Look at me, Avery."

She whimpered, her head turning slightly. The blindfold continued to keep me from seeing them, my mind going wild.

I groaned around the ball gag, pumping my hips.

"There we are," Mateo murmured. "You're so fucking close, aren't you, baby? So fucking close. He's going to fill you up with every fucking drop. I want to see him dripping out of you as you come on his cock."

Fuck, fuck, fuck.

"Keep going, Levi. Keep fucking her."

I felt his fingers brush the clasp on the ball gag. I moaned as he pulled it free, and it was as if a restraint were lifted. I grunted as his fingers glided against the base of my head, gripping my hair and turning my head. His mouth brushed against mine in a sloppy kiss, all of that pleasure rolling down to my cock.

I was so fucking close.

He nipped my bottom lip, his grip firm on me. Unyielding. Powerful.

"Fuck," I gasped against his mouth.

"I'm so close," Avery cried.

I could feel her tightening around me, the walls of her pussy gripping me like a vice. Being inside her without a barrier made every movement even more intense. I gasped, giving one more thrust right as an avalanche of pleasure crashed down on me. Cum burst from my cock, filling her up with every drop, just like Mateo promised her I would.

Avery's muscles tensed, her body bowing against me, muscles quivering as she came.

I collapsed in the chair, and she melted against me. Mateo pulled the blindfold free. I blinked like I was resurfacing from a dream. When I looked down, I realized he'd come all over her too, cum painting her latex bodysuit.

Mateo smiled and leaned down, kissing me gently this time,

and then kissing her too. "Let's move to the bed," he said. "I'll get a towel to clean up."

A couple minutes later, the three of us were dropping into her bed. I expected Avery to end up in the middle, but was surprised when Mateo pulled me to the center, wearing that damn smirk of his that always managed to make my heart flutter.

The two of them curled up next to me.

"How much longer are you here for?" Avery whispered.

I didn't want to answer. I felt Mateo adjust his head on my chest, his hand sliding into mine, fingers interlocking.

"Two more weeks as of Monday," I finally said.

She nodded slowly. "We'll make the most of it then."

CHAPTER THIRTY-THREE

I was up before the sun and in my studio.

I'd never felt this inspired before. But with all of the secret kisses and nights together with Levi and Mateo, my muse was running at full battery.

Between all the wild thoughts about those two, though, were cracks of worry in the foundation. I was all too aware of the fact that I'd missed family dinner last night and never received a text from my mother. All too aware that I hadn't heard a single thing from her since our blowout.

That weighed heavily on me, like it was my fault. It wasn't, and I knew that, but it still felt like it.

Then there was Levi.

Two more weeks.

We had two more weeks with him before he had to go back to Minnesota. A little ball of dread was forming between my shoulders.

I didn't want him to go, but I'd never be the person to ask him to stay. His career was there. His life was there. I couldn't ask him to change it all to be with me and Mateo. *That* would be selfish. And as someone who had walked away from all my big dreams of traveling the world and being *that* sort of artist, I'd never do that to someone I lov—*liked*.

I leaned back on my stool and stared at the canvas. The background was coming together, but the figures at the center were still missing. Cacti bloomed around them, the sunset dripping with magentas, oranges, and golden hues.

This was going to be one of *those* pieces. One that stuck with me. I wasn't sure I'd be able to let it go.

So who was going to go in the middle?

An idea started to scratch at the corners of my brain, but was interrupted. Footsteps outside my studio room had my head turning, but there were only two people it could possibly be—really only one, given how early it was. Evie's head poked into the doorway, but her eyes were covered, because she knew this room was off-limits to everyone.

"Morning," I chuckled.

"Morning. Come join me for coffee?"

I was already springing up from my stool. "Yep." I didn't bother to take off the apron I wore while painting. It was a beige canvas fabric once upon a time, but now it was covered in bright colors. I had a habit of wiping my brush off on it when I was deep into a project.

I followed Evie out of the room and let the door shut behind me. She uncovered her eyes and smiled, pure sunshine in a pretty dress.

"Hey," I said, giving her a hug. I noticed flour on her nose and wiped it away before releasing her. "How's it going?"

"Oh, you know," she said. "Working way too early, per usual."

"But you're closed on Mondays," I said. "I'm surprised you're here."

"I'm prepping for something later this week. And I wanted

to catch up. You've been so busy with Mateo and Levi, I feel like I've barely seen you."

She had a point. "Sorry about that," I said. "It's been a wild time. I'd love to catch up."

We left my gallery and crossed the empty street to her bakery.

Evie unlocked the door. "I think June will come over too. She's starting to get ready for mum season, so I saw her lights on early too."

"Oh god."

Mum season in Texas was a big deal. Every September, our little town celebrated the annoying, but cherished, game known as football by creating corsages quite literally the size of Texas. Given that June owned her own flower shop, mum season was one of the biggest events of the year for her—even more than Valentine's Day in a lot of ways, which was saying something.

"At least she's prepping early this year," I said.

"She needs to. Homecoming will be big this year. And you already know all the boy moms are gonna be up her ass for the best mum they can get."

"They terrify me," I said as we stepped through her shop's door.

"Me too. Coffee?"

"Yes, please." We rounded the bar and I hopped up, seating myself on the counter as she fixed each of us a cup. "What's on your mind?"

She wrinkled her nose. "That easy to tell?"

"Sure is."

She finished making my cup and handed it to me. I took a sip, humming as she finished hers too and leaned against the counter across from me. Her expression wavered.

"When are you telling Dallas and Austin about Levi and Mateo?" she asked.

Yikes. My stomach did a slow flip. "I don't know. I don't even know if we should. Levi leaves in two weeks."

"Fuck. I thought he was staying."

I shook my head as we took a sip of our lifelines. "He hasn't said otherwise. I don't know. I hope he stays. I want him to stay. Mateo does too. The three of us are just . . . not talking about it."

In fact, it was almost a taboo topic at this point. We were exploring the physical side of our relationship together, and occasionally comments about the future would make it through. Things like *I wish we could stay like this forever* or *It would be fun to wake up next to each other every morning.*

It was hard not to imagine a future where both of them were in it. When we were together, the three of us just clicked. There were things about each of us that complimented the other.

Like how Levi was quiet when he woke up. He needed a full hour to himself before he said much. He locked cute and grumpy at the same time, and Mateo and I loved it.

Mateo was chatty. And I was somewhere between. But that meant I could be quiet with Levi or I could be talkative with Mateo.

I didn't like cooking. Levi's idea of cooking was attempting to bake high-protein muffins. Between the three of us, Mateo was by far the best at it, and he was already talking about *meal prepping.* Meal prepping for the three of us like we were some married trio that had been together for a decade.

"Maybe he'll stay," Evie said softly. "I've got to say, I haven't seen you this happy in a long time. You've got a glow again. And I think Austin and Dallas are noticing. Dallas dropped by the other day and asked me if you were seeing anyone."

My mouth dropped. "What?"

"Yeah. I lied to him of course, so you're welcome. I'm always keeping all of y'all's secrets like I'm a human confessional." Evie sighed and shrugged her shoulders. "I just think they should know why you're happy."

"And you know why that would cause issues," I said. "I just want to enjoy my time with Levi and Mateo. I don't want my brothers getting involved. Ever since Kevin, they constantly overstep. But because that guy was their friend, I just know they would react poorly to Mateo and Levi. Not even just one of their friends, but two. And I don't think Mateo or Levi deserve that."

"They knew that going in, though, sweetheart. And keeping secrets from family is never a good idea."

I made a sour face. "I think more secrets might be a good thing."

Evie shook her head, clearly disagreeing. But that was the thing about our friendship. Sometimes we disagreed with one other, but at the end of the day, I knew she'd still support me.

"Maybe after Levi leaves," I said. "We can tell them. And at least he'll escape whatever stupid shit my brothers will pull."

"Or maybe they'll be happy for you," Evie said. "June and I are thrilled. A little jealous, maybe, but thrilled."

I grinned and took another sip of coffee. "I'm honestly so in —" I cut myself off, shocked by the words that had almost spilled out.

Her brows shot all the way up. "What was that, Avery Anne Whynot?"

"Oh god, not the full name."

"Yes, the full name. What was the end of that sentence?"

I covered my face, peeking at her through spread fingers. "I'm in love. I'm so in love. It's ridiculous and it makes no sense and I know my heart is going to get stomped on, but I'm so in love with both of them."

"Oh my god, you've lost it." She shook her head at me, but she was beaming. "June owes me ten bucks, by the way. Speak of the devil."

The door to the bakery chimed and I turned around right as June walked in. She raised a brow the moment she saw us.

"You owe me money," Evie said triumphantly.

"It's been like three weeks!" June exclaimed.

"I told you!" Evie announced. "Told you! I fucking called it."

"Y'all are bitches," I mumbled, chuckling as Evie fixed up another cup of coffee for our best friend.

June gave me a side hug, resting her head on my shoulder before joining us in our little coffee circle. "Don't get us wrong, we're happy for you. You seem happy, too. I'm just a little worried."

"I'm just going to soak up every moment I can," I said. "That's all I'm focusing on right now. That, and the fact that we have kinky times planned this week and I'm excited."

"What kind of kinky times?" Evie asked. "I want to know everything."

"No details left behind," June said. "And while we chat, the two of you can come over to my shop and help me organize my shipment of ribbons by color and size."

"Damn. I knew we were gonna end up doing this," I laughed.

"Mum season prep is the most serious time of the year." June drained half of her cup, which made me wonder how much caffeine she'd already had today. "Let's go, girls."

Evie and I groaned, but begrudgingly joined her. There was no getting out of mum season, no matter who you were. The closer we got to September, even a couple months out, the more I'd be cursing all of football culture in Texas.

The sunrise was starting to light up our little town. We

walked down the sidewalk together until we got to June's flower shop. The moment we stepped through the back door, we were met with stacks of a billion boxes.

"June," Evie said with wide eyes. "This is too much."

"This isn't half of it." She grimaced as she leaned against one of the boxes. "Avery, tell us about your mind-blowing sex life. I'll grab the box cutters so we can open these bad boys up."

I rolled my shoulders and cracked my knuckles. "You got me for an hour, then I have to go run my own business."

"Same," Evie said. "Avery, start talking."

CHAPTER THIRTY-FOUR

"You have to keep this secret," I said as I unlocked the backdoor to my studio.

Both Levi and Mateo sighed dramatically.

"Who are we going to tell?" Mateo asked, shouldering the leather bag he'd brought with him.

I'd told him to bring kink equipment, but now I couldn't stop wondering what was in there. Floggers? A ball gag? A paddle?

The kink list had come in handy for a variety of reasons, one of them being that I'd mentioned how much I'd enjoy watching the two of them. Voyeuring the two of them would be a major turn on, and it was Mateo's idea for me to draw them.

That man had all the good ideas. I shouldn't have been surprised—it was *Mateo*. I knew just how thoughtful and creative he could be.

As the three of us unleashed ourselves more, the kinkier it got.

"I'm excited to see what you're hiding in your studio," Levi said.

My stomach did a little flip. "I don't let anyone in here for reasons that'll make a lot more sense momentarily." Oh god. I was really going to show them my art. My *real* art.

"The antici . . . *pation*," Mateo teased.

"I'm also excited to see what's in Mateo's bag," Levi said.

"Me too," I admitted.

My cheeks flamed as I let them both in. This little idea to have them model for me was probably terrible, because the painting I was working on would never be able to be seen by the public. But, I was okay with keeping it for myself.

Was that selfish? Painting my boyfriends and keeping it somewhere in my house only I could see? Where would that even be? My closet?

Maybe. I'd find a spot, though. The heart—*pussy*—wanted what she wanted.

Also—*boyfriends?*

"Paint us like one of your French girls," Mateo said.

Oh god. I rolled my eyes, but led them down the hall to the door. I hesitated for a moment, feeling their presence looming behind me. It was hard to think with them so close.

"What's wrong?" Levi asked.

"Nothing. I've just never let anyone else into this room. There's a lot of . . . *art* . . ."

"Well, I for one am shocked that there's art in an art studio," Mateo said.

I stuck my tongue out at him. My keys jangled as I unlocked the door and pushed it open. I flipped the switch and stepped to the side, allowing them to go in first. Levi sucked in a breath as he entered the room and Mateo planted his hands on his hips in awe.

Mateo let the bag drop to the floor. It made a heavy thud. "Goddamn, Avery," he whispered. "You've been painting these the entire time?"

"Yes."

I let the door shut behind us and hung my keys on a hook on the wall. I hugged myself as I walked to the center of the studio, looking around and seeing my space through their eyes. Windows let in natural light during the day and I made damn sure they were the kind no one could see through from the outside. An ornamental rug spread over the wood floors, one of my favorite thrift finds I'd hauled all the way from Austin. A couple plants that were thriving, my ADHD stacks of random books and art supplies scattered around.

Then, there was the art. The erotic paintings combined with regular landscapes and a few experimental pieces too.

"These are so fucking hot," Levi whispered, gravitating toward one in particular.

"Jesus. Is that a self portrait?" Mateo asked, following after Levi.

I blushed so hard I thought I was going to faint. It *was* a self portrait of me on my knees in front of a mirror. I'd tied myself up and was fingering myself, my head tossed back in ecstasy.

I forced a slightly panicked chuckle. "I don't know what it says about me that I did a self portrait of me having an orgasm."

"I want this," Levi said.

"It's not for sale," I said.

"If he gets one, I also want one," Mateo said. "I'll hang it in my closet and look at it all the time."

I laughed. "Nope. It's all mine. For my eyes only. Well, and I guess yours now too."

The two of them continued to walk around my studio as I approached my canvas. I stole nervous glances at them as they murmured to each other.

"Conspiring against me?" I asked.

Mateo turned slightly and I caught the outline of his erection in his pants. His heated gaze met mine and any coherent thoughts disappeared.

"What exactly do you want the two of us to do?" he asked.

I sank my teeth into my bottom lip. Was I really going to ask them for what I wanted?

Preemptively, I'd put a twin mattress on the floor right in front of my canvas. It had blankets and pillows and would be good for . . . *posing.*

Levi turned around and was just as hard as Mateo. His attention moved to the mattress, an eyebrow raising. "I think she wants us there. Naked."

"*Modeling,* huh?"

"If you don't mind," I whispered.

The tension in the air was electric. My blood hummed with lust as I watched Mateo turn to Levi. He reached up, knotting his fingers in Levi's hair, and led him straight to the mattress.

Fuck. Levi hit his knees in submission, his head tipping back as he looked up at Mateo with an expression I could only describe as reverence. It was the same sense of longing and desire I'd seen in countless classical pieces on museum walls. It was almost spiritual.

Without taking my gaze off them, I leaned down and snatched my sketchbook from under my easel. I grabbed a black brush pen and sat down on the floor, crossing my legs as I flipped to an empty page.

Levi grunted as Mateo pulled his shirt free. His chest was bare, his muscles still defined, but stomach a little softer than when he'd first come to Whynot. I loved it. I loved his body and appreciated every inch of him, my drawing hand moving in quick broad strokes, attempting to capture their figures in loose lines.

It was about capturing that feeling. I'd fill in the details later. The sight of them together would live in my mind forever.

Levi's broad hands moved to Mateo's hips, tugging at his belt. "Good boy," Mateo praised. "Take off my boots first. Undress me for our little artist."

"Yes, Sir."

My breath hitched.

How in the hell was I going to focus while they were looking so hot?

Heat pooled in my stomach as I watched, lust rolling through me like a wave against the shore. I kept sketching them, never stopping, even as my body vibrated with anticipation.

Levi started with Mateo's boots and pulled them free, setting them aside and out of the way. The way Mateo's cock strained against his jeans was art in itself. I watched the way Levi ran his calloused fingers up Mateo's thighs until they met his belt. He pulled it free, the metal clinking, the leather sliding against denim.

He tugged them down to the floor and caught the head of Mateo's cock against his lips. My mouth dropped and hand paused as I watched him take Mateo's cock deep, Levi's moan echoing through the room.

I was so fucking wet already.

God, this was torture. Part of me wanted to throw down my sketchbook and crawl over to them and beg to be part of this. Beg to please one of them or beg for us to try out some of the threesome positions Mateo had been plaguing our chat with.

Mateo looked up at me as if he knew what I was thinking. The corner of his mouth lifted in a smirk, his mustache only making it more smug.

"You'd better draw our tough guy on his knees," Mateo said. "I want that framed for myself too."

Levi moaned and drew back on a breath, his hand closing around the base of Mateo's cock. Mateo's attention was immediately pulled back into the moment. He grunted and grabbed the hem of his shirt, tossing it to the floor.

"Put your hands behind your back," he said.

Levi did it so obediently. My breath hitched as Mateo took a step back and reached for the kink bag on the floor. The sound of the zip as he opened it echoed around us, amplifying the anticipation.

Just what had he brought for us to try?

He pulled a black piece of fabric from the bag and took it to Levi. He tipped his bearded chin up and leaned in, murmuring something I couldn't hear. Levi's eyes fluttered, the softest moan leaving him. He nodded eagerly.

Seeing Levi submit to Mateo was just as hot as me being dominated by him.

"Yes, Sir."

Without another word, Levi stood up and started to strip while facing me. My mouth watered and I started sketching again, only breaking eye contact with him to keep my lines moving. Drawing was second nature to me, which made this easier.

He looked so damn good. I sucked in a breath as he took his briefs down, revealing his cock—but there was something around his cock and balls. *A ring? A cock ring?*

"Oh my god," I whispered.

Mateo's smirk told me the bastard had planned this. Always two steps ahead when it came to who could turn who on. Precum dripped from Levi's cock, his eyes shutting as Mateo came up behind him.

"Kneel on the mattress."

His knees hit the cushioned surface and he put his wrists behind his back. Mateo held up the black fabric and I realized as he pulled it over Levi's head—it was a hood with a hole around his mouth.

"Feel good?" Mateo asked.

"Yes, Sir."

"Good. You'll tell me if anything hurts or doesn't feel right."

"I will, Sir."

"Good boy. I'm looking at our little artist right now and she's so flustered. I bet her pussy is dripping while she draws you with a ring around your cock and a hood on your head."

I could only see Levi's sly smile. "I'm sure she is, Sir."

"We'll see how long her concentration lasts."

Mateo returned to the bag. He rummaged around inside until he drew out a leather set of bondage cuffs along with a leash. *What is he doing?*

My hand kept moving and I glanced down at my page, seeing all of the loose sketches I'd made. I flipped to the next page, knowing I'd fill it up just as quickly.

It was getting harder to focus as I watched them. Mateo brought the cuffs and leash to Levi, clasping them around his wrists behind his back. He paused, his hands settling on Levi's shoulders and massaging them carefully.

"All good?"

"Yes," Levi said. "My shoulder isn't hurting today, but if it strains, I'll tell you."

"Good."

There was something so sweet and so sexy about the check-ins. Mateo was always so good about making sure we were okay, and it never took away from the scene. If anything, it made it hotter because I knew I could trust him.

"You look so fucking good like this," Mateo groaned, his cock pulsing.

He stepped in front of Levi and leaned down. I couldn't see

exactly what he was doing, but I heard the clink of metal against metal.

When he stepped back, the leash was gripped in his hand—and it was attached to the ring around Levi's cock.

My breath hitched. My hand stopped moving. My entire body shivered as desire punched through me.

Holy fuck.

Levi whimpered as Mateo tugged on his cock.

"Turn to the side so she can get a better view," Mateo commanded.

He used the leash to lead him by his cock. Levi groaned as he shifted awkwardly until I had the perfect view of the two of them from the side. My pen met the page, heart pounding as I watched Mateo slap Levi's lips with the head of his cock.

"Open."

Levi immediately did as he asked. Mateo thrust his hips, filling Levi's mouth in a smooth motion that had all three of us moaning. I couldn't help it. Watching them like this was turning me on in a way I'd never imagined before.

Mateo pulled the leash on the cock ring, drawing a whimpering sound from Levi. I adjusted my seated position, squeezing my thighs together. My breaths quickened as I kept drawing them, filling up pages and pages of poses and moments between the two of them.

I could do this for hours. Hours and hours until my hand cramped and vision blurred. Fuck, they were so hot.

"Good," Mateo praised. "God, you suck my cock so well. Take it deeper. There you go. *Good boy.*"

His words were lost to a long groan. Mateo tipped his head back, his hips driving faster, deeper. The sound of his cock pumping into Levi's throat made my thighs squeeze tighter. My hand shook as I imagined being right there on my knees to help.

"Fuck," I whispered.

"What was that?" Mateo called.

"Nothing," I mumbled.

"Losing focus?"

"Not yet." That was such a lie. All three of us knew it, too.

"Really? I bet you're soaking through your panties. Did you wear the set I told you to?"

Of course I had. "Yes."

"Take off your pants while you keep drawing us. I want to see your pussy and how fucking drenched you are for us, Blue. *Now.*"

Dammit. I tossed my sketch pad and pen to the side and unbuttoned my jeans, pushing them over my hips and legs quickly. I kicked them free as I spread my legs, showing Mateo proof that not only had I put on the cherry red lace panties he'd requested, they were in fact *wet* for him and Levi.

"You can't see her, Levi, and it's a shame. She's got her legs spread for me. She's wearing red lace panties, just like in the little fantasy you confessed to me the other night while I was fucking you."

What?! I gasped, staring at the two of them in shock.

Levi moaned in response. His cock throbbed and dripped as he yanked against his cuffs.

"That's right," Mateo huffed. "Avery, pick up your pen and keep drawing. But keep those legs spread. I want to see your pussy while I fuck our man senseless."

Fuck me. His demand only turned me on more. I grabbed my pen and sketch pad and kept my legs spread for him, my strokes shaky as my pen met the page again. I quickly sketched the two of them in their position, a quiet moan escaping as Mateo started to fuck Levi's throat again.

"That's it. Good boy. Fuck, you're taking me so well."

His thrusts turned into a consistent rhythm, music to my

ears. Spit dripped down Levi's chin, making more of a mess the longer Mateo took him.

I wanted to lick it all up.

I rolled my hips at that thought, sucking in another breath. I was so turned on, this was unbearable. I could barely focus. Could barely think.

Mateo dragged his cock back and circled behind Levi, uncuffing him quickly. He gave him a shove, pushing him down onto all fours. "Stay."

"Yes, Sir," Levi gasped.

Mateo released the leash and went back to the kink bag. I was eager to see what he pulled out next. I swallowed hard as I waited, my pen hovering above the page. He knelt down and pulled out a bottle of lube, a couple of condoms, and a leather flogger.

My heart skipped a beat. The scent of leather made my mouth water as he tossed it over his muscled shoulder and stood up. He turned, offering me a soft, knowing smile.

"I don't know how much longer I'll make it," I rasped.

"Your role is the artist, isn't it? Get all your material. We'll have enough energy for you after, I promise."

I believed him. I moaned and spread my legs further for him, enjoying the way his brows furrowed and eyes darkened.

"Okay, well, alternatively I drag you onto this mattress and we fuck you straight into it."

I tipped my chin up. "What if I want to see how long you last? Huh? What then?"

"Oh god," Levi snorted.

Mateo cocked his head and his expression damn near melted me into the floor. For a man I'd leaned on so much for comfort over the last couple years, there was a special sort of whiplash in feeling this sort of dominance from him.

I fucking loved it.

I knew I'd probably end up getting spanked now, but it was worth it.

Plus, I liked getting spanked. Win-win for me.

"I'll come back to you later," Mateo said.

"Is that a threat?"

"It's a promise."

CHAPTER THIRTY-FIVE

I couldn't see a damn thing.

It turned me on, though. Hearing Mateo and Avery go back and forth. Knowing what she was wearing. Feeling my body press into the mattress, my cock and balls still squeezed by the ring around them.

Every muscle in my body was relaxed. I trusted both of them so much that it almost scared me. The more we explored this part of our relationship, the more I learned new things about myself.

Relationship?

That word was haunting me at this point.

Two more weeks. Less than that now. The days were looming, flying by too fast, and I was holding on to every fucking moment.

"Relax," Mateo murmured.

His mustache brushed against my skin as he planted a kiss on my shoulder. He was intuitive. I released a slow breath until the only tension I felt was from the anticipation of not knowing what Mateo planned to do to me next.

Mateo knelt behind me, his hands settling on my hips. I grunted as I heard the jingle of the leash chain and then felt the tug on my cock. It was like constantly being edged, on the verge of coming for him but not quite there.

Not quite yet.

Mateo's lips skated down my back, his mustache soft against my skin. I whimpered as his hands massaged my ass cheeks. He sat back and I could feel him just looking at me.

"What are you doing to me?" I whispered.

"Whatever the fuck I want." Mateo rubbed my right cheek in slow, teasing circles. "Should I ask our artist what she wants?"

All I could do was nod. He let out a soft chuckle.

"What do you want to see, Avery?" he asked.

"Now you're asking me to make decisions? I can barely even think straight."

Mateo laughed like he'd won something. "All right. I already know what I want to do, I just wanted to hear you confirm just how turned on you are."

She mumbled something incomprehensible, and I didn't have a moment to guess what it was before Mateo dragged something down my back.

It took a moment for me to realize what it was. The scent of leather gave it away.

A flogger.

"Stay still for me and relax."

"Yes, Sir."

Mateo steadied his palm on my lower back. I heard the flays against his skin before he brought it down. The impact thumped through me along the right side of my back and I groaned, enjoying the full body feel of it. There was something both hot, painful, and soothing about being flogged. It pleased something deep inside me that had no words and was just a feeling. One I loved.

He brought the flogger down again along the left side of my

ass. I groaned, my muscles tensing slightly. He didn't let me rest, though. In a few swift movements, he flogged my right side, my left, my right—going back and forth over and over. I hissed between my teeth, my cock jerking in desire. Pain flared in my muscles, my skin tender.

It was the good kind of pain. The kind I craved more of. My body wasn't asking me to slow down—it was begging for more.

"More," I whimpered. "Please."

His answer was in the next thudding strike. It was harder, the impact rocking through me, reverberating all the way to my bones. Between the flogger against my body, I heard Avery's soft gasps and whimpers, every sound pushing me closer to coming.

I wasn't going to last. Not like this. There was no fucking way. Between the two of them, I was so wrapped around them that I could feel longing from my balls to my heart.

Mateo kept going until he was satisfied and I was trembling. I heard the flogger hit the ground and breathed deep as his palms spread over my back, massaging me with a gentleness that paired so well with his dominance.

"You did so good for me," he whispered in my ear. The leash jerked the ring around the cock and I gasped. "And now we're going to fuck Avery at the same time. Do you want to be on the mattress or standing above us?"

"Mattress," I said. "Please, Sir."

"Yes. You've been good for me."

He released the leash and uncuffed me, giving me a few moments to roll my shoulders and bask in the fact that I'd been good.

And that I was being rewarded.

Mateo grabbed hold of the hood over my head and pulled it

free. Light flooded my vision and I blinked a few times as my eyes adjusted.

And I immediately turned my head to look at Avery.

Fuck.

Her legs were spread, her pussy covered by a patch of wet red lace. Mateo leaned down and unleashed my cock, and then worked the ring free. The rush was immediate. I'd already been fucking hard, but I swore I was harder now than I'd ever been before.

"Did you get your sketches?" Mateo asked, his tone even, not giving away what he'd whispered into my ear.

She closed her sketchbook. "Yes, Sir."

"Did you prepare the way I asked you to?"

"Yes, Sir."

"How about you show Levi what that means?"

I swallowed hard as I watched her expression. Her cheeks were already pink, her eyes a little glassy. I loved it when she was just a bit nervous, and yet so incredibly turned on. I knew how that felt.

"Show him." Mateo's words were a command this time.

Avery looped her fingers in her panties and pulled them down her long legs, kicking them free. She rolled over onto all fours and reached back, spreading her ass for us and showing me the red plug.

Fuck.

"Have you been wearing that?" I rasped. "The entire time?"

"Yes."

"Fuck," I groaned, my cock throbbing. I looked up at Mateo, tempted to beg for us to do this now.

But I didn't need to. He was just as hard as me, just as fucking needy.

The corner of his mouth lifted. "Strip completely. Put your hair back with your scrunchie. Crawl to Levi."

Avery sat back and pulled her shirt and then her bra free. Her hair was swept up quickly, her blue ends dancing as they whipped into a messy bun. She turned around to face us and smoothed her hands down her body and then back up to her breasts. Her nipples were hard and dark pink and she pinched them, smirking.

"Fuck," I mumbled.

"She's being a brat," Mateo said.

There wasn't a shred of disapproval in his tone, though. He watched her with the same appreciation I had as she smiled and got onto all fours again, crawling across the floor to us.

The second she was within arm's reach, I hauled her close. I sat down, crossing my legs and guiding hers around my waist. Mateo knelt down behind her and grabbed her hair, pulling her head back.

She gasped as I kissed up and down her neck while he scolded her.

"You really think you're going to sit there and taunt me," Mateo muttered. "Teasing us. Mouthing off."

"I can mouth you off."

She squeaked as he yanked her hair again, but then smiled.

"You know," Mateo said. "I told Levi that we'd fuck you at the same time together. And I'm going to fulfill that promise after we take care of this."

My brows shot up as I met his gaze over her shoulder. Whatever he had planned now was going to be hot—and I was curious.

What did *punishment* look like to him?

"Take care of what?" Avery asked. "I've done everything you asked, haven't I?"

Mateo pulled her hair again, and her smile grew wider.

"Keep her here," he said roughly. "You can fuck her if you want, but she's not allowed to come."

"*What?*" Avery rasped.

"You fucking heard me."

Mateo met my gaze again and raised a brow in challenge. He held my gaze for a moment, then smirked as he walked over to the kink bag, leaving the two of us to our own devices.

Avery wrinkled her nose but then looked at me, waiting for direction.

My hands gripped her hips and I laid back on the mattress, putting her on top of me. My cock slid against her pussy and she moaned. She was driving me fucking wild already.

Flipping from submissive to dominant wasn't as hard as I thought it was going to be. I'd expected it to feel weird, but with Avery, it just felt right.

There was a very devious part of me that enjoyed aiding Mateo in her punishment.

"Take my cock," I said. "I want you to take every fucking inch."

Her hands planted on my chest, her eyes fluttering as she leaned forward, lifting enough so that she could guide my cock to her entrance. Heat gripped me as she sank down, doing exactly as I had asked her to.

It took every ounce of control to not immediately come. I'd already been edged for so long that it was torture, but I wanted to save it. I wanted to save it until she was right on the edge herself, and then I was going to pull out, and come all over her.

"*Fuck. Oh my god.*"

Every sound that she made was fucking perfect. Every single movement burned into my mind. My eyes fluttered, and I held onto her hips as I thrust up, needing to fuck her. Needing to breed her.

"*Levi,*" she whined.

I wrapped my arms around her, pulling her close to my chest as I started to fuck her. I didn't hold back. I needed this. I had already been so good for Mateo, and she was my prize. That little thought was almost enough to make me come again, and I sunk my teeth into my bottom lip, the pain grounding me.

Not yet. Not yet, I repeated in my head.

Mateo straddled my legs, the hemp rope dangling from his hands. He looked down with a smile, and I held his gaze as my cock slid in and out of her.

"Pin her arms behind her back."

"Yes, Sir," I said.

Avery writhed against me, her mouth right next to my ear. I moved her wrists behind her back, holding them in place as she whimpered.

Mateo leaned down, taking over her hands. I moved mine out of the way, gripping the backs of her thighs as she took my cock. She sank her teeth into my shoulder, biting me hard enough that I gasped.

But I didn't tell her to stop. I fucking loved it when she bit me. Our feral girlfriend was a vampire and I loved seeing her mark on me.

"There we go," I grunted. "Keep taking that cock, baby. I can feel you squeezing me. You're doing so good."

"I'm so close," she whimpered.

"*Stop.*"

Mateo's command was harsh and final.

Every muscle of mine seized up as I froze, a long groan leaving me as I stilled her body. Avery kept trying to move, but I tightened my grip until she couldn't.

"No," she cried. "But I'm so close. I want to come. Please let me come."

"You haven't earned it." She couldn't see his smirk or the way his eyes danced with amusement. He was getting off on this. "Hold her still."

"I'll try," I rasped.

It was fucking hard. My cock was still buried deep inside her. I could feel every fucking movement.

And then she started to flex.

"Avery," I growled. "Stop it."

She smiled against my neck.

Evil. Pure evil.

"Avery," I groaned. "*Stop.*"

Her inner walls kept milking me. Clenching my cock, pulsing around me with every intentional movement.

Mateo finished tying her wrists and then slapped her ass. She squealed, her body bowing, but I held her tighter. He smacked her again and again until I felt like I was wrestling a damn alligator.

"Brat," he said as he leaned down, kissing her shoulder. "Stop clenching."

"You can't stop me," she rasped.

And she did it again.

"Avery," I growled. "I'm about to pull out of you and bend you over my fucking knee."

"Do it then, if you can't handle me."

Mateo and I made eye contact.

A silent agreement was made.

He slid his arms around her waist and lifted her off my cock. I immediately sat up as he rolled her onto the mattress, the two of us working in tandem to put her in a position that worked.

Her ass ended up over the top of my thighs and Mateo straddled one of my legs and one of hers, trapping her in place, and spreading her just enough that her pussy was easy to access.

Between the two of us, there was no escape. Especially not with her hands behind her back.

"Want a paddle?" Mateo asked.

"Fuck no. This is a bare-handed job."

CHAPTER THIRTY-SIX

Avery was pushing us to the edge on purpose. The thing was, it was working. But she was now trapped between us, and there was no escape. Not until I said so. I intended to keep her here until she was a begging mess.

I slid my fingers against her pussy, feeling how fucking wet she was. *Drenched.* Her folds were slick as I worked two fingers inside her, keeping an eye on her ass as Levi warmed up each cheek with his palm.

I loved seeing him like this. Slightly unhinged and needing to put her in her place.

She looked really good bent over like this for us. She cried out as I slid my fingers in and out, pumping them like a cock. I could feel her clenching around me, but it wasn't going to do anything but drive herself wild. There was no escaping us. That was one of the best parts. I'd watched her sit there and draw us while I put Levi on his knees, while she teased us with her legs spread and that fucking wet pair of red lace panties.

But now here she was.

Exactly where we wanted her.

Levi's palm struck her ass hard. The sound of his skin against hers rang through the gallery, her breath hitching as she was forced to drape over his thighs. Her wrists tied behind her back, the rope digging into her skin. She continued to rock her body, trying to wriggle free.

Eventually, she would give up. Eventually, she would completely give in.

This time, he spanked her other cheek. She cried out, but he didn't give her a moment to rest. His palm smacked each side of her ass, going until her cries grew sharp enough we both took note.

He eased up, rubbing each side, massaging the pain away until it was just a dull ache. Her skin was shades of pink and red, and if he kept going, we both knew there would have been a couple of marks.

We both knew that she would love that.

"Every time you spank her, I swear she gets wetter," I whispered, thrusting my fingers harder.

Her ass wiggled as she mumbled our names repeatedly. Her wrists tugged against the ropes. Levi pinched one of the red marks he'd left on her ass and her voice filled the room, her head tossing to the side.

"Fuck!" she yelled.

"Too much?" he asked.

"No. No. Maybe. No. I want more. I'm so close."

I sped up the pumping of my fingers and added a third. She humped her hips, her voice muffled as she moaned into the blankets. Levi turned his head to watch, his eyes glazed over with lust.

My cock was angry at me at this point. I was so fucking hard, it almost hurt.

But I didn't want Avery to come yet.

"So close," she whimpered. "So close."

Levi was softening up to her. I could tell by the way he looked at her.

I pulled my fingers free and she cursed, turning her head to glare over her shoulder. It'd been awhile since I'd earned a glare from her, and in this context, I loved it. Her looking like she wanted to stab me turned me on.

"Mateo," she growled.

"Yes, my love?"

"Fuck you."

"Not yet, darling."

"And fuck you too, Levi."

He chuckled and replied by spanking her again.

"When you start behaving, you'll get rewarded," I said. "Or I can put you in a hog tie and Levi and I can fuck each other while you watch. And you can lay there and get nothing."

Her head tossed, but instead of insulting me again, her body relaxed. She moaned as she draped herself over Levi.

"Are you going to be good for us, Avery?" I whispered.

She was quiet for a moment, but then she wriggled her butt. "Yes. I'll be good. I promise."

I wasn't quite sure I believed her. I smiled anyway, though. Mostly because she was so fucking cute. Sexy, too, but *cute*.

For a moment, it hit me that I was really doing this with one of my best friends. That we'd crossed that line and the world hadn't ended. That we'd taken a leap, and now here she was, bent over for me and Levi.

I swallowed hard, trying not to think about what came *after*. Not after this scene or after tonight, but after Levi.

That pain swallowed me whole. I did my best to push it away and recenter myself, drawing in a breath to focus. It was something I'd deal with later, I reminded myself.

Besides, he was here with us now.

And that's what mattered.

I adjusted my body so that I was next to Levi and able to

spread Avery's thighs apart. I leaned down, planting gentle kisses against the hot marks blooming on her ass cheeks.

Levi sucked in a breath. "I don't know if I can keep holding out. I need to come."

"You will soon."

His eyes fluttered, his cheeks flushed as he watched me push my tongue inside her. Avery whimpered, her hips rolling, as I pushed my tongue deeper, getting a taste of her. It wasn't enough though. I wanted her to sit on my face and suffocate me.

I gave her ass a slap. "It's time to take a ride."

"A ride?"

"Yeah. On my mustache."

Levi chuckled as he let her up. I laid back on the bed, the three of us doing our best to stay on the mattress. It was almost impossible. We really needed a king-sized bed and days to spend in it.

I wanted Avery to be as wet as possible before the two of us fucked her. And I wanted to make her come with my mouth before that happened.

She stood up, looking down at me, unsure. "I don't know . . ."

"Sit on his face," Levi said as he knelt between my knees.

"I don't want to hurt him—"

"Avery," I snorted. "Sit on my mustache, baby. *Now*."

Levi didn't give her another moment to hesitate. Instead, he guided her over my body, and gave the backs of her knees, a tug, knocking her off balance. She squealed, but I caught her, lowering her down with ease. She straddled my head, her pussy right on my mouth.

But she still wasn't sitting all the way down yet.

I pulled her full weight down, burying my mouth against her cunt. My tongue lapped against her clit, and she immediately moaned, relaxing reluctantly. I could tell she was trying to hold some of her weight, but with her hands still tied behind her back it was almost impossible.

"Good girl," Levi praised. "Ride his face, baby. You look so fucking hot right now."

His voice was lost to the sounds she made as I fucked her with my tongue. She started to rock against me.

Levi's calloused hand closed around my cock.

I was in heaven. Truly. Pleasure shot through me as he stroked me, and then the heat of his mouth wrapped around the head like silk.

My head was spinning as the taste of her filled my mouth. I lapped at her, wishing I didn't need to breathe. Even so, I only took in a breath here and there, dedicated to making her orgasm.

It didn't take too long before her movements became jerky and her hoarse cry hit my ears. She tensed, going still as her orgasm wrapped around her, demanding more. More and more. More pleasure and more desire and need and everything pleasurable.

Levi kept sucking my cock, his grunts adding vibrations along my shaft. I thrust my hips up and he took me deeper.

I'd made him wait long enough. I lifted Avery up and pushed him back on the bed so that he was laying flat. I tugged the ropes around her wrists, freeing her so that she could plant her hands on his shoulders.

"Take his cock," I demanded.

"Yes, Sir," she whispered.

Levi's eyes fluttered as she slowly sank down on him, pausing as she tried to adjust. "I feel so full," she whimpered. "The plug . . ."

"Fuck. I forgot about that," he groaned.

"Keep going," I encouraged. "At your own pace."

She huffed as she worked his cock inside her. Even without the plug, it was a challenge to take all of him. But with that added fullness to her ass, I knew it made it even more so.

And made it even hotter too.

I stroked my cock as I watched her pussy spread around him, licking her off my lips.

"Fuck," Levi gasped. "Fuck. She feels so good. I needed her."

"I know you did," I murmured.

I rolled to the side and reached for the kink bag, dragging it closer. I pulled out the bottle of lube and a condom, tearing open the foil and pulling it on quickly.

I needed to be inside her.

I needed to know what it'd feel like to take her at the same time as Levi.

Avery moaned as I pushed her down against him, her head resting on his chest. I slowly pulled the plug free and set it to the side, studying her ass and how fucking hot she looked right now.

Was I dreaming? I'd thought about this for so long. *Fuck.*

I poured a generous amount of lube on my cock and then on her hole, working it around the rim and then using my fingers to push it inside her too. She whimpered as I prepped her for my cock, wondering if she'd be able to take me.

"This will be a lot," I said. "Between the two of us, if you need to stop, or need me to slow down, or need us to do anything—you tell us. Okay?"

"Okay," she said. "I promise. I've never done anything like this before."

"You're in good hands," Levi whispered.

That, she was. I positioned myself behind her, guiding the head of my cock to her. I nudged her entrance, watching as the two of them went very still.

"Relax," I said. "And for the love of god, don't do kegels."

She giggled, but thankfully, didn't do kegels. I slowly pushed inside her, and Levi moaned.

"I can fucking feel you," he hissed. "Holy shit."

I wasn't even halfway in yet, and it was a tight fucking fit. Avery took in several deep breaths, her muscles tensing until she remembered to make them relax. I waited, giving her time to adjust to the size of my cock alongside Levi's.

"You're doing so well, baby," Levi crooned. "You feel so fucking good."

She nodded, letting out a breathless, *"Thank you."*

He kept murmuring to her.

"You're such a liar, Levi," I huffed as I gave her another inch.

"Liar?" he choked out.

"Yeah. You always say you're bad at talking. And you're not. You're really, really not."

Avery gasped as she took more of me. Levi rubbed the back of her head, meeting my gaze over her shoulder.

He smiled.

It was a really wholesome smile despite the filthy, hot things we were doing. Sweet. Charming.

And dammit. Dammit, I was *falling* for him. And he was leaving us. *Soon.*

I swallowed hard as I kept sliding into Avery. I blinked and realized she'd taken all of me.

All of him.

"Fuck," I whispered. "You did it, Blue."

"I don't want to be congratulated, I want to be fucked," she groaned. "I want to come again."

She'd certainly earned it. Levi wrapped his arms around her and was the first to move, his cock pulling back slightly before pushing in deeper.

The three of us groaned together, even from the small movement. My eyes fluttered shut as I tried to take it slow.

"I'm okay," Avery rasped. "I'm good. I'm good."

She was the one to move this time. She shifted, our cocks pulling out and then pushing back. My hands held onto her hips as I started to thrust. Levi did too. We found a rhythm, one that was going to make me come sooner than later, but I didn't mind.

We were all past the point of trying to hold back. Something snapped inside me and I groaned, fucking her harder.

"Good girl," I huffed. "Fuck. You're taking us so well. So well."

Levi's thrust turned faster. Needier. I was already on the edge, but with the way I could feel his cock sliding in and out of her, I wasn't going to last too long.

Her next cry was sharper and her muscles tensed. Avery gasped as her head tipped back, her nails digging into Levi's shoulders as she squeezed the two of us.

Feeling her come while we were inside her was what sent me over the edge. I cursed under my breath as I slammed into her one last time, coming so hard that I felt the orgasm wrap around my entire body, pleasure rushing through me.

"Fuck," Levi rasped. "I can't—"

His words were clipped as he came, a long groan leaving him as he tightened his arms around her, and then *me* too. I always forgot how fucking long his arms were, but he managed to hug the both of us as he came inside her, filling up her pussy with every drop of his cum.

The three of us were panting. I pressed my face against Avery's back, breathing in the scent of her. My thoughts were barely able to form, every single part of me fully relaxed and . . .

Happy.

Really, really happy.

"That was as hot as I thought it was going to be," Avery whispered.

I nodded, savoring the moment.

"If you ever want to sell the art you make from tonight, I want it," Levi said.

A soft laugh shook her body. "Like I said. It'll never be for sale."

CHAPTER THIRTY-SEVEN

I knelt down in the dirt as I angled my lens, holding my breath as I tried not to move. A Montezuma quail perched just a few feet away from me, the high desert mountains rising up behind it, sunlight haloing his mottled feathers. The little guy was entirely too cute for his own good.

I'd woken up early so I could get out to the Davis Mountains before the sun came up. I wasn't the only soul in the park, but it felt like it. I'd only spotted the occasional ranger and then an ambitious couple hiking down the trail together. My backpack was packed with snacks, water, and a first aid kit just in case. I'd sent Mateo and Avery a good morning text to let them know I was shooting pictures today.

I snapped a few shots, my muscles straining as I tried to stay still. With all of the physical challenges hockey had, I was finding that photography had its own set of them. Sometimes if there was an angle I envisioned, I had to twist a certain way to get it.

Worth it. I got a few more pictures and then raised my gaze, smiling as I took in the scenery.

I still wasn't sure I was any good at this. But, when I was taking pictures and out in nature, I felt a sense of happiness. Of peace. And since my time here was winding down, I wanted to try to savor it.

My knees protested as I got up and stretched. The quail darted away and I chuckled as it disappeared into the shrubs that dotted the slope.

Maybe I was already adapting to the heat again, but it wasn't even eighty-five out yet, and it felt *cool*. I held up my camera, looking through the lens and scanning everything, snapping more pictures.

I wished this could be my life.

Why can't it be? That was the thought that was plaguing me.

Beyond Mateo and Avery, I was discovering just how much I loved this place. It was different from how I remembered it growing up. If anything, it was more boring in some ways. Quaint. Quiet.

And I loved that.

I loved the people. Even the old cranky lady that shot me a dirty look every time she saw me in town. I loved how everyone was in each other's business, even though that was inconvenient. I loved the landscapes and the beauty of the Chihuahuan desert.

It felt right.

But was it?

My phone rattled in my pocket and I pulled it out absent-mindedly, answering as I kept my gaze trained on the clouds that were turning a shade of blushing pink that reminded me of Avery.

"Hello?"

"Levi."

Dammit. I swallowed hard and looked down at my feet. This was what I got for not looking at my screen before answering.

"Mom," I said. "How's it going?"

She let out that sigh. The *mom* sigh. The disappointed one. It activated some sort of wall inside me, every brick going up in place as I tried to navigate whatever the hell she was about to say.

It wasn't that she and I were on bad terms. We'd never been on bad terms before. That would require her caring about me outside of the small parts of her life she included me in.

"How about you tell me? You know, I'm shocked you even picked up. I've been calling. Texting."

"Sorry I missed you. I've been keeping my phone off. It's been a lot lately." I hesitated, rubbing the back of my neck. "I guess you saw the news."

"I did. Weeks ago. Then couldn't get a hold of you."

Well, fuck. "I'm sorry. I'm doing fine."

"Did something happen?"

"Not exactly." I pressed my lips together, looking back out at the mountains. They grounded me. And my words flowed out before my thoughts caught up. "I just . . . I don't want it anymore."

The silence was deafening.

"What do you mean, you don't *want it* anymore?"

So she was definitely not going to be in support of me retiring from the league. That much was clear. I'd guessed she might react this way, but it still stung.

"I'm burned out," I said firmly. "I'm sick of social media. I'm sick of the pressure. I'm tired of eating like a machine. I'm tired of having to train. My body hurts all the time."

"Well, I hate to break it to you, kid, but that's part of getting older."

"It goes beyond that." My jaw tightened. "Did you call me just to berate me?"

"I called you to try to talk some sense into you. I heard

284

you're in Texas, of all places. Whynot? What the hell is in Whynot?"

"Well, it was my home in the summers." *While you remarried and had two other kids you loved and didn't get annoyed by.*

"But your home is up here. You could have visited me. You never do. And if you didn't want to see me, you could have gone to the lake house. Going back to the middle of nowhere, to where your dad used to be, just seems unlike you."

I understood that it probably hurt a little to know I'd picked coming out here over visiting her. If I were my own absent parent, maybe I'd be confused too.

"I needed to escape. I've met a couple of people here . . ."

I trailed off, thinking about Mateo and Avery. How did I describe *that* to her? That I was polyamorous? That I'd met two people I was thinking about moving to Texas for? That I was very much considering ignoring my agent for the rest of my life and fading into nonexistence? That maybe, just maybe, the idea of calling Texas home made me feel *excited.*

"I don't know. I'm kind of thinking about moving to Texas." My voice was a soft whisper, like I was confessing something. In a way, I was. I hadn't said this to anyone. "Why not?"

Her laugh was grating. "You can't be serious. Surely not, Levi. You've worked so hard to get to where you are. The countless hours I put in taking you to practice. Driving you to games. Spending money on your gear."

"This isn't about you, though," I said. "It's not about you having a hockey star for a son. It's about you having a son who is happy."

More silence. Long enough that I started to wonder if the cell service had dropped. Hell, I kind of hoped it had—

"All right, I'm sorry. I'm coming on a little strong, aren't I?"

"A little," I said tightly.

"I'm sorry. I was worried about you and when I didn't hear from you, I started to worry even more."

"I really am sorry about that," I said. "I didn't mean to ignore you. I've just been having a hard time. I've been ignoring almost everyone. Even my agent."

She laughed. "Oh god. I'm sure she hates that."

"She does. She's threatened to drag me back to Minnesota if I try to stay."

"Wouldn't put it past her." She let out a long sigh. "Listen. You've worked for years for this, Levi. And we both know most hockey players are out before forty. You're so close to that. You could ride it out for the next couple years and get those sponsorships. Set yourself up for the future."

"I've got plenty of money already," I said. "And I've been smart with it."

"I know. I just don't want you to do something you'll regret for the rest of your life."

The question wasn't if I'd regret walking away from my career—it was if I would regret letting Avery and Mateo go.

"I met someone," I whispered. "Two someones."

"Two?"

"Yeah."

"Like two people you're interested in?"

"Yeah," I said.

"Well. If it's meant to be, they'll still be there when you finish your career out. And if it's meant to be, they'll understand."

That didn't help at all. I closed my eyes. "I've got to go, Mom. I'm at a park taking pictures."

She hummed. "All right. Well, I love you. Whatever you decide."

"Thanks," I muttered. "Love you too."

I hung up and stared at my phone.

A text from Avery popped up.

> Avery: Good morning, Mr. Sexy Broody Man. Don't forget the dinner is tonight with everyone at my place :) You should stay over after. Mateo too . . .

> I'll be there ;)

I wanted to soak up every second I could with her and Mateo before Monday.

CHAPTER THIRTY-EIGHT

Today was a test on how good I was at keeping secrets.

I didn't feel that good, to be honest. Sick, even. I wished dinner with my brothers and best friends was something I could call in sick for, but it wasn't. They'd all show up at my doorstep and insist we watch a movie, just to keep me company —because that's how much they loved me. Germs be damned, we were having dinner together.

There was no escaping it. The whole reason our group was doing this was because of my falling out with my mom.

A text came through from our new group chat, titled: *Why NOT make a new chat?*

> Austin: I'm bringing BBQ
>
> Evie: I thought we agreed on sandwiches
>
> Austin: BBQ goes on sandwiches
>
> Evie: it doesn't because we all know you mean you got potato salad
>
> Austin: hey now
>
> Evie: Am I wrong?

Mateo: You're not wrong, I saw the potato salad in his fridge

Dallas: I got bread and lettuce for like turkey sandwiches . . .

June: I made enchiladas

Evie: Dammit, June LOL

Mateo: we can all bring whatever we want and it'll be great. Maybe missing some things like veggies, but great regardless

Dallas: hey, I said I got lettuce

Austin: I don't think that counts, tbh

Levi: Do all of you always text this much?

I snorted and tossed my phone down on my bed, studying myself in the mirror. I'd picked out a sleeveless lavender eyelet dress with a denim shirt tied at my waist. I folded the sleeves up my arm and rolled my shoulders, wondering if I was really going to be able to act like I wasn't completely in love with Levi and Mateo.

At what point did I tell my brothers the truth? Should I even bother if Levi was leaving?

If. I wished it was an if. I wished he liked it more here. That this place felt like his home.

But I couldn't ask him to stay.

Mateo was in the same boat. The two of us had ended up in this small town for different reasons, and neither of us could imagine trying to talk someone like Levi into staying. He had a job and a big career and money and a home in a state that wasn't Texas—all good things. Even with H-E-B and the toasted nuts from Buccee's and delicious Tex-Mex food, I knew it wasn't enough to keep him here.

I forced a smile.

I would be convincing. I had to be. I could play pretend, right? I could act like I was *totally fine* with Levi leaving in eight days, and my oldest brother not knowing I was dating his best friends behind his back.

Right, right, right.

Except over the last couple of years, I'd gotten really bad at pretending to be totally fine. Clearly—given I still hadn't talked to my mom. And frankly, I wasn't going to until she came to me first. *If* she came to me first.

When did everything get so goddamn hard? I tucked my hair behind my ears and ruffled my bangs, pressing my lips into a hard line.

My ass cheeks were a little sore. Every time I sat down, I thought about being spanked by Mateo and Levi. Thought about them sharing me between them, about me taking their cocks at the same time.

I wasn't ashamed to admit I wanted more. I was kinky, I already knew that. But actually getting to have all the kinky sex I'd always wanted? Made it even better and hotter. All of the sketches from our night in the art gallery were slowly turning into a series of paintings I had no business working on, but couldn't stop myself from doing.

For my eyes only.

Another text lit up my phone screen. I leaned over and smiled.

> Levi: I'm walking over. I'll keep my hands to myself . . .

> You don't need to until everyone else is here

Levi's knock echoed through my house and I was at the door in seconds. He leaned against the doorframe with a slight scowl, looking stupidly handsome and rugged and—

"I had a dream this morning that I woke up with you inside me," I blurted out.

His brows shot up and he stepped into the foyer, caging me against the wall as he kicked the door shut. "Oh really?"

"Yeah," I squeaked.

"What a wonderfully vivid dream." He leaned down, his mouth brushing against mine. "I dreamed that Mateo and I fucked you together in your bed. You took my cock down your throat and he took your pussy."

"Did you?" I gasped.

"No. But I've been fantasizing about that."

"We should—*fuck*." My words faltered as his lips sucked the tender part of my neck. A shiver worked up my spine. "*Levi*."

"We should fuck?"

"No—yes."

"We don't have time." He chuckled as another knock on the door interrupted us.

My mouth dropped and I glared, cheeks crimson. "Did you plan that?"

"No. Your brothers just have awful timing."

He stole one more quick kiss and I covered my mouth as he turned to open the door, and I took the opportunity to flee down the hall because I was *not* that good of an actor. I needed a glass of cold water and a fucking horny tranquilizer to get through tonight.

I opened the fridge as my brothers' voices echoed from the front door, followed by a few laughs. And then there was Mateo's voice rising above theirs—more laughter.

I pulled a pitcher of water out of the fridge and downed a full glass right as Austin came down the hall holding a foil-covered tray. The scent of barbecue filled my kitchen, and while we'd all agreed on regular sandwiches, I was glad he brought something aside from the potato salad he'd teased. He smiled at me, completely oblivious to *everything*.

"Hey," he said. "How's it going?"

"Good," I said, giving him a side hug. My gaze darted down the hall to where Dallas and Levi stood chatting. Mateo opened the door, and thank god—Evie and June came in holding stuff too. "I see you brought real barbecue."

"Of course I did."

"Did you grill it up?"

"Yep. Mateo has the potato salad. I think Levi was surprised I bought more. Dallas brought a few extra things. I think we're all going to have too much food."

"Probably. But then we all get leftovers. Does it need to go in the oven to stay heated?"

"Nah." He put it on the counter as Evie sauntered down the hall.

As always, she looked *perfect*. Today, she wore a white sundress, and her blonde hair was pulled up into a casual chignon. Was it possible to feel proud of a friend for being so damn sexy? Especially when it was hotter than a pit of lava outside?

Austin glanced up at her. "Hey, Evie."

"Oh good, you brought more," she said as she put three bags down on the counter. "I was worried there for a second."

"What did you bring?" I snatched the bags like a gremlin and took a peek. "She loves us," I sighed as I spotted an apple pie, a fresh salad, and paper plates.

"She loves *you*," Austin corrected, his gaze still lingering on her.

"Sure do." She tucked a strand of hair behind her ear, diamonds gleaming under my kitchen lights. "All right. Avery, I'm taking over the kitchen. Go sit with Mateo or Levi and look pretty."

My eyes nearly popped out of my head and her cheeks flushed as she realized what she said. Austin chuckled, though. "I'd rather her not do that with my best friends."

Evie rolled her eyes and the second of tension melted away. "Whatever, Austin. *Dallas!*"

Her voice rang through my house with an air of command that had even me jumping. My other brother materialized with Levi, Mateo, and June in tow. Mateo smirked at me as I met his gaze, and I narrowed my eyes.

"You and Austin need to set up the tables outside."

"We're eating outside?" Dallas sighed. "In this heat?"

"There's no way we're all fitting in here," I said.

"It'll cool down," June said. "It'll only be ninety in an hour or so."

Levi shook his head. "Too hot."

"You won't melt, Minnesota," Mateo said, his arms crossed and mustache permanently in line with his crooked smirk.

They were standing too close together. I wasn't sure if Dallas or Austin noticed it, but June and Evie sure did.

June cast me a side glance. "Let's just set the tables up in here. Someone turn on music."

It was a mess. Our little group was a tangle of chaos as we set everything up, and I did my best to interact with Mateo and Levi like a normal human being. One who hadn't had them both inside her at the same time.

Evie and June were the best wing-women. Any time one of them caught me being weird, they'd elbow me. Or interrupt. Or do *something* to run interference.

It took about half an hour, but we'd rearranged my living room to squeeze together two card tables with fold out chairs. They squeaked every time one of us moved, the tables were more wobbly than a newborn foal, but we made it work. Our seating arrangement was pretty good, too. Austin, Levi, and

Dallas sat on one side, and I was between June and Mateo. Evie was on the other end.

With Levi being right across from me, it was hard not to stare at him. I kept catching myself focusing on the way the corner of his mouth lifted when he smiled, or the heat in his eyes when they met mine or landed on Mateo.

"Thank you all for doing this," I said. "I know it's in the middle of the week and we all have work in the morning. But I'm glad we made this happen."

"Me too," June said, smiling at me. "I needed it."

"As did I," Austin said. "Even though I definitely put off work to be here."

"Uh-huh," Dallas said, shaking his head. "You gotta stop working so much. You're turning gray already."

"That's been proven to be a genetic thing," Austin quipped, not hiding his tired smile.

"It's also been proven to be a thing when you work sixty hours a week," Mateo said. "Too much."

"Well, someone has to do it," Austin said. "Levi, when are you leaving Whynot? Soon, right?"

His shoulders tensed. I couldn't help but look at him.

"Why? Trying to get rid of me?" he snorted, avoiding looking at me or Mateo.

"Of course not. I've just lost track of time. The last few weeks have flown by," Austin said.

"You should stay," Evie said casually.

"You absolutely shouldn't stay," Dallas laughed. "This place has nothing to offer you. I mean, I love it. I love our community. But you've worked so hard for your career, that would be such a wild change. Just make it your vacation spot and come visit us more often."

"I think he should stay," June said.

Levi opened his mouth to speak, but no words came out.

Mateo stiffened next to me, his hand sliding under the table and settling on my knee. No one else could see it, but just feeling the weight of his hand calmed me just enough so I could breathe.

"My flight is Monday," he said. "I'll have to drive my car to the rental place in Odessa and then I'll be heading back to Minnesota. My agent has a meeting set up for us the next day."

"Any idea what you want to do?" Dallas asked. "I don't know how the hockey world works. Honestly, I don't even know anything about the sport itself."

"I'm not sure yet," Levi said. "My shoulder has been feeling a lot better now that it's been rested. But . . . I don't know if I want to go back."

"You've worked so hard for it," Austin said.

"He can change his mind though," I said more firmly than I meant to.

Austin raised a brow and zeroed in on me. "I mean, yeah. He can. But that's like you giving up your gallery."

It wasn't like that *at all*. Did Austin even know Levi? "I think it's different. If he's not passionate about hockey anymore, then why do it?"

"The money? The fact that he's at the height of his career?"

"Okay," Mateo interjected. "This is none of our business. Levi should do what's best for himself. He *will* do what's best for himself."

Austin shrugged his shoulders and I wanted to launch myself across the flimsy table and choke him. And no, I couldn't just let it go.

"I just think Austin needs to think about what Levi is saying before trying to pressure him into doing something that he doesn't want," I said.

Austin scoffed. "Why do you even care, Avery? It's not like you know him."

"I know him better than you do."

Mateo's grip tightened on my knee. The room was so silent that I could have heard a pin drop. *Fuck, fuck, fuck.*

"I just mean you aren't listening," I mumbled. My cheeks were hotter than an iron. I looked away, looking at June and pleading for some sort of interjection.

Evie was the one to rescue us. "I have some gossip."

Everyone leaned in immediately, because she always had the best gossip.

Mateo's grip didn't lessen though.

And neither did the feeling that I'd just somehow fucked everything up.

CHAPTER THIRTY-NINE

"I'll walk you home."

I almost told Austin to fuck off, but restrained myself. After dinner, the rest of the evening was fun. Evie really did have the best Whynot gossip. I'd heard more about a couple of old women than I'd ever wanted to, but I also couldn't stop listening. It was like I craved the words of the grapevine.

Dinner flew by, and then we'd all settled in for a card game Dallas brought. I'd lost every single round, but I also hadn't really been trying.

I felt the clock ticking. Next Monday was breathing down my neck. I'd gotten my flight confirmation text, the Airbnb notification that my stay was coming to an end, and the Google Calendar invite from Robin about our meeting.

My decision loomed in front of me, and Austin was making it worse.

"He's across the street," Avery said, giving her brother a dirty look. "He'll find his way."

Austin kissed the top of her head and ruffled her hair. "Sleep well."

We were the last two out the door. Evie and June had

already headed home. Honestly, I felt like I owed the two of them for running interference all night. Having June and Evie on the inside was the best thing the three of us idiots had done, because they'd kept it all from imploding.

Mateo had offered to give Dallas a ride back to his place. On their way out, Mateo hadn't looked at me. He wouldn't look at me.

I didn't blame him. Part of me wished he and Avery would choose to hate me for leaving. It would be easier for them to just eject me from their lives than to deal with this awful, sticky feeling.

"Ready to head out?" Austin asked.

"Yep." I held Avery's gaze for a moment and smiled. "Goodnight."

Austin clapped his hand on my shoulder and led me out the door before she said anything else. He was *steering* me away from his sister.

Had I given something away?

It was hard not to look at Avery. It was hard to act like I didn't want her. And to make matters worse, I'd definitely found myself staring at Mateo instead. There were no rules against us flirting with each other.

The thing was, what she said at dinner had stuck with me. She had no reason to defend me and my choices, and yet she had.

The street was quiet. Stars speckled the dark skies above, the air still and thick with heat. Our footsteps echoed as we walked toward my place.

"What is it?" I finally asked as we hit my doorstep.

Austin pressed his lips together, his hands settling on his hips. "You know Avery is off-limits, right? You're leaving in just a few days."

So maybe staring at Mateo hadn't worked. "I'm aware."

"It's just . . ."

I raised a brow. I wasn't saying anything else though.

"The way she looks at you. The way she defended you. I know what a crush looks like. What's going on?"

I swallowed hard and met his gaze.

I'd known Austin for almost my entire life. Countless summers spent together. Countless hours of conversation over the years. Even with the omissions he'd made about his life recently, I still knew him.

He knew me.

Do I tell him? Do I tell him that I love—

"Because you wouldn't be right for her."

Every muscle in my body tensed. "What do you mean?"

"You wouldn't be right for her. Even if you stayed. Which I know you're not going to, otherwise you would have mentioned it by now. But you . . ."

"I *what*?" My voice was deadly calm, even as my heart thumped against my ribs. Wild. Angry. Hurt.

"I mean, your relationship history isn't the best," he said awkwardly. "You've never really been in a serious relationship. Anyone you date has to deal with the media frenzy that follows. You're away from home a lot during the season."

My throat felt like it was closing up. "Is that right?" I said softly.

"I'm just saying. You wouldn't be right for her."

"What about Mateo?"

"*Mateo*?" Austin's eyes widened, and if anything, they hardened even more. "I mean, absolutely not."

"Absolutely not right for him either?"

"No. I mean, he . . . He deserves someone that'll be here."

"Right." I reached back for the door knob and gripped so hard I wondered if an indent of my hand would be left behind.

"But you never answered me. Is there something I need to know about?"

"I'm leaving Monday, Austin. You have nothing to worry about."

That reply, while still not quite an answer, seemed to be good enough for him.

CHAPTER FORTY

> The spreader bars are taunting me.

> Avery: Sir, aren't you at WORK?

> What's your point?

> Levi: Are the spreader bars at the station with you?

> Nope. They're taunting me all the way from my house. I'll be home around seven tonight

> Avery: See you then ;)

> Levi: I'll bring dinner

"What are you smiling about?"

I damn near jumped out of my gear. Maria was standing in the driveway of the station, her brows raised as she studied me.

I'd been actively avoiding her. Mostly because out of all the people that knew me, my cousin always had this ability to see through bullshit. It was a talent. A terrifying one I did not want to endure.

"You scared me." I dropped my phone in my pocket and crossed my arms.

She crossed them right back. "You've been avoiding me."

Dammit. "No . . ."

"*Yes.*"

"Maybe."

"Why?"

I blew out a breath and leaned against the fire engine. The sun was shining bright, per usual. Water ran down the concrete and it glistened, along with the bright red of the truck. I'd been washing the damn thing because it was that time of the month, but it was an annoying job for one guy.

I raked my fingers through my waves. I wore my cargo work pants, suspenders, and my Whynot Fire Department T-shirt— one I probably needed to retire soon given how much I'd worn it. But the town had a budget, and custom shirts were fucking expensive.

"I can't tell you," I said.

"Sure you can." Maria smiled. "I'm too busy to be part of the Whynot clique."

"It's not a—"

"It is. It's fine. I don't care. But what I do care about is one of my only family members out here avoiding me. Abuela asked if you were still alive the other day. She asked if she needed to call your parents and complain."

I drew in a steady breath and released it. "I'll come over for dinner next week." *When Levi is gone.*

She narrowed her eyes. "What's that face for? What's wrong?"

"Do you have to be up in my business? Don't you have a library to run?"

"I'm on my way there now," she said, shouldering her canvas tote.

"Is that full of smut?"

Now, her glare turned wicked. "Do you want to die today?"

"I'm not judging."

"Whatever. It is, in fact, full of smut." She shrugged. "If you're not going to tell me, fine. I just wanted to check on you."

"I'm okay," I said. "I . . . I've been seeing someone. Two people, actually."

"You're cheating?!"

"No," I laughed. "No. Of course not. You know better. They're also seeing each other."

Her eyes widened. "See, that's like one of my books. Who are they?"

"Maria, if I tell you . . ."

"Who am I going to tell? The cat? My online friends?"

"Avery. And Levi. And you can't tell anyone because no one knows."

"Oh." Her eyes widened even more. "God*damn*. Both of them?"

I found myself relaxing. "If you tell a single soul . . ."

"I won't. So, why are you upset then? What's wrong?" she asked and then pressed her lips together, as if she already knew. "Wait. Isn't he leaving?"

I nodded.

"Oh. Soon, right?"

"Monday."

She winced. "And knowing you, you're already fully in love."

"I am."

"I mean, you've *been* in love with Avery."

I sighed. "That obvious?"

"It couldn't be more so. But Levi is new. And those two are together?"

"Yeah."

"Is Avery okay with him leaving?"

"I don't think either of us are. But why would we stop him?

He has a life in Minnesota. A career he's worked hard for. He can't uproot it all and come here, of all places."

Her smile thinned. "I've done crazier for someone I loved."

I raised a brow, but didn't press. Maria could get any info out of me she wanted, but when it came to her own, she was a vault.

"Have you heard from your dad?" I asked softly.

She blew out a breath. "God, what a subject change. No, I haven't. I'm sure we'll see him over the holidays. Are you going this year?"

"Of course."

"And maybe with your *lovers*?"

Despite everything, I was smiling again. "Maybe. If I'm lucky."

"You are. It'll be okay. I'll see you next week for dinner. You should bring Avery with you. I like her."

"If we're functioning at that point, I will." I spread my arms and gave her a hug, planting a kiss on the top of her head. "Go enlighten young minds or whatever it is you do."

"Right. Have fun saving cats and old people."

CHAPTER FORTY-ONE

Levi's idea of picking up dinner meant buying enough Chinese takeout to feed the entirety of Whynot.

But I couldn't complain. I'd worked up an appetite.

"I've never been to your place," Levi said as he came through my front door. Avery was right behind him and paused to lean up on her tiptoes, planting a kiss on my mouth that turned my cock to steel.

"Well, hi," I mumbled as my cheeks warmed.

"Hi." She winked and slid past me.

God, I'm fucking obsessed with both of them. I shut the door and locked it, trying to clear my head and keep up with our conversation. "It's nothing too fancy. I like Avery's place more. But my bed is bigger."

A lot bigger.

"And there are restraint points," I added causally.

Both Avery and Levi turned around with deer in the headlights looks on their faces.

Ha. "The dining room is straight ahead."

"I know where it's at," Avery mumbled, leading the way.

Levi looked around as he followed her and I was suddenly a lot more self-conscious of my house. I mean, it was a house, which was saying a lot in the world we lived in. It was entirely too small and there were parts of it that were outdated, but it was mine. Over the last couple of years, I'd taken cues from Avery and *attempted* to decorate.

My living room was cozy. My couch was definitely from my college days, which *was* slightly embarrassing. I did have a new leather recliner that made me feel like an old man every time I sat in it, but I loved it regardless.

"Your place is like mine," Levi chuckled as he put the food down on the table.

"Basic?"

His smile warmed me. "Just not like Avery's."

"I like it," Avery said. "It's . . ."

"Don't even try," I snorted. "If we ever live together, you can decorate."

It was easy to say that. Easy for the words to slip out, easy to say something so casually about a future together. And yet, the tension in the room became painful.

"I'll grab silverware." Avery practically fled to the kitchen.

Levi was quiet and broody as he untied the plastic bags. I could see his mind working. Thinking.

I wasn't going to shy away from the future, I decided. Even if it hurt. Even if it felt like a thousand tiny needles in my chest every time I thought about what happened *after* Monday.

"What's your schedule like next week?" I asked.

Levi's brows pulled together. "Busy."

"I'm sure. Meeting with your agent?"

He nodded. "The moment I land, I'll probably be in and out of meeting rooms for a full week. I'm sure they're going to come up with some sort of social media strategy for me."

Avery returned with bowls and utensils, but I'd lost my appetite. I tried to flip back to being horny, to being dominant, to wanting to do all the hot deviant activities I'd been wanting to do with both of them all day.

But it was hard.

It was hard to think about anything except the looming deadline.

Avery breathed out. "All right. I have a request."

Levi and I looked at her as we sat down around my table.

"What's that?" Levi asked.

"I want to pretend for the rest of the night that there's nothing else outside these walls. Can we do that?"

Could we?

Levi nodded. "I'd like that."

They both looked at me and I leaned back in my chair, considering. Finally, I nodded. "Okay."

"That wasn't very enthusiastic," she said half-heartedly.

All I did was smile and reach for the fried rice. "Maria knows, by the way."

Avery gasped and Levi's brows shot up.

"You told someone?" he asked.

"I did. She's my cousin."

"Oh, I've met her," he said. "At the cafe. She's a librarian?"

"The one and only," I chuckled. "Honestly, still not sure why she works at the cafe except she likes the extra money for some of her hobbies. But between being a librarian and watching the demon cat, I don't know where she gets the time."

"She's really cool," Avery said. "A little aloof."

She was that. "She is."

"So what did she say?" Levi wondered.

"She was happy for us." I shrugged my shoulders and decided to leave it at that. "What did you two get up to today? I see the marks on Levi's neck."

His hand immediately covered his throat and I laughed. There wasn't any such mark, but teasing them was enough to lighten the mood. Avery grinned as we dove into our dinner, and every topic we talked about carefully existed outside of *after*.

Once we were full, I got up from the table and headed straight to the bedroom, wondering how long it would take them to follow. I flipped on my light, listening to their murmurs as I pulled out my kink bag from the closet.

And the spreader bars.

The black metal bar had two cuffs that would be perfect for either of them.

Avery filled the doorway wearing nothing but her damn boots.

I cursed, breathing out as I took her in. "Ruining all my plans," I rasped.

"That's me." She smirked as Levi appeared behind her, wearing *nothing*.

"Did I tell either of you that you could undress?" I asked, unable to hide my amusement.

"No. We decided to save you the trouble."

"Ah, and I bet you want some praise for thinking so far ahead."

She tipped her chin up. "I sure do."

I smirked and snatched a pillow off the bed. I threw it to the floor at my feet. "I want you to kneel on the floor right here, Avery."

I felt the shift internally first. The dominant part of me taking over, desire washing away all my other concerns. We were safe in this space. Safe to be with each other, safe to explore our desires, safe from the future.

Avery entered my room and stopped in front of me. She held eye contact, never breaking it for a moment as she dropped down to her knees. Obediently. Willingly. Her sweet brown eyes watched me, waiting for more commands. The submission was pure and needy and all-consuming.

"Good girl."

Her breath hitched. Blush crept into her cheeks.

I tipped her chin up, cradling her face in my palm for a moment. There was so much trust here. So much that I cherished.

I turned my attention to Levi. His cock was hard, but he wouldn't look at me.

"Levi," I said.

Sad green eyes met mine. I hated seeing him like this. I needed to make him forget.

"Yes, Sir?"

"I want you to go into my closet and look to the right. There's a set of rope and safety shears. I want you to bring them both out."

Levi stepped into the room and moved past me for the closet, but not before I grabbed his wrist. His eyes lit up as I pulled him into a kiss, his lips smooth against mine, his beard rough against my skin. The scent of him was like a balm of comfort, his body leaning into me.

I wanted him to stay so badly it hurt.

I released him, smirking at the stars I saw dancing in his eyes. Levi swallowed hard and stumbled to the closet, flipping on the light and peering in.

"Fuck," he said. "You've got a lot of stuff in here. Have you been holding back?"

Avery started to get up, but I shook my head at her. "Stay kneeling."

I could see the curiosity eating at her, but her body relaxed into its place again.

Levi retrieved a bundle of rope and the scissors. I took it from him and unraveled the hemp, the roughness sliding

CLIO EVANS

between my fingers. Vibrations followed as the ends hit the floor and I smiled down at Avery.

Rope had been on the kink list. I knew Avery had never been tied up before. I wasn't going to do anything too intense, but seeing her chest in a harness would be enough to test the waters with shibari while also adding a layer of sexiness and control that appealed to me.

I also knew that Levi knew how to tie a chest harness.

I handed the rope back to him. "I want you to put her in a harness while I tease her."

"Yes, Sir," he whispered. He leaned in and kissed me once more before we both looked down at her.

Avery's eyes widened slightly, but then she licked her lips. "Am I going to suck both of you off at the same time?"

It was a damn good idea, but not what I'd planned.

"Put her in a harness first," I said roughly.

Levi looped an arm around her waist and lifted her to her feet. She wobbled for a moment, but we steadied her, the two of us boxing her in. I kicked the pillow to the side as her head fell back against his chest.

"This is hot," she whispered reverently. "Really, really hot."

My hands slid down her body as Levi lifted her arms, positioning her so he could move the rope around her breasts with ease. I slid two fingers against her pussy, not surprised to find her wet.

"Someone's so fucking eager," I whispered as I pushed a finger inside her.

"Oh fuck," she gasped, her eyes fluttering.

She squeezed my finger, pulsing around me as Levi slid the rope around her body. I watched it tighten around her ribs beneath her breasts. Then he looped it around, drawing the rope up between them. I leaned forward, catching her nipple in

310

my mouth and sucking as he tightened the harness, all while giving her a second finger.

Avery whimpered, her words lost to moans. Her hips moved, begging me for more. I sank my teeth into her soft skin, sucking her nipple hard enough that she yelped and gasped.

I could feel the rope vibrations through her body. Levi finished tying the back, meeting my gaze over her shoulder.

I released her nipple and stepped closer, her body pressed between ours. Her hands settled on my chest, her hips moving faster.

"Are you going to let her come?" Levi asked.

"I am," I whispered. "Because she's being so good, isn't she?"

"She is," he purred, kissing the sides of her neck. "Putty in our hands."

I nodded, holding her gaze. "She'd do anything we wanted her to. Keep fucking my hand, baby. There you go."

Her lashes fluttered, her breaths shortening as she kept moving, the wet sounds of my fingers fucking her turning my cock to iron. We kept working her together until her voice split my ears, her body shaking as her orgasm pulsed through her. I could feel it around my fingers, could see it in the way her expression twisted around the moment she came.

Avery moaned as I pulled my fingers free and pushed them between her lips. She sucked them as Levi cupped her breasts, rolling her nipples between his fingers.

"Thank you," she whispered, dazed. "That was so good."

"*You* were so good," I whispered. "Get on your knees."

She sank back down to the floor and grabbed the pillow, putting it beneath her knees so she wasn't kneeling on hardwoods.

"Can I undress you?" she whispered.

"Yes."

I pulled Levi around so that he was standing next to me, his cock already pointing straight at her. She licked her lips as she slid her hands up my thighs, unbuttoning my jeans swiftly.

They fell to the floor, followed by my boxer-briefs. Levi reached for my shirt and I let him tug it off, leaning to kiss him as Avery gripped both of our cocks.

Fuck.

Levi's tongue tangled with mine as she started to stroke me. A full body shiver sent a wave of pleasure through me, my knees weak as heat enveloped the head of my cock. She licked and sucked, alternating between Levi and me until we were both dripping, panting messes.

I tightened my grip on him and pulled our mouths apart. "Fuck," I mumbled. "We're going to fuck her together. And then I'm going to make good use of these spreader bars. Got it?"

"Yes." He sucked in a breath, looking down at Avery. "I'll do whatever you want me to do, Sir."

"Good." I took a step back because if I didn't now, then I'd be filling her mouth with my cum. "Pick her up. Put her on the bed on her back. I want her head over the edge facing you."

"Yes, Sir."

He leaned down and wrapped his arms around Avery's waist, picking her up and taking her back to the bed. She arched back, her lips parting as she stole a hungry kiss from him. My cock throbbed as I watched their limbs tangle and he pinned her down, his hands running up and down her body. She whimpered as he drew back breathless and stood on the other side of the bed.

Levi caught her head as it tipped over the edge. My hand slid around my cock and I groaned, needing to be inside her. I knelt on the bed, grabbed hold of her calves, and shoved her cowgirl boots together as I lowered my cock to her pussy.

"How's this angle?" I asked.

"Good. I need both of you," she gasped. "Rough. Please. *Fuck me.*"

She wanted it hard and fast and so did we. All of the tension broke free and I caved, *needing* this.

I tightened my grip on her calves, holding Levi's gaze as she opened her pretty mouth wide for him. I drank in the sight of the rope around her breasts, her nipples hard and skin flushed. She dragged her tongue over her bottom lip, meeting my gaze one last time before the head of his cock hovered and he nodded, the two of us thrusting into her at once.

"*Fuuuck,*" I rasped.

Her pussy pulsed around me, squeezing me with every inch she took. Her voice was muffled as Levi took her throat, his groan following.

His hand settled on her breast, pinching one of her nipples as he gave a pump of his hips.

"She feels so fucking good," he gasped.

I nodded, unable to form words. I tipped my head back, basking in the feeling of my cock buried in her slick heat. I thrust my hips forward, all the way to the hilt, shivering as I fought for control.

"Fuck," Levi muttered.

"Look at me," I grunted.

He looked up, his bright green eyes locking with mine. I gave a breathless nod and the two of us started to move in tandem, taking her at the same time, spitroasting her on our cocks. Her moans filled my bedroom and I wished I could listen to her forever.

"Good job," I whispered. "You're taking our cocks so well. Fuck, I can see him in your throat."

The outline of his cock was so apparent. That alone nearly made me come. I paused for a moment, catching my breath before I came too soon.

She rocked her hips, demanding more. My words slipped out in Spanish as I looked down, watching my cock slide into her, watching her stretch around me. *"Fuck. Me das caliento."* Her pussy glistened, wet and needy. I couldn't get over how fucking perfect she was.

"I love hearing you talk to her," Levi grunted. "Fuck. Look at her. Look how good she is."

His praise turned her on even more. I chuckled and drove into her harder, falling back into a rhythm with Levi until he pulled back completely, holding her head up to let her breathe.

"I want more," she whimpered. "I want to be fucked from behind."

That was a request we could happily do. I released her legs and moved back on the bed, pulling out as I flipped her over. Avery's squeak made me smile as I grabbed her hips and lined up my cock, thrusting into her with ease.

Her fingers gripped the blankets, her hair a mess as her head fell forward. "Oh god."

My grip tightened as I groaned. Levi knelt on the other side of her, stroking his cock as he watched us, his gaze stormy and full of lust.

"Suck his cock," I demanded.

She whimpered in reply, but reached up, closing her hand around his shaft. I knew just how thick he was, but seeing her stroke him reminded me so. His hips moved, his hand settling on the back of her head to steady himself. She lowered her lips to the head, swiping up precum with the tip of her tongue, her mouth making the most delicious sounds from every thrust of my cock.

They were perfect. Everything about them together and apart and with me. The way his expression turned euphoric, that worried mask slipping away until it was gone and there was only this moment left. The way Avery took every inch of our cocks, wanting more and more. I loved it when she was greedy. I loved it when she couldn't get enough.

"There you are," Levi groaned. "Fuck, look at you. You're taking every inch, aren't you?"

His praise even turned me on. I huffed, sweat turning my skin damp as I fucked her harder. None of us were holding back, and yet I knew he and I were fighting the urge to come fast.

"*I'm going. To come. Again,*" she rasped between sucks.

Levi pulled her hair and she took more. His head fell back and he moaned, our bodies melding together. I kept the same speed, the same constant motion, feeling her pussy around my cock and knowing she was close. *Feeling* that she was.

"*Fuck.*"

Her curse came the same time she did, her body going still as she gasped around Levi's cock. The sight of her between us like this was enough to steal my breath and send me over the edge. With one finally thrust, I buried my cock deep and came, giving her every drop.

I pulled out and watched as my cum dribbled down the sides of her thighs. I scooped up some with two fingers and pushed it back into her pussy, right where it belonged.

Levi released her, chuckling as he kept idly stroking his cock. Avery face-planted into the blankets, breathing hard.

And I smiled.

Because we weren't done yet.

CHAPTER FORTY-TWO

I expected both of them to collapse down next to me, but that's not what happened at all. Mateo's hands smoothed up and down my back, and he murmured something to Levi I didn't catch because I'd been launched out of earth's orbit by my orgasm.

I couldn't even remember my name.

I breathed deep, inhaling the scent of Mateo. His blankets were soft. I wanted to roll around in them and burrow deep and dream about the three of us.

Calloused fingers continued to shove his cum back inside me. I groaned, all of my nerve endings prickling back to life. My boots were tugged off, more murmuring. What the hell were they even saying?

I felt something around my ankles and groaned, pushing my ass back. Slowly, but surely, my pussy was pulsing back to life as they continued to move me and tease me how they wanted.

"I think she's out," Levi chuckled.

"She'll come back around. I think she's hornier than both of us combined."

"Fuck both of you," I mumbled with a smile. They weren't

316

wrong though, I was insatiable.

Levi pushed his fingers deeper and I gasped as he pumped them slowly. I tried to move my ankles, and then realized they were firmly spread.

I finally peeled my face from the mattress and looked over my shoulder, seeing the spreader bar. Mateo knelt at the edge of the bed, his eyes dark and full of sexy promise, a riding crop in one hand and his cock in the other.

Levi rolled me over onto my back and drew my hands above my head. I looked down at his cock, realizing he was still hard and still hadn't come yet. He pinned my wrists down with one hand and looked back at Mateo.

"What are you going to do to me?" I taunted.

"Whatever I want to."

"Do your worst, if you dare." This was turning me on more than I thought possible. Then again, my mind had been running off fantasy fumes for years at this point, and now that I was actually getting to have kinky sex—I was *loving* it. "I doubt you'd even leave a mark."

"You're such a brat," Levi chuckled, his weight keeping me in place.

"I already know you want to remember this moment," Mateo said.

The mustache only made him hotter, like a deviously sexy villain. Hot and flirty and someone I trusted explicitly.

I stuck my tongue out at him.

That earned me the first strike from the riding crop. It was quick and at the top of my thigh. I gasped as the sting of it registered, pain followed by . . .

A rush of endorphins. My nipples hardened, my eyes widening as Mateo rubbed the spot he'd just hit with the flat of the crop. The leather was cool and almost soothing.

The anticipation was driving me insane.

Mateo shook his head at me. "Hold her down."

"Yes, Sir."

Levi smirked. I started to squirm beneath him as Mateo inched closer. I eyed the riding crop nervously, but it was the horny kind of nervous. The *curious* kind of nervous.

The riding crop dragged down my leg. I whimpered as Mateo grabbed hold of the spreader bar before I could twist, keeping me in place as he brought the crop down.

"*Fuck.*" My eyes closed, a moan following. It hurt. It really fucking hurt, but it also felt so good that I was turned on all over again.

When I looked at Mateo again, I was in awe. There was a darkness in his gaze that was swallowing me whole. A lusty, depraved need to own me. To have me.

He could have it all.

I trusted him. I trusted Levi. They were both the kind of men I'd leave my drink with in a bar or I'd ask to drive me home. They were both someone I could trust to leave bruises on my body and still treat me like a queen. Both of them worshiped the ground I walked on, and knowing that . . .

Knowing that made this even hotter.

Mateo smacked my other thigh, the sound snapping around me. I bucked, whining as he did it *again, again, again*—

"Fuck," I gasped. "Fuck you."

Again, again, again.

"It hurts," I cried. He hesitated, but I shook my head. God, the last thing I wanted him to do was stop. That's why we had our safe words, right?

Again, again, again—

He pried another gasp from my lips, and Levi caught it in a kiss. I whimpered as our tongues met, the taste of Mateo shared between us. The pain and pleasure created the perfect shade of desire in my mind, every breath shared with him. Every kiss all-consuming. Every stinging ache soothed by the euphoric rush pumping in my veins.

Levi's other hand settled over my pussy, the weight surprising me. His fingers slid against my clit right as Mateo smacked my thigh again, earning a sharp cry.

"Oh god. *Oh god. Fuck.*"

His fingers against my clit felt so fucking good. I couldn't move. I couldn't get away. I just had to take what they gave me.

My muscles tensed, my lungs sucking in jagged breaths as I chased the high. My skin felt raw, every strike from the riding crop growing more and more intense until tears squeezed out the corners of my eyes. A punchy orgasm rolled through me, quick and raw. By the time it finished, neither of them gave me a second to recover.

"Levi," I whimpered. "*Fuck. Fuck.*"

"Give us more, baby," he whispered. "You can do it."

"She *will* do it."

I don't know what I said to him. Something between a *fuck you* and *more, please.* Either, both, it didn't matter because he was right—I would come again.

My hips bucked against Levi's firm hand. The tops of my thighs burned with every delicious smack until I was shaking, another orgasm relentlessly taking me, tears rolling down my cheeks.

Levi leaned down and licked one, humming softly as he peppered kisses over my face. "Beautiful," he murmured. "You're beautiful."

I huffed out my thanks, melting into the bed as Mateo tossed the riding crop to the side and unclasped my ankles. He crawled between my legs, kissing up to the marks that were already bruising.

He pushed my thighs back and held them, my mouth dropping as he looked at my pussy.

"I want your cum inside her too," he said to Levi.

Levi let out a soft grunt. "Is that a . . ."

"Yes. I'm going to fuck you while you fill her up."

He blew out a long breath and nodded eagerly. "Please."

Mateo slid off the bed and opened a drawer and Levi nestled his hips between my thighs. I reached up, winding my arms around his neck and kissing him. Savoring him.

I don't want him to go. I blinked back tears, holding him a little tighter.

The head of his cock nudged against me. I wrapped my legs around his waist as Mateo joined us on the bed with lube and his condom. Levi kissed more tears away as he slowly eased forward.

Gentle. He was being gentle. Even after waiting to be inside me, even after the heated kinky things we'd just done—he wasn't *taking*. He was giving.

"You feel so good," I whispered.

"So do you, baby. Ah, fuck."

His words were soft, his eyes squeezing shut. I felt Mateo's hand on my leg, giving me a gentle pat, and I realized—Mateo was filling Levi at the same time.

"Okay?" Mateo checked in.

"Yes. More than."

Levi knelt his forehead to mine. I could feel his cock hardening even more inside me, stretching me around him. I kissed him softly, making myself relax and enjoy the fullness of him. The connection between the three of us.

I slid my hand around his back and smiled as Mateo's fingers tangled with mine.

Perfect. For a few moments, everything was perfect. Everything was how I wanted it to always be.

A thousand brushstrokes made a bigger picture, and every moment with Mateo and Levi painted a life together I wanted more than anything else. I wanted this to be us forever.

I could feel my heart shattering. Little breaks in slow motion, like I was watching it happen on a big screen. I knew what came next, but I couldn't stop it, and I couldn't look away.

Levi's lips searched for mine and he moved his hips, taking me deeper. I groaned, letting all the sadness slip away into the pleasure that took me—deep and lazy.

Mateo moved his hips, his fingers tightening in mine as he pumped his hips, making Levi thrust his. I gasped as I felt him, felt them together.

"Oh yes," I rasped.

He pushed my bangs out of my face, kissing me as we moved together. We took everything slow—almost painfully so. It was intimate. It was sad. It was full of longing and yearning and my ungranted wish for Monday to never come.

"I'm so close," Levi whispered.

Mateo picked up the rhythm, the change enough to push me right where I wanted to be.

Levi groaned as I came again, my pussy wrapped around him, milking his cock. He thrust deeper and buried his face against the curve of my neck, his breaths puffing as his movements jolted.

"Fill her up," Mateo commanded. "Give her everything. She's earned every single drop, hasn't she?"

"She has." His lips grazed my skin as he pumped harder.

I moaned as Levi gasped, his movements hurrying. Faster and faster until he planted his hands beside my head and gave one last movement, burying himself deep inside me as he came.

Mateo's groans joined Levi's. Awe washed over me as they came together, their orgasms syncing. Mateo's face twisted with pleasure, his head tipping back as Levi kept slowly rolling his hips. Hot cum jerked inside me until it dripped out.

"Fuck," Levi moaned.

He drew back, the two of them rolling to either side of me. The three of us were a mess, but the right kind.

My eyes drifted shut as I basked in the afterglow of that. The tops of my thighs hurt, but the ache grounded me.

Plus, it was really hot.

Mateo planted a kiss on my cheek, his arms slinging over me. "We should all drink water."

"We will," I mumbled. "But it's nice here in your arms. Don't get up yet."

"Wouldn't dream of it."

I smiled as the two of them curled closer.

For a few minutes, I was blissful. But then those pesky *what ifs* started up in my mind. Annoying questions about the future and things I wanted to know.

Fuck it.

"In this perfect world where the three of us don't have secrets and where we could be together," I started. "Would either of you want kids?"

Mateo rolled onto his side, drawing tiny circles on my hip with the tip of his finger. Levi let out a long hum, and I knew he was going to answer first.

"Yeah. In a perfect world."

"I would too," Mateo said. He smiled as I turned my head to look at him, his eyes dancing with . . . hope? Something inside me melted. "I'd want a big family with dogs. Hell, maybe even something weird like a bearded dragon. I want a chaotic life. I want it to be fun and full and happy."

"The world doesn't need to be perfect for you to have those things," Levi murmured.

We both turned our heads to look up at him.

"Yes," Mateo said. "But in any world—perfect or imperfect—to have those things, I'd need you here too."

Levi's throat bobbed as he swallowed. I breathed in the scent of his aftershave, tracing every line of his face and committing it to memory. The soft wrinkles alongside his bright green eyes, the couple flecks of silver I'd spotted among the blond of his beard. His thick brows and soft lips and the way he scowled.

"Both of you will be fine," he said. "You'll be happy together."

I frowned at him and propped myself up. "Levi, why do you think that? Both of us want you to be in our lives, together but also separately."

"I just mean that when I leave, the two of you will be okay," he said. He sat up slightly, his muscles tensing, and frankly—it pissed me off how casual he was about us moving on without him.

"You don't know that," I said. "I don't think I'm going to be okay. Honestly, I don't think I want you to leave."

"I have to. I can't stay here."

Mateo's hand tightened slightly on my hip. "Maybe the three of us should talk about something else."

"I don't want to though," I said, sitting up completely. Cum rushed out of me and I cursed, squeezing my thighs shut.

"Should I get a towel?" Mateo asked quickly.

"No, I don't even care right now. I'll wash the sheets." I narrowed my gaze on Levi as he got up without a word, grabbing a towel from the floor and handing it to Mateo. This conversation while trying to clean up was going to send me over the edge, especially since Levi refused to look at me. "Am I losing it? I thought you wanted to be with us. This was starting to feel like . . ."

"Like what?" The bed shifted as Levi sat on the edge and

finally looked at me. "Like a real relationship? Like we aren't sneaking around behind your brothers' backs? We all know that I'm going to leave in a week without them even knowing. I'm going to go back to Minnesota, and both of you will move on. You can have the life that Mateo—"

"In a perfect world, would you want it too?" Mateo cut in.

Levi's words stumbled into silence. "What?"

"Answer the first question," he said. "What would you want?"

We already knew the answer. I *knew* the answer. Mateo *knew it*.

Levi knew it too, right?

That even if he didn't want that, he wanted *this*.

He swallowed hard again. His muscles tensed again. And then he just looked sad.

And didn't say a single thing as he stood up and pulled on his T-shirt and jeans.

Mateo sighed and raked his fingers through his dark waves. "I'm not going to beg you to move to a place like this, Levi. I don't think Avery will either. Neither of us planned to end up in Whynot. Your life is still in Minnesota. You have a career. You have everything you've worked for. But, if you leave next week, you should know that you always have a place with us. You always have a home with us. No matter what."

CHAPTER FORTY-THREE

Forty-eight hours.

That's how much longer we had with him.

Every hour counted, but I was in my studio. Painting was the only thing that was soothing the unease I felt. The plan was for us to have a date tonight, but I felt like I was constantly on the verge of crying.

I didn't want Levi to go.

I'd known from the start that he was leaving. Maybe I was delusional, but for the last few weeks, I'd been living in a bubble. A bubble where there was no end in sight. There was no plane ticket, no set day he was leaving. Our time together was never-ending.

But it wasn't. It *was* ending.

"Whatcha painting, Blue?"

I looked up from my canvas, but wasn't startled by Mateo's presence. He smiled as he lingered in the studio doorway. Like a vampire, he wouldn't step into the room without an invitation.

"Hi," I said. I kept my paintbrush and palette in hand as I slid off my stool and went to him. I leaned up on the toes of my sneakers and kissed him hard, smiling as his mustache tickled my skin. "You're early."

"I am. I just wanted to creep," he said. "Levi will be here in a few, too."

I nodded and kissed him once more before returning to my canvas.

The cactus piece was almost done. The landscape around it was finished aside from a few highlights I wanted to add. Mateo and Levi stood in the middle, and I felt pretty damn proud of how I'd captured them. I'd gotten the sparkle of mischief that always twinkled in Mateo's eyes and the soft, steady expression of care in Levi's. It *felt* like them, but was missing something.

"Can I see?"

"Yeah," I said. "But don't critique me or I'll have a breakdown."

He snorted as he followed me to the canvas. "I can't paint to save my life, Blue . . ."

Mateo trailed off as he stood behind me. My muscles tensed as I realized I was letting him see something unfinished. Not only unfinished, but a painting with him in it. What if he hated it? What if he thought it was bad?

"This is amazing," he whispered. "Baby, you're so talented. I don't say it enough. I could stare at your art all day and night and never grow tired of it. I want to always be surrounded by it."

I breathed out and smiled as his arms slid around me. I leaned back against him, aware that the door was open. Knowing that it wasn't some odd hour of the night where we could openly love each other.

A little weight lifted off my shoulders as we continued to study the painting.

"Something is missing from it," I sighed. "I'm not sure what."

"Would you like my thoughts?"

I considered it for a moment, then nodded. "Gently."

He pressed another kiss to the top of my head. "It's missing you, Blue. The three of us are supposed to be together."

My chest squeezed.

He was right.

"I want him to stay," I whispered.

"I do too."

"I don't know what we'll do without him."

"I don't either."

"I'm not going anywhere, though."

"I'm not either. I know we're in this together, Avery. I just . . ."

Want him too. We both wanted him. Without him, I wasn't sure what life would look like. The ache in my chest was the same sort of pain I'd feel if Mateo left. Equally sharp and, if anything, *worse* because I wasn't sure I'd ever see Levi again once he flew back to Minnesota.

Mateo pressed his face against the top of my head, his arms tightening around me. I dropped my palette and paintbrush on the stool and turned around to face him, pressing my face against his chest and breathing him in. Soaking up his comfort.

"It's going to be okay," he whispered.

"Will it be?"

"I hope so."

He tipped my chin up and cupped my face. He leaned in, his lips brushing mine. I melted into him, fighting the tears. Fighting the little monster in my head that screamed it wasn't enough. Whatever I was, I wasn't enough to keep Levi here.

"What in the hell is going on?"

My heart dropped. Mateo immediately whipped back, the two of us spinning.

Austin.

In my studio.

Not just at the doorway, but *in my fucking studio.*

"What are you doing?" I asked quickly. "Get out of my studio! You know you're not allowed in here."

I watched my brother's expression roll through a few different emotions. Shock, like he was looking at two ghosts. Betrayal, because we'd lied to his face. I'd lied to his face. Shock again as his eyes wandered around the room and then to the floor, where there were countless sketches of Levi and Mateo.

Countless sketches of the three of us too.

None of them were sexual, luckily, but that did nothing to lessen the fact that we'd been found out.

"Austin," Mateo breathed out. "We can explain—"

"I . . ." His eyes drifted from me to Mateo and then back again.

"Austin," I growled, panic clawing at me. "Get out of my studio. This is my space. Get out!"

He wasn't hearing me. He wasn't listening. His gaze moved to the tops of my thighs.

I was wearing shorts, and the bruises from my spankings were visible.

I saw the click happen.

Austin's eyes lit with rage as he marched towards us. "*What the fuck?*"

"Austin, it's not what you think," I said quickly.

I tried to intercept him, but he pushed past me and straight to Mateo. I grabbed at my brother's shirt as he grabbed onto Mateo, anger pouring off him in waves.

"Austin," I pleaded. "*Stop* this. It's not what you think—"

Mateo's voice was steady despite the fact Austin was in his face. "I need you to calm down and let me go, Austin."

"What do you mean, calm down?" Austin yelled.

"It's not what you think," I insisted, trying to stay calm. Ice crept through my veins as he shoved Mateo back, the tension in the room making my heart race. I didn't like this. "The bruises were consensual. It's not what you think."

"Did he hit you?" Austin asked, turning back to look at me. "Did either of them hit you?"

"Austin, it's not—"

"What's going on?"

Levi emerged in the doorway, filling up the frame. He immediately barrelled toward us, straight to Austin.

My brother spun around, his grip still on Mateo as he glowered at Levi. "You fucking lied to me, Levi. Did you sleep with her?"

Levi's expression blanked, his eyes darting to me and then Mateo.

"I slept with both of them," I blurted out. "We're dating. We've all been together the last few weeks."

"*What?*"

"I'd really like you to take your hands off both of them," I whispered. "Please. You're making me nervous. I don't like this. I don't like this at all."

Tears blurred my vision as the panic crept up. Icy, freezing, making everything spin. I didn't want him to find out like this. I didn't want any of this. I—

"Did they do *that* to you then?" He growled, gesturing at my thighs.

"It's none of your business. They're not Kevin. They're nothing like him. I need you to calm down because you're making me—"

"Really? Because I just walked in on you kissing my best friend and you have fucking *bruises* on your legs, Avery. And then you're also sleeping with my other friend too?"

"Hey," Mateo interjected. "We need to take this outside. Not in Avery's studio."

"Fuck you," Austin growled, tightening his grip on Mateo. "Why the fuck have you been hiding this from me? Why the fuck have either of you been hiding this from me? You know Avery is off-limits. I've said that for weeks. For fucking years!"

"*This* is why we didn't tell you," I said.

"Avery is an adult," Levi said. "And if you don't let go of Mateo right now, I'm going to make you."

"Fucking make me then—"

Levi grabbed Austin's wrist and twisted him away from Mateo, but he was ready for it. Mateo stepped toward me and looped his arm around my waist, pulling me back as Austin threw a punch.

I screamed as it landed. A crunching noise followed from Levi's nose, but he was hardly fazed by it. Even though I knew he was a hockey player and could take a punch, my heart dropped. Mateo cursed, pulling me back further.

"I have to separate them," he said quickly. "Will you be okay?"

No, I wouldn't be. Nothing was okay. Nothing. "Please," I rasped as Austin took Levi to the floor.

Mateo released me and put his arm around Austin, putting him in a headlock and hauling him off Levi with ease. Austin grunted, clawing at Mateo's arms and kicking out.

He released him and Austin stumbled forward—and straight into my canvas.

"No!" I gasped, covering my mouth as he and the easel tumbled to the floor.

"What in the fuck is going on—*oh shit.*" Dallas, Evie, and June all filled the doorway, but Evie grabbed Dallas' sleeve before he came in.

Levi sat up, blood dripping down his nose. Mateo helped him up, horror painting their faces as we all looked at Austin.

The canvas had snapped.

My knees felt weak. I sank to the floor, tears streaming down my face as I stared at it. Austin rolled to the side, getting up, paint sticking to his back. He looked down, his expression softening.

"Fuck," he whispered. "Avery . . ."

"Get out."

"Avery—"

"Get the fuck out. Now."

Austin glowered at Levi and Mateo as he staggered to the doorway. "I'm not done with either of you."

"Austin, *stop!*" I yelled, a sob breaking free. "I've been dating both of them behind your back because of how you act. This is your fault. Not theirs. You never listen to me. You don't listen—"

"Avery, I listen all the time. I—"

"No, you fucking don't! You broke my number one rule which is that this is *my* space. No one is allowed in here."

"Mateo was in here."

"Because I let him," I cried. "I let him in here. I wanted him in here. But that doesn't give you an excuse. This is my space. Mine. It's all I fucking have in this place. I've spent weeks on that painting—"

"On a painting of *my* best friends kissing?"

"Fuck," Levi sighed, wiping his nose. "Austin, Mateo and I have been together too."

He blanched, looking around the room until he finally noticed our other brother. "Did you know this?" he asked Dallas.

Dallas shook his head. "No, but you're over-reacting and you need to come out of Avery's studio."

"*I'm* over reacting? You're not even fucking reacting, Dallas. You're not doing anything. Per fucking usual, it's on me to handle everything."

Dallas leaned forward without crossing the threshold and grabbed Austin by the shirt, dragging him out.

"I need everyone out," I whispered.

Mateo gave me a pain-stricken look, and I looked away from him. From Levi.

"Please. I need to be alone for a few minutes."

Mateo slid his hand into Levi's and led him to the door. "We'll come back. We're going to go talk with Austin. Okay? It's going to be okay."

All I could do was nod. But nothing, absolutely nothing, was going to be okay.

CHAPTER FORTY-FOUR

It was very rare that I lost my temper. But between the blood on Levi's face and the tears in Avery's eyes, the moment we were out of her studio, I grabbed Austin by his collar and punched him hard enough that he dropped onto the sidewalk.

"Holy shit," Evie gasped, tugging June out of the way.

Levi put his hand on my shoulder, pulling me closer to him. Despite everything, having him at my side was a comfort.

"Fuck, Mateo," Dallas gasped, kneeling down next to his brother.

Austin stared at me, dazed as he sat up. "You lied to me," he said. "You went behind my back. Why didn't you just ask me about Avery?"

"Because I know how you are," I said. "And because Avery asked us not to tell you. And I agreed because I've been in love with her for two fucking years, Austin. Two years."

"Why haven't you done anything?"

"Because you act like *this*," I said. "Ever since she's come back to Whynot, you've been completely overprotective. You haven't given her any space. You've been constantly over-stepping."

"It's really none of your business—"

"It is now," I said firmly. "I *am* dating your sister, whether you approve or not."

"Then you're not my friend anymore."

That hurt. Every muscle stilled as I blinked at him. "Really?"

He slowly got up, glaring at both of us. "Neither of you are friends. Levi, I asked you earlier this week after dinner. And you—"

"I told you that you have nothing to worry about," Levi said firmly. "Because I leave on Monday. And that's the truth."

My stomach twisted as he said that.

"That makes it even worse!" Austin yelled. "So you sleep with my best friend *and* my sister, and then just leave? Is that really who you are?"

Levi's hand left mine. "Yes," he whispered.

Dallas tightened his grip on Austin before he could lunge at Levi. "And you lied to all of us about it."

"Well . . ." Evie interjected, trailing off. "June and I have known."

His mouth dropped. "What?"

"We've known," June said. "And we've supported this too, because Levi and Mateo have made Avery happy. I don't think they intended to hide from either of you for so long, but you guys have been too much since Kevin."

"Kevin *hurt* her," Austin rasped. "And then to see bruises on her—"

"Austin," Evie cut in. "We all need you to drop the bruises. Avery consented to those. It has to do with BDSM."

He blanched to the white of a ghost. He slowly turned to look at me and Levi again, but Dallas shook his head.

"We all need to take a breather," Dallas said calmly. "This all blew way out of proportion. Austin, we both owe Avery an apology."

Austin shrugged Dallas off and shook his head at us. "Neither of you deserve her. And you never fucking will."

Levi remained quiet as Austin spun and stomped down the sidewalk. Dallas cast us an apologetic look and then stalked after him.

Evie blew out a long breath. "Please go check on her."

"We'll take care of her," I promised. "If I need anything, I'll call both of you."

"Good," June said. "We trust you."

I blew out a breath, feeling the weight of that. Coming from June, it meant a lot. She didn't hand out trust easily.

"We're headed home for the night," Evie said. "But remember, we're just a call away."

I nodded and reached for Levi, but he stepped away before I could touch him. Evie and June left us, heading across the street to their cars.

"Levi," I said softly. "We need to go back inside."

"I can't face her right now."

My heart stopped. "What do you mean? She needs us."

"She needs you," he said. "Not me."

"She does need you," I argued, my brows pulling together. "I need you."

Levi shook his head, wiping the blood in his beard on his sleeve. "I can't . . . I can't. I just can't, Mateo. I need to go."

He started to turn around to *leave.* Panic sprang up and I reached out, grabbing his hand. "Levi," I rasped. "Please. I need you. We need you. I—"

Levi yanked his hand around and spun back. "I told you what this was from the beginning. I told you I'm not good at relationships. I told you that I'm going back to Minnesota."

"I know, I know." Tears sprang to my eyes. "But this is different. This relationship is different. It means something, Levi. Every time I'm with you, I feel whole. We fit. We work."

"No." He shook his head. "*None* of this works."

"It could. We can figure things out. We can work together to create a future—"

"I'm not in your future, Mateo," he whispered. "I don't belong there."

Levi stared at me for a moment longer.

"I'm sorry, Mateo. Love her for me."

But what about me? I wanted to scream. But I didn't. I couldn't. I couldn't speak or move or cry or breathe or think as he walked away. His steps quickened, and he was running. Running away from me. From Avery. From everything we could have had.

I couldn't go after him.

Tears streamed down my cheeks. I rubbed my eyes and raked my fingers through my hair, trying to pull myself together, but the parts just wouldn't fit. Not without him.

"Fuck," I cried. "*Fuck.*"

My body trembled as I opened the gallery door and walked down the long hall like a zombie. Her studio door was still wide open. When I looked in, my heart crumbled.

Avery held the ruined painting in her lap, cheeks red, shoulders shaking with sobs. She looked up at me with wide, glassy eyes.

"Can I come in?" I croaked.

She nodded and scrambled up as I stumbled to her. I wasn't sure who grabbed who first, but we both sank to the floor.

"Where's Levi?" she whispered.

"He's gone, Avery. I'm sorry." Her hair was damp from where my face pressed. "I'm so fucking sorry."

"I love him."

"I know. I love him too."

"And it's not enough."

I tightened my hold on her, squeezing my eyes shut. My words had run out and I just . . .

I just couldn't . . .

I couldn't lie . . .

I couldn't tell her it was fine . . .

And I couldn't stop crying.

My heart couldn't stop breaking.

CHAPTER FORTY-FIVE

The knock at my front door did nothing to rouse me from bed. I tugged my blanket around myself tighter, staring at the wall as the knocking came again. And again.

But then there was a jingle of keys.

"Avery?"

I sat up immediately as my heart launched to my throat. That voice belonged to the very last person in the world I thought I'd see right now. Before I could hop out of bed, my mom appeared in the doorway.

"I . . ." I trailed off, meeting her gaze.

Her brows pulled together. "Are you okay?"

"No."

She swallowed hard and nodded. "I know I'm probably not who you want to see right now."

I couldn't spare her feelings right now. "You're not. But no one is."

June and Evie had been in and out the last few days, keeping me fed. Hell, keeping Mateo and I both fed.

Levi hadn't even left Monday. He left on Sunday. Took the earliest flight out of Texas and went back home without saying another word to me. To us.

Mom pressed her lips together and nodded. "I understand."

We stared at each other until my shoulders relaxed a fraction. I let my body slump back into bed, blinking back tears as she entered my room and sat on the edge of my bed. Her hand settled on my hip, and she didn't say anything.

"The last time you checked on me like this was when I broke up with that guy in high school," I whispered.

"Oh, god. I remember him. He was a dumbass, too."

I smiled even though I didn't feel it. "He was. I don't even remember his name."

"I think it was Taylor. Tyler?"

"Yeah." I sniffled, curling in more. "You don't need to be here right now."

"I know." She was quiet for a moment, letting out a slow breath. "Your brothers called me. Well, more like Austin came over and told me everything. I . . . Avery, you never told me about Kevin."

"We had other things happening."

"But he hurt you."

"He did."

"You never told me."

"I didn't."

"I didn't know he'd done that. And I gave you hell for leaving him."

"Would you have cared?"

Her breath was shaky. "I don't know. I would like to think I would have. I would like to think I would have been a good mom to you. But on top of losing your dad, I don't think I would have been. I haven't been."

"Mom, I don't know if I have the strength to fight right now. I'm too sad."

"I'm not here to fight. I'm here to tell you I'm sorry. I . . . I started therapy. I have a lot to work on. I don't know how long it's going to take me, but I'm going to try." She took a deliberate breath, her words barely above a whisper. "Avery, I'm sorry. I'm so sorry, honey."

I didn't tell her it was okay. I didn't say I was sorry. But for once, she didn't prod for me to do either.

"I really loved him," I whispered. "Mateo and I really loved him. I wanted to go all the way with both of them. I wanted to be with them forever. And Mateo and I still have each other. We always will. But I'm so fucking sad that Levi left. I knew he was going to leave, but . . ."

"You hoped he would stay."

"Yeah, I really did." Tears burned against my skin. "I just want to be held right now."

"Can I hold you?"

I nodded. She leaned back on the bed next to me and put her arms around me.

A sob loosed in my chest as it hit me.

Sometimes a girl just really needed her mom.

CHAPTER FORTY-SIX

Non-stop meetings.

Over the last week, from the moment I touched down in Minneapolis, I was in meetings. Meetings with PR. With my agent. With my coaches. With teammates. Everyone and god wanted to know what the hell I was thinking with my stunt, but they were glad I was back.

I felt sick.

Robin slid into the backseat next to me and let out a breath. She looked like she'd aged five years, and that was probably my fault.

"Let's go get dinner," she said.

"I'm tired."

"I know you are," she said. "I don't give a fuck. You owe me after this absolute shit show."

I shrugged my shoulders as she gave directions to the driver. Our last meeting had gone well for the most part, except that she kept *looking* at me like she knew something was wrong.

The silence. I hated it. I hated everything.

I wanted to go . . .

Home? I was home.

My throat felt thick.

The car slowed to a stop after a few minutes and Robin opened her door. I sighed as I got out, giving her an annoyed glance, but her annoyed look back certainly beat mine. I'd known her for years, and in a lot of ways, she'd become a mom to me. She'd been in this business a long time—long enough that she sported a silver bob and wrinkles and a manicure that could tear up any cisgender white man's ego.

Robin led the way to the restaurant. It was a nice sit-down place that had insanely expensive steak, but I owed her after the shit she'd been putting up with.

It took a few minutes before we were seated, but the moment we were, she ripped off her badge, folded her hands on the table, and looked at me. "All right, Rayburn. What the fuck is wrong with you?"

I opened my mouth, but no words came out. What was I supposed to say? That I'd fallen in love with two people then had left them both crying in Texas? That I'd fucked up? That I'd lied to my best friend?

"Spill," she demanded. "Or I start spilling blood."

"I visited my hometown in Texas, met two people, and fell in love."

Her perfect brows shot up. She never broke eye contact as the waiter put down a basket of fancy rolls with grains and butter. She held up a finger.

"Bring us a bottle of Syrah."

"Yes, ma'am."

The moment he left she leaned back in her seat. "Two people? Were they cheating on each other or something?"

I laughed and shook my head. "No. The three of us are—were—a thing. Avery is my best friend's sister. And Mateo is his best friend. And the two of them are also in love, but they didn't do anything about it until I showed up. And her brothers are overprotective, so we kept it a secret."

Robin's expressions ranged from surprise, to amusement, to her eyes rolling. "This is some real Texas shit."

"How so?"

"Who gives a shit about her brothers?"

"I mean, I did. Considering they're both my friends."

"Uh-huh. Okay, so. What happened?"

I snatched a roll from the basket, earning an arched brow because in the past, I'd never touch bread on the table. Especially during a season. I took a bite and then sighed. The carbs didn't fix a damn thing, but they gave me enough bravery to tell her everything.

By the time I finished, she was on her second glass of wine, our order was in, and it was clear Robin was mad at me too.

"You're a fucking dumbass," she hissed. "Why in the fuck are you back here?"

My mouth dropped. "What do you mean? Because this is my job. You would have literally come down to Texas to retrieve me."

"Sure, I would have. But also, I think you and I both know you're done."

I opened my mouth but then shut it. She'd said that so . . . "Are you firing me?"

"No. I make a lot of money off you. But based on how you've acted this week, I don't think you want this. Especially after hearing about those two back in Texas."

I sat back in my chair as the waiter put our plates down. I'd ordered a massive chopped salad topped with steak and knew it wouldn't disappoint. Robin had ordered something that was going to cost me a lot of money.

A soft, sad laugh bubbled up. "I came back here. I'm not done."

She raised a brow. "So this isn't a goodbye dinner?"

"Not unless you're firing me." We both fell silent as she cut into her steak, her lips pressing together.

She didn't approve.

"You think I should quit?"

"I think you should do what makes you happy."

"That's . . . not something I thought I'd ever hear you say."

Robin sighed and leaned back in the booth, studying me like I was a bug under a microscope. "I got someone too, you know. I met her a few months ago, but she lives in Nashville. Works as an assistant at some record label. She's funny and smart and perfect."

"Really? You've never said anything." I frowned. "Do you do long distance?"

"We're trying. But long distance can be hard. You can make it work, of course."

"I think the ship has sailed for that . . ." I hadn't even texted Avery or Mateo since the day of the fight with Austin. I owed both of them an apology. I owed both of them a lot more than that.

"From what you've told me, I'm not so sure they'll just move on."

"Well. Would you move to Nashville for her? For your person?"

"I would if I lost my star client."

"Surely you don't mean me."

Robin shrugged. "I don't feel like blowing smoke up your ass."

I shook my head. "Well, I can safely say you've never done that."

Her laugh was harsh but comforting. "Whatever you decide, Rayburn, you need to make up your mind. A season off will be good for your recovery with your shoulder, but you still need to be maintaining your body. And I need to get you on some social media campaigns and maybe even modeling."

Ugh. "I don't know about modeling."

"People would pay a lot of money to see you in your underwear."

"If I wanted to do that, I'd just start an OnlyFans."

She paused for a moment as if she were considering it.

"Robin, *no*."

"Sex positivity. You'd make a lot of money."

"Absolutely not. I respect the hell out of sex workers, but I don't have the temperament for it."

"You don't have the temperament for anything," she sighed. "Except for pining. And torturing yourself. Are you sure you're not a Jane Austen character?"

"I'm sure I'm a dumbass, and that's about it."

Another dry chuckle. "I should be glad you're staying."

"But . . . ?"

"You look miserable. It's pathetic."

I felt miserable. But I'd made the right choice for everyone, right? I'd left so they could get on with their lives. Avery and Mateo would move on and buy a house together and probably get married and live happily ever after and I'd . . .

Wish I was with them.

"Take some time to think," she said. "You've got the weekend. I need an answer by Monday."

"Okay."

"And Levi?"

"Yeah?"

"If you stay, you need to be in this one hundred percent. I can't handle a half-assed, sad hockey boy. There's no market for that."

I stepped into my apartment building, autopilot kicking in. I was full from dinner and tired from the mind-numbing activities of this week.

In a way, I was grateful for it.

It was easier not to feel anything when other people were around.

My keys jangled as I unlocked the package room and poked my head inside. There was a small stack in the corner on the shelves and I winced, realizing they all belonged to me. I'd probably pissed some neighbors off after not checking the mail for . . . seven weeks. *Jeez.*

I gathered all the packages and balanced them in one arm as I locked the door behind me and went to the elevator. By the time I made it to the ninth floor, the loneliness had settled in.

Unavoidable. Eventually it would go away, right? Eventually this decision would feel right.

Even my apartment felt lonely. I closed my door behind me and leaned against it. The view of the city was beautiful. Everything was nice and clean and modern and didn't have a single drop of kitschy Texas charm to be found.

I set everything down on my kitchen counter and started sorting through it all. A couple T-shirts. A sponsorship package with some sort of hydration powder. A couple new books, a new set of sticky notes, a new set of folders.

The package at the very bottom made me freeze.

It was square. A red fragile sticker was stuck on the brown paper, a hand-scrawled address on it.

I traced the ink with my fingertips, and my heart wedged in my throat.

Part of me wondered if this was going to be a binder with a long-ass letter on how much of an asshole I was. I wished it would be. I wished that they hated me because that was easier than the idea of them being sad.

Leaving Mateo on the sidewalk . . .

Leaving Avery in her studio . . .

It haunted me. Every night.

I peeled the paper off in strips, my hands shaking as the gift beneath was revealed.

It was a sketch. A small one of the three of us. Nothing lewd or evocative, just us standing together, looking at each other. The lines were loose, but they captured . . .

They captured what I wanted more than anything else.

Tears dripped onto the frame and I wiped my eyes quickly, breathing out. I pulled my phone out and pressed call.

"What do you want?"

"I need your help," I said. "Do you know a real estate agent?"

I heard the smile in Robin's voice. "I sure do."

CHAPTER FORTY-SEVEN

Nothing was okay.

Not really.

There were moments where it felt okay. Like when Avery woke up next to me and tangled her fingers in my hair. Or when she kissed me on the forehead. Or when I held her and we both did our best to forget about the world outside the walls of our bedrooms.

But it wasn't okay.

Life had a way of bringing people into it that you never knew were missing to begin with. Levi was that for us. Every time I was at Avery's, my gaze crossed the street to the yellow door.

One morning, there'd been a car in the driveway. I'd run across the moment I saw it, only to discover someone else was staying there. And they were really fucking confused as to why a Whynot firefighter was waking them up at six in the morning.

Another afternoon, I saw a photographer shooting pictures of the town on the street. From a distance, he'd been a tall muscled man—but the closer I got, the sooner I realized that he actually wasn't. I still wasn't sure if I'd seen a ghost or if I'd made him up in my head. Either way, he hadn't been Levi.

It'd been six weeks. That was the fucked up part. We'd been apart from Levi as long as we'd known him, and the ache was still there. This giant, awful wound was prying apart my soul.

Avery and I had always been meant to be together. I knew that now more than anything. It'd taken us two years to get here, but if there was any sort of comfort, it was knowing I was in love with my actual best friend.

I was worried about her, though. She wasn't painting. She hadn't gone into her studio since Levi left. I was pretty sure the broken painting was exactly where we'd left it.

Austin had tried talking to her, but she was still avoiding him. She and Dallas had talked a few times, and were on better terms. He could at least own up to the fact that he'd fucked up by being too overprotective.

A knock on my truck's window made me press my lips into a thin line. It was like the bastard knew I was thinking about him. There was no way to completely avoid Austin, but I was still mad.

I rolled down the window for Austin and he raked his fingers through his hair. The circles under his eyes had gotten worse. He looked like shit. It didn't make me feel better.

"Can we talk?" he asked.

"I don't know," I said plainly. "Can we?"

"Please."

I sighed and gestured to the passenger seat of my truck. I was technically on call, but was just sitting here waiting for something to come up. I had a thousand things I needed to knock out on the department checklist, but they could all wait.

Austin went around to the passenger side and opened the

door, climbing in. The moment he shut the door, he ran his palms over his denim-clad thighs.

"I fucked up," he said. "I really fucked up."

"Again? Or do you mean what happened recently?"

"You know I mean recently," he said.

"It's been six weeks, and you haven't apologized for a single fucking thing."

"I tried to apologize to Avery—"

"Avery isn't the only person you hurt."

"I know. I have my reasons for overreacting but they aren't an excuse. I'm sorry for what I said to you. I'm sorry for hurting you. I'm sorry I haven't apologized yet, but I just needed to try to make things right first. When I found out Levi left, I tried to reach out to him, but haven't heard anything."

"I just . . ." I trailed off, thinking long and hard for a moment. In my head, I'd gone over this conversation a few different times. Countless times, really. There was one thing that bothered me the most. "You know I would never hurt Avery the way Kevin did."

"I know that. But I saw the bruises and lost it," he whispered. "I know you're kinky. And fuck, man. I don't want to even think about that with my little sister. I jumped to conclusions. I didn't stop to ask. I didn't stop to do anything other than hurt everyone, Levi included."

My hand tightened on the steering wheel. "Have you heard from him?"

"No. I've called. I've emailed. I even messaged his damn agent. I think she blocked me, actually, after I called fifty times in a row."

Despite everything, I chuckled. "Wouldn't be surprised."

Silence settled between us and I knew he was doing everything in his power to not ask me about Avery.

"She's okay," I said softly. "She's still hurt. I mean, it sounds like she's doing better with your mom at least. That's a first."

"Mom started therapy. She's trying. She's also mad at me."

"I think everyone is."

Austin blew out a breath. "Yeah. Rightly so. Dallas and I had to work through some stuff too. I think I've been running myself into the ground and I haven't taken a single second to work on myself since Dad passed. None of this is an excuse."

"It's not."

"I don't know what to do. I'm sorry, Mateo. You're one of my best friends—"

"Was. At least that's what you said."

Austin winced. "I treated you like shit. I treated Levi like shit. I don't know how to make it up to any of you."

I held out my hand, palm up. He hesitated for a moment and then slid his into mine. I gave him a gentle squeeze and just sat there, watching the quiet street in front of the station.

"I can't really function without you," he whispered. "Ever since you came to Whynot, we've been friends. And you've quickly become one of the only people, if not the only person, outside of my family who really knows me. I shouldn't have jumped to the conclusions I did. I shouldn't have reacted the way I did. I don't have any excuses for it, Mateo. I'm sorry."

I was quiet for a moment, letting his words sink in. I squeezed his hand and then let him go. "I forgive you."

"What?"

"I forgive you."

"You . . . you do? Why?"

"Yeah. I do. I can't forgive you for Levi or Avery, but I forgive you." I looked over at him. "I've been waiting for you to come to me, because you did owe me that apology. And you owe one to your sister and Levi too. But the thing is, I don't think we should have hid anything from you. I don't necessarily regret it, but the moment I knew I wanted forever with both of them, I should have talked to you."

"I wish you would have," he said. "I think I still would have been mad. Probably would have overreacted. Kevin really fucked everything up. I think I became obsessed with keeping her safe. Especially after our dad died."

I nodded. "I get it. I do. I don't have a sister, but I have Maria. I have my grandmother. I have my mom and aunts. And if I ever found out something was happening to them, I would scorch the earth on their behalf."

Austin let out a slow breath. "Yeah. Well, and to make it worse, I went into her studio. I ruined her painting. I ended up hurting her by not listening. Has she even gone back? All the classes have been cancelled. All the Whynot elderly population are up in arms. I've started getting hate mail."

I fought a laugh. "Oh god."

"Let me tell you something. Ms. Carlson is *mean*."

I grinned. "She really is."

The two of us smiled until I sighed, relaxing in my seat.

"Avery hasn't gone back to the studio yet. She's been sketching a lot at the park. Reading. Doing yoga. Started looking up how to design a house."

Austin's eyes widened. "Are you wanting to build?"

"Maybe? It's been in our long-term talks. Just an idea for the future. I wish . . ." I trailed off, swallowing hard. "It would be big enough for three people. In case Levi comes back."

"I've been really focused on my sister," he said. "But I haven't asked you how you are."

"I'm . . . I'm heartbroken. It's weird to be with someone I've wanted for so long while losing another person I want to be with. We're both still healing and I don't know how long it'll take."

"She's loved you for a while," Austin murmured.

My brows shot up. "What do you mean?"

"I mean that I've known for a while that she's had feelings for you. Avery is shit at hiding things." Austin shrugged his shoulders. "I've known."

I kind of wanted to punch the idiot. "There's no fucking way you've *known*."

"Yes fucking way. I'm busy, but I'm not an idiot. I've known since she came back. I've seen the way she looks at you. Then I kind of noticed how you looked at her, and I always wondered. But you never made a move and it became easier for me to be the asshole older brother. The thing is, Mateo, you deserve her. I was wrong when I said that and I didn't mean it. I can't think of another person in this world that you should be with, aside from Levi."

He held out his hand this time and I squeezed it, holding back tears. "Thank you. I wish he were here."

"Well . . . I have a confession."

I scowled. "What?"

"I lied about something."

"Ugh. *What?*"

"The thing is that you've been sitting in your truck for a really long time this morning."

"Okay, and?"

"Well, you haven't been watching the station. You've been watching the street."

I narrowed my eyes. "Am I fired, Mr. Whynot?"

"No," he laughed. "No. But it *was* convenient."

I had no idea where he was going with this. "Spill."

"So the thing is, I did get a hold of Levi."

I sat up and leaned forward. "What?"

"Yeah. He sold his place."

"He what?"

"And I picked him up from the airport and just got back to

Whynot. I've been up since 3:00 a.m. because his damn flight landed at 6:00 a.m."

"*What?*"

"And I think you should maybe go inside the fire station."

I couldn't breathe. I stared at him for a moment and immediately unlocked the truck. "If you're fucking with me—"

"Mateo." Austin gave me a soft smile. "Go get your man."

I couldn't believe it. I jumped out of my truck, my limbs feeling like jello as I sprinted to the station door. I shoved it open, sucking a breath as flowers covered the floor, all making a path to—

"Levi." My voice was hoarse. Tears blurred my vision. Was I imagining things? It wouldn't be the first time I'd imagined him standing in front of me.

"Mateo," he whispered.

Our eyes locked, and—god—the pain in his eyes killed me, because it was the same pain I'd been carrying for weeks.

Before I knew it, I was throwing my arms around his neck and he was lifting me, holding me tight. His lips searched for mine and I kissed him until we were both breathless.

"What are you doing here?" I rasped.

"I'm here," he said, pressing his forehead to mine. "And I'm sorry, Mateo."

He slowly let me down, but his hands slipped into mine, holding them as he met my gaze.

"I shouldn't have left, especially the way I did. I'm sorry. I've thought about you—both of you—non-stop, but I needed to work through some things."

"It's okay," I said quickly.

His expression softened. "Mateo."

My breath hitched. "It's not okay."

"It hasn't been."

"No," I said. "It hasn't. I've missed you every fucking day.

And I think Avery and I have cried enough to fill up an ocean. We talk about you all the time. We needed you."

Levi swallowed hard and nodded. "I'm here."

"Visiting again?"

"No," he whispered. "I'm *here*, Mateo. I sold my place. I had to work through some contract stuff with my agent but she got me taken care of. I'm officially done with the NHL. All of my stuff will be arriving in the next few days and I have no idea where I'll even put it, but I'm here. Texas is my home. And you and Avery will be my home, if you want me."

"If we *want*." An ugly, snotty little laugh bubbled up. "Yeah, Levi. We *want*. I mean, you'll have to see her yourself. But I want. I want this."

"I do too. More than anything else."

"What took you so long? Why didn't you reach out?"

"Because I fucked up. I've spent the last few weeks torturing myself. I've dreamed about the two of you every night. Then I was afraid to reach out. So I did what I do best and started planning."

"Did you make your little spreadsheets?"

"I did." The corner of his mouth tugged. "There's a column full of things I wanted to do to earn your forgiveness."

"Oh. Is there?" I couldn't help but smirk. "What kind of things?"

"Mostly romantic things."

"Like flowers on the floor?"

"Yes."

"And . . ."

"And you'll find out if you want." He chuckled. "When I came back, I wanted to prove to both of you that I'm in this."

"What if . . . What if we didn't take you back?"

He thought about it for a moment. "Well, I really hoped

that wouldn't be the case. But if it were, that doesn't change the fact that this place is right for me."

"Good thing that's not the case."

I kissed him hard, every part of me feeling light. Like I could breathe again. I slowly gave him a wild grin and he narrowed his eyes.

"Don't you dare say it."

"I'm going to," I said. "I *have* to."

He sighed dramatically, but I could tell he wanted to hear it.

"*Why not* move to Texas and fall in love with two people who love you more than anything else? And want to share a life together? And grow old together? And make love together?"

Levi's eyes softened. "Why not?"

CHAPTER FORTY-EIGHT

My heart would eventually unbreak, right? Was that possible?

I ran a brush through my hair. This time, I was wearing gloves. And this time, I was following a set of instructions from June on how to dye my hair the color I wanted.

It was the same anime blue, of course. It was my favorite. But over the last few weeks, I'd let it run out until the ends turned seafoam silver. It was not my least favorite color on canvas, but certainly my least favorite color on myself.

So it was time. Time to put the blue back in, time to glue my heart back together, time to go back to the studio.

I crossed my legs on my stool and went strip by strip, pinning them back with clips June had given me. The first half wasn't too bad, aside from the occasional wisp of hair that would cling to my cheek and leave a blue line.

"Avery!"

I squeaked as Mateo's voice startled me and a glob of blue dropped straight onto my nose. "Dammit. No. Oh god. Fuck." I pushed all my hair over my shoulders and tried to flick the glob off my nose. It spattered against the porcelain sink as I stripped off my gloves and grabbed a makeup remover wipe, quickly trying to salvage my skin.

That was what Mateo walked in on.

His eyes widened and his hand clamped over his mouth. "*Avery.*"

"Don't laugh," I hissed as I scrubbed my nose. "It was going great until you startled me."

"Well, you see, I need you to come with me."

He wasn't serious, right?

"I'm literally in the middle of dyeing my hair."

"I'm aware. I need you to come with me."

"I'll come with you later," I teased.

"*Avery.*" His expression became serious. "You want to come with me."

Had he hit head? I stared at him for a moment but his brows wiggled and he disappeared, off to the kitchen or somewhere else in the house. I sighed and shook my head as I attempted to put my hair up.

I looked like Weird Barbie. I shook my head but slid off the stool. I wasn't wearing a bra. I was in an old paint-stained T-shirt and ratty cut offs, but the man wanted to show me something.

I sighed and followed him down the hall to the living room. A soft voice made me freeze before I rounded the corner.

"She's coming."

"What if she doesn't want to see me?"

Levi? Tears sprang to my eyes and I leapt forward, rounding the corner to see if I was hearing things.

Levi stood in my living room. He wore a T-shirt and jeans and boots, as if he'd never left. As if he'd never gone back to Minnesota.

My breath whooshed out. "You're here."

"I am," he whispered with a soft sniffle.

Was he *crying?* Or was that me?

"What are you doing here?" I said. I couldn't hear anything

but my pounding heart. "What . . ." I looked over at Mateo, my breaths quick. "Did you . . . What . . ."

Mateo offered a smile, but didn't say anything.

Levi took a step closer, his gaze locked on me. "I'm here, Avery."

"Here?"

"Yes. To stay."

"*To stay,*" I echoed. Another sniffle. This time, it was definitely me.

He took another step. Just a little closer. So close. "The tip of your nose is blue."

"I see you still have no manners." All of the broken parts of me started to slowly knit back together. *Hope.* Was that it? "What are you doing here?"

"I'm here to stay. I'm doing what I should have done to begin with." Another step. "I'm here, Avery. I never should have left. I got back to Minnesota and got your sketch, and I . . . I knew how much I'd fucked up."

I stared at him. I'd forgotten about that. I'd dropped that in the mail as some sort of . . . I don't even know what. A giant *fuck you, look at what you lost?*

"I realize that I've hurt you. I've hurt both of you. And I don't know if I deserve another chance, but I love you. I love both of you. There's not a life I want without the two of you in it. I would give up anything, *everything*, to be with you."

Mateo sucked in a breath and looked at me. I held his gaze as I registered what Levi said.

"Wait. You love . . . ?"

"*I love you.*" Another step closer. There were just a few inches between the three of us now. He looked at me, and then Mateo. "I love you. I love you." Back to me. "*I love you.*"

I couldn't stop myself anymore. I grabbed both Mateo and Levi and dragged them into a hug, letting the tears flow. "I love you. I've loved you for a while. Maybe since you caught my hair on fire."

"I've loved Avery since I came to Whynot. And I've loved you, Levi, since you tried to feed me bad protein muffins."

Levi's chuckle was also a sob. His arms wrapped around us, and we sank to the floor, a pile of tender words and tears and laughter and *love.*

I love you, I love you, I love you.

It turned out the way to *un*break a heart was those three little words.

Levi

"I think we should start with a dog."

Mateo and I were both sprawled out on the pavement in front of the fire station with towels beneath us and sunscreen spread generously over our bodies as we tanned. At any moment, we'd maybe need to hop up and get dressed in our gear, but I hoped we could soak up the sun a little longer.

"A dog?" I asked.

"Yeah. I've always wanted one," he said.

"What kind?"

"A big dog. The sloppy kind. Not one of those neurotic chipmunks people claim to be dogs."

I grinned and pushed my sunglasses back up the bridge of my nose, turning my head. "Well. We've been together for a few months now. We're already buying a big house."

"Right. Why not get a dog?"

"Why not?"

"Don't look," Avery demanded.

Mateo snorted as the two of us did our best to not immediately turn around. His hand was firmly in mine and he'd occasionally give me a squeeze as the anticipation built.

Sunlight filled her studio, turning all of her artwork vibrant. In the corner, the painting that Austin and I had crashed into months ago was patched up, but unfinished. Avery had started a new one that she'd been hiding from us—until today.

"Can we look now?" Mateo asked.

"No."

He shook his head as we listened to her shuffle behind us. The scent of paint was stronger than normal, but I'd gotten used to it. I'd also gotten used to seeing it all over Avery or somehow on my things.

Just earlier this week, Mateo and I had discovered specks of blue and pink on our boxers.

Although, we all knew how *that* had happened.

"Okay." Avery blew out a breath. "I think it's ready. I've been working really hard on this."

My chest squeezed with excitement. Mateo was buzzing next to me.

"Can we look?" he asked.

"Yes. Turn around."

Mateo's hand tightened in mine before releasing me, and we both turned around together. My eyes widened and my mouth dropped as a large canvas was revealed. Avery was hiding her face with her hands next to it, her cheeks pink.

"Oh my god," Mateo whispered.

It was beautiful. It was even better than the one we'd seen before.

It was the three of us, but with our backs turned. We all sat together on a blanket in the desert, the sun setting and turning the landscapes a thousand shades of pink. Cacti bloomed in the foreground, and everything about it was full of a bright hopefulness that filled me with warmth.

"Avery," I said. "This is amazing. You outdid yourself, baby."

She peeked at us through her fingers. "Really?"

"I need this in our house," Mateo said. "As soon as you walk in. With a spotlight. And a plaque."

"And the plaque says it was painted by the most beautiful woman in the world."

"Yes. And next to it is a photo of you—"

"Oh my god," she laughed, finally pulling her hands away from her face and revealing a big grin. "Both of you are ridiculous."

Ridiculously, completely, hopelessly in love with you.

Stars sprawled out in the sky above us, completely untouched by humanity. This far out from town, it felt like the three of us were the only people in the world. There was no light pollution. *Nothing.*

"Do you ever get bored of living here?" Avery asked.

Mateo raised his head and looked at me. "That's a good question. Are you bored of us? You've lived here for a year now. It's so different from how your life used to be. Volunteering at the station and taking photos for a living isn't very glamorous."

I snorted and tightened my grip on both of their hands. They had no idea how much happier I was now. It'd taken some work to figure out what I was doing with my life after my hockey career ended, but I'd figured it out.

We'd figured it out.

"I could never get bored of either of you," I finally said.

Avery rolled onto her side and placed her chin on my chest. I was in between her and Mateo, which happened more often than not. Our Dom liked being the little spoon.

"I didn't say bored of *us*, silly. I said of *living here*."

"No," I said. "I miss Minnesota sometimes, but we visit enough that I never truly long for it. Texas is hot. And there's not much to do out here. It's a quiet way of living. But you know what? I've never been happier."

Avery's smile was bright enough that it touched the stars.

Avery squealed as she knelt down on the floor of the animal shelter, holding out her hands as a hoard of puppies rushed toward her. I wasn't resistant either, immediately plopping on the ground next to her as the pack of blue heeler mutts surrounded us. We'd driven almost three hours out to a shelter in Odessa just so we could find *the one*.

Avery and I had been planning on surprising Mateo for over a year, but the moment had never felt right until now. Well, until June saw a video online about the mama dog that'd been rescued and then had given birth to a big litter of puppies.

I laughed as three of them fought to climb into my lap. One nipped at my beard, another went for the tip of my now well-worn boots, gnawing like it was a bone.

Avery was a goner, her giggles giving me a thousand butter-flies. I laughed with her, the two of us cooing and playing with them until they calmed down.

"How are we going to pick just one?" she asked. "It's not fair."

"I know." I looked around us, wondering if we could reasonably adopt eight puppies. The answer was no, we couldn't.

One of the shelter volunteers grinned at us. "They'll go

fast. It's always the older dogs that end up staying here for a while, like their mom."

Something flickered in Avery's gaze and she frowned. Dammit, I knew that look all too well. "Has the mom been adopted yet?"

"Not yet."

Avery turned her pleading gaze on me. "What if we adopted her instead?"

"I thought we wanted to go through the puppy process together. It's a trial for having children . . ."

"I know . . ." She trailed off. "What if we adopted the mama and a puppy so they can be together?"

"*Two dogs?*"

Avery grinned, her eyes sparkling.

"Don't you dare say it," I said, narrowing my eyes on her.

She laughed as she held up the plumpest puppy of the pack. "Why not? I have two boyfriends, don't I? We could have two dogs."

I groaned, but didn't say no. Instead, I looked up at the volunteer. "Can we meet the mom?"

Later that night, Mateo spent an hour crying on the floor as he hugged our new dogs and told us how much he loved us.

***

"Hey! I know you."

I looked up from the booth at the cafe in the hotel, surprised as a random guy approached me. Austin raised a brow, seated across from me with our usual peach pancakes piled high in front of us. It'd been our monthly tradition for eight years now.

"Do you?" I asked.

"Yeah. You're Levi Rayburn," the stranger said. He let out a hum, nodding as if he'd made the coolest discovery ever. "The hockey star, right? Number ninety for Minneapolis? You were such a great player, man."

I smiled and held out my hand, giving his a shake. "Thanks. Nice to meet you. What's your name?"

"Bryan. Mind if I get a picture with you? I got some friends up north who are gonna lose it when they find out I ran into you on my vacation to the middle of nowhere."

Austin was clearly holding in a laugh. "I can take it for you, if you'd like."

"Man, that would be great."

I eyed my pancakes and held in my sigh as I got up, towering over the stranger. He handed his phone to Austin eagerly and he snapped a picture of us.

"Thanks," Bryan said. "It was so cool to meet you. Was it worth it? Leaving it all behind?"

"Daddy!"

I turned around immediately and knelt down as my daughter ran through the hotel. She threw her little arms around me and I laughed as I picked her up, holding her tight. Avery came around the corner with Mateo, and he was cradling our son. The four of them were everything to me.

I love them so much.

I smiled. "Yeah. It was worth it."

About Clio Evans

Clio Evans writes contemporary and monster romance books that are kink-positive, queer-normative, steamy, and full of heart. They're from Austin but are now living their best life drinking lattes and writing happy endings in Chicago. When Clio isn't writing, she's either painting, swing-dancing with her partner, or discovering new coffee shops in the city.

Join them on Instagram, Facebook, TikTok, or their newsletter for new releases, updates, and more!

www.clioevansauthor.com

Also by Clio Evans

Contemporary/Small Town Romance:

WHYNOT SERIES

Cactus Heart (Whynot 1)

Thorn Kiss (Whynot 2, releasing 2026)

Prickly Pair (Whynot 3, releasing 2026)

CITRUS COVE SERIES

Broken Beginnings (Citrus Cove 1)

Stolen Chances (Citrus Cove 2)

Hidden Roots (Citrus Cove 3)

STANDALONES

Mine: A Reverse Age Gap Romance

The Perfect Gift (Christmas Cuckold Novella)

The Perfect Escape (Summer Spanking Novella)

Lasso Lovebirds: Rainbow Ranch Novella

Monster Romance:

CREATURE CAFE SERIES

Little Slice of Hell

Little Sip of Sin

Little Lick of Lust

Little Shock of Hate

Little Piece of Sass

Little Song of Pain

Little Taste of Need

Little Risk of Fall

Little Wings of Fate

Little Souls of Fire

Little Kiss of Snow: A Creature Cafe Christmas Anthology

Little Drop of Blood

Little Heart of Stone

Little Spark of Flame

WARTS & CLAWS INC. SERIES

Not So Kind Regards

Not So Best Wishes

Not So Thanks in Advance

Not So Yours Truly

Not So Much Appreciated

FREAKS OF NATURE DUET

Doves & Demons

Demons & Doves

THREE FATES MAFIA SERIES

Thieves & Monsters

Killers & Monsters

Queens & Monsters

Kings & Monsters

GALACTIC GEMS SERIES

www.ingramcontent.com/pod-product-compliance
Lightning Source LLC
Chambersburg PA
CBHW021954130726
47903CB00014B/1350